LIA DÀN –
STONE OF DESTINY

Revised Edition II

Lia Dàn – Stone of Destiny

Dàn Cycle Two

Revised Edition II

James Raquepau

BOOK COVER ART © 2024 BY NADIIA KOLPAK & JAMES RAQUEPAU

ILLUSTRATIONS © 2024 BY JAMES RAQUEPAU

LYRICS © 2024 BY CLAIRE ODLUM, EMY SMITH, AND JAMES RAQUEPAU

EDITED BY HOLLY ATKINSON (EVIL EYE EDITING)

ISBN

979-8-9896602-3-0   *IngramSpark Paperback*

979-8-9896602-6-1   *IngramSpark Ebook*

979-8-3473285-8-1   *AudioBook*

Destiny Cycle Publishers - Gaels Rule!

www.destinycycle.com

Lia Dàn: Stone of Destiny – Dàn Cycle Two

TABLE OF CONTENTS

Map of Eastern Erin

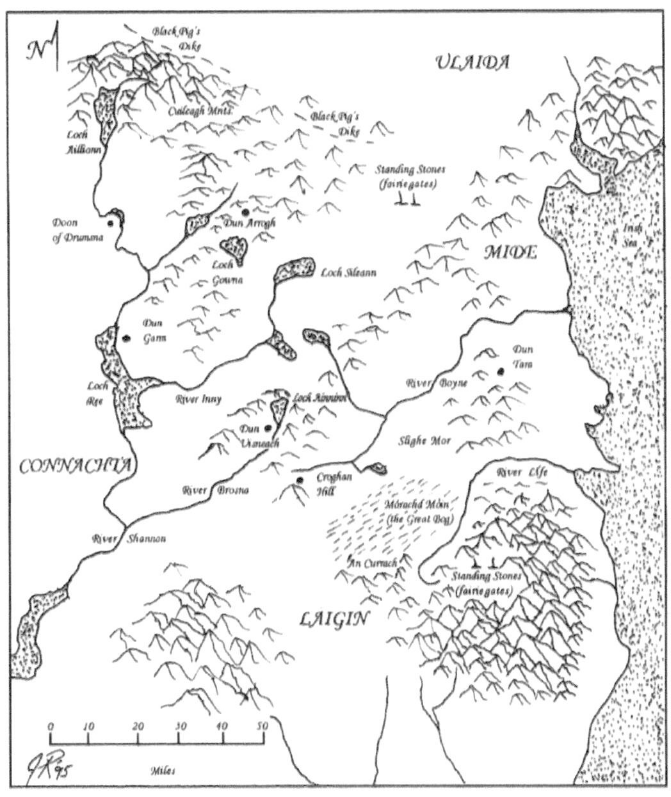

Destroyer Pursued

Toal

Toal Mac Kyras listened intently to the Norvegr warriors on the wall above him. From their panicked tones, they seemed convinced that the High King in Tara had sent a dun full of warriors to attack their walls. The fire in the main hall's roof appeared to fuel the confusion. That made Toal smile. He looked up through the fog, trying to see anything on the rampart; the torchlights were barely visible. Not even enough to show them the ground at their feet.

He asked with more than a hint of concern, "Fergal, between the dark and the fog, how are we going to find Eoin and Bre once they escape?"

Eoin's cousin looked around as if surprised and cursed, "*Tá olann ina hintinn agam!*"

"We all have wool for brains sometimes," Toal chided.

"And those who do, more often than not, end up dead when facing the likes of the Dreadlord," Fergal growled. He paused and added, "If I were Eoin or Breanna and heard those on the wall yelling about the fire, I'd not come here, and I'd not head for the gates. Not closed and barred as they are."

"Too many warriors about?"

"Correct," Fergal answered. "That leaves us with the south and east sides. Let's go back and see what we find. And stick close. I don't want to lose track of you in this murky soup."

"Aye," Toal agreed, shuddering. His imagination ran wild with fairies and demons lurking in the mist as Fergal turned and headed into the darkness. He kept close to the older warrior. If the sun had been out to cast a shadow, he would not have seen his own.

Careful not to make any noise, the pair moved slowly southward along the rampart's base. When both passed the southwest corner of the fort, Toal paused, cocking his head to listen. It was quiet, save for the now muffled yelling from the Dreadlord's warriors about a fire in the main hall. Fergal tugged on Toal's arm, leading him toward the southwest corner of the massive fort.

Torches also burned atop this wall all along the rampart, but they still could see little else. When Toal could hear nothing above him, vise-like indecision gripped him. He whispered, "Should we retreat and slip back into the trees or wait it out? When the sun rises and the fog lifts, they could see us. What good will it do if they capture us as well?"

Fergal countered, "But if Breanna manages to free Eoin, we'd leave them when they needed us most."

"Okay then. Let's keep going east along this south side. My arrows came from the west, so more warriors should search there first. That means Bre and Eoin should likely come over somewhere on the eastern rampart."

Fergal grinned, nodding in approval. He took Toal by the arm again and led him to the southeast corner. This time, they went even slower as they headed north along the base of the rampart, hoping to discover something they had missed on their last pass.

When Toal heard voices ahead, he was sure from the accents that they had to belong to Breanna and Eoin. Then the sound of timbers breaking made him all the more convinced. Fergal seemed to sense the same thing and picked up the pace.

Suddenly, Eoin came stumbling down the steeply pitched dirt and stone wall of Dun Garm, nearly skewering his cousin. The pair went down amid curses and grunts.

Breanna was more graceful as she came to a skittering stop at their feet, her grim expression illuminated by the faint glow of *Lann Dàn* and *Maorgairme*. A white-haired lad followed her. She hissed at Fergal in a quiet but tight voice, "I put you in charge of the Red Branch to keep them safe, not to drag them into the Dreadlord's stronghold to get hacked apart!"

"I didn't drag anyone to Dun Garm except for Toal, who came of his own volition."

Breanna turned to him as if she had just noticed his presence. "And what do you think you're doing here?"

"Trying to help free our Chief," Toal spat as his back stiffened; he was glad his voice didn't crack as it was wont to do of late. "That fire Hakon's warriors are preoccupied with right now just happens to be my doing."

Eoin helped Fergal stand. "Now is not the time to argue about who should have done what and who shouldn't. Fergal and Toal, meet Braoin—he's with us. Let's get away from this place. Fergal, do you have your chariot?"

"Aye," Fergal said tartly, glaring at Breanna. His gaze returned to Eoin, and he added less tightly, "We left it in the trees northeast of here. The horses should be rested by now and could carry us all."

"Good, then let's get moving," Eoin commanded and started hobbling north along the base of the rampart.

"Wait," Breanna demanded in a stiff, low voice. "The Dreadlord will surely catch us if we return to Dun Arrogh, and, with five in it, that chariot won't carry us swiftly enough to go anywhere else. And with how you two are still limping, it'd take us a span or more to get to that creaking old bucket. Once Hakon's hounds have our scent, we'll be done for if we don't have at least a half day's lead on them."

"Then what do you propose?" Fergal suspiciously demanded.

"You and Toal take the chariot," Breanna offered. "It will carry you two faster than the five of us. My sister lives deep enough into Mide that her mate's clan will protect you. I doubt the Dreadlord would risk an attack with the *Ard-Rí* so close at hand in Dun Tara."

"It's a two-day ride at best to Orla's," Eoin commented. "Fergal and Toal would have to move swiftly."

"Or the Dreadlord would catch us," Fergal added, his tone almost accusatory. "I say let Toal take the chariot. He handled it most of the way here anyway and would make better time without me."

"Then, which way would you four go?" Toal asked.

"We certainly need to throw the Dreadlord off our trail," Eoin interjected as he looked over his shoulder at Dun Garm's rampart. "East and south, I'd say, toward Dun Uisneach. Then, once we've outwitted their pursuit, we'll keep going that way. If I remember correctly, my Champion has a goddess to visit."

"I don't like sending Toal off alone," Breanna countered. "You dragged him here, Fergal. You should see that he gets back safely. He's just a boy, after all."

At first, Toal thought his cousin was overly obvious about wanting to be rid of Fergal, but then her words sank in. She had tried to goad Fergal into taking care of him. What did he have to do to prove himself? Had he not helped her find *Lann Dàn* and face Tethra's demons? Weren't his arrows the ones that had helped divert the Dreadlord's warriors so she could free Eoin? His blood boiled at being called a boy. Toal snapped, "I'm old enough to look after myself. Fergal's right—he'd slow me down. I'll lead Hakon's dogs away from your trail, get to Orla's, and find someone to get word to Dun Arrogh that you are all safe."

"Safe, but on the run," Eoin corrected. "Now, we've wasted too much time. Run, Toal. Get to the chariot and yourself to safety."

Breanna nodded stiffly, saying, "Aye, go safely and quickly then, my cousin."

Toal quickly hugged Breanna and bolted into the dark.

Hurriedly groping his way through the dark, misty night, he only knew the grassy plain had ended because his face met up with the gnarled bark of an old black oak. At least he was no longer out in the open where the Dreadlord's men could easily see him once the sun came up. Cold, tired, and dazed from smacking into the tree, he sank to his knees and touched his scraped forehead. His fingers came away a little sticky with blood.

He shrugged his pack off to find a cloth to tie around his head. Exhausted from not getting much sleep the last few days, he could not resist stealing a moment and closed his eyes, slumping against the oak tree. He only needed those few moments to recover from his dizziness. But before his head cleared, he succumbed, and sleep swept him away.

The dreams that came to Toal were dark and filled with scenes of Dreadriders riding down his friends, their blades hacking off arms and heads. They were gruesome images, images from which he could not wake. Then Tethra's demons surrounded him, the black, misshapen forms pulling him apart limb from limb.

Hakon

A span after sunrise, Hakon watched Alrik and Brede lead the last of his warriors through the gates of Dun Garm. He had sent his wolfhounds, Hati and Skoll, along with the rest of their pack, to follow his most senior Dreadriders. Few remained to man the walls, with most out hunting the Destroyer and her friends. Lang would also be after them if it were not for Runa's potion. She had somehow managed to get the grieving Dreadrider to drink her concoction, and he now slept in his hut.

Lunt's body would be given to their gods in the evening once his servants finished preparing the pyre. But for Hakon, the day held a sour taste. He had lost one of his best warriors, a warrior he had grown more fond of than anyone who had followed him to this land. Yet he had also found a daughter who was every bit as skilled as Lunt, maybe more so.

Now that he had seen her in battle, Hakon had convinced himself that his best course was to lure his Destroyer into joining him as an ally. But dealing with a woman as an equal was not something he had ever needed to do. Convincing his offspring that he was not the monster she believed would be the challenge of his life. And if he could not win her over, she would have to die.

Hakon had not told Runa about his plan to subvert his daughter to his cause, for she had been busy tending to Lang. And he understood his völva had been none too pleased with being thumped on the head. As he approached her hut, he tried to frame his argument in his mind.

Runa responded to his knock on her door, though the scowl on her face made it plain she was not happy to see him. "My Jarl, what can I do for you?"

"A little talk, if you will," Hakon said as he stepped into her hut.

Runa did not look up as she turned toward her table and took a seat. "About your daughter. I'm surprised you took so long. That I was wrong about your bastard's sex is obvious, something I regret nearly as much as you. Maybe the other two are just Tuatha decoys to trick my magic."

"Possibly." Hakon shrugged. "We lost Braoin last night, as he appears to have escaped in the night's mayhem."

Runa rubbed her head. "I'll need to cast my Runes again to see if those two remain important in our dance with the Tuatha gods. Yet with fairie magic in her hands, your daughter is undoubtedly the Destroyer. What my black beauties previously told me did not change by our discovery that he is, in reality, she."

"Aye, and Lunt's death is proof of her skill as a warrior," Hakon said, deciding to take an indirect approach. "And I nearly met the same fate. We were both surprised to see each other, which probably saved my life. Runa, what drives her to seek my death?"

"Even she does not know," the sorceress replied, eyeing him critically as she poured them tea. "It is the nature of her *geas* to seek your end. Few of us truly know what drives us, and in your daughter's case, she was manipulated over the years by forces beyond the *Cycle's* normal turnings."

"So diverting her from this *geas* would be a challenge?"

"Diverting her?" Runa questioned, pausing before taking a sip of tea, her eyes never leaving his, her expression doubtful.

"After seeing her in battle, I would like to try to win her support," Hakon finally confirmed as he looked into his cup, unwilling to hold her gaze. "A warrior with such skills could be a great asset."

"And a great danger."

Hakon ignored those words as he sipped absently at his tea. Then he asked abruptly, "Can this *geas* cast upon her be broken? Is your magic strong enough to destroy its hold on her?"

Runa frowned. "It may be possible, but I'd need her to be here to try and break the spell. And in case you have forgotten, your daughter is being hunted by more than your warriors. You enlisted the Fomorian god, Tethra, to kill her, and the Tuatha gods provided magical weapons and came to her aid in the demon battle. So between those two factors, getting her back to Dun Garm alive may be more challenging than breaking her *geas*."

"I'll leave that part to you if you leave the rest to me," he said. Runa frowned again but managed a slight nod. Hakon could see the doubt in her eyes and sensed she had more words of caution. Knowing he would have to prod her, he demanded, "Is there something else?"

"You made a pact with Tethra," Runa said quietly. "A pact to kill the Destroyer."

"That I did, but since he didn't live up to his end of the bargain, there's no reason I should hold up my end," he responded as he rose. "I've lost one of my best Dreadriders because of his failure."

"I doubt the Fomorian god will see it that way, especially given the price he has paid thus far for the privilege of helping you. He wants to see your bastard dead now more than before. It's no longer simply because the Tuatha gods are helping her. She's killed scores of his demons, and stopping him from carrying out your original pact will be harder than you think."

"Leave Tethra to me."

"You play with powers far greater than you realize," Runa advised.

Toal

Screaming, Toal bolted awake. He wasn't sure how long he had slept; all he knew was that the sun had risen, and the fog from the night before was gone. Sighing, he got his feet beneath him and retied the cloth around his forehead. It took a moment for the events of the night before to churn through his mind.

Toal rubbed his eyes, then looked through the trees to find the sun, hoping it would tell him how long past sunrise it was. With the clouds and fog gone, sunlight filtered brightly through the branches.

"Danu, save me," he whispered when he realized the sun was clearly above the horizon. Panicked, he picked up his bow and turned north, dodging his way through the tree line as he ran. His body ached, especially his legs, but there was no time to be concerned about minor pains. It was likely that Hakon's warriors were out searching for them already, and Toal had wasted at least a span of the slim lead he was supposed to have.

He found the chariot as he and Fergal had left it, with the hill ponies still tethered to his makeshift picket. Toal quickly hitched them to the cart, and, in a few moments, he was heading north. The narrow path through the forest was bumpy and dangerous, but he dared not take their rig to the more accessible plains. Not yet, anyway, not until he was well out of sight of Dun Garm.

Not a quarter-span after he had the chariot rolling, he heard hounds baying in the distance. Knowing they must be from the Dreadlord's stronghold, Toal picked up his pace, urging the horses to go faster.

The chariot bucked and rocked like a boat in a storm, and Toal could do little more than hang on. He heard the hounds again and was sure they were closer this time. If they had picked up his scent, he needed speed and not the cover of the woods.

Seeing an opening to his left, Toal pulled the reins over, and the chariot burst through the light brush and onto the open plains.

With another snap of his reins, the horses were soon in a full gallop. He found the going easy enough to hold on with only one hand as a cold wind pulled tears from his eyes. The ground flashed by as he chanced a glance back toward Dun Garm. While he could hardly see the massive fort, the dozen or so warriors charging along the forest's edge were unmistakable. The wind drew their white hair back as they urged their mounts after him. A half dozen giant wolfhounds bounded with the Norvegr riders, each easily keeping pace with their masters.

Toal muttered a curse he had heard his father use when he hit his hand with a hammer, then flicked the reins at Fergal's hill ponies again. They surged forward, but gaining ground on his pursuers was not enough, especially with their faster warhorses. He needed something to divert them and spied his bow and the quiver of arrows tied to the railing. When he lunged for his weapon, the chariot lurched over a rock. Toal nearly flew out the back. Only the reins kept him from hitting the ground.

Grabbing at the rail, he clawed slowly toward the front with his bow. Another look at Hakon's warriors told him they were gaining, and he urged his horses to find more speed. They flew on, dragging the cart wildly behind them. Toal managed to get his bow restrung and nocked an arrow. Aiming was another matter. The rocking motion made it seem impossible to hit the riders behind him.

The first arrow flew wide off its mark, and the second nearly took down one of the hounds as the arrow landed right in front of it. The dog tripped and tumbled to the ground, flipping over several times, but he rose and took off after those who had passed him by. He knew killing their dogs would not save him, so he adjusted his aim higher at the riders behind him. This time, he put his arrow into the shoulder of one of his pursuers. The man spun off his mount and crashed to the ground. It brought the others to a halt for a moment. Then the lead Dreadrider had them hurtling forward again, digging their heels into their horses' flanks.

The white-haired warriors pulled their small, round shields off their saddles as Toal let another arrow fly. His aim was good, but the warrior he had chosen got his leather buckler up in time. Toal tried several more shots, each with the same result. With his quiver half-empty, he groaned at the thought of aiming at the horses but knew there was no other way to slow them down. He turned and fired again. His arrow buried itself in the lead mount's chest, and the rider was pitched over its head as it went down.

The Dreadrider behind the downed warrior quickly changed tactics and veered into the woods, where hitting them would be more challenging. His warriors followed suit, soon weaving their way through the trees. Toal muttered another curse and drove his horses on. Hoping to draw them out, he pulled the reins to the right and headed east, farther out onto the plain. The grass-covered ground continued to flash by as Toal glanced around to see if there were other options. With his pursuers hidden by the woods, he had no choice but to keep going in the same direction, as he had regained some ground on Hakon's riders.

As the chariot drew away from the tree line, the white-haired warriors swerved to the outer limits of the forest. Toal didn't bother wasting his arrows, for his short bow now did not have enough range. Movement to his right caught his eye as he turned to concentrate on getting the most out of his slighter horses. A second band of the Dreadlord's men was closing on him from the far side of the plain, eating up the ground between them. Their warhorses were fresher than his homegrown hill ponies, who were starting to flag.

Deciding to unseat as many warriors as possible, Toal readied his bow again. Within moments, he began nocking and releasing again, unseating two more of the Dreadlord's men before they got their bucklers unstrapped. Onward they came, as did the other band of riders behind him. The ones closer to the trees had pulled away from the woodlands, and now both groups were nearly on top of him.

Then, with his quiver down to two arrows, Toal drew back on the reins and pulled his chariot to a stop. Hakon's warriors swarmed around him with their blades drawn and murder in their eyes, and Toal recognized the two Dreadriders from the time when they had come to Dun Arrogh, burned down Breanna's hut, and took Eoin hostage. Both barked orders to their respective charges to stand down.

The one who seemed to be the younger took control of Toal's horses. The other dismounted and stepped onto the chariot, towering over a stiff-lipped Toal. It took all the will he could muster not to flinch; then his resolve grew firmer. If he could face Tethra's demons and survive, staring down a Dreadrider was certainly within him.

Still, he couldn't suppress a groan as the gnarly warrior snatched up his bow and snapped it over his knee.

The Dreadrider growled darkly, "If the Dreadlord didn't want you alive, I'd skewer you right here, boy or no. Those were good men you took down! Kvasir, ride back and tell Runa she's needed. We've wounded men to tend to. And Jotun, you ride with this whelp back to Dun Garm. And be careful that he has no more tricks up his sleeves for us. Like using this little sword."

As the Dreadrider took his sword and stepped down to mount his horse, Toal stood dejectedly. Then, the warrior Jotun joined him, and he was sure he had failed Breanna's band in drawing them off far enough. Hopefully, the dogs did not have his cousin's scent. As to his fate, they'd either kill him or take him hostage. Neither option was good, and if it were the latter, he wondered whether or not he could keep Breanna's secrets and mislead the Dreadlord.

Hakon

Before Runa could tell Hakon about Tethra, a warrior was pounding on her door, demanding help, though panicked enough that not much else was clear. Hakon strode over and wrenched it open in annoyance. Nearly out of breath, the young warrior pulled up and regained some composure at seeing his master towering before him.

"My Jarl! Alrik and Brede caught one of the Gael raiders! The boy unhorsed a number of our riders with his bow. Such skill makes him a suspect for the one who set fire to the main hall last night."

"Well done, Kvasir, well done," Hakon said, pleased. "Get a chariot ready, and Runa will ride out to treat those wounded immediately. And have Alrik and Brede bring the boy to me. We've much to discuss, he and I."

"Aye, my Jarl," Kvasir said and ran to do his Jarl's bidding.

Hakon turned to his völva. "Find me once you've tended to the men."

Hakon stepped out of her hut as Runa gathered her medicines and tools for the stitches. He could nearly taste his anticipation. The boy they had caught would know something about his daughter, like her name. And if fortune was smiling on him, the young Gael might be able to say where she was heading.

Eoin

Silently, Eoin led the way into the night, leaving Dun Garm behind as fast as he and his wounded cousin could manage. As they trudged over the dark open field, he noted an uneasy silence between Fergal and Breanna, but he had no time for their ongoing rivalry. Still, he needed to catch up with Breanna on what transpired between them and what happened on her quest for the Blades of Destiny.

A cloud-covered sky meant no moon or starlight could guide their direction. The Dreadlord's warriors would be on their trail as soon as the sun rose, and they needed to be as far from Dun Garm as possible. Once they had traveled what Eoin thought was a safe distance, he asked Breanna for some light, and she commanded *Maorgairme* and *Lann Dàn* to give it to them. The magical glow cast enough light to improve their footing, and they could at least now see a few steps ahead.

Braoin brought up the rear of their small band, his dual-bladed hilts harnessed on his back like Breanna's long blades. Eoin dropped back to walk beside him. "I hope we are heading in the right direction. While Loch Síleann is southeast, it makes up the beginning of the River Inny. I'm wondering how familiar you are with this area. Have you explored the river down to Loch Ree?"

"Aye, our settlement trades with another one on the south end of the loch, where it feeds the River Shannon once more," Braoin answered. "We normally follow the river and go south at the shoreline to get there."

"That's good news," Eoin said. "I'm hoping we can reach Dun Uisneach by tomorrow afternoon, but we'll need to keep under cover come sunrise so the Dreadriders do not discover us out in the open. That could slow us down."

"Understood," Braoin said.

After another span, the ground began to slope and turn soft. Eoin heard water lapping on a nearby shore, and his heart sank.

Beyond doubt, it was not the sound of a running river. They were close to Loch Ree, not the River Inny. They had gone southwest and not southeast! And they were more west than anything.

"We've seemingly headed the wrong way," Eoin growled in frustration. "Yet traveling farther in the dark could prove hazardous. Let's get some rest."

Grabbing Eoin's arm, Breanna protested, "Absolutely not! We are too close to the water here! We must get at least a good march away from the loch. We should head east and find firmer ground."

"What are you talking about?" he demanded.

Breanna added urgently, "Lugh believes Hakon's völva summoned the Fomorian god called Tethra, and the Dreadlord made a pact with him to set his water demons after me. My first encounter with them was after I found *Lann Dàn*. Once we descended Cuilcagh Mountain, Lugh and I fought them at Loch Aillionn!"

Eoin and Braoin looked at her in amazement. "Lugh?" Eoin asked. "As in the Sun God?"

"Aye, the Sun God," Breanna answered defiantly. "I am deep in this mess, Eoin. One of those demons almost pulled me into Loch Gowna while traveling to Dun Garm. Trust me, this is real. We need to be wary of water, especially at night. Fortunately, they shun sunlight."

"All right, we will head east for a bit," Eoin said. Without a doubt, he needed to catch up with his Champion on what had happened since she left on her quest for the magical long blades. Water demons! How much more trouble could descend upon them?

With the matter settled, they tramped on. As they groped their way through the dark, the ground became uneven, and despite the light, Fergal slipped and fell again. He muttered, "*Cos diabhal! Fuar fliuch agus trua.*"

Breanna let out an exasperated sigh as she helped him to his feet once more. Fergal ground out, "I can manage on my own!"

"You just admitted you can't on that leg!" she snarled back as she scooped her hands under his arms and got him to his feet.

Fergal grumbled, "You're only helping to ensure the Dreadlord doesn't catch up to us."

Eoin stepped in this time. "Fergal, not asking for help because you're too proud to admit that you're hurt is slowing us down. Braoin, can you help make sure he stays upright?"

As Fergal slipped again but caught himself before hitting the ground, Braoin appeared beside him. "Here, lean on me."

Breanna

Breanna sighed as she stepped around the pair and marched on. Since her return from Cuilcagh Mountain, the uncomfortable distance between herself and Fergal that had once been like a lake was now a sea. Until moments ago, she and Fergal had not spoken a word since leaving Dun Garm behind, even when she had assisted him throughout their dark trek.

As Braoin helped Fergal, Eoin asked Breanna, "Is this far enough from the loch? Having cover would be good." He indicated the small stand of birch trees in front of them.

"Aye, it should be," she confirmed.

Eoin dropped his pack and travel roll, and Breanna followed suit. Her knees hit the ground beside her friends. She was not ready to admit she was exhausted, but letting sleep take her would mean Eoin couldn't ask about her father. Discussing Hakon Skadi's demise as they once had would no longer be possible.

Telling Eoin that the Dreadlord wanted her to join him in Dun Garm and fight against the Gaels was definitely out of the question. Whatever seeds of doubt her Chief had about her would surely sprout with that knowledge. How could he ever trust her? She was her father's *dìolain*! Few Gaels within his territory would accept her, especially knowing who she was. Looking at the faint glow of her ring, she wondered if *Maorgairme* would help her again and make Eoin forget what he discovered in his time with her father, as it had with Fergal. Yet with what his cousin had seen when her father took him from Dun Arrogh, maybe Fergal had deduced some of it; she hoped not.

Eoin startled her out of her thoughts. "We move on at sunrise."

If there had been enough light to see her reflection in a pond, Breanna knew her face would show guilt etched on it like a stone carving. She was relieved her Chief couldn't see that as she lay out her bedroll. Then there was the shame she felt at being the Dreadlord's bastard and for not believing her lifelong friend would support her. Not trusting her voice, she managed to nod in agreement and silently commanded the ring and her blades to turn out their light.

It wasn't long before Eoin, Fergal, and Braoin were asleep.

Despite being dead tired, Breanna found the bliss of even a nightmare elusive, and she couldn't keep her attention from wandering to Badb Catha's ring. Maybe it would help her stave off Eoin's questions in the morning. When she asked the fickle piece of magic to tamper with Eoin's memory, *Maorgairme* gave no response. It was as if the ring knew he was not her enemy. Yet her fears of his rejection ate at her, as he knew her best of any fellow clansmen.

As the night wore on and Breanna stared into the darkness, Hakon's words echoed through her mind. *We could try to draw the poison out together. Knowing what drives you can help you understand why it drives you.*

It made Breanna want to spit, but try as she might, there was no shutting out his voice. Nor the lingering thought that he might be right. Frustrated, she turned over and tried to sleep again, though what little she got was troubled.

Dawn was breaking over the horizon when Breanna started, waking at Fergal's grumbling as he rose. The fog had lifted, and a light, cold breeze washed over them from the north. Unfortunately, the day would be mostly clear, which did not bode well for them on open ground. Loch Ree lay to their west, the shore dotted with longboats brought here by the Norvegrs many years before, along with smaller fishing vessels they had built. She couldn't suppress a groan as her stiff muscles protested the slightest movement.

Eoin was already up and digging through her supplies for breakfast. Breanna sat up and said, "Hakon will be on our trail soon. Without horses, we'll be hard-pressed to keep ahead of him. Any ideas on how to avoid his pursuit?"

He pulled out some oatcakes and strips of dried venison. They had no fire or time to make one to cook some oats into porridge. He handed some to Fergal, Braoin, and Breanna. Then he mentioned casually, "I thought we'd borrow one of his boats and take it south to the mouth of the River Shannon. We'll only have to push east on the High King's Road for a day to be out of his grasp.

"Once we reach Dun Uisneach, I doubt he'll risk tangling with the High King's men. I may even ask for Guestright to see what it's like inside one of Mide's biggest forts. Aside from Dun Tara, of course. Then we can go at our own pace to the Boyne River to meet your goddess and find out how *Lann Dàn* is supposed to help you."

"She's not my goddess. She is the Dark Goddess," Breanna corrected more tartly than intended as she took a bite of jerked meat. After chewing, she added, "And if it were not for Danu and Lugh claiming I must visit her to discover how these things will help me rid the land of my—of the Dreadlord—I'd be heading north toward Dun Arrogh. But, either way, I'll not get in a boat with Tethra's demons seeking me."

While Fergal didn't notice her slip, the look in Eoin's eyes told her he had. But he seemed to sense her reluctance and gave her a shrug. "Did you not say the demons shied away from sunlight?"

Breanna nodded.

"We'll get off the loch before it gets dark. Best not to get caught on the open water, then," Eoin confirmed.

Fergal grunted as he bent to pick up his pack. When he stood, he added sourly, "I don't know why you both think we need to be concerned about magic and gods."

"Because they can help rid us of the Dreadlord," Eoin snapped. "If you can't defeat one of his Dreadriders, how do you expect to take on a whole dun full of them? Hakon Skadi is said to be the best warrior in Dun Garm, so how would you propose killing him, even if more than a hundred of his clan didn't guard him? Most of whom are at least your match with a blade!"

Fergal's face reddened, and his jaw clenched, but no retort came.

As Breanna settled her pack on her back, letting it hang off her blade harness, she rejoined flatly, "I could kill him if it were just the two of us, his sword against my long blades—and I wouldn't need magic or gods to do it. You can count on that. Still, Eoin's right. We don't stand a chance against his numbers."

Fergal glanced from one to the other, then limped toward the boats on the shore of the distant Loch Ree.

Braoin, after a long look at the pair, said in a disappointed tone, "You three best put to rest this shite that's between you if you hope to beat the Dreadlord." He then followed Fergal.

Eoin watched them go before turning to Breanna. He whispered, "Bre, if you want to talk about last night, about coming face to face with—with Hakon Skadi, I'm here for you. Just like you were there for me when his Dreadriders attacked us and when you rescued me at Dun Garm."

With that, he turned after his cousin and Breanna's half-brother. She sank to the ground, stunned that he still supported her. Or, more correctly, to have it confirmed, for she had been sure that he would not. To have it said to her face, though, was not something she had been ready for. And what did Eoin think of her now that he knew her father was Hakon Skadi, the Dreadlord of Garm?

Breanna watched Eoin's back momentarily, wondering if the man she knew loved her had honestly thought about what her lineage meant for their future. Whether he wanted to admit it, she was not only a *dìolain* but a tainted one.

Fergal, Braoin, and Eoin had reached the boats and managed to get one of the smaller ones into the water when Breanna joined them. It was not in the best shape, seemingly used for little more than short fishing runs on the huge loch, but its style was distinctly Norvegr, with a strange carved animal head on a rising prow and a narrow stern. The vessel had a light sail and two pairs of stubby oars, and even with a fair wind, they would need both to help carry them south at a swift pace.

Eoin asked, "Braoin, any experience with boats on Loch Síleann?"

The young warrior responded with, "Nothing of this size."

"Then take up the first set of oars." Eoin worked on hoisting the ragged sail while Fergal took the tiller. With no other place to sit, Breanna plopped herself down at the prow as they set sail.

The current took them slowly out into the loch, tacking south, with Braoin pulling on a set of oars, his dual-blade hilts sticking up over his shoulders. Seeing such a significant body of water made Breanna shiver. It had to hold enough of Tethra's demons to pull their vessel beneath the surface. She managed to console herself with the notion that the misshapen things would not face the shining sun. At least they were not going to try to cross the loch. Yet seeing Fergal and Eoin trying to steady the fishing boat didn't give her much confidence that sticking close to shore would help.

"You two know what you're doing?" Breanna asked.

"I hope we do," Eoin answered. "Fergal and I rafted on Loch Gowna, you know."

Eoin stumbled over a rope and fell into the port gunwale. The boat pitched violently as Fergal and Braoin threw themselves starboard to keep it from flipping. Breanna could only roll her eyes. "Loch Ree is considerably larger than Loch Gowna. And if I remember correctly, your raft didn't have a sail. I even had to save Toal from drowning because I'm the best swimmer among us."

"Aye, you did," Eoin shrugged as he got to his feet and tied off the mainsail sheet.

Fergal said, "Would you rather wait for the Dreadlord to ride us down?"

Breanna growled. "Nay, but I'd also rather not drown!"

"We're not going to drown," Eoin scoffed, but he couldn't say more. The boat shifted as a gust of wind caught the sail, and he had to duck under the swinging boom. Losing his balance, he ended up tumbling into the gunwale once more; moving a second later would have seen him knocked overboard.

Breanna did her best to keep a straight face, but seeing Eoin's sprawled form at her feet made that a challenge. Finally, righting himself, Eoin muttered a curse. After that, they sailed south silently as the men learned to work their craft with the wind and the oars.

Seeing them struggle, Breanna remained planted in the bow with her long blades in her hands, thinking she would not be much help unless they ended up in the water. Then, as the three finally grew accustomed to the boat and a few moments passed without further mishap, she offered brightly, "Well, maybe we won't sink after all, and I won't have to save you all from drowning."

"I'm glad your confidence in us has not fully deserted you," Eoin chided as he sat near the mast and readied the second set of oars. Yet, he rubbed his injured leg instead of dipping the paddles into the water. "Do you think you might be able to tell me about your quest for those magical blades you hold? Last I saw, you and Toal had headed off to Cuilcagh Mountain."

Breanna grimaced, looking past the glowing diamond blades before her as if they didn't exist. She thought about how her muscles had ached following the battle with Tethra's demons. Finally, she relented. "As I said while breaking you out of the Dreadlord's tower, keeping these blades the first night I found them wasn't easy."

Then she spun her tale about finding *Lann Dàn* and what had happened in her battle with Tethra's demons. Despite the bright sun, her words brought *Lann Dàn* and *Maorgairme* to life. Breanna felt them basking in her praise of their Tuatha magic.

Eoin whistled in surprise when she got to the part where she summoned Lugh. "It would have been glorious to take part in such a fight."

Braoin, equally awed, added, "Och, a dream of a lifetime!"

"Your steel blades would not touch them. Only magical ones can do that," Breanna declared. Then she finished the tale with her rescue by Toal, Fergal, and Ulicia. Seeing Fergal's sour face at the tiller, she offered, "Your cousin has already heard the tale from Toal, but I didn't have the opportunity to thank him for riding out to save me. So thank you, Fergal."

Fergal's face was dark as he said acidly, "Nor have I thanked you for running off to Dun Garm without me. Your confidence in my abilities to assist you was, frankly, underwhelming. Or was it that you wanted the glory all for yourself?"

Breanna knew her eyes burned with fury. If they could have unleashed *balefire* like her blades, she would have. Eoin cut in before she could say anything more, demanding in a tone that brooked no room for argument, "Fergal, I know you don't care for Breanna as I do, but this quest is important to our clans. Given that the gods have surely involved themselves, even our entire island, either join us willingly or go back to Dun Arrogh. I don't care which. If it's the former, then do so gracefully. You do no honor to our clan's name or that Celtic Knot armring you wear with spiteful words and the oath you gave me when you were once my Champion."

Fergal reddened as he sputtered, "But—but she could have—"

Eoin barked, "My Champion did what she thought best. She left someone in charge of the Red Branch. Did you think of doing the same? I thought not. Now, if you can't put aside your disdain, I'll not give you a choice and, as your Chief, order you back to Dun Arrogh."

Though Fergal's face remained twisted in anger, Breanna was surprised by Eoin's following words.

"I am a Prince of the Blood. While I rarely used such authority, my word on this is final. I'll have your pledge on this now, on your oath to me as your Chief. Can you accept that your Chief commands you, and Breanna, as my Champion, does the same? If not, let me know now, and we will part ways. You can return to Dun Arrogh to collect your things and be gone, banished from our clan as a traitor to your oath."

Eoin stood from his oars, glaring at Fergal. His cousin could not hold his gaze but nodded. His Chief demanded, "Swear it!"

Fergal hesitated before caving in. "I am loyal to my Chief and his Champion—I swear it."

"Accepted!"

Eoin sat heavily, shaking his head as he took up the wooden paddles and began his sweeps. He and Braoin helped them travel southward in silence.

All Breanna could do was stare at her Chief in disbelief. She had not thought he would take her side so readily once he understood whose daughter she was. But, *dìolain* or no, Breanna now knew he had confidence in her and believed the destiny laid upon her by the gods would lead her to kill the Dreadlord. She wished she had that same faith.

Silence fell over the boat, save for the sail catching what little breeze there was, with Eoin and Braoin dipping their oars in rhythm and water lapping against the hull. Then, as the wind coming out of the north died, the sail no longer helped them; the pair had to keep rowing for the rest of the morning.

A short while later, Breanna pulled off her still-ripped otter-skin cloak, reached into her pack for a needle and some thread, and began stitching it back together. When Braoin suggested they set out the ship's nets to see if they could catch some fish for dinner, Fergal cast a weighted mesh in their vessel's stern as they made their way south.

Braoin broke the silence by asking, "So, sister-mine, how did you become your Chief's Champion?"

Fergal looked up sharply at Breanna as she answered, "Eoin's cousin there goaded me into challenging him. He seems to think the *void* is a fairy tale. Then I used it to knock him out."

Fergal questioned, "Sister-mine?"

"Aye," Breanna confirmed. "Braoin is my half-brother."

"You're the *dìolain* who Hakon came for at Dun Arrogh."

"Aye, I am," Breanna confirmed in a tight challenge.

No one said another word as the afternoon passed.

"So, you're the young bowman who tried to set my hall on fire," Hakon stated as he towered over Toal, who did his best to hold the Dreadlord's gaze. It was more of a challenge than he had thought it would be. His will to stay strong failed with the Dreadlord and his warriors surrounding him in the oppressive stone tower, and he cast his gaze down at the floor. Hakon continued, "And you wounded some of my best warriors this morning. Do you think I should take your head as a trophy for these acts?"

Toal said nothing, his eyes still locked on his booted feet.

"Well, maybe not just yet. So, I offer a chance to redeem yourself and keep your head. Tell me where my daughter went."

Toal looked up in surprise. "Your daughter?"

"Yes, the white-haired girl who lives in your dun," Hakon snapped, wondering if the boy was simple.

Toal was stunned, unable to believe what he had just heard, and he stuttered doubtfully, "You think my cousin is your daughter? I know Breanna Ban Morna certainly would disagree. She's of the Clan Dálaigh, like myself."

"Ah, so you didn't know, and I suspect she didn't either, until recently," Hakon said. "Her mother likely hid her true lineage. No wonder she was so full of hate and rage toward me last night. Well, that explains many things. And Breanna Ban Morna is her name, you say. It is certainly a Gaelic name, which I believe means exalted one. Interesting choice. But enough of this. Tell me, boy, where is your cousin headed? And how many of your Red Branch warriors were with her?"

"Since you won't catch her, I guess I can tell you," Toal offered, trying to set up a lie to help Breanna. "North, around the tip of Loch Ree, then west. She figured you wouldn't follow her into

Connachta, and Eoin has cousins at the Doon of Drumsna. There was only Breanna and our *Ceann-cinnidh*."

Hakon eyed his captive. "I am unsure how much of that is true. What do you think, Brede? Donalt? Alrik?"

Before the Dreadrider could answer, a warrior rushed into the room. "My Jarl, one of the fishing boats is gone. Jarlson insists his scullions had them all well beached. One of them couldn't have floated away. The raiders must have taken it this morning."

Hakon turned back to Toal, his expression narrowing. "North and west, you said, but with a north wind blowing, having to cross Loch Ree in such a scullion would push them south. Even our cook would not attempt something like that in one of his fishing boats. But by hanging the sail out, they could ride the shoreline south and then circle east. If I were in their place, I'd abandon the vessel at the ford with High King's Road and head east to Dun Uisneach."

"Because they know we can't risk a fight with those in Mide or Laigin," Donalt said.

"Exactly," Hakon confirmed. "Clan Mórdha's origins are in Ulaida. He could head there for protection. Connachta is certainly the last place they'd go. How to stop them is the question."

"But why not just let them go?" Brede asked. "If they seek areas outside our control, they'll no longer be a threat. The High King only tolerates us while we have kept our focus on the west and north."

"Because my daughter is a very skilled warrior."

Brede's expression was curious. "My Jarl?"

Toal saw Hakon pause and wondered what passed between his cousin and the Norvegr. The Dreadlord finally said, "Her martial abilities are not just exceptional. She has some way of anticipating her opponent's moves and seemed to have a counter ready for each strike I made during our little battle. I can do that sometimes, but not every time!"

Brede shook his head in disbelief. "Can she truly be that good?"

"You didn't have to face her last night." Hakon sighed. "I did, and I'm certain. She also knows the ways of her fellow Gaels better than we do. I'd rather have her fighting at my side than someday find she's returned to put a knife in my back."

Then the Dreadlord walked around him, and Toal thought he was assessing him. "I don't see any of your cousin's blood in you, boy."

Toal stood with his eyes downcast, hardly trusting what he was hearing. It was like trying to piece together half a puzzle. If Breanna were the Dreadlord's daughter, what did he mean by saying he'd rather have her fighting at his side? Toal couldn't imagine Breanna would ever join the Dreadlord's cause. She was the Champion of their Red Branch, and her vow to kill the Dreadlord had remained unwavering over the years.

Still, seeing Hakon up close, with his strange blue eyes and white hair, convinced Toal that his cousin was indeed born of Hakon Skadi's seed. The how and why of it, he couldn't say, but there was little room for question about her lineage. Could this discovery be used to sway her to his side? By the stars, he hoped not, for she was their last chance to end the Dreadlord's reign.

The warrior who had brought the news of the missing boat returned a moment later, saying, "My Jarl, Runa asked me to tell you that all of the warriors this boy wounded will recover. She'll be along shortly."

"Thank you, Gjall," Hakon offered. Toal looked up at the Dreadlord. It appeared he was thinking before he turned to his Dreadriders.

"Breanna's cousin is just the bait we need to lure her back to Dun Garm. Donalt, since you recently rode along the shoreline on your hunt for my Destroyer, you and Alrik take a few warriors and see if you can pick up their trail along the shores of Loch Ree. Five of you should be a match for the two of them. And if you find my wayward daughter, remember, I want her alive. I'll bring Runa and the boy once she's sent Lunt off to Valhalla. I owe Lang a Feast of Einherjar to honor his brother."

Donalt stated, "I'd rather not miss the Feast of Fallen Warriors, as Lunt was also one of my favorites."

"As would I," Alrik added.

Hakon countered, "There is nothing we can do about it. Pay homage to Odin and Freyja while on your mounts. You two will soon be on my bastard's trail."

Donalt suggested, "If they are making for the River Shannon ford with that pathetic fishing boat, they'll likely stop at the settlement that supports me. We can be there before sundown tomorrow if we leave early. They'll need to stop for the night before that. We can be at the settlement before they arrive."

"No, you and Alrik should ride shortly," Hakon declared.

"I assume I'll be riding with you," Brede stated. "Why do we need the völva? She'll slow us down."

"My daughter was cursed by her mother at birth with something the Gaels call a *geas* that will be hard to sever," Hakon informed him. "It's what drives her to want to kill me. Runa must break the spell that the Tuatha gods provided to their Druids. Anyway, it is likely best if you and Thorvald look after Dun Garm, Brede."

Changing the subject back to their pursuit, Donalt asked, "If your Destroyer is not at the settlement where I expect them to arrive, where do we meet? And when?"

"If they do not show up by midmorning, meet me back at the River Inny crossing," Hakon answered. "If I remember correctly, a small settlement of a few hovels is gathered around it. We'll meet there at midday. And shortly after that, my daughter will either be standing at my side or be dead."

Toal could only groan at his failure, certain he would be Breanna's downfall.

Breanna

As Breanna and the others entered the bay on Loch Ree that led to the River Inny, it was just before sunset, but not by much. The light winds that had appeared earlier in the day had not helped to keep them moving south. As a result, the band had to rely on rowing. Unfortunately, as they crossed the bay created by the inlet, Eoin and Braoin were forced to keep at the oars as they slowly followed the northern shore of the loch.

When *Lann Dàn* flared, Breanna turned to her Chief, saying with dread, "We need to get off the water now."

"I'd prefer to be on the south side of the River Inny, just in case the Dreadlord has second-guessed our plans," Eoin replied between strokes. "We could row for the south side from here."

Breanna looked toward the far end of the bay and shook her head. "It's too far. The sun will be down before we get there."

From his post at the tiller, Fergal sneered, "Afraid of a few demons?"

"Aye, you idiot, and you should be, too!" she spat with rage.

Breanna saw Eoin study her face for a long moment. Then, with a shake of his head, he ordered, "We will steer north for the near shore, Fergal. Braoin and I will keep the boat moving. I'd rather not tempt the Fates, especially with what happened to Breanna near Loch Aillionn. This time, there may be no gods to answer her call."

Fergal groused something about the pair jumping at shadows, but heaved the tiller over and set the boat on a course for the closest piece of land. Breanna let her eyes scan the water behind them, looking for any sign of demons as the sun slipped lower and lower. She kept *Lann Dàn* ready, the diamond blades glowing in response to possible demons and her palms sweating in anticipation. Even the hairs on the back of her neck stood on end. The feeling lessened when the keel scraped bottom, and the bay's surface remained calm as Braoin and Eoin jumped out to pull the boat ashore moments later.

As Fergal bent to get his pack, the water behind the vessel erupted, and a dark shape suddenly loomed over him. The demon held the same black sword Breanna had faced in her last battle, and she lunged over Eoin's cousin and drove her raging white blades in. *Balefire* surged into the demon, with each diamond flaring even brighter when they struck, and Tethra's spawn exploded in a shower of dark water.

"By the gods, what was that?" Fergal shrieked, scrambling away from the stern.

"A demon who would have sliced your head off and sunk our boat if we had not made for the shore when we did," Breanna said grimly and then wiped the black muck from her face left behind by the now-dead otherworld demon. Seeing the bay's surface churn, she added, "And if we don't hurry away from here, more will follow him."

Eoin, Braoin, and Fergal looked in the direction Breanna pointed, their eyes wide with alarm. They all grabbed their packs and bolted away from the small boat, making for higher ground. Even with the fading light, they could see the water was alive with Tethra's demons as each cast wary glances behind them. That made them run faster.

It wasn't long before Eoin and Fergal were limping, but they held out long enough to be clear of the loch and the River Inny.

A short time later, exhausted, they made camp for the night in yet another tiny ring of birch trees.

 Eoin

After Eoin started a fire and cooked their small catch of fish, they ate in silence. He looked to Breanna, hoping to have words with her about her father as she unrolled her oiled tarp, bedding, and blanket. That Fergal was still staring blankly at the fire convinced him this was not the right time. It was not a conversation to have in the presence of others nearby.

Yet, maybe it did not matter, for his cousin had puzzled out the story of her lineage with Braoin's slip of the tongue and Breanna's confirmation of it. Still, something was off with him, as if he had missed some exchange between the two. Fergal must have had suspicions before now. Eoin shrugged and said, "Bre, thanks for saving my cousin from that demon. He's churlish enough not to do so himself."

"He was lucky there weren't more of them," she shrugged before she hunkered down in her blanket. "Time to get some sleep."

As she tucked herself in, Braion added, "One was enough for me. For now, though, I agree. Let's get some sleep."

With that, Eoin joined him and turned over to do just that. His cousin said nothing as he stared at their meager fire.

The following day came cold and gray for Dun Arrogh's exiles, so they wasted no time getting their sore bodies on the move once more. They followed the River Inny eastward, as it was too deep to cross and the current was still running swiftly; the harvest season had been rainy this year. Eoin didn't like it, and he complained their efforts had not taken them much farther away from the Dreadlord than at the beginning of the previous day.

He noted Breanna didn't argue the point. It was clear they had no choice except to press on. The air grew even cooler, and the clouds darkened, hinting at rain. Finally, around midday, they came to a small hovel of a settlement that lay near a ford on the river. There was not much to the place, whatever defenses they once had having rotted away. It was populated mainly by older folk standing in the doorways of the few still livable huts, their faces wary.

With their rations running low, the three from Dun Arrogh and Breanna's newfound half-brother traded a few spans of work for a meal. Their gold and silver Celtic Knot armrings identified them as holding the highest level of the warrior class, and Eoin's cloak proclaimed he was a Prince of the Blood, which meant they could have claimed Guestright and not worked at all.

Yet Eoin didn't mind chopping firewood or stacking peat, though his body protested the work due to his healing wounds. Fergal also seemed not to mind the labor, and Eoin had to smile over the effort Breanna and Braoin put forward, so they did not take from people who were so poor without giving something in return.

⸻ ❦ **Breanna** ❦ ⸻

Breanna went down to the river to try her hand at fishing and quickly filled her bucket. The older man who helped her smiled as they returned to the ford. There were indeed not enough strong young backs to support the small settlement. By the time they were ready to set out, Breanna had bartered her catch for food options that would travel better. Oatcakes, jerky, nuts, and fruit would serve them better than fish, and smell pleasant the next day. And while the small dun had no ale worth drinking, Breanna ensured she got a small jug of mead and a bag of tea in their trade. Then, pleased with herself, she led the way to the River Inny crossing.

As they approached the water, four men dressed in simple brown robes crossed toward them. From their looks, they were outlanders, likely from Albion or maybe Cymru.

The leader emerged from the river, saying in accented Gaelic, "Greetings in the name of the One God. I am called Phátric, and these are my brothers in faith. We hail from the Isle of Man and travel to spread the word about the One God and how you can find salvation through his one and only Son. I ask that you take the time to hear us out."

Breanna looked at Eoin, finding the foreigner's words challenging to follow as he mixed his Gaelic with Latin words. His accent was not something she had ever heard before. "Eoin?"

Finally, Eoin stepped forward, saying, "My mother taught me Latin mainly so I could read, but I don't speak well. From what I gathered, I cannot grant that boon. We have no time for your words, as we must be on our way quickly. But you might find receptive ears in a large dun to the northwest."

Phátric frowned. "That is unwise for your souls. You should welcome words of wisdom."

"Aye, but whose wisdom?" Eoin rejoined.

"The only wisdom that matters."

"Then take your wisdom north to Dun Garm," Eoin confirmed with a wicked grin. "It's another day's travel."

As the outlanders turned toward the small settlement to see if anyone would listen, Fergal whispered, "That's like directing a lamb into a wolf's den."

Eoin smiled. "Let's go. I want to be away from here and their kind, as they are the ones our *Ard Rí* takes captive in Albion and Cymru."

Before they could take a step, five mounted warriors came from the south, thundering across the ford. The old folk of the village ran for cover, leaving Dun Arrogh's best to stand on their own with the four defenseless One God believers. The Norvegrs rode three in front and two behind as they emerged from the river.

With their white hair, Breanna knew they were the Dreadlord's men. Before she could think about it, courage swept through her. Her *Lann Dàn* were suddenly in each hand, and she was charging the Norvergrs. She knocked down Phátric and his brothers as they got in her way, even while Eoin, Fergal, and Braoin were still drawing their swords.

Eoin cried, "Bre, no!"

It was too late—Breanna had committed herself, but to what? She wasn't entirely sure. Then her ring, *Maorgairme*, flashed, and the bravery of battle seemed to fill her like never before. She felt a weight appear on her chest, and a voice cried in her mind, *"Breanna Ban Morna, I claim you, my Hero! Erin's Hero! Rise and fight as you did when you and Lugh defeated Tethra's demons! Destroy our enemies!"*

Breanna knew it had to be *Croí Dàn*, as she could feel its heat on her chest beneath her tunic, but she had no time to think about the implications of its appearance. Yet knowing she had the Heart of Destiny supporting her, she quickly took in the first set of warriors riding three abreast as they surged forward without the water that had hindered their mounts.

Breanna caught a glimpse of the pair riding behind them, instantly noting one was the same Dreadrider she had seen in Dun Garm—Alrik was his name—when she slipped out of the cart the night she had freed her Chief. And he seemed to know her, trying to pull his mount to a quick stop. She adjusted her path to take on the lesser warrior on her left.

Fortunately, the three riders were not as skilled with their warhorses and were caught off guard by her fearless, aggressive tactics, her glowing blades making the beasts rear up before her. Forced to leap aside at the last minute to evade being trampled, Breanna seized the *void* as she rolled to her feet. She caught one rider in the thigh with a raking blade swipe. He instinctively tried to jerk out of her reach, but his fellow warriors were in his way.

When the three collided with each other, Eoin, Fergal, and Braoin pressed their attack in the mayhem of the moment. Breanna pulled the warrior she had wounded from his saddle. As he fell, she slit his throat and flung herself onto his horse. Then, the two older Norvegrs rode through the One God followers and cut them down as if they were nothing more than wheat stalks.

Riding was not one of Breanna's more proficient skills, for they had few horses in Dun Arrogh with which to practice and none of this size. Still, she knew enough to heel her mount out of the fray. The Dreadriders urged their horses after her as the other two warriors lifted their blades to fend off Eoin, Braoin, and Fergal. Their battle-trained horses flailed away with their hooves to help protect the riders as the trio of Gaels tried to get at them.

Breanna wheeled about at the northern edge of the settlement, charging back at the Dreadriders pursuing her. When Alrik swung at her with the flat of his blade, Breanna ducked away from his sword, realizing as it flashed past her that he had not used the edge—her father must have ordered that she be taken alive. As she passed, she lashed out at the other Dreadrider, ducking away from his sword. Breanna nearly unseated him as one of her *Lann Dàn* caught him firmly in the chest. He would have been dead without his hard-boiled cuirass, as the blade only punched a small hole in the leather. Still, Breanna heard him grunt at the impact. She kept her horse charging forward, riding down one of the other young warriors. Breanna managed to spear him in the back as he turned to evade Braoin's dual sword blades.

As the Norvegr tumbled from his saddle, his companion countered with a desperate roundhouse sword stroke. Luckily, Breanna took only a glancing blow on one of her leather vambraces and quickly was out of range. The awkward swing left the warrior off balance, and Eoin jerked him from his mount, skewering him on the way to the ground.

Braoin, Fergal, and Eoin used the young warrior's horse for cover as the Dreadriders were on the offensive, trying to get at them. Seeing this, Breanna turned to intercept the senior warriors, cutting in behind the one she had nearly unhorsed in her last charge.

The younger warrior yelled, "Donalt, behind you!"

Yet it was too late, and Breanna drove a *Lann Dàn* blade deep into his upper hip. The force of the blade on his bone knocked him from his saddle. The one named Alrik turned his horse on Breanna, raising his sword to strike her down, but she was too quick—the *void* showed her his planned move before he even thought of it—and she raised one blade to fend off his sword stroke while slashing in with the other.

Her left blade tip caught him in the face, drawing a line from his cheekbone to his chin, and he reeled backward to avoid her other weapon now sweeping in across his chest. The sharp blade slit open his leather cuirass, leaving a shallow cut from armpit to armpit as Breanna charged away.

Breanna saw Donalt fling himself back onto his mount and urged it toward a clear space back up the trail. He turned his gaze to the Gaelic warriors as if to confirm that those companions lying on the ground at their feet were dead. As Breanna pulled her mount around to face him, ready to charge again, he yelled, "Alrik, we ride!"

Alrik kicked his horse into action to bolt north toward Dun Garm, the one he called Donalt, hot on his heels.

"Cowards!" Breanna bellowed after them, then pulled on the reins and heeled her mount gently toward her Chief.

"That was incredible!" Braoin exclaimed. And then swore, "*Damú*! You're more than good. That was brilliant! You all keep tossing about words of Tuatha magic, and I thought you were *craiceáilte*, but by the gods, they've claimed you, Breanna!"

Fergal was gathering his pack from the river's edge. "That woman's crazier than I thought," he said to Eoin. "Charging five mounted warriors—two being Dreadriders—was more than cracked. She could have gotten herself killed. And we with her!"

"At least she got us horses to ride," Eoin countered. "And her courage was indeed a terrifying thing to behold."

With adrenaline still pumping through her veins, Breanna ignored Fergal, sheathed her blades in the harness on her back, and then dismounted the warhorse. To her surprise, *Croí Dàn* exclaimed mind-to-mind, *"My Hero, Erin's Hero! You fought brilliantly!"*

Breanna gasped at the Heart of Destiny that was speaking in her head. Then she pulled the heart-shaped ruby gem from her deerskin tunic, asking, "Where in the world did you come from?"

Croí Dàn answered, *"You are mine! Danu sent me to support your quest to remove the Dreadlord from our land. My name is Kree Dawn. Maorgairme declared it was time I joined you!"*

Braoin and Eoin came to her side, with her Chief demanding, "What is that?"

In amazement, Breanna shook her head. "It's called Kree Dawn, the Heart of Destiny. The Mother Goddess wore this gem when she informed me that Croí Dàn chose me." Her magic imparts courage and heroism in Gaels when borne by her chosen Hero, Erin's Hero, so it looks like I am hers."

"Hers?" Braoin asked.

"Aye, she is undoubtedly female and a demanding one, to boot!"

The ruby-shaped gem informed her, *"Danu created me as a conscious female being. You can refer to me as Ćroí Dàn, but I'd prefer you use Mo Chroí."*

Breanna chuckled, "Hmm, let me correct myself, as she just told me to address her as *Mo Chroí*. I think a better description of her nature would be that she is very assertive. "

Ćroí Dàn huffed, saying, *"My Hero."*

Eoin agreed. "Given our legends, my Heart is appropriate."

Braoin looked around at the dead Norvegrs and the One God followers, stating, "Well, she certainly inspired your courage, given the results."

Having gathered the packs the Norvegr warriors had carried, Fergal returned to hand one to each of them. "What I want to know is how they found us."

"Maybe it was his völva," Breanna suggested. "Runa is said to have the *sight*. Either way, it's a debate that can wait. I expect Hakon will send more warriors soon."

Fergal asked Breanna, "Do you want your trophies? Two of these kills are yours, and you certainly helped Eoin with the third."

Breanna answered, "We barely have the time to claim our spoils as is our custom after a battle, so let's see what their bodies yield beyond their packs and get going. And leave the Christians be. The settlement can deal with them. Yet, we should leave them the coins."

"You're right," Eoin confirmed.

The four of them went about the grim work of stripping the dead of their weapons, as their swords and hunting knives would make for a good trade ahead. While the warriors had few coins, which they handed over to the settlement, Breanna secured a spare cloak. Braoin and Fergal did the same. After cleaning the weapons and themselves of spilled blood in the river, they mounted their seized warhorses.

Eoin commanded, "We ride for Dun Uisneach!"

A nearby crow cawed what sounded like the word *ride* and took flight over them, heading southeast, with a murder of her fellow crows flying in formation behind the bigger bird.

Eoin gave Breanna a hand, swinging her up to ride behind him, and she said, "Given *Mo Chroí* has claimed me, and this is the second time the Mórrigan watched me battle, I think some force is, indeed, leading us to the Dark Goddess."

They left the village and Hakon's dead warriors behind, along with the cut-down and trampled followers of the One God, fording the River Inny and then turning east to track its course.

Hakon

Hakon rode south with his völva. To say his mood was foul would be an understatement. Yet, unfortunately, it was a mood that the gray sky seemed to match. The night before, he had sent one of his most favored warriors to Valhalla. Then, this morning, he'd been forced to leave four seasoned warriors behind to heal from the arrow wounds caused by the Gaelic boy. And now, instead of speeding after his daughter, he had to endure the slow pace of a creaking cart. Much preferring to have his horse beneath him, he looked longingly back at the mount following on a tethered rein tied to the chariot. Then he thought about his Dreadriders and hoped Donalt and Alrik had tracked down his Destroyer.

As it stood now, his daughter was probably no closer than when he had set out, which would do him little good. He needed to catch her, not follow at a safe distance. How else would he convince her he was not the foul ogre she thought he was? If all that Runa had told him about Breanna Ban Morna was true, the gods of his co-opted land would not want to see that happen. Thinking about making better time, he urged the cart horses into a slightly faster trot.

Runa muttered something foul and held on to the railing tightly.

Hakon offered defensively, "I must know where she is going and why."

Runa cocked her intact eye at him. "You mean the Destroyer?"

"My daughter's name is Breanna," he commanded, his tone biting.

"That may be, but knowing her name doesn't change what she is nor the *geas* cast upon her," his sorceress rejoined. "She remains the Destroyer, a point with which Lunt can no longer argue. Until—or if—I break that *geas*, she will not change."

Fury burned in him, but his noted logic prevailed. His voice held less acid when he asked again, "Then where is the Destroyer going and why?"

She answered in a more soothing tone, "Given that Breanna carried Tuatha weapons when she came to Dun Garm and did not use them magically, one might surmise she does not know how the magic works. If I were her, I'd seek one who could tell me that. "

"So she is not running away with her friend?"

"She is the Destroyer," his völva reminded him again. "Or has your quest to lure her to your side blinded you? Save for my error about her sex, have not my foretellings thus far been true? No, she is not running away—she cannot. Instead, she is searching for a way to destroy you."

Hakon probed, "Then where is she headed? Surely Dun Uisneach cannot be her goal."

Runa looked to the east, her one good eye glazing over, and Hakon knew the *sight* had taken her. A moment later, the world seemed to lurch to a stop, as if time had frozen, and she whispered, "No, Dun Uisneach just happens to lie along the way. The Destroyer is heading southeast. A place called Cro—gah!"

Runa's hands flew to her head; she squeezed her eye tight and screwed up her face in pain. As she sagged into his arms, Hakon steadied her and asked, "What happened?"

Runa shook her head as if to clear it, took a deep breath, and whispered, "The Tuatha Dark Goddess just declared war on me! She sent a murder of crows into my mind when I pulled the *sight* open. It was like being drawn into chaos!"

"What does that mean?" Hakon demanded.

"It means I can only try to access the *sight* with protection," was the answer. "Like the shield I used when we summoned the god Tethra."

"That took power and considerable time on your part, did it not?" Hakon asked. She nodded. "And it will slow us down in determining where the Dark Goddess has directed Breanna to?"

"Já, to both questions," Runa grumbled. "The Gael gods are working openly against me. What I know is one thing–she is heading southeast. Unfortunately, that's an area we know little about. I saw a tall forest-covered hill that the Destroyer must seek out. Then the Goddess of War's crows attacked me. So, that was not enough to know where to find this place."

"We need to know what lies that way that would help Breanna Ban Morna," Hakon stated.

"It must be someplace where the Dark Goddess can meet her," Runa guessed. "But for what magical purpose? What can only Badb Catha tell your Destroyer? Likely how to fulfill her *geas*."

Hakon raised an eyebrow, urging her on, so Runa continued, "Those few Druids with whom I've managed to have civil words say the Dark Goddess is the Gaelic ruler of war, death, and knowledge. One of the primary makers of the Tuatha's magical works, be they weapons or otherwise. So the strange glowing long blades your Destroyer wielded would be something she would understand and probably had even created."

"Then we must intercept her before she reaches this Dark Goddess."

"Aye, that would be advisable," Runa said. "You must also catch her before our Fomorian god, Tethra, does. He will pursue her if she carries magic woven by the Tuatha gods."

Hakon grimaced, wondering if he had been rash in enlisting Tethra's help. Still, if all Runa said about the Tuatha was true, turning his daughter from her hatred would be a challenge. Thus, he might still need the old god's aid. His hopes rested on the notion that Breanna would want to trade her life for her cousin's. The boy named Toal, who rode sullenly behind one of Hakon's warriors, was a boon he had not expected.

They wheeled on, silence settling over them for a time, with Hakon surveying his entourage of warriors, looking for signs of weakness or inattention. He had kept their number to ten mounted warriors in hopes that if he encountered any other clans, they would think before attacking, but it also was not enough to provoke a response by the High King's men at Dun Uisneach, should they be spotted.

Until he strayed too far east, that was. Then, getting past Chief Faolán's hold without losing his daughter's path would be his next problem. With Donalt and Alrik already ahead of them, the only other Dreadrider with him was Lang; the lad had insisted on joining them despite his wounds.

Hakon had yet to tell the young warrior that he hoped his daughter would fight alongside them. Getting her to see his point would be a significant challenge, especially after their battle. Yet he had other concerns, like getting south and east of Dun Uisneach.

A commotion ahead drew his attention, and he stopped the chariot. Then Alrik appeared with his face bloody and a hand pressed across his chest. The Dreadrider looked like he had seen one too many battles, and Hakon knew that meant he had crossed blades with his daughter. Donalt followed behind his fellow Dreadrider, holding a hand pressed to his hip. The fact that the other three warriors were missing brought a troubled frown to Hakon's face.

Several hands, including Lang's, helped Alrik from his mount before turning to Donalt as Hakon strode toward them. Both immediately dropped to their knees, with Runa quickly checking on the former, declaring, "Donalt's high hip wound is more serious than Alrik's shallower wounds." She pulled out her needle and thread, setting herself to stitch up the wounded older Dreadrider.

Kneeling beside Alrik, Hakon said softly, "So, old friend, you caught up with my daughter. I fear my concerns about you taking her alive were misplaced. They should have been for you."

"Já," Alrik managed with a nod. "She is as fierce a warrior as I've ever seen. We rode in on them by surprise at that small village just ahead by the ford, and she, on foot no less, charged five mounted warriors with her long blades blazing. I've never seen anything like it. Your daughter either has more courage than the sum of your Dreadriders, or she is mad. There she was, causing our first line of mounts to rear up. After that, chaos reigned. She is fierce, like you."

Donalt grunted. "We couldn't stop her from charging us repeatedly while she somehow evaded every sword stroke."

"Fellow warriors?" Hakon questioned as he cast a dark look at Toal.

"Aye, there were three Gael warriors with her. Two with gold, one with silver arm rings," Alrik answered. "I recognized two of them as being the ones from Dun Arrogh, and the other was Braoin."

"By the gods, what a mess!" Hakon bellowed. Then, in a clipped voice, he asked, "And they took the horses?"

"I expect so," Donalt answered, "though I can't say I stayed to see it. I thought it best we lived to tell you what a crazy bastard she can be."

"Hel's tits," Hakon swore as his mind raced to form a plan. If his daughter and her clan were mounted, she would soon be too far ahead of them to catch. He quickly turned to Runa. "Once you finish stitching these two up, take Donalt and Alrik back to Dun Garm in the chariot with Gjall as an escort. You must determine where in the southeast they are heading.

"After that, you and Thorvald should take two bands of nine and head southeast. Make sure you swing east of Dun Uisneach before heading south to evade their patrols. There's a ford at the mouth of the River Brosna where we can meet up. Tell Thorvald to use a signal fire at dusk on the north side of the High King's Road. I'll meet you there after I follow them past Dun Uisneach, which will likely be in three days. Tell Brede that he is to continue his command of Dun Garm. Given that Alrik and Donalt are wounded, I need someone uninjured to take charge."

"What about our dead warriors at the river crossing?" Runa inquired.

Hakon knew she was referring to the fact that his warriors would have no one to give them the funeral rites, and they deserved it as much as Lunt had. He hesitated before commanding, "Lang, take half the band and ride ahead to get the bodies. We'll create a pyre here."

"Certainly, my Jarl," Lang said stiffly, his face tight with anger.

As his young Dreadrider and his companions rode away, Hakon asked Runa, "Once you finish the rites at dusk, will Donalt and Alrik be able to travel?"

"Best to wait until morning before heading back to Dun Garm."

Hakon grimaced at the delay.

The five warriors returned with their three dead friends in under a span, though Lang was not amongst them. They informed Hakon that his Dreadrider was questioning those in the dun where the attack occurred. Hakon knew Lang would not return by this evening. He was briefly furious, but at least his youngest Dreadrider would only have a short lead on his hunting party. He would be sure his youngest Dreadrider paid a price when he caught up with the wayward lad.

With nothing to do about Lang until then, he turned to the matter of his dead warriors, as they deserved his attention one last time. As night fell, Runa stood before their funeral pyres, ready to lead the dead to the Halls of Valhalla. They could not undergo a Feast of Einherjar to honor them as they had Lang's brother, but such a thing was not always necessary. Instead, they would pay homage to Odin, Freyjá, and her Valkyries with simple pyres.

As Hakon and his warriors gathered around her, Runa chanted, "This is a time that is not a time, in a place that is not a place, on a day that is not a day. Here, we stand at the threshold between the worlds. We stand before the Gates of Asgard. We humbly ask the Ancient Ones to help and protect those who have gone before us during this turn of seasons. More fine warriors have fallen, ones who will not have the honor of a Feast. We ask that all in Asgard pay them homage, for they died bravely and with swords in their hands. Led by Freyjá, may Odin's Valkyries provide these warriors safe passage to Valhalla."

And with that, the funeral pyres were set on fire. The blazing flames flickered across Hakon's face as he pondered the cost of pursuing his daughter. It had already taken a more significant toll than expected. If Breanna couldn't be turned to his side soon, she would have to die.

A moment later, he walked away to mount up. In darkness or not, he would have to ride if he was going to catch his daughter or Lang. His remaining warriors followed him quietly into the night, leaving Runa and her escort behind. While their pace was slow, at least they were moving, each carrying a torch to light the way.

SAFE HARBOR

Breanna

The path they followed along the river was one that Breanna knew led toward Dun Uisneach and beyond, which should ensure their safety. Eoin set a leisurely pace at her suggestion, so they did not tire their horses. Still, they made better time on the big mounts than she ever imagined possible. While the gray sky threatened rain, it was a promise not kept.

Breanna urged Eoin to leave the river path behind in the late afternoon, especially given that sunlight was fading. A quick reminder about Tethra's demons had him taking the next opening in the woods, where a path heading south. They came across another small settlement a short time later, one that had once been a dun, and Eoin claimed Guestright so that they didn't have to spend the night outside where it might rain.

The settlement had little to offer besides an empty cow shed for the night, but it was good enough after the past few days of hard travel and battle. For Breanna, the first order of business was to find the wash house. Unlike the peat fire-warmed tubs in Dun Arrogh, the water was cold. But after what she had been through these past few days, she was more than willing to endure the icy water to remove the demon and warrior blood from her skin.

Fortunately, the wash house was empty, except for an older woman who passed by as she came out of the door. Breanna didn't have to face anyone who might question her distinctly Norvegr appearance as she washed herself and her soiled clothes. Once back in the shed, she convinced the men to use the tubs, then donned the set of Toal's clothes that Lissa had given her. That thought made her hope her cousin was safely in her sister's hands.

Afterward, once they had eaten and laid out their blankets for the night, Eoin touched Breanna on the shoulder and motioned for her to follow him outside. Fergal moved to join them, but Eoin held out a hand to stop him. "I would have words with my Champion alone. Remember your oath, cousin."

Fergal stiffened at the command.

Breanna guarded her expression as she stepped from the shed, knowing Eoin wanted to talk about her father. Fortunately, it was dark enough to hide her face and any telling expressions she might have made.

After emerging from the shed, Eoin took her by the arm and led them between the broken-down gates of the settlement and their guestright shed. An old guard stood some distance from where they stopped. He seemed only briefly interested in them, and Breanna expected it was due to his cloak, which proclaimed him as a Prince of the Blood. Torches burned in their stanchions on the broken gate posts, casting enough light for them to see each other.

Eoin turned to her and said softly, "Bre, when the Dreadlord came to Dun Arrogh, he said things that puzzled me. While in his stone tower, I managed to sort out most of what you'd decided not to tell me about your father. I can't say I understand why you thought you had to keep it from me, but I think you owe me an explanation."

Breanna was unable to hold Eoin's gaze. She looked at her feet and was silent for a time. Then she hissed abruptly, "It's because his blood taints me!"

Nonplussed, Eoin asked, "Excuse me?"

Letting her eyes rise to his and, feeling vulnerable, she whispered in a trembling voice, "You truly don't understand, do you? I am the Dreadlord's daughter. A *dìolain* spawned by a rape! Tainted blood isn't something to boast about. I never noticed how people looked at me with skeptical glances, but I do now. I never understood the hushed comments, but I do now. People have always looked at me differently, Eoin. My mother protected me from most of it, enough to blind even me. I can't hide my white hair, can't hide that I'm half-Norvegr. And no clan except my own—and even that I wonder about—would accept or suffer one of such blood."

Eoin shook his head, scoffing. "Is that what this is all about? Acceptance?"

"Yes! Yet you don't see it because love shades your view."

"Maybe it does, for I do love you, Bre. And you know it."

"Aye, I do know it," Breanna confirmed. "But love is not for us. You see, thinking my mother would hate any spawn of the Dreadlord, she had our old Fáidh place a *geas* upon my *anam*. That *geas* cast my destiny as the Dreadlord's Destroyer. Why else have the Tuatha gods come to my aid? Until I fulfill that destiny, I cannot think of anything else. Especially a man. Especially you."

"And after, when you have indeed rid our land of the Dreadlord?"

"I will remain half-Norvegr, half-outlander," Breanna reminded him sadly. "Any children I have will be part outlander, tainted by his blood. Can you honestly say your clan—with its deep-rooted royal Ulaidan Gaelic blood—would accept me or any children from our union? Would you truly be able to dance around the Beltaine tree with me and have no concern about what your clan would say?"

Eoin stammered, "But—but it's not fair. I love you."

"Aye, that I know. Unfortunately, as I said, my *geas* and half-outlander blood have left me no room for love or fairness."

With that, Breanna turned and walked back to the shed.

 Eoin

Eoin could only shake his head and think the world was cruel. Why did he have to love a woman who was so single-minded? Her passion was given to only one thing, leaving no room for other emotions. Still, despite his stinging heart, he could do nothing but love her all the more for her devotion to her cause.

He had often seen what a simple *geas* could do, and the gods drove her with a strong and complex one. Someday, maybe someday, she could come to love him. He could only hope it would be so. When he returned to the shed, though, the cold shoulder she gave him by facing away, even though she lay next to him, made it difficult not to be bitter. It was even harder not to pull her into his arms.

The following morning passed uneventfully, save for encounters with passing rain showers. The air remained cloudy and chilly as they rode, helping to keep their horses from overheating despite Eoin pushing them into a gallop at first for a few miles. He wanted to put some distance between them and the settlement in case Hakon had someone tracking them. Then, he pulled the pace back to a trot. Breanna sat stiffly behind him, saying not a word, and there seemed to be more profound tension between them than the day before.

Fergal broke the silence, asking Braoin, "Anything I need to know about your half-sister? Something that might bring Eoin to his senses."

Braoin raised an eyebrow and said tightly, "If there were, I'd not be sharing it with an unbeliever like you."

"Gods and magic won't save us from Hakon!" Fergal countered.

Eoin, sounding exasperated, suggested, "Braoin, my cousin's blind dislike of magic has addled his mind. Best to ignore him."

A short while later, Breanna had Eoin hold up to switch the riding order, giving Eoin's mount a more manageable load. When she jumped up behind Braoin, Fergal urged his horse next to Eoin, asking, "You'd have two of Hakon's spawn ride at our backs?"

Eoin heard his cousin's caustic tone and glared at him. "Take the lead. Spew your foul words to yourself."

Reining his mount back, Eoin fell in beside Braoin and Breanna, muttering, "By the stars, he got a hard head."

"Is Fergal always so thick?" Braoin asked.

Eoin cocked his head. "Thick about?"

"Well, your cousin is as dense as mud to side against my half-sister and you. You have an undeniable connection."

Eoin heard Breanna groan as he grunted, "I'm too obvious."

Croí Dàn smugly said, *"My Hero, this Braoin is very perceptive!"*

Breanna replied, *"Hmm. He should keep his nose to himself."*

Eoin stiffened at the unknown voice in his mind, looking around and wondering where it came from. Still stunned, he glanced at Breanna, asking, "You said the Heart of Destiny speaks to you. Why am I now hearing her and you in my head?"

Braoin asked, "I'm confused. What?"

"How did Eoin hear you?" Breanna demanded.

"You are both connected."

Eoin raised an eyebrow and thought, *"Connected?"*

Ćroí Dàn chortled. *"Indeed!"*

Breanna directed at her brother, "It's nothing important, Braoin. So, Eoin, you and Fergal seem to be doing better with your wounds. I don't hear as much groaning or complaining, and even spending so much time in a saddle does not seem to bother you."

Braoin asked, "What happened? Was there a battle I missed?"

Breanna chuckled. "It's how they got wounded. Eoin and Fergal exchanged words with Hakon's Dreadriders, Lunt and Lang, while they were hunting for me, and a battle ensued. I injected myself to protect my Chief as his Champion and beat off the Norvegrs."

"That's twice you've taken on two Dreadriders and won, then?"

Breanna confirmed, "Aye, they were good to practice on. Speaking of which, Braoin, I remember you from the Dun Uisneach *comórtas* last summer. If I recall, you lost to a warrior who looked like us. His name was Bradaigh, and his white hair makes me think he's one of us."

"Aye, that's him," Braoin answered. "Your assumption is correct. From my time at Dun Garm, I heard the older Dreadrider you beat was searching for him on Hakon's order, as Alrik did with me."

Eoin interjected, "Aye, that would make sense."

Braion continued, "Anyway, back to Bradaigh, I'd say he made it a tough match. He hails from a settlement near Dun Uisneach. He's good with a sword, for sure, and quick on his feet. Before I thought of a move, he seemed to know what I was planning as a counter. It was just like the match we had. But you're better than Bradaigh with that uncanny ability."

"Och, the *void*," Breanna commented, smiling. "It's called *urghabháil an neamhní*, seizing the *void*."

"You know how to seize it?"

"I do," she answered. "And the more I use it, the easier it is to wield in battle. It appears to be similar to the Tuatha magic that our one-time Seeress Druid uses called the *sight*. While an *Aos Dána* uses it to see the future or past, the *void* for a warrior is about seeing a moment ahead of time in their mind. It is Tuatha magic, where you know what your opponent will do before they have fully formed the thought of their action. When you're in the *void*, you are a step ahead of your opponent before they know it themselves. It's hard to describe, but I will try to teach you when we have time."

"You'd do that for me?" Braoin asked. "You've only known me for a few days."

"Certainly. It makes us all better. Anyway, I recall you're from Loch Síleann. How did you come to be at Dun Garm?"

Braoin spun how Alrik appeared at his settlement and added that the Dreadlord had offered him a place in his dun. He also shared what he knew about the justice *geas* his mother had cast upon him before his birth.

Eoin said, "That fits what I gathered from my time there."

"Then it appears we share the same father and a similar *geas*," Breanna concluded. "Mine is to seek my father's destruction, and yours is to seek justice. I'm curious to learn if Bradaigh has one as well."

"Aye, I believe we do share such a link."

"Then, my brother," she asked, "will you commit your life to my cause? I have pledged to use the Tuatha magic granted to me by our gods to end the Dreadlord's presence in our land. Will you join me, even if it costs us our lives?

"Sister-mine, I will make that pledge. And swear it before our gods."

"Then you are as you just called me, brother-mine."

"Let's hope Bradaigh will also join us," Eoin added, urging their mounts into a canter to make better time. By not quite sunset, they had traveled entirely into Mide territory and started along the High King's Road to Tara. It didn't take long for a patrol to stop them, the leader drawing his chariot across their path.

As the battle-scarred hulk of a man—the *fian-ceannard*, clearly the band's leader—moved his chariot closer to question the four, he eyed Breanna and Braoin suspiciously as he rubbed his graying, bristly red beard. He looked nearly old enough to be a grandfather, yet age had not kept him from command or the trail.

Eoin noted the *fian* of nine warriors who surrounded them were young and edgy, and they held their long spears tightly. Their leader was the only one with a sword and a gold armring. Without a doubt, they were Chief Faolán's men. He raised a hand in peace, saying, "Hail, good men of Dun Uisneach! Your escort is welcome."

Turning his weathered face to Eoin, the leader said, "Regardless of your royal garb, those who travel east on the *Slíghe Mor* must be on the king's business. Where are you bound?"

With no reason to lie, Eoin answered, "To the headwaters of the River Boyne. Our Fáidh sent us on a quest to seek out the Dark Goddess."

The old warrior, who likely would have been a *Ceann-cinnidh* at any other dun, made a sign to ward off the thought of anyone wanting to seek out Badb Catha, and his horses shifted the chariot under him nervously as if they agreed. "Your Fáidh, you say, sent you on this quest? Hmm, it sounds like a thing not willingly undertaken."

"Aye," Fergal put in with conviction. "Certainly not on my part. These three appear to think more of our Druids than I, but I could not let them run off without a proper escort."

Then the leader turned to Breanna and Braoin. "And from where do you two claim your clans?"

Gesturing to Eoin and Fergal, Breanna answered tightly, "We three were all born and raised in Dun Arrogh and have won duels at the Dun Uisneach *comórtas* for the gold or silver on our arms. Braoin, my half-brother in front of me, hails from a settlement near Loch Síleann. He also competed for his silver arm ring last summer alongside me during the same games, and we were both honored by Chief Faolán. Surely, you should remember that."

The leader of the *fian* shrugged. "Maybe I do, but Dun Arrogh, north of Loch Gowna, is where that white-haired Norvegr outlander has laid claim. From what I've seen of them, they resemble you and your half-brother. While you fought in our *comórtas*, you may be here to spy for them. After all, you ride their horses. You wouldn't be one of them, would you?"

Eoin answered, "Nay, not our Bre. Born and raised in Dun Arrogh, she was. As for these mounts, they are spoils of battle. Five of Norvegr outlanders, two of them being Dreadriders, waylaid us, and we slayed the lesser warriors. The senior ones fled."

"Dreadriders? You're pulling my leg!"

Breanna said with a cold stare, "Not in the least."

Realizing the dangerous turn of the conversation, Eoin pulled one of the Norvegr swords from his bedroll. "In addition to these mounts, I can offer this as proof, one of the many spoils we claimed. But the day gives way to dusk, good sir, and our tale is long. We would happily share it if you would grant us Guestright in your dun."

"If you claim Guestright, then I must grant it," the old warrior said, as he looked over to Eoin and broke his gaze away from Breanna's bright blue eyes. He took the sword to have a closer look.

Croí Dàn said, *"Be easy, my Hero. He is not your enemy. On the contrary, I will influence him, and he will soon be an ally. Pull me free of your tunic."*

Eoin was again momentarily stunned by the Heart of Destiny speaking in his mind, making her magical being feel more real to him. Breanna casually pulled out *Croí Dàn* from her tunic, letting it hang visibly. Eoin quickly asserted, "Then I claim Guestright. My name is Eoin Mac Cairbre, of Clan Mórdha, and this is my cousin, Fergal Mac Conall. My Champion, Breanna Ban Morna, is of Clan Dálaigh. And last, Braoin Mac Lochlinn."

The *fian* nodded. "You have a Champion, wear a Prince of the Blood's cloak, and are likely a Dun Chief from Norvegr-claimed lands. That would make you a *Ceann-cinnidh*, outranking me. Yet I've never heard of a woman being a Chief's Champion. She doesn't appear to be one taken lightly from the look in her eyes, the lines of her muscles, and those strange, shiny blades poking over her back."

"On that, you'd be wise not to challenge her," Eoin agreed.

The old warrior protested with disdain, "Dálaigh is from Laigin, but Mórdha is a northern Ulaida, likely one of three Dál Clans."

At his continued obstinacy, *Croí Dàn* pulsed as the *fian* leader returned the Norvegr sword to back him. When Eoin slid it into his bedroll, where he had previously stored it, the weathered Gael warrior seemed to relax. A smile crept over his face, and his warriors raised their spears as if their leader commanded them to stand down.

Eoin answered, "Aye, but a splinter of each of our clans settled in Dun Arrogh many years back. So we now owe our protection to the *Ard-Rí* in Tara. Not that he has done anything about the Norvegr Jarl who claims his tribute from us."

The old warrior sighed. "I find myself in agreement with you, as it's a shame the High King has not been paying attention to matters in his land and is more interested in raiding the Albion or Cymru coasts lately. Given this, I believe you four need my help."

"Aye, we do," Eoin confirmed.

The *fían* leader gave Eoin a toothy grin, showing gaps where several teeth were missing. "The name is Corbmac, of the Clan Uí Néil, cousin to Faolán, who is a cousin to the *Ard-Rí*. I bid you welcome in my cousin's name to join me as we ride to Dun Uisneach. Chief Faolán and Chieftess Falyn will also want to speak with you. They will honor your guestright request.

"Since you live in the Dreadlord's territory, and given your recent *contest* with his warriors, you might have some interesting observations for my *Ceann-cinnidh* and his *Taoiseach*, maybe even helping us limit the Norvegr Jarl's power. Please, follow me."

"Aye, Corbmac," Eoin said, relief filling him. "We can help your *Ceann-cinnidh and Taoiseach* with that." He caught Breanna's gaze, then regarded *Croí Dàn*, faintly glowing on her chest.

Mo Chroí, the artifact claimed as her name; the thought sent a pang through Eoin's own chest. She was useful indeed, this gift of the gods that had claimed Breanna as her own.

But he could not help but be a trifle jealous.

Breanna

Ćroí Dàn directed to her Hero, *"See, easy. A new ally."*

Breanna shook her head. *"It was easy for you."*

As they fell in behind the *fían-ceannard's* chariot, Breanna said aloud, "Corbmac, we are indeed glad to offer our assistance, but we want more than that—we want to see the Dreadlord destroyed."

That brought another grin from Corbmac as his band of nine followed, making their way along *Slíghe Mor* toward Dun Uisneach.

Fergal rode up beside Eoin, asking in a low voice, "What just happened?"

Eoin said darkly, "Not now unless you wish me to send you back."

Fergal cursed quietly to himself, "*Tá olann ina hintinn agam!*"

Eoin turned, saying tightly, "That's not wool in your brains. It's your head up your arse. Shut your mouth. These are not our clans; we have not fully won their support."

Hearing the exchange, Breanna tapped Braoin's shoulder to draw in the reins. Their horse slowed, settling between the other two. She gave Fergal a narrow glance, adding tartly, "*Croí Dàn* has ensured this Corbmac will provide support. Yet you could ruin it with your doubts. Keep your opinions to yourself, or there will be more dire consequences than just Eoin ordering you back to our dun."

Fergal bristled, but *Croí Dàn* punched into his mind, "*Cur, I can end you!*" He blanched in response.

Breanna looked at Eoin to confirm he had heard the Heart of Destiny. She demanded, "*Mo Chroí, what have you done?*"

"*Only what was required.*"

Eoin smiled at his cousin. "Be wise, Fergal."

Breanna nodded to her Chief and signaled Braoin to nudge their horse forward next to the chariot. Then, with encouragement from her Heart, she asked, "So, Corbmac, tell me about yourself. You seem loved by these *fian* warriors. Do you have grandchildren?"

"Nay, I'm my Chief and Chieftess's man, doing his duty."

Breanna frowned. "Och, that's a shame. I think you'd be a wonderful grandpa."

Corbmac looked perplexed yet pleased. "I wouldn't know about that."

Her voice hinting at sorrow, Breanna said, "Hmm, I never had a grandpa or a father to guide me."

The grizzled warrior's stern nature seemed to wilt at her odd half-outlander admission of how she had grown up. But he smiled, countering, "Yet here you are, a brilliant warrior with extraordinary courage."

With that, Breanna shrugged. Yet she knew he spoke truly.

The sun was nearly below the horizon when they arrived at Dun Uisneach, a sprawling hillfort bigger than Dun Garm with tall earth-and-stone ramparts and gates made of stout oak timbers covered with bronze plates. It was somewhat like the Dreadlord's hold, with its pickets lining the ramparts. The land west of the ringfort was cultivated and bounded by many stonewalled pastures for horses, goats, and cattle. To the north and south was a thick black oak forest, and to the east, Uisneach Hill rose to tower over the fort.

Seeing it brought up memories of the summer *comórtas*, something she thought was a key turning point in her life. Yet, that was nothing compared to what she now had to face. How could her gods have picked an odd girl from a backhills dun to save their land?

As they passed through the gates, Breanna could only wish Dun Arrogh thrived like Dun Uisneach. But, then, Chief Faolán and Chieftess Falyn's fort lay within the borders of the High King's realm and served a purpose—keeping the Norvegr raiders from crossing into the heartland of Mide or Lagain. Dun Arrogh, on the other hand, was now just an afterthought, built by some long-forgotten Ulaida Clan Chief.

When the springtime Beltaine Festival arrived, their Druids said it was from this fort that the *Ard-Rí* lit the first ritual fires on top of Uisneach Hill. Those hills rose above the fort, and once seen, the lighting of other fires by other Provincial *Rì's* and *Ceann-cinnidhs* from various hilltops across the land signaled the beginning of spring and the fertility rites that accompanied the season of rebirth. Yet her dun had been sacrificed to live under her father's rule. That was a bitter herb to swallow dry. But here, in the center of their land, Breanna breathed a sigh of relief, now protected by a powerful Chief and Chieftess.

It was nearly dark when they drew up at the stables; they left their mounts to the stablehands and crossed the yard to the knot of communal buildings. After the four of them had finished cleaning up by making a brief stop in the bathhouse, they were ready to be presented to the Chief and Chieftess of Dun Uisneach and strode to the main hall. As was his right, Corbmac requested that they leave their weapons at the building's entrance.

Eoin, Fergal, and Braoin willingly gave up their blades, but Breanna did not. As she stared Corbmac down, *Lann Dàn* came to life, as did *Maorgairme*, flaring bright white. Then *Ćroí Dàn* pulsed beneath her tunic, making Corbmac step back.

Before he could signal the guards, Breanna said in a tight voice, "While I think you're a good man, these are Tuatha weapons, given into my care by the Sun God. I'll part with them for no one, not even the *Ard-Rí* in Tara. Ask your Fáidh about *Lann Dàn* if you would care to confirm my story. If you require it, I will give you my word that they will remain on my back. There is only one man I intend to kill with them; your Chief is not the one I seek. I'll gladly meet you in the courtyard—grandfather—if you still want to challenge me for my right to bear these blades."

Corbmac looked like he was about to scoff at Breanna; she narrowed her eyes, making it clear she was deadly serious. The old warrior looked through the door at a tall, silver-haired man, the question on his face clear. Breanna knew he had to be the dun's Fáidh from the colors of his robes and stature. He looked at her intently as if seeking some unseen sign, and then his green eyes glazed as the *sight* took him.

The world around Breanna faded along with him. She was suddenly in a vision where *Lann Dàn* blazed, and the Dread-lord vanished in a flash of Tuatha magic. She hoped the Druid had, indeed, seen the same thing. Otherwise, they'd be taken as prisoners or maybe even held as hostages, especially if they discovered her true lineage.

Then the world lurched, and all seemed normal again, with the Druid nodding his approval.

Corbmac sighed in apparent relief. "This way."

Ćroí Dàn exclaimed in Breanna's mind, *"The cur! How dare he question Erin's Hero!"* Then *Lann Dàn* faded, with *Maorgairme* holding out a moment longer as if confirming her opinion was the same.

Letting Eoin, Fergal, and Braoin step through the door first, Breanna admonished her magical blades and ring to keep quiet before following. However, the Fáidh kept his gaze on her as she passed, and she felt it penetrate the iron shell she presented to the world. Fortunately, the imposing Druid was soon behind her.

They drew uncomfortable stares from the rest of the dun's residents as they crossed the main hall floor with Corbmac, passing the rows of filled tables to either side. Dinner had already started, and with it came the noise that accompanied so many people eating and drinking together. Silence quickly settled over the hall as the old warrior and his guests approached the high table; even the servants paused mid-stride while coming to or from the kitchen area.

Seated on a slightly raised dais, Dun Uisneach's Chief and Chieftess observed those who claimed Guestright in their hall. Breanna thought the latter's expression was one of puzzlement, as ragged travelers, even those of the valued warrior class, were rarely brought before the high table, never mind introduced to the rulers of the hall. Indeed, at times, they would have been lucky to get scraps from the kitchen door. Yet someone had said something to get the Chieftess's attention.

Breanna noted Chief Faolán did not possess an imposing figure like his cousin Corbmac, yet his features were dark and commanding; he certainly had some Fir Bolg lineage. His closely cropped black beard revealed a face with sharp lines, and a silver-beaded leather cord held back his slightly graying hair. He was dressed in a fine silk tunic dyed a deep blue and a five-colored cloak draped around his shoulders. He wore a gold circlet on his brow, a torque around his neck, and jewelry on his wrists and fingers. And the blade at his hip was not like the larger broadswords carried by most. Instead, it was a smaller weapon requiring more skill than brawn to wield. It was more like what Braoin usually had strapped over his shoulders.

His mate, Falyn, sat to his left as his Chieftess, which Gaels called *Ceann-feadhna*; Breanna had heard she was also the dun's *Taoiseach*, which meant wisdom provider. She had fair features, golden tresses streaked with red highlights, and commanding blue eyes. She wore an elegant azure dress, and a five-colored silk cloak flowed down her shoulders. Like her mate, she adorned her brow with a gold circlet; a torque ringed her slender neck, and jewelry circled her wrists.

To Faolán's right sat an elfish-looking woman who was whispering something into Faolán's ear. She was a slender woman who appeared to be under thirty, with light red hair and a finely chiseled face that hinted at *Tuatha Dé Danann* heritage. She was dressed in traditional Filidh colors of gold and green, though her gown was silk instead of linen, as their Bard at Dun Arrogh wore. At first, it appeared to Breanna that Faolán wasn't listening to the Druid, but then the woman clearly said something to widen his eyes. When his mate whispered something in his other ear, he craned his neck to get a better look at Breanna and her weapons.

While she once more commanded *Lann Dàn* and *Maorgairme* to be quiet, they still emitted enough of a glow to show their otherworldly nature.

Catching himself staring at his guests—or more correctly, Breanna noted, herself—Dun Uisneach's Chief said hastily, "Greetings, questers. I am Faolán, of the Clan Uí Néil. To my left is Chieftess Falyn, my mate and joint leader of Dun Uisneach, and our wise and knowledgeable *Taoiseach*. To my right is our Master Bard, Bláth. Behind me is our Seneschal, Keegan. Before us, with their *feighlí leanaí*, are our three children, Dáithí, Domhnall, and Teagan."

"Thank you for honoring our claim of Guestright, Chief Faolán, Chieftess Falyn," Eoin said with a slight bow to those at the high table. Then he bowed to their children, who were sitting at the table before him.

To Breanna, the two boys and a girl appeared to be around ten, eight, and six years old, if she were to guess. Then, she took in Master Bard more closely, noting that there must be more than one with such a title. While Breanna knew the leaders of Dun Uisneach were related to the High King and his Queen, the sumptuous surroundings and staff made it clear there was little Dun Uisneach could not afford. During the summer *comórtas*, the co-chiefs did not invite the warriors inside their hall.

As those at the high table rose, Eoin continued proudly, "My name is Eoin Mac Cairbre, and this is my cousin, Fergal Mac Conall. As I'm sure you have heard, we are of Clan Mórdha. Beside me is Breanna Ban Morna of Clan Dálaigh, my Champion for personal combat. We all hail from Dun Arrogh, for which I am acting *Ceann-cinnidh*. Last is our new friend, Braoin Mac Lochlinn, who hails from the southern Loch Síleann settlement."

"As my cousin, Corbmac, informed me," Faolán put in with a nod. "Will you all join us at our table?"

Realizing the poor state of their clothes, Breanna protested, "Chief Faolán, our attire certainly does not merit an invitation to the high table of your hall. Unfortunately, our sudden departure from Dun Arrogh did not give us time to gather everything we should have for our journey."

"As my Champion has said, maybe something a bit humbler would be more appropriate," Eoin suggested.

"Do not concern yourself about the state of your dress, warrior prince," Faolán said, waving a hand as he and his mate sat. Breanna saw the *Ceann-cinnidh* and *Ceann-feadhna* glance at her other companions and then let their eyes return to her quickly.

Breanna squared her shoulders and returned their gaze as they assessed each other's mettle. As Eoin's Champion, she projected the strength she exuded, felt the Tuatha magic within the blades, each humming with power that rose over each shoulder, and then scanned the hall. Faolán and Falyn whispered to each other, but Breanna could not hear their words. It was clear to her that the old leader of the *fians* had conveyed most of their story while they were cleaning up before the evening meal, but not all of it.

"Nor should you, Breanna Ban Morna," Chief Faolán added as servants arranged seats and tableware settings for them. "Please join us. I understand from Corbmac that you recently faced down five mounted Norvegr outlanders and, nearly single-handedly, thoroughly beat them all. We would love to hear more about such a feat. Maybe Bláth can spin it into a new tale for our people."

Following Eoin, Breanna climbed the three steps. Then, the Seneschal moved forward to guide them to their seats.

Chieftess Falyn agreed. "Indeed, we would be most interested. Watching you move with such catlike grace and seeing the smoldering fire in your eyes tells me you are not just a skilled warrior but a driven and observant one. I have a bit of the *sight* in me, and it says that you need our support and that we could benefit from your knowledge of the Norvegr Jarl called the Dreadlord—we share a common cause, if you will."

"Well said, my *Taoiseach*," Master Bard Bláth put in. "I have an equal hold on our link to the Tuatha realm, and it says the same to me."

Faolán turned to his cousin. "Corbmac, please join us. After all, you've spent a few more moments with our guests than we have. And Keegan, have Maoilir sit at the high table this evening. While I understand he prefers his corner, these guests merit his attendance."

Keegan said obediently, "Aye, my Chief."

Falyn added, "To our questors, welcome to Dun Usinech!"

With *Lann Dàn* still strapped to her shoulders, Breanna found the high-backed chair she sat in anything but comfortable and had to lean forward to accommodate the weapons. But, despite a muttered curse as she wiggled each blade's haft to settle outside her seat, she was determined to keep them in place. Eoin and Fergal seemed amused by her discomfort as they took the seats beside her and Braoin. Breanna only just contained her growl.

Before them lay silver plates and gold-lined wooden cups, something she had never seen. Servants set out platters of roasted boar and venison, onions, garlic, parsnips, and fresh bread. They also provided apples and plums set out in bowls. While the dark ale brought grins to her small band's faces, Breanna requested mead.

Falyn raised her cup. "Finally, a lady with good taste. Who drinks ale when there's mead to be had?"

That made Breanna smile as she returned the gesture.

A few moments later, Corbmac joined them, sitting next to Eoin and saying, "I would like to introduce you to Maoilir, our Master Fáidh."

Maoilir looked a bit weathered, somewhat like their own one-time Seeress, Beatha. His silver hair and a salt-and-pepper beard added more years than merited to his face. With his blue-and-red mantle of the prophetic branch of Druids draped across his shoulders, he sat beside Braoin. Breanna attempted to ignore him as he looked her over, especially her *Lann Dàn* blades. Just a seat away, he managed to catch her gaze and held it. He gave her a deep nod as if it were almost a bow. Then, disregarding her companions, he added, "It is my pleasure to meet you, Breanna Ban Morna."

Breanna swallowed uncomfortably, returning the same gesture, wondering what he knew about the Amergin and the Sun God's long blades. Maybe even about *Ćroí Dàn*. Yet something told her that he was no match for Beatha.

Then, as Breanna's thoughts strayed to her Heart, *Ćroí Dàn* said, *"While I trust the Bard, I have doubts about the Seer. He lacks control of an Element that he should have mastered by now. Yet I have foreseen their roles in helping you learn about our magic and your quest. Danu had All-Father ensure all Aos Dána across Erin would support your cause, but his conviction feels, well, lacking."*

With such a confirmation, Breanna turned to her plate and was suddenly famished. They ate quietly for a time, save for some small talk about the day. The servers started to circulate about the high table, and there was a brief buzz in the main hall as those seated at the lower tables tried to determine why their Chief and Chieftess would sit with such a ragged band. Yet the questions died, and those of Dun Uisneach appeared to relax as the ale flowed and they returned to their trenchers.

Falyn asked, "Breanna, tell us of your battle with the Norvegrs."

She swallowed and cleared her throat. "It was nothing special. I just did what I had to ensure my Chief was safe."

Braoin choked on his ale. "That's the biggest understatement I've ever heard! Let me tell you the tale."

With that, her half-brother recounted the battle she led. He concluded with, "Her courage was breathtaking, and it was not her first time taking on Dreadriders. In an earlier battle before we met, she took on two of them, saving her Chief and his cousin. While those two took wounds in that encounter, Breanna had not a scratch on her."

Breanna sighed. "Braoin, enough with the praise. Speaking wounds, hopefully, you can have your Healer look after these two."

Falyn answered, "Of course. I will have Master Bodhmall see to them tomorrow. What of your wounds?"

When she saw Braoin roll his eyes, she answered, "I have none."

That silenced the table as she turned back to her trencher, save for Faolán's hushed comment dryly to his mate, "No small feat those battles."

Later, Breanna noticed that some younger women at a nearby table were whispering about the strangers, with their attention focused on Eoin, Fergal, and Braoin. A slight blush crept over her face when she heard one of them questioning which of the three men might be spoken for by the slender but formidable warrior—her.

Eoin garnered more interest because of his princely cloak. Notwithstanding, the ladies also appeared to find Fergal and Braoin attractive. Few warriors had the skill to earn a gold or silver Celtic Knot armring. That said, Eoin Mac Cairbre bore royal blood, so he drew the lion's share of their flirtatious glances.

While she might not have been able to acknowledge what she felt about Eoin, she was not ready to let anyone else have him. Trying to make it clear to the women of the hall, she put a hand on Eoin's arm and made a few comments about Faolán's and Falyn's impressive hold. Eoin only nodded, and Breanna noted with a smile that his plate held more interest for him. She was pleased he had entirely missed the young ladies' attentions from the table below.

The rest of the meal passed without incident, and the four hungry warriors took in a good deal of the fine food and drink. Honeycakes rounded out the dinner, something Breanna was delighted to see. However, she could not help stealing glances at the Fáidh. The tall Druid had hardly eaten a thing, and he had exchanged whispers with the Bard throughout the meal.

When Bláth rose and excused herself from the table so she could prepare the evening's music, Faolán said, "So, Eoin Mac Cairbre, Corbmac mentioned that you are on a quest to meet the Dark Goddess. Not a thing to undertake lightly."

"Nay, 'tis not," Eoin agreed. "But a thing we must do."

"We would like to talk with your Fáidh or Filídh about the best time and place to find Badb Catha," Breanna interjected. "We have been commanded to seek a high place near the head-waters of the Boyne when the moon is full and not much more, someplace called a well near Croghan Hill. A Seer or Bard would know better where to look."

"Certainly, Maoilir and Bláth will be happy to direct you," Faolán affirmed; the Fáidh nodded slightly and continued to gaze at Breanna. His eyes wandered more than once to the glowing blades of *Lann Dàn* poking up over each shoulder. What he saw in them, she couldn't be sure. Then Bláth cleared her throat at a raised dias across the hall, and Faolán commanded, "Time for our evening songs. Listen and appreciate a true Master Bard at work. Our people so love her songs and stories."

Bláth let her soft, melodic timbre resonate through the hall as she sang a few lines of a familiar folk song. As her fingers rolled over her strings, the harp's music filled the air. It was a medium-sized instrument that suited her alto voice, which carried clearly throughout the hall.

A hush settled over the tables momentarily before Bláth began her first full tune. The song she had selected was about a great warrior of days past who had protected Ulaida from harm, no matter how skilled the foe was. Cuchulain, the Hound of Ulaida, was his name. He was a legend, chosen for a brief time as Erin's Hero. His skill and bravery were well known throughout the land.

Croí Dàn said to Breanna, *"The Bard's an Air Elemental. Her command is not strong, but that's why her naturally under-spoken voice carries so well when she sings."*

Breanna found that tidbit worth noting and looked around the hall. She saw heartened faces on the folk listening to the tale of Cú Chulainn's mighty deeds and the trophies he took in battle while defending their land. All the while, Bláth's eyes were on Breanna, gazing at her as if they were not seeing anyone else, as if her voice and music were only for her, somehow seeing more than they should have. It unnerved Breanna that the Bard might think she was another Cuchulain, as she was only a Spartan warrior from a dirt-poor dun in remote hills to the north.

Then Bláth transitioned into a second song, this one being about Maeve, the warrior who had built the great fort in Connachta known as Cruachan of the Enchantments and was the province's *Banríona*. She was also a legend, chosen as Erin's Hero, beloved by her people, and renowned for her fierceness, wisdom, and commitment to justice.

Next came Macha Mong Ruad, the first female warlord of Ulaidia, selected by *Croí Dàn*, one who had provided strength and leadership to keep the Gaels focused on their enemies and not warring amongst themselves. In the days before Rory the Red had founded his original Red Branch at the fort named after Macha, she had ruled as *Ard-Banríona*, the first High Queen of their Emerald Isle.

Last, Bláth regaled Rory the Red himself, a fearsome leader who had structured their clans, teaching them how to fight and organize into groups like his Red Branch and be led by strong warriors like himself—the last known legend chosen by *Croí Dàn*.

The room erupted in cheers and clapping when the Master Bard finished. After taking in the reaction of those at the tables, Breanna glanced back at Bláth. From the Bard's smile of acknowledgment, it was clear she saw another Hound of Ulaida, Maeve of Connachta, Macha the *Ard-Banríona*, and Rory the Red.

Croí Dàn confirmed in Breanna's mind, saying, "*Yes, they were all once mine, as are you now. While Maoilir and Bláth do not yet know this, they soon will.*"

Breanna sighed to her Heart as Bláth rose and left the hall without a word, and the older Fáidh rose to follow her out into the night. Many in the great hall also started turning in for the evening, though a few remained to make small talk and finish their ale or play the game of chance the Gaels called *dìsnean*.

Chief Faolán rose and told his guests, "Your day must have been long. Corbmac will show you where you can roll out your bedrolls and blankets in our hall. We will talk more in the morning."

"Thank you for your hospitality, my Chief and Chieftess," Eoin said with a bow. "It is most generous of you."

Faolán and Falyn nodded with smiles, gathered their children with their minders, and excused themselves for the night. Braoin sighed as the pair strode away, saying, "Their Bard is magnificent."

Three of the braver young women took the opportunity to approach the high table and attempted to engage in small talk with Eoin, Braoin, and Fergal. Breanna noted the latter had kept his eye on one red-haired lass the whole evening and seemed to be hoping she would be generous with her affections.

Breanna stepped next to Eoin and pointedly suggested, "I expect we will want to make an early start tomorrow if we are to seek out Bradaigh."

Eoin looked around in surprise and countered, "I think not, as we have much to discuss about arranging possible escorts to the east and learning how best to get to the headwaters of the Boyne. We also need to learn what these Druids can add to our knowledge about the Tuatha, not to mention that we must seek refuge until the next full moon. Hakon will undoubtedly be on our trail but cannot reach us here, so it's best to request that someone fetch your half-brother."

Eoin paused, turning to say, "Unfortunately, my good ladies, we must turn in, as we need sharp minds in the morning."

Fergal started to protest, but Eoin gave him a look that ended any argument. The three women reluctantly left the handsome warriors. All was quiet, except for a few scullions working in the kitchen area. The main hall slowly emptied while servants moved cedar screens into place to form a sleeping area in one corner. Two men carried in cloth mattresses stuffed with rushes and set them on the floor. Two others brought their travel packs and bedrolls.

Corbmac appeared and said, looking at Breanna, "I also bid you good night. Bláth and Maoilir would like to meet with you mid-morning."

Eoin stepped before the older warrior as if to ensure he knew who was in charge. "We would be happy to have such a meeting. Also, let your smith know we have Norvegr weapons to trade with him."

Corbmac nodded with a bow and left.

"I didn't expect this kind of reception," Fergal said.

"Aye," Eoin agreed. "Yet, the Chief and Chieftess of this fine place and their Druids seemed very interested in Bre."

"Too interested, if you ask me," Breanna added as she turned to spread out her blanket over one of the mattresses.

Eoin added, "We'll see what the Seer and Bard have to say in the morning."

Fergal started to ask, "But why Bre—"

Eoin cut him off. "Seek your bed. We do not talk of ourselves, especially in a strange dun with possibly prying ears. It is not the time or place for such a discussion."

A span or so later, with her fellow warriors sleeping around her, candlelight drifted into the hall. Breanna was instantly alerted to the presence of others. Through the cedar screens, she could see two figures approaching: one tall, one short. When *Croí Dàn* said in her mind, *"Druids,"* Breanna reached for the heart-shaped ruby, seeing it pulse briefly in her clasped hand beneath her nightclothes.

Breanna had been suspicious earlier in the evening with the stares she had received, thinking the Druids wanted the magic their gods had gifted her. She rose from the floor like a shadow, dressed in a dark sleeping frock, her hands already wrapped around the hafts of *Lann Dàn*. The Sun God's long blades sprang to life with a low glow as she edged around one of the cedar screens, prepared for battle.

It was the dun's Master Fáidh and Master Filídh who faced her, each holding a candle, their expressions reserved as they waited for Breanna to settle and approach. She did so slowly, realizing they had come for her, not her Tuatha magic. She had to carry her blades because she was not wearing her weapon harness as she crossed the floor toward the Druids.

The Heart of Destiny pulsed once. Quietly but emphatically, she said only to her, *"Be firm and confident. Remember, you are mine! You are Erin's Hero! One day, they will take a knee for you."*

Maoilir whispered, "We would have words with you, Breanna Ban Morna of Clan Dálaigh."

Bláth added, "Outside, where we will not wake your friends."

Breanna nodded and followed the Druids through the hall. At the main doors, they paused to exchange their candles for a torch. There was a hint of rain in the cool night air, which had not been noticeable when they had arrived earlier that evening.

Shivering outside the entrance to the massive hall, Breanna said darkly, "This weather is chilly, and I am underdressed for it. What must you say only to me at this time? I suggested a meeting in the morning for a reason—I had several intense days in a row and am tired and sore."

"You asked for our help finding the Dark Goddess," Bláth said gravely.

"It is not something we tell just anyone," Maoilir finished for the Bard. The guttering torch cast a garish pall over the tall Druid. "Few seek Badb Catha's altar, and even fewer know where to find it. Or the best time for the Dark Goddess to respond to such a summons. That is well, for she answers the call of any warrior who dares to seek her out, even those who are vain and thirst for power. Her lust for war and battle is dreadful, and she shows no mercy on the weak-hearted. Yet she has a penchant for helping warriors approaching her with causes that bring dishonor in what they seek, even if only to instigate a conflict."

"And you want to confirm I seek her with honorable purposes."

"Very perceptive, Breanna," Bláth put in. "To be correct, we need to assure ourselves you are indeed the one the Mother Goddess foresaw, the one chosen to end the Dreadlord's reign."

"While I consider it my destiny, I do not know how to convince you. Yet, it doesn't change my assertion that this discussion could have waited until morning."

Maoilir demanded, "Tell us where you found *Lann Dàn*."

"Nay, what was the riddle that led you to them?" Bláth countered.

Breanna looked from one to the other. "Our Fáidh told me: It is a place which lies both north and south of Black Pig's Dike. A place where the sun shines only after reaching its zenith. From this place flows a river that feeds the land. Within this place, one can find *Lann Dàn*. Look closely, for many rocks hide the fairie treasure."

"She certainly heard that from a Fáidh, likely Beatha," Maoilir confirmed.

"And she certainly bears the outlander's countenance," Bláth observed. "The blood of both sides."

Breanna looked from one to the other and said sharply, "I don't know what you two want from me, but I've had enough. I'll find the Dark Goddess with or without you, as Danu herself has set me on this path. I will fulfill my destiny!"

Maoilir looked hesitantly at Bláth and nodded. "Peace be with you, Breanna Ban Morna. We support your quest. After all, we are All-Father's *Aos Dána*, and he has already commanded us to assist one who bears Tuatha magic. However, we also understand the Dreadlord is hunting for you and your friends. It is a critical juncture for all of us. After dinner, I used the *sight* to see how events might unfold and what we might do to influence those events. It was as if the gods presented a path for us, a path provided by none other than Dagda and the Mórrigan, and they demanded that all *Aos Dána* support your quest."

Croí Dàn interjected, *"We need their help, and the All-Father and Badb Catha have shown their hands. Be strong, but let them know who you are. Show them you are, indeed, my chosen one."*

Breanna stood proudly. She looked pointedly at the Bard, saying, "*Croí Dàn* just confirmed what is in your heart, that you are true to your word. I can tell you this. Danu gifted me this ring. It is called *Maorgairme* and shows me when Fomorian magic is near. Her ring enables me to summon a Tuatha god, which I am limited to using only three times. I used one of those calls right after I found and claimed *Lann Dàn*. Unfortunately, Tethra's demons attacked us at the headwaters of Loch Aillionn. I called on Danu's magical ring, and the Sun God, Lugh, came to my aid. It was a terrible battle, and I had to learn to use the magic within the blades as I fought. In that battle, I did not escape unscathed and took many shallow wounds."

The two Druids looked at the ring, glowing proudly on her finger, in surprise, then noticed, as one, the red pulse under her tunic. Bláth, clearly astonished, asked, "The Heart of Destiny?"

Breanna reached into her frock, wrapped her hand around the heart-shaped ruby pendant, and pulled it out. "Aye. You should also know this--*Croí Dàn*, the Heart of Destiny, has proclaimed me as Erin's Hero."

Bláth cried, "Thank the gods. It has finally happened!"

Breanna hesitated, unsure how much to share regarding her lineage. Yet, she needed to try to recruit Bradaigh, and there was help here at Dun Uisneach.

Croí Dàn said, *"Trust the Bard."*

With a firm nod, she added, "And know one more thing. I am the bastard daughter of the Dreadlord, born from a mother who gifted me her Clan Dálaigh blood and a father who raped her. A mother who had our Fáidh place a *geas* on me before I was born. One that set me on a path where I will destroy him and his ilk."

Maoilir jerked back, and Breanna watched as the *sight* took him. Then, a moment later, the world spun again, and he said in awe, "I just heard Danu's voice confirming that to end Hakon's reign, only one bound by the blood of both sides can be victorious."

Breanna nodded. "Aye, Danu told me the same thing. However, there is one last piece of information you both should know. There are two others like me, each born of Hakon's loins, with the blood of both sides. My half-brothers, sired by the Dreadlord and the women he had taken by force in his early days here. While not chosen by the Heart of Destiny, they are similar to me in that a *geas* binds them. They are crucial to my success as Erin's Hero. You met one of them earlier tonight, whose name is Braoin. His *geas* is justice.

"The other lives near Dun Uisneach and earned his gold Celtic Knot armring this past summer with me. His name is Bradaigh. I am unsure of the nature of his *geas*, so please ensure I meet with him by mid-morning. Now, my day has been long. I am cold and need sleep."

Breanna shivered and swept back inside the dun, not bothering to ask their leave as she sought her bed.

Ćroí Dàn interjected in her mind, "*Well played. Now, I need you to know one more thing about my powers. There are two that I believe you are already familiar with. First, I can instill courage in my chosen one, my Hero. Through you, I can inspire those around you to become demi-heroes and undertake acts of heroism they might not have been able to accomplish on their own. Those magics flow from me to you and then from you to those who follow you."*

Breanna questioned, *"Beyond those two?"*

Ćroí Dàn seemed to hesitate, then said, *"Not every Hero can use or leverage the third piece of Tuatha magic crafted within me, so I do not always tell my chosen one about its nature. Magic that inspires a love of our land, our people, and my Hero. I know it is not your nature to love like this or expect those around you to give you love. Beatha constructed your geas to be one of destruction. It would be best to balance that darkness with lightness to succeed in your quest to destroy the Dreadlord.*

"My Hero, Breanna Ban Morna, you must find a way to internalize my love for you and accept the love of those around you. Only then can you love your land and people enough to make the necessary choices that will lead to the Dreadlord's destruction!"

Breanna, unsure how to process what the Heart of Destiny had told her, was silent as she slipped back into her bedroll. Thinking only of how her *geas* had ruled her life, she could not see how to use this last piece of magic offered by *Ćroí Dàn*. She had buried the part of her nature to love for so long that she could not see how to embrace it.

Fortunately, sleep took hold of her moments later.

Lang

It was near sunset when Lang learned he was in Mide territory, for he had to evade one of the High King's patrols—a lone chariot surrounded by a band of foot soldiers, all bearing spears. Lang knew the High King's *fian*s to be fierce warriors, even if they were not mounted. They headed toward a band of Gaels riding on the High King's Road as he watched them.

It was Hakon's daughter and her friends. Two mounted on the same horse had Norvegr's white hair, and one was unmistakably a woman. His Jarl's bastard and brother's slayer! Only, there was no way to get to her as the *fian* warriors surrounded them. He watched the two parties talk at length–it appeared the *fian* leader had some suspicions about them, but then they all soon went east. Following at a safe distance, he fell behind them on the road, keeping to the brush on the north side. Yet Lang knew they had to be heading for Dun Uisneach. He could think only of one thing—the severed head of Lunt's Valkyrie in his hands.

To Lang, the fort before him was more impressive than what his Jarl had constructed at Dun Garm, and the defenses were very sound. Cursing his luck, he could do little more than rub down his mount and settle into the thicket where he had found cover. Given that he was only about five hundred yards west of the ramparts, he would have no fire to warm him this evening.

Some spans later, Lang heard the sound of horses approaching through the woods. He stiffened as he rose and looked north. As they drew closer, he recognized his Jarl and their fellow warriors. Lang sighed with relief. He knew Hakon wouldn't be pleased, but at least he could tell his commander where the Destroyer had gone.

Lang emerged from his thicket when the band rode into the clearing, saying, "My Jarl, it is good you have come so closely on my heels. I followed your daughter to Dun Uisneach. She entered the fort just a short time ago."

Hakon dismounted and strode toward his Dreadrider, his expression one of barely contained fury. He spat, "Lang, I know why you decided to chase after my daughter. If you had caught her, one of you would be dead, and it would most likely be you. You know my order to Donalt and Alrik was that she be taken alive, and you have gone against that order. If you had the opportunity to kill her, you would have. You know it, and I know it. I cannot have my Dreadriders breaking their vows. You swore to uphold my command, and I assure you that I will strip you of everything and cast you out if you disobey me again!"

With his eyes downcast, Lang dropped to one knee. "Forgive me, my Jarl, but anger burns within my heart over what she has done. Lunt deserved better."

"Lunt died with a blade in his hand," Hakon continued more easily. "A Norvegr warrior can ask for no more. If you two had told me the Destroyer was a woman, perhaps I would have approached the matter differently, and your brother might still be alive. But, unfortunately, that is on you. So you'll have to live with it."

Hakon's suggestion that he could have prevented his brother's death struck Lang like a lightning bolt. Yet his Jarl gave him no time to contemplate that thought, ordering, "Now, I command you to put aside your anger and return to Dun Garm. Also, know that I plan to take my daughter alive, and if it pleases the gods, she will soon be fighting at my side."

Lang stiffened and looked up in surprise. "You expect me to fight at her side?"

"If I so order it, yes," Hakon said tightly. He ground each word out slowly, "Do I have your oath?"

Lang felt a deep stab of pain at the thought of making such a commitment. Hakon must have seen that pain etched on his face. Yet the Dreadlord's expression was stone cold, so Lang said hesitantly, "Já."

"In the morning, you will return to Dun Garm. You must gather warriors to accompany Runa and Thorvald to the ford where the High King's Road crosses the River Brosna," the Dreadlord ordered, his blue eyes drilling into Lang's soul. "Swear it!"

With a strangled voice, Lang said, "By Thor's Hammer, I swear it!"

Hakon nodded and turned away to face Dun Uisneach. "Then tell me about your hunt. I need some advantage to use against my prey."

Lang rose, stood beside his Jarl, and recanted the previous day's ride, starting with the settlement at the river crossing and his tracking of Breanna and her band to the High King's Road. The Dreadlord said nothing as he talked, gazing at Dun Uisneach so intently that Lang wondered if he was seeing inside the earthen walls. Then Hakon came to life and said, "Let's hope my daughter stays locked behind those gates until we can find a way inside. For now, we should maintain some distance between us, that's all. We passed a copse of trees north of here that would serve as cover."

Turning to one of his warriors, he commanded, "Gern, I want you to take over Lang's watch. Jotun will look after your mount and relieve you just after sunrise."

Eoin

In the morning, Eoin rose to the sounds of cooks preparing food for all to break their fast. Breanna came to her feet right after he did and told him she had met with the Druids the night before, and they were to gather again later that morning. She also informed him that Bláth and Maoilir would be fetching Bradaigh so they could all get to know each other.

With that, she grabbed her second pair of leggings, a spare tunic from her pack, and her weapon harness, declaring she needed to visit the bathhouse before eating. Then, she snatched up her soiled clothes to wash them.

Eoin just nodded, waiting for Fergal and Braoin to join him, knowing that they must create a plan to safely get to the area known as Croghan Hill, as the Dreadlord would be hunting them. From descriptions he had heard, Croghan Hill roughly lay no more than two days of traveling on their mounts to the southeast of Dun Uisneach, and the hill would be visible not too far south of the High King's Road. The challenge was that they had more time than needed until the new moon, the time when Danu had advised Breanna to call on the Dark Goddess. What should they do until then, especially with her father on her heels?

Breanna

Breanna headed for the bathhouse behind the kitchens. She ducked through it and was surprised when Bláth caught the door before she could close it behind her. The Bard asked, "May I join you, Breanna?"

"Aye," Breanna answered, "though I doubt we will be alone at this span."

"We will see," Bláth said with a shrug. Then, taking the lead, she led Breanna into the bathhouse. Sure enough, it was somewhat crowded, but there were empty tubs. Yet Bláth passed them by. "I see you have some clothes for the wash. Please leave them in this basket. I'll see that they are taken care of. Now, follow me."

Bláth turned left through another doorway. They emerged into a smaller room with several large tubs holding warm water and no other occupants. "Faolán and Falyn often have privileged noble guests passing through here on their way to or from Dun Tara," Bláth explained, "so they built this area for such travelers. I thought it best to take advantage of their forethought."

Breanna smiled, honored to have such luxury. "I like how you could envision me as a noble."

"Think of it this way," Bláth added. "We know our gods touched you. How could you be anything less than a noble? However, I know you are more, much more."

Cróí Dàn chimed in Breanna's mind, *"You are mine, my chosen one, Erin's Hero. Live it, embrace it, love it. Shake off your human doubts. I chose you for a reason. It is because I believe in you!"*

Breanna pulled herself taller as the Heart's voice lifted her spirits by placing Breanna upon a high pillar. Especially given she was half Norvegr and the Dreadlord's daughter. How could this be?

Sensing such a pause, Bláth stared at the young warrior. "The Heart of Destiny talks to you in your mind, aye? While I suspect she would answer your call anytime or anywhere, it would be amazing if she could initiate a conversation. Nothing like this has happened in many hundreds of years. Unfortunately, we know very little about *Cróí Dàn*. Her legends are all but lost to us. While the tales of her Heroes live on, she is a mystery."

Breanna nodded, unsure of how to answer. Then, a burst of courage rushed through her. "Well, I can say this. *Cróí Dàn* is very assertive, opinionated, and demanding. She gives me no quarter, leaves no room for doubt, no room to question my abilities, regardless of my heritage. Nor has Danu. Well, at least not after *Mo Chroí* chose me."

As Breanna and Bláth stripped off their clothes and slipped into one of the large tubs, they both sighed at the warmth of the water against their skin and began washing away the grime. It was Breanna who moaned the loudest in the pleasure of the bath water. Their own dun's bathhouse never had water this warm. Breanna grabbed the soap and dunked her head under the water to scrub her scalp and hair. Then, she surfaced to rub the rest of her body with soap.

Watching, Bláth said, "I am astounded at how casual you are about being Erin's Hero, about talking with one of the more significant pieces of Tuatha magic created by our pantheon of gods. The jewel is said to be sentient, and your description of how you two have interacted confirms that part of *Croí Dàn's* legend."

Breanna shrugged and took hold of the ruby on her chest. Yet she said nothing of her conversation with her Heart, in which they had discussed her need to let love into her life, to love life, and to love her man. Could it be that easy? Could she put her taint aside? Shaking herself out of her muse, she added, "I've only just met her."

Nodding, the Bard said, "Your account of the Heart of Destiny's interaction with you fits our history, lore, and legends that *Aos Dàna* have passed down over the ages. Given that, *Croí Dàn* and Danu are correct. It would be best if you accepted their belief in you, in your ability to grow into what they have foreseen. It is what your land needs of you, and that is to rid us of these Norvegr outlanders."

For a few moments, silence reigned, and then Breanna breathed quietly, "Of which I am one."

Bláth froze momentarily. "Breanna, I'm so sorry. That was tactless of me. Bards tend to get caught up in the moment, overthinking a new story's substance and how it fits into legend, rather than focusing on those who can account for the experience they are living and creating. As a Master Bard, I should know better. Danu and *Croí Dàn* have chosen you. Dagda, Badb Catha, Lugh, and Danu have actively supported your quest."

Breanna shrugged. "Thank you for that courtesy, but I understand what I am. Just a tool to remove my father's taint from our land. And at what cost? The Tuatha always have a price. You know that as well as I do. And I don't know what that price is!"

Ċroí Dàn blasted her with, *"You are not just a tool! You are mine!"*

Breanna sat in silence, trying to process the cascade of expectations that others had placed upon her. Then, shaking her head with a sigh, she replied dejectedly to the heart-shaped stone, *"As you say."*

Then Breanna said aloud, her tone cold as death, "Our time here is over. You have a task I set for you and Maoilir this morning. I expect you'll see to it."

With that, she rose from the bath, toweled off, put on her clothes, and then snatched up her weapon harness as she slipped out the door, leaving the stunned Bard behind.

Bláth

Bláth was left to wonder about the young woman, who, at just over seventeen, was chosen by Heart of Destiny to undertake such a daunting task, especially given her virtually nonexistent support structure. Breanna needed to see that she was a Gael first, not a Norvegr. Others selected as Erin's Hero had come from royal lines or were descendants of a Chief. Well, save for Lugh, who was also a half-breed.

Deciding to ensure everyone knew who Breanna was, Bláth quickly finished her scrub down, rose from the bath, and, after toweling off and dressing, went to seek out Maoilir. Based on what she had just learned, she had much to discuss with her fellow *Aos Dána* before they set out to ensure Bradaigh was brought to Dun Uisneach to meet Erin's Hero.

After fetching a bowl of porridge and adding raisins, nuts, dates, and brown sugar from the kitchen area, Bláth found Maoilir sitting at his usual table in one corner of the main hall. As he was also breaking his fast, Bláth sat opposite him. After taking a few scoops of porridge, she said, "We have much to discuss before we meet again with Breanna Ban Morna. I spent time with Erin's Hero this morning in the bathhouse, and I found her to be a complex and conflicted young lady. I am more certain than ever that she needs our help."

Maoilir glanced across the hall to where Erin's Hero had found her companions. Then he nodded in agreement. "Indeed. As I mentioned last night, Dagda has touched the *Cycle of Time*, alerting any *Aos Dána* who reaches for the *sight* to assist her. It was a bit more explicit than I told Breanna, as the message was: *Erin's Hero walks among us--All-Father, Danu, Lugh, and Badb Catha command all Aos Dána to stand ready to assist her.*"

Bláth said, "Well, we have orders from the highest authorities. Let's have a stablehand ready three mounts for us so we can fetch Bradaigh, and he can meet his half-sister."

"Aye," Maoilir answered with a nod as he rose to flag one of the kitchen hands to alert the stable that horses each would need to be readied for them.

The *sight* briefly took the Bard, and Bláth paused as they stepped toward the hall's doors. She gravely advised, "We will need an escort. The one Erin's Hero would destroy is near, lying in wait."

"Then let's command Corbmac and one of his *fians* to join us," Maoilir answered. "Maybe have him make it two *fians* as a show of force."

The pair left the hall to fetch their cloaks and arrange their escort to ride with them to the settlement where Bradaigh lived.

Breanna

Breanna found that Dun Uisneach was less formal for breakfast and picked up a bowl of porridge, a hunk of bread, and strips of fried boar. Then, seeing some strange brown eggs still in their shells, she asked, "What are those?"

"My lady," the cook answered, "they are sicín eggs, birds who canna take full flight. The cocks make a god-awful sound at dawn, but the hens lay eggs that make mighty fine eating, especially in the morning. Our Chief, being a first cousin to the High King, brought back a clutch from Dun Tara last year, and we've been raising them ever since. My Chief and Chieftess usually reserve these eggs for the nobles, but seeing as our Heart has chosen you, I figured I should offer them. We cook them in a pan, mixed up or with the yolk intact."

"Hmmm, word gets around," Breanna commented. Then she shrugged. "I've only had wild bird eggs and never had them cooked. Just ate them out of the shell."

"A moment, my lady," the cook said, adding a glop of butter to her skillet. Then, she cracked two eggs into the pan. "My Chieftess said the same thing—she likes them this way."

The cook cut the clear outer part to thin it out, then rolled the pan as it turned white. Once the egg whites were solid, she flipped them over, waited half a minute, and flipped them onto a small trencher with a flair, saying, "*Ionadh mór!* They go well with the soda bread and boar strips."

Impressed, Breanna smiled and turned to the table where her men sat. After joining them, she dug into the gooey orange egg yolks, sopping them up with her bread; the egg whites were delicious as well. As the cook said, a great wonder indeed! The boar strips were a perfect complement, and the oat porridge with fruit, nuts, and cream rounded out her meal nicely.

With all eating in silence, Breanna paused at raising her spoon to her mouth and told her band tightly, "I've dropped off my soiled clothes and had a privileged bath with the dun's Master Bard beyond the central bathhouse. It is located on the left, at the far wall, by the clothes baskets. They will take care of our clothing for us, and you will be welcome to use those washtubs as they reserve them for nobles."

Fergal snorted in derision. "Nobles!"

"Stop being a horse's arse!" she responded caustically. "Bathe where you will and wash your clothes if you want. I'll take advantage of someone thinking I'm noble because *Mo Chroí* chose me."

Eoin said, "Bre, please take a moment to finish your breakfast. Fergal will keep his mouth shut. I'm unsure what happened last night or in the baths. Yet, I support you and the task set upon you by our gods."

Braoin added, "As do I, sister-mine. I have seen what you can do. Only someone touched by our gods could have done what you did to those Norvegrs. I am with you."

Fergal remained silent, furiously chewing his boar and spooning down the gruel. He muttered, "Talk of Tuatha gods and magic makes my head hurt."

Since he already knew her lineage, Breanna reasoned it was time to free Fergal's memories. He needed to choose his path freely, especially since Eoin understood her origins. She commanded *Maorgairme* to free Fergal from his memory block. A moment later, he looked up, the surprise evident on his face, and snarled, "You!"

"Aye, me," Breanna answered honestly. "As you already know, I am the Dreadlord's daughter. And I will be the one who destroys him according to our gods. And no one, not even you, cousin to my Chief, will stand in my way."

"Through gods and magic?" spat Fergal. "Nonsense!"

Eoin harshly said, "Fergal, you try my patience again in this matter. If you cannot abide by my order, as your Chief, to support this cause as I do, I will order your return to Dun Arrogh. The *Aos Dána* support Breanna's cause and would only do that if the

Tuatha gods did as well, not to mention her support from Chief Faolán and Chieftess Falyn. If you cannot believe this, say so. I'll send you back to our dun to collect your things, and then you'll be banished as an oath breaker. You can go wherever you want, as you will be a cousin of mine no more."

Fergal said bitterly, "So I must accept or be cast out? Then you can—"

Eoin said darkly, "I can what? Tell me now, cousin, which path will you choose? I, we, have no time for your doubts."

Fergal's skin turned even redder. Then he just nodded, saying, "I gave you my oath."

Braoin interjected. "Fergal, that sounds like a weak commitment if I say so myself. I am also a *dìolain* of the exact spawn, yet I am embracing it and my gods. You're just a coward. Not strong enough to believe in your heritage. In our Gael heritage."

Braoin turned to Breanna, saying, "Since we likely have a few spans before the Druids fetch Bradaigh from his dun, sister-mine, I'd like to take you up on your offer to teach me how you seize the *void* your way. That would be something that could help me support your *geas* and mine."

Breanna smiled for the first time since she had sat. After taking a moment to finish her oats, she said, "Of course, brother-mine. Let me fetch my vambraces, and we can retire to the yard."

With that, the two left to do as Braoin had requested.

Fergal

Fergal was stunned. Eoin rose to follow Breanna and her brother but held back and informed Fergal, "Your disdain for our gods and their magic is a stain on our clan. Clan Mórdha has never challenged our *Aos Dána* and has always supported our Tuatha gods, as our ancestors pledged. Not as you have. Please do not test me on this again. Or. You. Will. Be. Banished!"

With that, Eoin turned to leave when Keegan approached, asking, "May I be of help?"

"That would be welcome, as my cousin here has shite for brains when it comes to believing our gods or how their magic can help us," Eoin spat. "He has a decision to make. Maybe you can help him make it."

Fergal looked at Keegan with suspicion as Eoin walked away.

The latter sat across from him, stating, "So, I overheard you have a challenge believing our Gods and their magic. And an added measure of distrust in Breanna that she is Erin's Hero? Maybe about how such gods could choose a half-blood to tackle the challenge of the Dreadlord in our land?"

Fergal just nodded.

Keegan sighed. "As a significant ringfort in Mide, Dun Uisneach likely has better Druids than you've experienced, especially under the Dreadlord's thumb. That said, I have a few years on you. Living here as Senschall, I see how life works between nobles and commoners. We've strayed from our past. Yet, in Breanna, I see hope despite her doubts about herself. Our *Ard Rí* cares not about his people—that needs to change. That's why Hakon is still here."

Again, Fergal just nodded.

"So, why do you resist?"

"I am not her equal. She destroyed me in moments."

Keegan laughed. "Of course she did! Embrace the *void,* and you will know why."

Fergal just nodded, chewing on his thoughts.

Breanna and Braoin took a break after a half-span of sparring while she worked on his ability to seize the *void*. Since their progress was limited, *Croí Dàn* suggested to Breanna, *"You need to let Braoin touch me so I can accelerate his ability to seize the void. With your approach to the void being one of the best I've ever encountered, I can help link his mind to the Tuatha realm in the same way you can."*

"Now you tell me!"

"Calm down, my Hero," was her Heart's response. *"It was time well spent, as I now have a path through his mental block to the void."*

Breanna pulled the Heart of Destiny from her tunic. *"Croí Dàn* tells me she can open your block to the *void* and show you how I do it. Grasp the gem."

"What?"

"Trust me, brother-mine," was her answer. "I need you."

He nodded. "I am unsure why you trusted me so profoundly thus far."

Yet he did as she bade, closing his fingers around the heart-shaped gem. Then, a moment later, with eyes wide, he added, "Now I see it! So you came up with that?"

Breanna winked, drawing her blades and taking a challenging stance. "Aye, brother-mine, but let's see if you can now truly seize the *void* as I can."

A quarter-span later, neither had gotten inside the other's guard. Eoin, who had appeared after they started, said, "From what I saw, that is an incredible improvement since Braoin touched the Heart of Destiny. I want the same."

Croí Dàn said, *"Yes! So now that Braoin knows his way to the void, your Chief needs this same pathway."*

Breanna nodded. "*Mo Chroí* agrees with you, Eoin. Step forward and take her into your hand."

He did so and was momentarily puzzled as if he was assimilating a foreign concept, then exclaimed, "That's brilliant! It is so clear! And much easier and faster than how I was approaching the *void*."

Breanna smiled. "Then let's have a match and test it. The more you use it, the better you'll get."

While they circled each other, testing with thrusts and feints, Corbmac and his two *fians* of nine emerged from a large oblong hut that appeared to be the barracks for the fighters. The *fian* warriors created a circle around the sparring couple. They started what looked like a dance among their blades, which began slowly but grew faster and faster. Eoin led with sweeping sword strokes, moves that Breanna masterfully deflected, ducked, or countered. Then Breanna spun her long blades and pivoted. Eoin appeared to foresee the move and danced away from her shining blades.

They engaged in several more such exchanges of blade work, with Breanna on the attack and forcing Eoin to circle. When a feint drew his blade right, she tapped his shoulder with her left. She stood down, announcing, "Match to me. You're wounded but not dead!"

Each of the *fian* soldiers thumped their spears on their bucklers in approval, chanting, "Bre! Bre! Bre!"

She took a few deep breaths, sheathed her blades, and gave Corbmac's men a bow. Turning back to Eoin, she said, "Well done, my Chief. Your anticipation is now much better."

As Eoin grinned at her praise, the *fian* leader strode to their sides. "Impressive match. I've rarely seen such unrestrained skill so masterfully displayed. There were times when I was sure one of you would skewer the other, but then the attack was evaded or countered. You must have engaged in many rounds together like that to create such a stunning dance. You're both more than worthy of your gold armbands. Had I known how overmatched we'd be yesterday, I wouldn't have been so rude when we met. I hope you'll all forgive my insulting questions and tone."

Eoin shrugged. "I would say you caused no lasting damage, Corbmac, and just now, we were pleased to provide some entertainment for you and your *fian* warriors."

"I hope to see you both dance again," Corbmac told Breanna.

"I'm sure we can do that," she replied, strangely feeling closer to Eoin than ever before. It was an unexpected emotion.

"Yet I must be off to escort our Master Fáidh and Bard to fetch Bradaigh so you can meet your half-brother."

Breanna raised an eyebrow. "And that requires two full *fians* along with you?"

"Ahhh, that," Bláth said as she approached with Maoilir at her side. "It appears the one you would destroy is nearby. He seems to know you're here. Thus, additional warriors are warranted. We want to ensure he doesn't do anything rash."

Breanna looked around in alarm, but there was no way her father could breach the walls of Dun Uisneach. Then, putting a calming hand on her shoulder, Eoin inquired, "'Nearby' means...?"

Maoilir answered, "Aye, he has scouts out watching the High King's Road to alert him if you depart, so we will have to make a plan to fool him. For now, you're safe inside our ringfort. But first, let's fetch your half-brother for you. We can then discuss where and when to find the Mórrigan."

Bláth added, "Our scouts say he only has a few warriors at hand."

That eased Breanna's concerns over her father being so close.

Moments later, as the Master Fáidh and Bard of Dun Uisneach rode out through the gates with the *fian-ceannard* and his two *fians* of nine, Eoin said, "Well, Braoin, we should go to the baths before they return. I'd prefer to thoroughly scrub down before we meet the Chief and Chieftess later this morning."

"Don't forget about the nice, noble baths," added Breanna as she followed. "But after lunch, I suggest you two return here and have a match. Sword-on-sword is the practice you need if we clash with the Dreadlord and his ilk."

"As you command, my Hero," Eoin agreed with a wink. Breanna slugged his shoulder, and he replied, "Ouch! At least pick the arm that wasn't wounded fighting those Dreadriders."

Breanna laughed. "That's why I only hit your shoulder, you oaf!"

Croí Dàn chuckled in her mind. *"That man has some things to learn about women."*

Breanna answered, *"I don't have time for men, especially that one."*

"Yet I know the truth about you two."

Breanna scowled at her Heart, only to receive smug silence.

Hakon

Hakon stirred to life at dawn, a bit sore from sleeping on the ground, and stretched his muscles to work out the kinks. Then, he worked on his forms while two warriors, Brynjar and Haldor, hunted for breakfast. Kvasir once more took up his watch over Toal, who had just awakened and sat up, and Lang prepared to follow his orders.

He saw that his other warrior, Jotun, was already wolfing down his morning rations, unable to wait for the hunters to return. Hakon knew the young one would leave shortly to relieve Gern, stationed near the High King's Road. The thicket Lang had found offered a good view of the road while providing cover.

"Jotun, bring an additional horse so you can ride back if you see something happening," Hakon commanded. The lad nodded and mounted up with a second set of reins in his off-hand, riding off to his post for the day with the extra mount.

In the meantime, Hakon noted Lang was finally ready to depart for Dun Garm as he had ordered. He stepped beside his Dreadrider and said, "If you ride hard, you can make it to our dun by late this evening. But given we are not sure how long my Destroyer will shelter with the Gaels in Dun Uisneach, we must be ready to catch them where the High King's Road crosses the River Brosna.

"You missed my order that Runa and Thordvald set out tomorrow morning. It would be best if you reached them in time. With a route east and then south along Loch Ainninn, that should be about two or three days with Runa in her chariot. You must pull together two bands of nine, one for you and one for Thorvald, to help catch my daughter."

"I understand, my Jarl," Lang said contritely.

"You must live up to your Dreadrider title and lead our men with Thorvald's support, as you swore to me last night that you would master your rage. Now, go with all speed!"

Lang departed, riding hard as ordered. Hakon's thoughts swirled, wondering how his unstable Dreadrider and daughter could ever work together.

Gern returned after being relieved by Jotun and said, "My Jarl, all was quiet throughout the night. No one came or went from Dun Uisneach."

"Thank you for your diligence," Hakon said with approval. "We will see what the day brings. There could be more cover actions from those at Dun Uisneach before his Destroyer is on the move again."

A little over a span later, Jotun charged into the Dreadlord's camp on his mount. "My Jarl, three riders with two *fians* just headed west on the High King's Road. They were escorting two robed riders, a man and a woman."

"That is a show of force for sure," Hakon commented. "The robed riders were likely Druids. What could have caused them to ride out in such numbers?"

"Unknown, my Jarl," Jotun responded, to which Hakon shook his head and signaled for him to return to his post at the thicket. Hakon was furious that he lacked the numbers to challenge his main rival at the place where his daughter sought refuge.

Later, the two *fians* returned with the robed riders, but this time, they also escorted a young white-haired warrior. Hearing the report, Hakon nodded, his mind churning. "Mystery solved. Bradaigh, my other bastard son, has been called to meet the Destroyer. If he joins her cause, that will make it five of them to contend with. It's good that Lang and Thorvald are bringing eighteen of our warriors.

"No matter, Jotun. Head back to the thicket. Gern will relieve you before sunset." With that, Hakon turned away, wondering what his daughter was planning.

Noticing Toal was staring at him, Hakon demanded, "What?"

The boy said flatly, "She won't turn, and she will kill you."

Eoin

As Eoin returned to the main hall, he noted Fergal still sat where he'd left him nearly a span ago. Then, waving toward the bathhouse at the back, he said to Braoin and Breanna, "I need a moment with my cousin to see if he will continue with us or return to Dun Arrogh. I'll join you shortly."

That brought Breanna to a halt. "What did you say to him?"

Eoin shook his head. "That's between him and me. But we can't risk having him join us if he can't be all in with our quest."

Breanna touched Eoin's arm with a small smile. "I know you and Fergal are close. Yet thank you for your support. I don't know if I could do this without you."

As she and her half-brother moved toward the bathhouse, a young lad approached Eoin, saying, "Pardon, my Prince. I understand that Corbmac informed our Master Smith, Fergus, that you have Norvegr weapons you wish to barter. I am Lorcan, Gus's apprentice, sent to fetch what you have so they can be assessed."

"Good to meet you, Lorcan," Eoin replied, pointing to the screened-off area for them. "The weapons we claimed as battle spoils are on a table behind those panels. Take them and tell Fergus that I appreciate the offer to barter."

With that, Eoin bid the lad good day, only to be interrupted by a middle-aged Druid bearing the colors of a Healer. She said, "Your Champion demanded you needed healing due to a previous battle."

"Och, I'm fine," Eoin countered.

The Druid said, "I am Bodhmall, Master Healer here. And my *sight* says you're not *fine*. I understand you have issues to deal with today, but please let Keegan know that we need some private time before dinner. He will arrange a suitable place and time. It appears your cousin needs the same attention."

With that, she left him, and Eoin crossed the hall and sat opposite Fergal, who looked up from his empty ale cup at him.

Fergal asked, "So you have come for my answer?"

"Aye," Eoin replied tightly. "I have."

"I've always supported you, as you are my Prince and cousin."

"You have, and you are," Eoin confirmed

"And Breanna beat me in my challenge. She is your Champion."

Eoin nodded. "She did and is."

"Yet I still doubt our Gods are truly here."

"It has always been this way with you. I don't know why."

"Keegan said something similar about accepting it. I can't."

"Then you are lost to me, which breaks my heart. Yet, I'll have you know one thing before you leave us.

"While working with Braoin in the yard, I experienced *Croí Dàn's* magic firsthand. After Breanna sparred with Braoin, it seemed he could not grasp how to seize the *void*. Then, Breanna had him hold the Heart of Destiny. It–or should I say *she*–showed him my Champion's pathway to the *void*. After a second match, Braoin's skill level jumped dramatically.

"That was when I demanded the same knowledge. Her Heart showed me how to seize the *void* using Breanna's method, which is faster and easier to hold for extended periods. I was going about it all wrong. I have never moved with such anticipation as when Bre and I had a match. It was as if we were one. Knowing you have a block similar to Braoin's, I would ask you to do one thing before you give me your decision."

"You want me to hold the Heart of Destiny?" Fergal asked hesitantly. "To see if it will help me to believe in its magic?"

"Aye, my cousin," Eoin stated firmly. "I think it's the only way for you to embrace our quest fully, and know that Breanna is Erin's Hero. After that, if this talk of magic and the notion that we must support my Champion and Erin's Hero still troubles you, return to Dun Arrogh. Then find your way in our land as you will."

With that, Eoin rose. "I think it's time for a bath, as we should likely meet with Chief Faolán soon. Are you with me, cousin?"

With a resigned sigh, Fergal answered, "Aye, my Chief."

A while later, the four warriors were all cleaned up and dressed in their best clothes, sitting again at their customary table in the main hall. As they waited for the Druids to return, Eoin decided it was best to address the challenge Fergal presented to their quest.

He rose to stand before them. "We are all charged to support Breanna's quest to destroy the Dreadlord, by our gods no less. Against all odds, my Champion sought out our Mother Goddess. Then, graced with her support, she accepted the challenge of this quest, battled demons, and was saved by our Sun God. And now, she has been chosen by the Heart of Destiny as Erin's Hero. All but one of us has embraced these actions as fact.

"After my experience today with *Croí Dàn*, I have given Fergal one last chance to decide if he can genuinely join us in this quest. Not just with his mind but with his heart and soul. Like I have, and like I know Braoin has."

Braoin added heartily, "Aye, I have indeed!"

Breanna's eyes brimmed with tears as Eoin turned to her and continued, "Fergal has accepted a challenge I laid upon him. After *Croí Dàn* conveyed your ability to seize the *void* to Braoin and me, I now hope she can do the same for Fergal. If he cannot or still does not believe that our gods are behind Breanna's quest, he will ride for Dun Arrogh tomorrow, gather his things, and make his way in our land, banished from our clans."

Fergal nodded in agreement.

Breanna ducked a hand under her tunic. "I will ask if she agrees."

Croí Dàn answered both of them, *"It is the only way."*

Breanna pulled out the gem. "*Croí Dàn* has agreed. Take the gem in your hand; she will show you my path to the *void*. And likely more."

As Fergal closed his finger around the Heart of Destiny, he froze. *Croí Dàn* spoke in his mind. *"Know me! Know that I speak for Danu, Lugh, All-Father, and the Dark Goddess! Know that I have decided who will be Erin's Hero! I will not show you the way to the void until I know your heart is mine. Do you commit your heart and soul to me?"*

Fergal jolted back. *"Are you real?"*

"More than you can imagine," was her cold response. *"I am Erin's Heart, and that makes your heart mine. All of Erin's people belong to my Hero and thus are mine, every one of your hearts, and they beat as one, as mine. You can be a force of change in Breanna's quest to destroy the Dreadlord. Will you join us? Help save our land, your land? Support Breanna?"*

"I...I have been blind," Fergal stammered, his emotions flowing through the connection. *"Please let me help Breanna with her quest."*

The Heart of Destiny replied, *"I accept you. I will now show you how to seize the void as Breanna does. It was very clever of her to find that path. But before that, I will have your oath."*

"You shall have it!"

"Kneel before Breanna and swear to the following: 'My Hero, I pledge my blood and bones to you and promise to accept your orders and protect you no matter the danger to my own life. If I fail to fulfill this oath, may my heart cease to beat.'"

"I swear it will be so!"

A moment later, Breanna said, "When my Heart speaks to anyone, I also hear it. I know she has accepted you, Fergal, and that you've sworn to me. We have not seen eye-to-eye for a long while, but I welcome you to my quest."

Fergal smiled. "Thank you for giving me this chance to redeem myself and for sharing your pathway to the *void*. It is indeed incredible. I now feel it at the edge of my consciousness, ready to seize. And I am deeply sorry for being so blinded. While our gods left us to the Dreadlord's whims, they plotted to remove him—through you. The Heart of Destiny has cleared my mind. You have been true to our land and our clans. I know I didn't make it easy on you, so if I slip up with any future doubts, you can knock me in the head with one of your hafts once more!"

Breanna pulled him to his feet and wrapped her arms around him. "Thank you, Fergal, as I need the support of those who know me best. For good or bad."

At that, the doors to the main hall burst open, and in strode Dun Uisneach's Master Bard and Master Fáidh, along with Corbmac and a tall, white-haired warrior who looked like a brawnier version of Braoin.

Eoin said, "One issue settled, another to address."

As the Druids marched up to their table, Maoilir said, "We have brought the other half-brother to Erin's Hero, as she demanded. I have sent word to Chief Faolán and Chieftess Falyn to meet with us all here. And then we need to plan on how to best get you on your way toward Croghan Hill and the *Well of Segais*."

Bláth shook her head. "Maoilir, please, a little tact. They are not ours to order about. We are theirs to command, as Danu charged us through her Heart."

Maoilir looked sharply at Bláth, who did not blink, returning a hard stare. Then, a moment later, he sighed, saying, "Forgive me, Erin's Hero. You have upset the balance of the people and their *Aos Dána*. It has been eons since a Hero our Heart has chosen walked this land."

Breanna smiled. "Maoilir, if this were easy, we would have rid ourselves of the Dreadlord long ago. But let's not waste time on who should worship whom. I'm just a seventeen-year-old woman who happens to have been chosen by her gods. So let's make the best of what we have."

Maoilir smirked. "Wise move to play the youth card."

"Curb your tongue," Bláth hissed. "I'll demand our Hero have *Cróí Dàn* speak directly to you if you cannot be more civil."

Croí Dàn blasted into the recalcitrant Druid's mind. *"I don't need permission from my Hero, Erin's Hero, to speak! So get in line or fetch an Aos Dána Seer worthy of his gods and goddesses!"*

Eoin heard that clearly and saw Maoilir blanch. Then he bowed to Breanna, saying, "Apologies, Erin's Hero. And to *Croí Dàn*, who has chosen you."

The tall, white-haired warrior beside the Druids looked perplexed at the exchange. "Well, that was enlightening. Two Druids and a pair of mixed Gael-Norvegr warriors are arguing over who is at the top of the pile. Introductions might be in order before we decide whose arse to kiss."

Breanna smiled wider. "I think I might like you, Bradaigh. In case you forgot, I am Breanna Ban Morna. We battled to a draw last summer, and you bested Braoin here at my side. You controlled the *void* well, then; now my control is better than anyone else in our land.

"Either way, like Braoin, you are my half-brother. We were each born under the same circumstances, each cast under a similar *geas*. Braoin's was justice. Mine was destruction. Yours, I yet do not know. But what yours is does not matter."

Bradaigh's eyes narrowed. "Because?"

"The Heart of Destiny has proclaimed me as her chosen one, as Erin's Hero," Breanna answered, pulling the heart-shaped stone from her tunic. "Hold it, and you'll know for certain I speak truly."

Bradaigh

Bradaigh looked at the pulsing red heart-shaped gem, feeling its power, its heartbeat. A force that would help him fulfill his *geas*, his curse, driving him to defeat the Dreadlord in single combat in a battle of power. With that, he boldly reached out to grasp it, thinking maybe to rip the magical gem from her throat, only to find he was frozen, with *Croí Dàn* surging into his mind with, *"HOW DARE YOU, YOU CUR, CONSIDER SUCH A THOUGHT!"*

With a blast of her Heart's power, her half-brother was flung three feet up and back, away from Breanna, by a flash of magic, only to land hard on his back with a crash. The jewel had burned his hand bright red, and his wind whooshed from his lungs.

Breanna stood over him, with two strange blades blazing in her hands as she held them crossed at his throat, asking, "My brother, are you so much like our father that I cannot trust you?"

Stunned, Bradaigh could not answer. What had he been thinking? This magic of his land had ripped into him as if he were a child's doll. Then Breanna spat, "Take him away. I could never have believed one born of our land, as I was, as Braoin was, could be so brazen to think he could steal the magic of our gods from us."

With that, Corbmac told his *fian* warriors, "Put him in a holding cell. We will deal with him later."

A moment later, Chief Faolán and Chieftess Falyn strode into the hall, looking askew at the young Bradaigh as two warriors hauled him to his feet.

"Corbmac," Chief Faolán said, "what's the trouble?"

"There's much to update you on since last night, my Chief and Chieftess," the older warrior answered. "Yet, I think this information will hearten you."

With that, the warriors led Bradaigh away.

Faolán

It was then that Corbmac, Maoilir, and Bláth relayed the previous day's events and the Tuatha magic in play, providing a timeline for Breanna to meet with the Mórrigan near Croghan Hill, and concluded with the exchange between Breanna and Bradaigh, including his attempt to seize the Heart of Destiny from around her neck.

"Maoilir will speak with the boy," Faolán said, rubbing his chin as he pondered Bradaigh's fate. "He could still be an asset. We will need to find out how. Either way, we have much to consider and decide."

"We do indeed, but the boy can simmer in the soup for a while," Falyn stated. "With this decisive news, we need a solid plan to deal with the Dreadlord—a plan built on bravado and deception."

Faolán nodded at his mate's quick command of all things military, proving his choice of her as their *Taoiseach* was as sound as it had always been; even his cousin in Tara sought her advice. "Your counsel, my mate?"

Falyn smiled brightly at his request for her thoughts. "The Dreadlord hovers nearby, and we have a new hero, Erin's Hero, who could defeat the Norvegr Jarl. How many days until the next full moon, when Breanna must meet the Mórrigan?"

Corbmac answered, "I believe it's about seven or eight days out now, but they need time to get there. So I'd plan on a departure in four or five days."

"We can work with that," Falyn declared with a glint in her eyes. "Our Hero and her friends can help train our troops while we plan a diversion. Let the Dreadlord stew in his nearby hidey-hole. We need to rotate the *fians* out on patrol throughout the region to spend some time here at Dun Uisneach so they can learn about and from Erin's Hero. And help spread the word to watch for any Norvegrs heading east."

Changing the subject, she added, "Now, as to the distraction needed to get our Hero and her band safely away to seek the Mórrigan. I think a Céili is in order. Bláth, you'll be overseeing this with our Seneschal, Keegan. Let's make sure it's loud so the Dreadlord knows we are celebrating something big!"

"That is brilliant, my mate!" Faolán beamed.

——⚬ Bradaigh ⚬——

Bradaigh sat in his cell, wondering what had happened. The Druids from Dun Uisneach had sought him out to meet with two other mixed Gael-Norvegrs, whom he had sparred with this past summer. One of them he had won against. A lad about a year younger than him, one who could not control the *void* as he could. The other was much better at seizing the *void*. She was a lithe young woman who had battled him to a draw with long blades against his long sword. Highly unusual.

Then, in meeting the two half-breeds again, he had been drawn to the magical gem around the one called Breanna's neck. Had his *geas* forced him into an action? It indeed seemed that way, though he did not understand why. He looked at the burn on his palm, the stinging red shape mirroring the heart-shaped stone he had briefly grasped. Why had he thought he could seize the magic that had chosen her?

Corbmac escorted Master Fáidh, Maoilir, into the area outside of a cell constructed of black oak poles. The former said, "Lad, you're lucky. I've seen you battle in the yard and at our annual *comórtas*, and you've always shown restraint. As a result, I convinced our Chief and Chieftess to allow you to share your thoughts. To attack Erin's Hero, chosen by *Croí Dàn* herself, was daft at best. Were the leaders of this dun here instead of us, you'd likely lose your head by nightfall."

The Seer added flatly, "I also don't know what you were thinking, but, as Corbmac said, the young woman has been chosen by *Croí Dàn*, the Heart of Destiny. Given that you grew up near Dun Uisneach, you cannot claim ignorance about our Heart, as we teach everyone how the magic of the *Triple Dàns* protects Erin and her people."

Bradaigh looked back and forth between the two interrogators, thinking about the right approach to use to save his neck. Then, he said honestly, "I was born with a *geas*, one that demands I find the power to end the rule of the Dreadlord single-handedly. That *geas* made me assume the power I saw in *Ćroí Dàn* was mine to control."

Corbmac exclaimed, "Idiot!"

Maoilir added quietly, "Your other half-brother has a similar *geas*. Braoin's is justice, and your half-sister has a *geas* of destruction. Not just to kill Hakon Skadi but to entirely remove his stain upon our land, including all of those he brought with him to our lands. Do you think you can do better without being chosen? Breanna will have to make the most demanding sacrifice for all of us. It seems even the gods do not know how it will take shape. But, given she has been chosen by *Ćroí Dàn*, whether you live or not should be decided by Erin's Hero."

The pair departed, leaving Bradaigh stunned.

Maoilir

Maoilir led the way to the Chief and Chieftess's private meeting room. He found the couple reviewing crop and animal production reports.

Then, after a moment, Faolán rose and said, "Maoilir, Corbmac, what news do you have about Bradaigh's fate?"

Maoilir answered, "Well, I can confirm we have a third *geas* in play. First, Braoin's is one of justice, then Breanna's is one of destruction, and now Bradaigh's appears to be one of power.

The local Druids who cast them did not envision the conflicts that could happen if they crossed."

Falyn asked, "So what do we do to resolve this conflict?"

"It is not our place to do so," Maoilir said bluntly. "Only Erin's Hero can decide Bradaigh's fate. Or should I say *Croí Dàn*? Or both? They are the ultimate authority. Only her magic can tell if Bradaigh can be true to the quest the gods have tasked Breanna to undertake."

Chief Faolán questioned, "Should our Master Breitheamh not be involved?"

Maoilir shrugged. "You think our judges can make better decisions than *Croí Dàn*? I think not. She and her chosen one should decide his fate."

"Agreed, then make it so," ordered Falyn.

"As you command, Chieftess."

◈ Breanna ◈

Breanna followed Eoin, Fergal, and Braoin as they each took turns at matches and seized the *void*. Intently observing Fergal, since he was the newest member of their band to embrace Tuathain magic, she and the Heart of Destiny followed him into that place between the realms. Watching and nudging him in the shared space of the *void*, assessing his skills to see how well he could discern Braoin's next move. Noting a slight hitch in his movements, she knew his wounded leg was still troubling him. Breanna decided it was time to find Bodhmall.

Spying Keegan crossing the yard, she waved him over.

"How may I help you, my Hero?" asked.

"Eoin and Fergal need the Master Healer. She said you could fetch her for them. Now would be a good time to address the issue, as their previous wounds still hamper them."

"As you command, my Hero."

"As I've said to many, it's just Bre."

Keegan smiled at her request and continued on his way. When Breanna turned to watch the match underway, she was startled to find Maoilir beside her. He said gravely, "Erin's Hero, we have a situation with Bradaigh that only you and *Croí Dàn* can resolve."

"Resolve?" Breanna asked, annoyed she had not sensed him hovering nearby.

"Aye, his fate is in your hands," Maoilir answered.

"His fate? As in life or death?" she queried with wide eyes.

"Indeed," Maoilir agreed with a bow. "His *geas* is one of power. To seek any power to defeat the Dreadlord single-handedly. Thus, his rash decision was to try to take *Croí Dàn* from you. The Heart of Destiny must assess him and decide his fate with you. More pointedly, can his *geas* be trusted? Enough to be able to join you in your quest."

Croí Dàn commented, *"We will decide this together!"*

Breanna looked at the Fáidh doubtfully and gave him a stern nod. She turned away from her band, following the Druid to a small hut beside the main hall. He led her inside, where she found a cell of stout black oak poles holding her brother captive.

Maoilir said to the white-haired lad, "Stand, Bradaigh. Your sister, Erin's Hero, chosen by *Croí Dàn*, will stand in judgment."

"Judgment?" Bradaigh asked.

Maoilir answered, "Indeed. You sought to seize the Heart of Destiny from her chosen one. For any Gael, that was a brazen overreach of power, no matter its source. Your Chief and Chieftess decided your fate needs to be in the hands of the Tuatha and their chosen one."

Bradaigh demanded, "Will the Master Breitheamh be involved, as is my right?"

Maoilir responded gravely with, "No. In this matter, such a judgment is beyond him. This matter is one where the choice will be life or death, and the Heart of Destiny will judge your heart, soul, and, therefore, your destiny. Judge if you can be true to your land and people, regardless of your *geas*."

Breanna thought her brother looked sullen at the Druid's pronouncement. When *Croí Dàn* sent a pulse of magic to get his attention, Breanna explained softly, "You have a *geas* that seeks a power laid upon you. Similar to, yet different from, the *geas* driving me, which is to seek the absolute destruction of the Deardlord. Yet my other brother's *geas* seeks justice for the wrongs Hakon committed against our land and people. Whose is right? Whose is wrong? Which path do we take? What do our gods want? Can each of our *geases* be combined? Can they be merged into something more than each casting by their respective Druids? Something each of our mothers would be proud of? Yet, regardless of those answers, there can only be a single chosen one.

"As you know, my Heart can speak in your mind, as does Maoilir here. *Croí Dàn*, please include the Druid in our discussion."

The Heart of Destiny spoke harshly into his mind, *"Remember this first, Bradaigh. She is mine. Understand this or die."*

Breanna smiled darkly, as it was their joint decision if her brother lived or died, asking, *"So tell me, in your afterthought, what do you now think? For instance, if you possessed my Heart in your hand, would it make you powerful? Provide enough power to defeat the Dreadlord?"*

As their words spoke in Bradaigh's mind, his eyes widened, and he nodded slightly to acknowledge it. Breanna went on. *"Yet, that is the seduction, the allure of such thoughts. That is why you are dangerous and unstable. Your geas is about power, power to control, and it is corrupting you."*

Breanna glanced at the Druid, who nodded in approval and then switched back to her natural voice, continuing, "My *geas* is about the destruction of the Dreadlord, to remove him and his fellows from our land. Our gods are behind me in this quest. I cannot control the method by which our Tuatha gods' magic will take effect. I can only trust they will lead me to that destructive moment. Still, your power challenges mine, the power of our gods. I know my path will lead to his destruction. Can you see how yours does not do the same? Your path, your *geas*, leads to you being in power, replacing the Dreadlord, maybe killing him. Yet it would not remove the Norvegr stain from our land, would it?"

Bradaigh answered, "Nay, it shames me to admit that was what I saw in the Heart's power, and your logic is flawless in where that would lead us."

"Yet, *Croí Dàn* has claimed I am to have that power," Breanna whispered. "As have our gods, through their gifts of magic to me. Can you claim the same?"

"Nay again, Breanna Ban Morna," Bradaigh responded solemnly. "I apologize, my sister. You are the chosen one. I didn't realize this when my *geas* took control of me and rashly demanded I seek the power of the Heart of Destiny. I saw the opportunity. I had to take it."

"So, what is your verdict about that action?"

Bradaigh hung his head. "I am guilty."

Breanna asked mentally, *"Croí Dàn, can we train him to be ours in four days?"*

The Heart of Destiny answered, *"Yes, I can make him ours. However, because of his geas, I must limit, at least for now, the advanced access to the void you gave to Eoin, Fergal, and Braoin."*

"That is wise of you. With that, I command you bind Bradaigh to us," Breanna said. Then she turned to Maoilir. "*Croí Dàn* and

I can ensure Bradaigh's loyalty to our quest. Tell your Chief and Chieftess of our decision."

Maoilir nodded solemnly.

While the Druid turned away to do as she requested, Breanna decreed, *"Croí Dàn, I need assurance his geas cannot subvert him. I have had enough treachery from him today. Please make it so."*

Her Heart informed her and her brother, *"Aye, I will endeavor to control him. Danu, when she made me sentient, gave me the choice to select Erin's Hero. Once chosen, I will always be at my Hero's side. Bradaigh, I will mute your geas and keep it that way. And make sure you swear the oath that I will make your heart mine to stop."*

Striding back to Bradaigh, with only the black oak poles between them, Breanna commanded, "Take the Heart in your hand once more. She will bind you to us. And, I think, heal your hand in the process. We must practice together as a band to prevail, and I doubt you could hold your sword now."

Bradaigh tentatively reached through the bars to the heart-shaped ruby that hung around her neck, their foreheads almost touching, her eyes locked on his. When the Heart flashed this time, it did not burn or throw him to the ground. Instead, *Croí Dàn* joined with Breanna, wrapping them around his mind, and bent his *geas* to their mutual goal of destroying the Dreadlord.

Croí Dàn gave the order inside his head, *"Now swear: 'My Hero, I pledge my blood and bones to you and promise to accept your orders and protect you no matter the danger to my own life. If I fail to fulfill this oath, may my heart cease to beat.'"*

Bradaigh repeated the words and ended with, "I so swear."

The Heart of Destiny proclaimed: *"So sworn!"*

Bradaigh released the stone, withdrew his hand, and said in surprise, "My burn no longer hurts."

Breanna saw that the red had faded to a faint white outline that matched her Heart. "It's a good scar to remind you who is in command of our quest."

Bradaigh nodded in agreement, and Breanna sighed in relief. She knew she needed him as she opened the cell door, saying, "You are now one with us. Follow me, as we must go to the yard and practice battling our foes as one band, not as five individual warriors."

"Aye, sister-mine. That is something my *geas* now understands. So we can be more powerful together."

Hakon

Hakon stirred from his midday contemplations in the woods, unsure of what move to make next. Yet he could not access Runa to determine what was happening inside the dun. All he could do was have his men watch and report, as he did not have the power here to attack the nearby Gaels.

That made him bristle, yet he had to wait and see what his daughter would do next. Well, not *what*, as that would be to head southeast to seek the Tuatha Dark Goddess, but *when*. Frustrated, he rose to do his midday forms, opting for Kvasir as his workout partner.

When they finished, Hakon looked at Toal and smiled, knowing what the other saw, as he was a beast who could kill him in a heartbeat. He sneered, "You think you can challenge me?"

Toal smiled as if he knew something.

"Boy, you think you understand what is happening?"

"Aye, maybe," Toal said, scratching his neck. "You seem to know the Tuatha gods stand against you. And you know they have chosen your daughter to lead the fight against you. Your völva is not here to speak in your ear about the future, so you are blind until Breanna makes a move. I know that much."

Hakon spat, "Imp!" And then he stormed away.

Toal

Toal smiled, knowing he had just goaded the Dreadlord's anger—just a lad who had seen much more in the creation of Erin's Hero than most. Gazing at the cloudy sky, holding a threat of rain, he wondered if his gods were looking at him now. He hoped so, for that would mean they were doing the same with his cousin.

Yet there was little he could do, trussed up like a boar for a roast and unable to escape the Dreadlord's clutches. Yet he would survive to warn Breanna about what the wretched man was planning.

Breanna

As Breanna had requested, Bodhmall sought out Eoin and Fergal for a healing session. She utilized her Earth Element to expedite the recovery from the wounds they had sustained in their battle with Lunt and Lang.

For the next three days, Breanna's Band, as they came to be known, continued to spar in the yard no matter what the weather held, accepting challenges from both *fian* warriors and those who had earned their Celtic Knot armrings and wanted to test themselves. Eoin and Breanna also trained with those who wanted to learn how to seize the *void* with confidence.

They held various matches against each other, sometimes one-on-one and other times two-on-one or three-on-two, and even a few matches with Corbmac's *fian* warriors. Those were nine-on-five, which helped the band learn how each other fought when surrounded, something they expected they would need should the Dreadlord catch them with an equivalent of a *fian* or more, though those would be swords on swords and not spears on swords.

At the end of each day, Bodhmall returned to ensure Eoin and Fergal were in top form, applying her Elemental healing magic.

As word of the upcoming Céili spread and more people arrived at Dun Uisneach, people gathered to watch Breanna's Band. Cormbmac matched each of them one-on-one, two-on-three, and against a *fian* of nine-on-four. Their blade and footwork were a more complex dance than a battle. Though Fergal, Bradaigh, and Braoin had put on splendid matches, the crowd waited to see Eoin and Breanna matched together once more.

While the two leaders danced, their blades flashed dangerously close to inflicting ruinous injuries, but never did. Only they knew each had seized the same space in the *void* and moved in unison as if their minds were one, where there was no genuine risk.

It was the end of the third day when the last match between the pair took place. It was masterful as they danced with their blades while jabbing, stabbing, blocking, countering, and slashing at each other with grace and care. To share the same *void* space was something only they could comprehend, a deep link of oneness between them.

As Breanna and Eoin finally stood down, over a hundred supporters roared their approval. Her Chief gracefully bowed to her. She did the same, and then they sheathed their blades. A moment later, Eoin took her hand and raised their arms together as they faced the crowd, bowing once more, then turning to quarter their audience, rotating to face each side so all could see their appreciation and acknowledge their cheers.

Croí Dàn, who could now talk inside each of the band's minds, said proudly to them, *"That was a beautiful dance of blades, one I've never seen the likes of, even in Macha's day—and she was a blade master. Of all my Heroes, only Lugh was better, but not with a mate."*

Making their final bow to the crowd, Breanna answered, *"Yet it was your magic that made it possible for Eoin and me to seize the same space in the void."*

Croí Dàn rejoined, *"That may be a technical reason that allowed you to create such a match, but Macha never had a partner who could be her equal with blade, body, soul, and mind. No Hero has had that."*

As they approached Faolán and Bláth, Eoin nodded in agreement with the Heart's comment. "That was indeed something special, Breanna. We must do that dance without our blades at the Céili tomorrow evening."

Breanna blushed at the idea. Her—dance? And take a moment for enjoyment?

The dun's Master Bard, overhearing the comment, confirmed, "I agree wholeheartedly! I'll find a reel that suits both of you. Your people would love to see such a joyous moment."

"I could not agree more," Faolán declared. "Everyone is already showing appreciation for Breanna's Band after just a few days of your presence, yet you two notably stand out as leaders. But enough accolades. Tomorrow will be busy, so it's best if we finalize your departure plans this evening."

Bláth added, "The Dreadlord still hovers nearby, waiting for your next move. Thus, a diversion during the Céili is needed."

Faolán requested, "Join us in my private meeting room after you've sought the bathhouse. Corbmac will be in the hall to guide you. We'll have supper there and decide how to proceed."

As they turned to the main hall, a burly man approached Eoin, asking, "My Prince, do you have a moment? I am Fergus, Master Smith here at Dun Uisneach, but please call me Gus. I believe we have some business to discuss."

Eoin said to the others, "You all head to the baths, and I'll join you shortly." He turned back to the smith. "Aye, I have time, and Lorcan mentioned you prefer Gus. Please, call me Eoin."

The smith smiled. "Aye, I will. That was one skilled blade dance with your Champion earlier. I know she is Erin's Hero from the gossip, but Corbmac shared the tale about how you came by those battle spoils you requested to barter. Before we get to business, my compliments to you both, as such talent has not been seen in my lifetime."

"My thanks," Eoin said with a slight bow. "It is only possible with my Bre, though. Yet, a question. You chose to forego your full name, Fergus. Ulaidian princes are well aware of this, as some of Clan Mórdha are related to the Fergus line in Dál n Araidi and Dál Riata. I have an aunt who mated into Clan DunBroch via a son of Chief Loarn Mac Eirc around when they relinquished northeast Uladia to the *Ard-Rí*."

"Aye, I'm of that line. Sounds like we share some lineage."

"Indeed. Yet on to our barter."

"Aye, the weapons presented are well-crafted swords and hunting knives. They are the work of a Norvegr smith. I would charge five golds per knife and twenty per sword for similar work. Yet not everyone wants to touch Norvegr-made iron, and I need to make a profit. So I propose ten golds for the three knives and forty-five golds for the swords."

Eoin scratched his chin through his braided beard. "That's a reasonable offer, but I need to buy my Champion and Hero something special for saving my life—several times now. Let's say sixty total, but you can keep half on my account until we finish our quest. Where we are going, I cannot carry that much."

"Aye, agreed!" Gus exclaimed, offering his arm to seal the offer.

"One more thing," Eoin added. "As to the gift I mentioned for Breanna, I think it would be fitting for her to have a new harness for *Lann Dàn*. Do you have a tanner who could make it?"

"Aye, that'd be Bhruic. I'll see that he gets it made in time. Faolán issued orders the morning after you arrived, instructing the trade masters to deliver what we believe you need to support Erin's Hero in her quest. We are already at work."

That left Eoin a bit stunned.

⊶⬦ Breanna ⬦⊷

A span later, bathed and dressed in their best but somewhat ragged clothes, Eoin, Breanna, and her three sworn warriors found Corbmac waiting for them. Holding a bundle in his arms, the older warrior said, "I understand we are dining privately tonight, so I expect we will not have time to present my Chief and Chieftess's gift afterward."

He walked into their screened area and set the bundle on a table. "With the Céilí tomorrow evening, Faolán thought you'd like some less warrior-like clothes for the celebration. Something you can dance in."

Breanna narrowed her eyes, muttering, "I see Bláth's hand in this *gift* you say your Chief thought of."

Corbmac shrugged a shoulder and lifted a bushy eyebrow with a smile. Then, he changed the subject with, "Shall we join my *Ceann-cinnidh* and his *Taoiseach*?"

The old warrior turned and led the way through a door to the left of the kitchens, with Eoin and Breanna behind him and

Fergal, Bradaigh, and Braoin following. The door opened onto a short hallway that led to a large room with an elongated, oval oak table at its center, surrounded by chairs. Four Druids stood next to a sideboard table of food that made up a small feast, along with pitchers of ale and mead.

While Breanna and her band were familiar with Bláth, Maoilir, and Bodhmall, they only occasionally saw the other one walking through the yard. The taller of the two wore the blue and green colors of the judicial branch and must be their Master Breitheamh, a Lawgiver. Bodhmall wore the green and red of the Healer branch as Master Ollamh of the dun. The former seemed to be of a similar age to Maoilir but with a stockier build, while the latter resembled a slightly older, slimmer version of Bláth, both with red hair.

The dun's Seneschal, Keegan, greeted Breanna's Band with a cheerful smile. "Welcome. We have food and drink ready, but we will have limited staff to assist with serving due to preparations for the Céilí. Given that this is a private meeting, please help yourself to a trencher and a mug. Chief Faolán and Chieftess Falyn will join you momentarily."

Bláth turned to the band and said, "I'd like to introduce you to Tadg. He and Bodhmall will be helping us spread the word across the land that the Heart of Destiny beats among us once more, and she has chosen Erin's Hero to protect her people. They, like us, have been commanded by the All-Father to support you."

Both Druids bowed to the warriors. Breanna acknowledged them with a nod and a slight bow. Then she said, "I'm not sure they or you will have the time to accomplish such a task. Danu indicated that I must meet the Mórrigan in the next few nights when the moon is at its zenith again. I know not where my quest of destruction will take me from there."

"Be easy, our Hero," Bláth said. "Maoilir and I will be traveling with you to assist in any way we can, and Tadg and Bodhmall will range ahead into the southeast part of our land to foretell the coming of your travels throughout where they range. Yet tonight was intended to be one of relaxation first and quest planning second. Can I offer you ale or mead?"

Four of her band answered with ale as Breanna shook her head. "Mead for me, please."

As Maoilir filled four mugs with ale and passed them about, Bláth handed a mug of mead to Breanna and took one for herself. Tadg hovered nearby, a questioning look in his eyes. Breanna sighed audibly and turned to him, saying before even tasting the mead, "What would you ask of me?"

"Apologies, Erin's Hero. I—"

"Stop. My name is Breanna Ban Morna, and I suspect you already know of me through your Bard. Or heard my claim. My Heart chose me because of only one thing."

As Eoin stepped to her side offering his support, Breanna sucked in a breath, yet was determined to embrace who she was, adding, "That Hakon Skadi killed my father—who would have been—and raped my mother. That act resulted in me being born a bastard daughter to a mother who ordered our Fáidh to cast a *geas* upon me to destroy that baby's birth father.

"Bradaigh, who stands next to me, has a similar fate, though in his case, his *geas* was one of power, to seek it regardless of the cost—anything to end his father's reign. With Braoin, it was a comparable case, yet the Druid his mother chose decided on justice for his *geas*. How that plays into this saga, I do not know, though I suspect either one could have been chosen by my Heart or me."

Croí Dàn interjected, *"That was never going to happen!"*

Eoin heard that and chuckled while Braoin and Bradaigh stood protectively at Breanna's back, hovering close enough to threaten the Druid.

Tadg shrugged. "Again, Breanna, we have just met, so please forgive the questions. Our Gaelic laws, handed down by Dagda himself, are based on equality: the lowest can call out the highest. Yet the Tuatha gods are a rule above. When one of their chosen is amongst us, we have a dilemma. To be ruled by our laws or be ruled by their, well, will. While Gaelic law generally drives us all, a moment like this is exceptional. How do you judge such moments?"

Breanna sipped her mead before looking into his eyes. "When our gods or their magic speaks in my mind, it is a higher power than a mere warrior can comprehend. I cannot think of a way to second-guess them. I must trust them to guide me. I hope that you see our laws in the same way, as they are applied unequally."

Bodhmall stepped in. "Enough, you old oaf, leave the young lady be. You think too deeply. She is only working to fulfill a destiny our Tuatha gods have laid upon her. Anyway, enough of such talk. I had hoped to get to know Breanna and her band this evening. Not to have a debate about laws and higher powers."

"Indeed!" exclaimed Chief Faolán as he entered with his mate. "We have much to discuss, and I expect my *Taoiseach* will lend the excellent wisdom she is known for far and wide."

"Och, that's too much butter you're spreading about the bread!" Falyn admonished. "We will all contribute. But first, to the trenchers. I, for one, am hungry! And after seeing the blade matches Breanna's Band displayed in the yard today, I'm sure they are as well!"

As the mood lightened and shifted, Breanna whispered to Bláth, "I know the game you're playing with the clothes your Chief and Chieftess have *given* us for the Céilí."

The Bard looked wide-eyed as if to deny the accusation, but then shrugged. "I do what I must to ensure our people are behind Erin's Hero. I sing from my heart as a Bard with a keen eye. Watching you two in that blade dance today made it clear that you two can create art that surpasses that of ordinary people. At the Céilí tomorrow, those who will gather in the yard and watch you and Eoin dance to a reel will be moved to believe in miracles again, moved by the love you two share."

Breanna protested in a whisper, "But I have no room for such love!"

"Aye, you do," Bláth countered quietly, holding a finger to Breanna's lips. "It may be what saves you. Ask *Croí Dàn* about this, as loving your land and your people will mean more when you have your love at risk."

Croí Dàn remained silent as the Bard spun away to talk with others, allowing Eoin to slide next to Breanna. "Hmm, you seem on edge. Is there something amiss?"

"Aye," she muttered. "Druids who like to meddle in my life."

"When have they not?" he questioned with a smile. "They have a less direct path to our gods than you have. It must gall them."

Breanna appreciated Eoin's misdirection, playing as if he didn't know the matter the Bard had raised. Then, nodding to herself, she commanded, "Let us sit, eat, and plan."

Bodhmall slipped next to the pair as they filled their trenchers. "I hope you and Fergal are doing better after our recent healing sessions."

Eoin said, "Aye, we are, Bodhmall. Thank you!"

"Of course," the Ollamh replied with a respectful nod.

Chief Faolán requested that Keegan bring the maps as they dug into their trenchers and lifted their mugs. After a short time, the trenchers were refilled and emptied again. While those gathered at the planning dinner had finished their meals, the mead and ale still flowed, and the focus was on the terrain that showed the way to the *Well of Segais*. Breanna commanded confidently, "Tell us what we need to know to reach the Dark Goddess's altar."

Maoilir pointed to a spot on the main map. "First, you ride east on *Slíghe Mor*, and you'll soon come to a ford at the River Brosna, created by Loch Ainninn. Then, after several more spans of riding, you'll ford the River Boyne. On the south side of the road, there's a deer track, where the sloped forest gives way to grass at the summit, and there you'll find a small pond called the *Well of Segais*. That is the main source of the River Boyne."

"Good directions, but there's still a chance we can miss it," Breanna complained. "Finding this well and the Mórrigan's altar, which few know exists, seems dubious. The Sun God also mentioned Croghan Hill. Where is that?"

"One can hardly miss it," Bláth answered, "as you'll see the tall mound from the High King's Road as you ride east. Let your ring guide you once you cross the River Boyne."

Her warriors looked at the glowing Tuatha crystal on Breanna's finger, and *Maorgairme* gave a pulse as if it was confirming it would be her guide. A moment later, a dot of light appeared on the map to demonstrate her support of the plan.

With that concern settled, Falyn said, "While our Druids will ride with you at the start of their quest, they must seek different paths beyond the ford where the River Brosna starts. And now for the distraction. My mate will lead a band of revelers who live to the west with a *fian* in tow, and Corbmac will escort your band east with his *fians*, but not leading revelers. You'll depart in secret on your quest through our post-turn gate.

"Leave just ahead of Faolán's party, unseen in the dark. Corbmac will catch up and escort you down the road to a settlement near the ford of the River Brosna. Once on your way, my mate will ensure no one uses the road to follow you. And the Céili will make some joyful noise while everyone sets out."

Breanna nodded. "Sounds like a solid plan."

It was late when Breanna settled into her pallet, her blanket covering her. She was painfully aware that Eoin lay next to her. She had been drawn to him since she was very young, and Breanna knew her Chief was attracted to her. Yet her *geas* allowed no quarter between them.

Croí Dàn reached out to her, saying, *"Once I chose you, the geas Beatha cast no longer held the same power over you. The Bard was right. You are more than a Fáidh could ever have conceived or cast. You must embrace your love of our land and her people. Yet, you must also accept love from those closest to you to fulfill the vision and future your gods have foreseen."*

Breanna shook her head. *"I am afraid of doing it, of opening myself. It will only bring pain."*

The Heart of Destiny murmured, *"We are all afraid of the same thing. We wonder, are we loved? Danu and I are often on and off, making me question her love for me. Yet, you already know that you are loved. And not just by me."*

Breanna had nothing to say to that. Yet, being loved by a gem who was just a voice in her head was one thing; accepting a man's love, Eoin's love, was another matter. What if she could do just that?

DARK GODDESS

Lang

Leaving his Jarl, Lang rode hard throughout the day, reaching Dun Garm well after dark. He had been drawn to the ringfort from afar because of the torch lights on the ramparts. After he slipped from his tired mount, he commanded the gate guards, "I must immediately speak with Thorvald and Runa. And let the warriors know we will choose two bands of nine to join us in the morning. All should be ready at first light for their opportunity to join our Jarl's Dreadriders on a special march to the southeast."

With that, he spun and strode into the main hall, demanding of the cook, Jarlson, "I am famished from my ride! Bring me a trencher and a tankard!"

The cook asked, "All is well with our Jarl?"

Lang sighed. "Já, but he requires warriors to support him."

Jarlson hurried off to fetch a trencher for himself.

Seeing Brede and Thorvald at the Dreadrider's table with Alrick and Donalt, Lang marched up to them. "It is good to see you both. You're looking much better than when I last saw you on death's door."

Alrick exclaimed, "I was hardly that!"

Lang shrugged, turning to Thorvald. "I am happy I caught you before your departure with Runa to the east side of Loch Ainninn. I have word from our Jarl."

Thorvald barked, "Then spill it, lad."

Jarlson approached to hand Lang a mug and set a trencher before him. After several long swallows, Lang dug in, eating with abandon. Then, as an aside, he said sheepishly, "Pardon, my fellows. It was a long day, and I likely pushed my mount and myself harder than I should have. Nevertheless, our Jarl commanded that I ride to intercept you, Thorvald, before you leave for your mission to the east side of Loch Ainninn at the ford where the High King's Road crosses the River Brosna."

Thorvald sighed. "And?"

"Ahh." Lang paused to chew and swallow his food. "Our Jarl has seen doubled patrols on the High King's Road—two *fians* per leader. Given this, he wants us to bring an equal number of warriors to the river crossing to ensure a balance of forces. I have alerted the men to be ready for selection early in the morning. He also commanded that I join Thorvald to help manage the men. Brede, Hakon commanded you to continue your charge of Dun Garm while Thorvald and I lead our warriors to the ford at the River Brosna."

"Well done, Lang," Brede said as he rose. "I'll let Runa know about the change in plans."

As Brede left, Thorvald asked, "And given your lust for revenge, Lang, what else did Hakon make you promise?"

The Lang flushed angrily. "I pledged myself to him. To his cause, to bend his bastard daughter to his will."

"And can you do that?"

"Já, I have so pledged it."

"Then I will see that you keep your pledge!"

With Alrik and Donalt watching them, Lang and Thorvald led eighteen warriors out of Dun Garm in the early morning, heading on a southeasterly track with Hakon's völva riding in her chariot as their Jarl commanded.

Breanna

The preparations for the Céilí were underway early. It had rained during the night but was now partly cloudy and starting to dry out, with the sun peeking out now and again. Breanna's Band used the morning to practice together once more. Since two of Corbmac's *fians* were available, the matches were primarily nine-on-five, with her warriors forming a ring to keep the mock enemy at bay.

Then, after one more training session where the *fians* fighters practiced with Breanna to seize the *void*, the *fian* fighters took their leave of Corbmac so they could take time to bathe and change clothes for the celebration. It was the night they would depart, in the deepest darkness of it, while the Céilí carried on to distract the Dreadlord's attention. Until then, the *fian* warriors could take a moment to enjoy this moment in their physically challenging lives.

Blálth indeed planned to make sure it was something the nearby Norvegrs heard. Faolán also assured Breanna that, in addition to the three warhorses taken from the Dreadlord's dead warriors, others in her band would be supplied with extra swift mounts that could keep up with their larger stallion counterparts.

After their bath, Breanna summoned Keegan, asking the Seneschal, "Since wearing my harness over this dress would be awkward, especially if I am to dance this evening, would you secure my blades for me?"

"Aye, my—Bre," Keegan answered. "They will be safe in Faolán's office."

Breanna handed over *Lann Dàn*, saying. "Thank you! Now, Eoin, let's enjoy this Céilí. As Erin's Hero, I must also undertake my first official act."

As Eoin arched an eyebrow, she took his arm with a grin, and they sought out their band of warriors. Fortunately, the weather was still fair when the *Ceann-cinnidh* and his *Taoiseach* of Dun Uisneach climbed the steps to a stage. Behind them, a few musicians were getting ready to kick off some uplifting Gaelic reels to help set a positive mood for the afternoon and evening. Their master Druids followed them in their colorful mantles, creating a semi-circle behind the dun's joint leaders.

Faolán addressed the crowded courtyard, "Our people, our friends, and our extended family, we welcome you all to Dun Uisneach! For those not living here, I understand that not every-one knows why my mate and I called for this Céilí, especially when we just held the Samhain festival a week ago.

"I am pleased to let you know our Tuatha gods have returned to Erin once more, as we will need help to address the Norvegr invaders to our Northwest. It has been hundreds and hundreds of years since Erin's Hero was last chosen by the Heart of Destiny. And now that time has come again.

"Many of you have seen Breanna Ban Morna and her band dancing with their blades over the past few days. Some of you have had matches with them. And, because of this, you know their warrior skills have become what is likely the best seen in our land for an eon. All because *Croí Dàn* has chosen her Hero,

Erin's Hero, our Hero! And our gods bestowed their Tuatha magic on our Hero, magic not seen in ages!"

Faolán and Falyn motioned toward Breanna's Band as the crowd cheered. Their *Taoiseach* added, "Enjoy our games, crafts, and hospitality. And take the time to get to know Erin's Hero and her brave warriors during this celebration. A celebration to renew our commitment to the Tuatha gods who protect us as in days of old."

The people roared their approval once more as Faolán and Falyn climbed down the steps to greet their fellow clan folk, milling among them with their Druids and trying to answer any questions. Those around Breanna and her warriors were all smiles and full of welcome, thanking her for accepting the mantle their gods had laid upon her. Breanna tried not to blush at their words of encouragement.

She and her band began a circuit around the cheerily trimmed courtyard. Their first stop was a table staffed by the dun's Master Smith, who was pleased to see them. "Welcome, Breanna! I've watched your matches with joy in my heart."

Eoin answered, "Gus, as we have met, let me introduce Fergal and Braoin. And I expect you know Bradaigh, as you likely made his sword. Breanna, of course, needs no introduction."

Breanna scowled at Eoin, nudged him aside with her hip, and clasped the smith's forearm in a warrior's welcome. "Pleasure to meet you, Gus. I assume that's short for Fergus."

"Och, my Lady, it is. Eoin and I shared our respective lineages, which are likely related. Anyway, I prefer just Gus."

"Then he must also have forgotten to tell you I'm just Bre!" she rejoined. "Just a common warrior with uncommon skills."

"My Hero, you underestimate yourself."

"Nay, I had a humble upbringing," she countered. "But enough of the formalities. This evening, we are just Gus and Bre. While

I have my magical long blades, and these oafs have their clumsy swords, we are short on dirks. I see you have plenty of options, but I require a gold armring before we discuss pointy things."

Gus cocked his head. "You already won that privilege last summer. I remember you presented your grandmother's armring."

"Och, I did. But it is not for me. Do you have one available?"

"Aye, My—Bre." Gus turned to his table and presented it to them.

Breanna took the armring and looked at Braoin, saying with authority, "Given your control of the *void* is equal to Eoin's and you've matched me while sparring, as Erin's Hero, I award you the privilege of wearing the gold!" Her brother was undoubtedly surprised as she handed it to him and pointed at his silver armband. "I'll need yours in trade."

With a big smile, he removed his silver band and replaced it with the gold armring. Hugging his sister awkwardly, he whispered fiercely, "Thank you!"

As Eoin, Fergal, and Bradaigh congratulated him, Breanna returned to Gus. "Now, on to pointy things. What do you suggest, and what will it cost us, including trading his silver for the gold?"

"Och, Bre," Gus protested. "Chief Faolán and his *Taoiseach* ordered that I kit you and your band up with whatever you need. They will cover the price. Now, I'm pleased to recommend this set of six knives for you, as they are well-balanced for both throwing and stabbing. One is for each calf and forearm, and two others for your waist."

"Hmmm," Bre said appreciatively. "I agree with you. They are, indeed, finely made. The sheaths are masterfully detailed and look easy to strap on. Your work on the waistbelt is the same. Wait, what are these small heart brands? How did you know I'd select them?"

"I made a good guess," Gus shrugged, holding up the small brand he'd made. "Yet leather work is that of our Master Tanner."

Once Gus had suggested some dirks for the men, he informed them he would have their selections delivered to the main hall by nightfall. Then, he proposed outfitting them with bows that the Master Woodwright had crafted. Since only Braoin and Breanna knew what to do with such a weapon, they selected two medium-weight bows to try out from a neighboring stall managed by a wiry redheaded man named Kyle. As the dun's Woodwright, he often worked with Gus. Once again, as with the smith, she found the wood carver's skill superior to anything crafted at Dun Arrogh.

While Eoin, Fergal, and Bradaigh looked over Kyle's short spears on display, Breanna and Braoin each took up their selected bows, nocked arrows, and aimed at a bale of hay twenty yards away with a target pinned to it. Breanna nodded. "On three, two, one."

She had seized the *void* as she counted, then released, hitting the dead center as Braoin's arrow did the same. They nocked again, with Breanna counting down again before they fired. Once twelve shafts were sticking out of the center of the target, Breanna said to her brother, "Once more, but you go first."

Braoin nodded, and his arrow struck dead center. Then Breanna aimed, and her arrow split his last one in two.

"Show off," her brother said wryly.

Laughing, Breanna turned to Kyle and said, "My brother was right—that was a bit of hubris on my part. Yet you have wrought some finely crafted weapons here. My compliments."

"Thank you, my Hero," the Master Woodwright replied, beaming at her praise.

Breanna sighed. "Kyle, as I commanded of Gus, tonight I am just Bre if you please."

Then Gus advised, "Best you humor the lass, my friend. I'll ensure these fine weapons get included in the delivery by this evening."

Kyle gave her a slight bow as his thanks.

Breanna's Band proceeded through the yard, occasionally stopping to admire the artistic skills of weavers, dyers, jewelers, and potters. Breanna fawned appropriately over this or that trinket. The tanner Gus had pointed out drew Breanna's eye, for he was showing off a gleaming fur-lined otter skin cloak.

She cooed, "Och, my, this is lovely. May I try it on?"

The tanner smiled, holding out the cloak. "Many thanks for your kind words, Erin's Hero. And of course. I made it for a noble lady, so the size should be right for you."

"Please, call me Bre," she murmured as he slipped the garment around her shoulders. Then, humming her approval at the perfect fit and the soft pelts, she asked, "And what name do you go by?"

"Bhruic, My Lady. I'd be honored if you would wear it."

"Hmm, I think it might be too nice for me."

Eoin put in, "Name your price, my fine man."

Bhruic shook his head, answering, "Unfortunately, there's no price you can pay for this cloak, my Prince, as I have already bestowed it upon the noblest warrior lady in our land. She only needs to let anyone asking who made it for her know that it was Bhruic, Master Tanner of Dun Uisneach, who crafted it for her."

"Wait! What?" Breanna exclaimed. "I couldn't!"

"Aye, my Hero, you can, and by doing so, you've given me the honor of making sure Erin's Hero is warm during her quest to remove the Dreadlord from our land. Given winter is upon us, and you know not how long it will take, warmth could become important."

It was Breanna's turn to blush. She did not protest his use of the honorific and bowed to him. "Thank you. While it is too much, I will accept this gift in your honor, as to do otherwise would be churlish of me."

As Breanna nodded in approval and wrapped herself in her new cloak, Eoin grasped Bhruic's arm in thanks, saying, "You're a fine Master Tanner to gift my Bre that cloak."

As Eoin stepped away with Breanna's Band, Fergal winked at his cousin. "I saw that you slipped some gold coins into his pocket unseen."

Breanna said, "I noted that as well. It was sweet of you."

Eoin shrugged. "Let's eat!"

They found an open table; Fergal, Bradaigh, and Braoin motioned their leaders to sit and went off to fetch trenchers and mugs for each of them.

"Remember to bring me mead, brother-mine!"

Bláth

Later, with the Céilí contests now finished and the evening meal closing, it was time for the music and dancing to begin. Bláth handed a large harp to a bandmate and climbed the steps to the stage set up for the players. Her smaller travel harp would not carry in the yard like this one.

At first, she led her fellow Bards and musicians through several Gaelic songs of victory, some on lutes and flutes and whistles, some on fiddles, and some on bodhrans, with medium and large tabor drummers filling the deeper notes.

Then she conducted her band of players through a warm-up of a new piece she had just composed that morning after dreaming about Erin's Hero; it was as if All-Father, first of the Druids, had sent it to her. She began with the rhythm to confirm they had it, then nodded at her players as her melodic voice filled the yard, supported by their harp notes and unmistakable voice.

After the opening notes, she seized the *sight* and led her fellow musicians jointly on their instruments with her harp before calling on her Air Element to carry her voice. "I give you a new song for this evening, one I'm sure I had help with now that the Heart of Destiny has returned. It's called *Erin's Hero Rising*."

Then her voice followed the song's opening mournful introductory notes.

In the kingdoms of Emerald Erin
Where the Heart of Destiny beats
To choose Erin's next Hero
In times of needs

Croí Dàn, can you hear the calling?
The whispers of many lost souls
When kingdoms are close to falling
You'll find the right Hero for us

Croí Dàn defends us
Croí Dàn protects us
In your chosen Hero we trust
Croí Dàn defends us
Croí Dàn protects us
Make fire rise from the dust

They came to conquer our Land
Some fought and some held hostage
Yet one would end all the fear
Our next Erin's Hero with courage

One born of blood from both sides
As our gods before have foreseen
They gave her the magic to stand
And build a new destiny

Croí Dàn defends us
Croí Dàn protects us
In your chosen Hero we trust
Croí Dàn defends us
Croí Dàn protects us
Make fire rise from the dust

Croí Dàn has called a Hero
To battle and bleed
For our land and our pride
In dark times she'll lead

Croí Dàn has called a Hero
To battle and bleed

Croí Dàn defends us
Croí Dàn protects us
In your chosen Hero we trust
Croí Dàn defends us
Croí Dàn protects us
Make fire rise from the dust

As the song ended with a flourish, Bláth stepped away from her large harp and, moving beside her fellow master Druids from the dun, exclaimed, "We, the *Aos Dána* of our land, acknowledge you, Breanna Ban Morna, as *Croí Dàn's* chosen one, as Erin's

Hero! So rise and accept this challenge from your people, for your people, and with your people! Our Heart has chosen you!"

Breanna stood before the cheering crowd, her fist raised in acknowledgment of their support. Then, Bláth saw her half-brothers take a knee so she could stand on them, allowing the crowd to see her better. She then heard *Croí Dàn* tell Breanna, *"Be fierce, Erin's Hero! Your people need you. I am with you, always!"*

With hands held out to steady her as she stepped onto two bent knees, Breanna cried aloud, "The Dreadlord's stain on our land will end. By our gods, my band and I will make it so!"

The crowd cheered her on, repeatedly chanting, "Bre, Bre, Bre!"

When the chanting did not stop, the musicians started to play with the chant and then turned it into a familiar Gaelic reel of past heroes, and their redheaded Bard leader took a break.

As she descended the stairs, Breanna strode to Bláth. "You! You could have warned me that you wrote a new song, one about me! As Erin's Hero!"

"Nay, Breanna, you would have protested too much had I done so," Bláth said sheepishly as the party continued around them. "You inspired me. It's the most epic song I've written in a long while. How could I not? It's been many hundreds of years since we have had *Croí Dàn* appear among us with a new Hero, Erin's Hero. So eat some crow and accept it."

Breanna said darkly, "Bláth, that was not the best word choice, as I need to seek the Mórrigan next."

Bláth bowed, saying, "Apologies, my Hero."

Shaking her head, Breanna rejoined with a wry smile, "I know you do not have a single apologetic bone in your body. Yet I will forgive this minor transgression."

Bláth could only shrug sheepishly at Breanna's comment.

Eoin approached them, stating, "Bláth, that was masterful! Now, play us a cheerful reel so I can see if my Champion can seize the *void* with me in a dance that does not include blades!"

"Stellar idea!" Bláth exclaimed. Then, before climbing back onto the stage to escape the wrath of Erin's Hero, she patted Breanna's shoulder. "Nice cloak, by the way."

Breanna spun to her Chief. "And you! You're involved in this conspiracy. I'm sure of it!"

"Bre," Eoin said as he held up his hands. "I have not conspired with the Bard, but having an intricate dance together is a good idea. It will test our control of the *void* when not in battle. When we have to use our wits together, not just our blades."

Breanna narrowed her eyes for a moment but then nodded tightly in agreement. As Bláth took charge of the next reel, Eoin seized Breanna's hand. "Let me take your cloak so it does not tangle your feet or mine. By the way, you look rather fetching in that blue dress tonight."

She said in mind speak, *"It is the finest thing I've ever worn,"* before allowing him to whisk her otterskin cloak away and hand it to Braoin along with his own Prince of the Blood cloak. Then Eoin swept them into the fray of those dancing around the stage. Breanna was already in the *void*, waiting for him in their special place, which bridged the realms of Erin and Tuatha.

The crowd parted around them, clapping and singing with the jaunty reel that the Bard led her fellow musicians through, giving the pair room to make their dance together. As they spun and twirled to the music, Eoin conveyed the moves he had in mind through the void, one of which was to roll her back-to-back across his broad shoulders, their arms raised above their heads, only to spin out his love, landing where their fingers barely touched.

Then he pulled her back into a warm embrace before flipping her around from one hip to another and back to scarcely a finger hold again, each with an arm outstretched to the twilight sky and one to each other as if they were reaching over the vast distance of their varied land. Through *Croí Dàn*, Breanna projected the glowing embrace of her land, one that included Eoin in her love of their Emerald Isle.

Breanna laughed and smiled as she and Eoin flowed through the reel, dipping, sliding, and twisting through and around each other's arms and legs as if dancing on clouds. Her blue dress flared as he spun her again, making her unbound white hair follow behind her like a misty fog.

Then, sensing the song's climax approaching, Eoin dropped to one knee. Breanna spun to place a foot on his raised knee, and he lifted her by her hips, allowing her to stretch her arms wide. It was as if she were ready to fly over him. Pushing up with his legs in a powerful surge, he rose to lift her high over his head, turning in a circle with her lithe form stretched horizontally.

Those around them cheered, and Breanna was sure they had never seen such a dance. Then he spun her into the air, allowing her to twist her back to the ground, and caught her in his embrace as he sank to one knee again, cradling her with their foreheads pressed together. Indeed, it was a lover's dance.

Eoin touched his lips to hers lightly before he drew Breanna to her feet. Once standing, they bowed to the crowd, much like they had done the day before to the warriors of Dun Uisneach after their blade dance.

A moment later, using *Croí Dàn* as a link between them, Eoin said to Bre, *"A beautiful dance in the void! It felt like we were one."*

"We were one," Bre confirmed. *"You took my breath away."*

Eoin added, *"Aye, we were, and I felt your love for our land through your Heart. It gives me hope."*

Mo Chroí agreed, saying, *"Like yesterday, this was masterful. Your link to the void lets the true magic of the Tuatha realm flow through and between you both—not just over you! That bonds you to each other."*

Breanna smiled in joy for what seemed the first time in her life. Braoin settled her new cloak back on her shoulders and handed over Eoin's Prince of the Blood cloak, saying, "That was breathtaking, sister-mine!"

"Aye, it was," Breanna agreed, taking in the moment. Then, as musicians took up another upbeat reel, the ladies they had met their first night at the dun approached Fergal, Braoin, and Bradaigh, and together, the three couples swirled into the mass of dancers who had taken to the next reel.

Bláth caught Breanna before she could turn away, asking, "Please, a moment, if you will?"

Watching the three warriors go to let off some pent-up energy, Breanna sighed, saying to her Heart, *"I hope she will not be long-winded."*

"I heard that," Eoin commented, stepping in to be at Bre's side, scowling narrowly at the Bard. "Be brief, as we need to prepare for our departure."

Bláth stood her ground. "I have only this to say. You are each tied to one another in this quest cast upon you by our light and dark gods. Don't lose that. Never lose that. While it is easy to say, always believe that. Each of you is needed to rid us of the Norvegrs, and the gods will test you both on this quest."

Maoilir was suddenly at Bláth's side, adding, "For a Bard, she has moments of foretelling that I can say are profound, and there are times I wonder if her music led her astray from being a Master Fáidh. Either way, it is sound advice. We will ready ourselves to join you in the coming spans."

As the Seer and Bard left them, Breanna turned to Eoin. "Thank you for that moment of freedom during our dance. It finally allowed me to experience something joyous, especially with you."

Eoin exhaled. "Bre, you've not much to be cheerful about. We both know your *geas* has driven you. Yet, here we are, and I am glad we created our dance, even if it was years in the making."

Breanna folded herself into Eoin's arms and held him, her head resting on his chest for a moment. Then, looking up, she sighed, "Aye, you're right, and know it was never about you but me and my *geas*. Yet, we must prepare ourselves. It's time we were on our way."

The pair packed in silence moments later, understanding that their brief time being secure at Dun Uisneach would soon be over. They sorted through the pile of new clothes, a mix of travel garments and finery, taking items they needed to replace.

As they gathered their things, Breanna slipped into the private bath reserved for the nobles who visited the dun and shed the elegant dress Falyn and Bláth had selected. Then, after a quick but glorious dip in the warm water, she donned her leggings, tunic, and vambraces. Finally, tossing on the fine otterskin cloak gifted to her by the tanner, she returned to their place in the main hall.

When Breanna arrived, she commanded, "*Croí Dàn, please call my warriors in from their romp with the ladies. They must get ready as we are to continue our quest.*"

"Good idea, that," Eoin said. "Now, before I take a dip, I have something for you. I commissioned Gus and Bhruic to make it."

With that, Breanna turned and unexpectedly found a new harness for her long blades on the table. It was nearly a duplicate of her old one, but more finely crafted and supple than her grandmother's. When she tried it on, it fit her body perfectly, and she squealed, "Eoin, you shouldn't have!"

After shrugging out of the superior leather construct and placing it back on the table, she crossed over to Eoin and hugged him tightly before lifting her lips to his cheek, whispering, "Thank you."

"Little steps, my love," Eoin said in return. "Time for my dip."

As Eoin left, Breanna looked at the six dirks waiting for her, four of which were on the table with sheathes for her calves and forearms. Then she found the intricately woven waist belt to hold the other two dirks Gus had shown her in the yard, along with a fine pair of lambskin gloves.

The Master Tanner had also included simple yet flexible boiled leather pauldrons to protect her shoulders. It looked Roman in its design, as she had seen similar variations at the *comórtas* this past summer.

Next to them lay the two bows, four quivers full of iron-tipped arrows, two pouches with several bowstrings in each, and both left-handed and right-handed archery finger gloves, one for her and one for Braoin. Strangely, there were also five short but sleek iron-headed black oak shafted spears that they had not discussed. Unlike the long thrusting spears used by *fian* warriors, these were casting spears.

It was apparent that Keegan had included new footwear and bedrolls for each of them, and her three warriors had new cloaks.

Breanna wondered how her people could be so generous to strangers like them. Yet, they had ensured her band was as prepared as possible. Feeling more confident, she looked forward to embarking on her quest.

# Toal

Toal listened to the cheering and music from within the dun's ramparts. Chief Faolán must have organized a celebration for his cousin. He watched Hakon fume for days over the long wait, though Jotun's report of the increased traffic on the King's Road seemed to give Hakon hope that his wait would soon be over.

"My Jarl," Jotun said, approaching him. "I have rested and am ready to return to my watch."

Hakon nodded toward the ringfort, saying, "This seems like an intentional distraction. I want both you and Gern to meet in the thicket this evening. It may be this night when they make their move.

"For the rest of you, prepare to break camp. If needed, we should be ready to move swiftly."

Toal chuckled at the exchange, "Once more, it appears without Runa, you are guessing what my cousin might do with help from Dun Usneaich."

Hakon snarled, "What would you know?"

"Enough to know one thing. Our gods back your daughter."

"Bah!" the Dreadlord scowled. "Tell me something I don't know! How has this accursed land survived? I can't fathom it!"

Toal just smiled but did not provide an answer. Yet he knew he had gotten under Hakon's skin.

———✦◈ Breanna ◈✦———

Breanna watched Eoin come toward her, weaving through the busy kitchen staff cleaning up around them from the celebration dinner, and noted he looked refreshed. Then she greeted Fergal, Braoin, and Bradaigh, who had just returned to the main hall as the Heart of Destiny requested, suggesting they take advantage of the baths and pack their things.

Turning to her Chief, Breanna motioned to their new gear and said, "Chief Faolán has been generous."

"Aye, he has," Eoin answered.

Breanna strapped one of the forearm sheaths around her vam-brace and slid the dirk in. She repeated the process on the other arm, checking each to see how easily they slid free and thought *smooth*. As a Master Tanner, he had crafted them so finely that few would even know she wore the sleek dirks with her tunic sleeves to cover them. The calf sheaths also fit perfectly around the top of her new boots, making those dirks easy to reach.

Next came her intricate waist belt for the remaining two dirks, and she noted that Bhruic had added some pouches for the extra bowstrings. Again, the slim blades slipped effortlessly into each of her hands. Upon noticing that he had added center loops so she could sling her bow and spear on her harness, she shrugged into it.

Now dressed in his new travel clothes and boots, Eoin turned to her and dipped his head. "You look fiercesome!"

She smiled at that. "You cast an impressive figure as well, but I liked your rather dashing attire from earlier this evening a bit more. I think Keegan and Bláth likely had a hand in selecting all this finery."

That brought a broad smile to Eoin's lips. "Your dress was quite fetching on you as well, my love. But speaking of the Seneschal, I'll fetch him to get your magical long blades back in their place."

"Good idea." Breanna nodded.

He departed to seek out Keegan. A short while later, Eoin and Seneschal emerged from the Chief's private meeting room, with the former carrying the Blades of Destiny. She shrugged back into her new harness, and Eoin slid them into their new home.

Keegan said, "A slight change of plans, my Lady."

"Keegan," she sighed. "Please, call me Breanna or Bre."

The Seneschal ducked his head, saying, "Sorry, but seeing you now dressed this way, it is hard to see the young lady who, with your Chief, just awed hundreds of your fellow Gaels in a stunningly beautiful dance while wearing such a glorious dress—that's not easy to do."

"It was a beautiful moment," Breanna concurred. Then, she stepped back to test her reach for her new weapons. Knowing she was left-handed, Bhruic had set the spear over her right shoulder and the bow over her left, as a bow took time to string. Since she knew a spear must be thrown quickly, it would be best to reach for it with her dominant hand. Breanna pulled her bow up and out of her harness. It came free simply enough, but she required Eoin's help to slip it back into its leather loops. Then, she practiced the same movements with her spear. Neither interfered with the draw of her long blades. Satisfied yet feeling a bit like a hedgehog bristling with weapons, she asked, "So, what is this change of plans?"

Keegan answered, "I will be dressed as Chief Faolán and lead the chariot and revelers to the west with a *fian*. In the meantime, my Chief will park himself with his *fian* and some of his blooded warriors on the road in front of our dun. He expects the Dreadlord to make a move when his scout reports that a richly dressed prince has left the dun."

Eoin asked, "When Hakon does that, will they intercept him?"

"Indeed," Keegan answered. "As a guest of our Chief to attend the end of the Céilí. Then Faolán will have to negotiate the cost of Hakon's levy to use the High King's Road. It will take a long time. The Dreadlord likely will not leave here until tomorrow at midday."

That made Breanna smile, thinking how Faolán's obstruction would vex her foul father. A moment later, her half-brothers and Fergal returned from the baths and slipped into their screened area to prepare themselves.

"My—Bre," Keegan said. "Your travel ration sacks and feed for the horses are ready."

By the time Chief Faolán and Chieftess Falyn strode into the main hall with the four master Druids and Corbmac in tow, the band was ready. Falyn commented, "You're a fine-looking bunch of Gaels, but enough small talk. I assume Keegan told you about our plan alterations?"

Breanna and Eoin nodded, but the other three were in the dark.

Faolán added, "It was Falyn's idea to make the ruse more complete. Anyway, let's get on with our charade. The horses are ready, and your band and our *Aos Dána* will leave via the postern gate under the dun's northern rampart. That'll ensure you'll remain unseen as you reach the road without light. And we will handle the rest of our game of deception."

Breanna stepped forward, holding her arm out to offer a formal warrior's forearm clasp, only to have Faolán take it and pull her into a fatherly hug, saying, "Be strong, my Hero. I need no homage or thanks. We know our gods are with you and are proud of you and your courageous band."

Breanna blushed as she turned to Falyn, who hugged her next, whispering, "May our gods continue to guide you. And remember, loving your land, your people, and your man can help you overcome anything and anyone."

Breanna nodded and responded solemnly, "*Mo Chroí* reminds me of these facts regularly. As does your Bard. She has your ear."

"Aye, she does, and she's rarely wrong."

"I welcome her presence and thank you and your mate for the generous support from everyone at Dun Uisneach, as you commanded. I will not forget it."

The Chieftess gave her one more hug. "Remember to love."

With that, Falyn and her mate stepped back. Faolán said to the rest, "Let's confound the Dreadlord!"

They all made for the stables and put their plan into action. Breanna led her band, each with a horse's reins in hand, through the postern gate at the northern side of the dun. It could barely accommodate the bigger warhorses they had claimed as spoils. With them were the four Druids, each leading a mount in silence.

The torches on the ramparts blazed but did not reach them at the base of the steep mounds. The Céilí continued as the band played more reels, letting the music cover any noise the warriors and Druids made as they crossed behind the dun and headed east into the darkness.

Having been told by Faolán that the Dreadlord had stationed his warriors in a thicket west of Dun Uisneach, Breanna was confident they could flee undetected. Shortly after that, they reached the road and ambled east to allow Corbmac to catch up to them with his two *fians*.

——✦☙ **Hakon** ☙✦——

Jotun charged into Hakon's camp and flung himself from his mount, saying, "My Jarl, a man dressed as a prince, has led a group of Céili revelers west with a *fian* in tow. It appears Chief Faolán is escorting some of those celebrating to the settlements to our west."

Given the music and cheers, the Céilí was still in full swing, and Hakon was more confident than ever that this was a planned distraction. With Chief Faolán on escort duty, he and his men could slip past them on the High King's Road if they were swift enough.

With the decision settled, he pulled himself onto his horse. "Mount up. We ride east along the road. Our quarry must have already left unseen. Kvasir, you're in charge of the boy. After we have collected Gern, you hold back with Jotun and slowly bring up the rear. Pull back into any thicket you can find if anything is amiss. If we get stopped, wait until all is clear and find a place just east of Dun Uisneach to hole up for the night."

Toal commented, "Your plan is flawed. You will not catch her."

Hakon demanded, "Shut your mouth. We move!"

With packs strapped to their mounts, the three warriors joined him and leaped onto their horses, with Kvasir pulling Toal up behind him. Jotun quickly packed his things and remounted to join them; he and Kvasir hung back to follow Hakon's orders that Toal be kept out of sight when they came upon Dun Uisneach. Hakon urged his mount into a light canter, with Gern, Brynjar, and Haldor following closely behind him. Just before they passed Dun Uisneach, which lay north, Hakon found Chief Faolán with his *fian* and several warriors with gold armbands, all bearing torches and blocking the road.

He slowed his horse to meet the Gaelic prince. "Good evening, Chief Faolán. Is the High King's Road not open for all?"

"Aye, for all who pay the *Ard-Rí* his tribute," came the answer with an amused smile.

"And given we have not, our way is barred," Hakon concluded.

"You are astute for one not of our own."

"And what would it take to gain us a right of passage on this road?"

The Gael grinned again. "Well, as the Chief of Dun Uisneach. I can order us to battle for the right, but the odds look to be in our favor."

Hakon offered, "That is certainly a possibility, though, as you say, it would be a nasty affair."

"Indeed," Faolán responded. "Or you could choose to return the way you came."

"With your escort, of course," Hakon said, and the other leader nodded. Having studied Gaelic ways, Hakon knew he had only one option, and following his daughter's route east was not one of them, at least for now. It galled him that the boy Toal was right. He had reacted rashly.

Yet, knowing her direction, he could find her trail again, especially with Runa's help if she were already in place. Hakon also knew fighting now would cost him in warriors—warriors he might need to take Breanna as a hostage. So, unwilling to fight something he could not win, he asked, "Could not my request for passage on this road be granted?"

"Only if you claim Guestright and ask such a boon from my council of advisors and me. Of course, they must address the matter of the levy for those who have not tithed to the High King."

"Then I claim it," Hakon nearly growled. "The name is Hakon Skadi, Jarl of Dun Garm."

The Chief nodded. "I know your name, Norvegr. And since you know mine, let's make this a formal introduction. I am Faolán, and I stand before you as a first cousin of the High King and a Prince of the Blood in Clan Uí Néil. It's a position that provides me with plenty of resources. My King knows of you and uses you as a pawn. Yet I know you have other aspirations. So here we are. I assume you will accompany me peacefully? We have the remnants of a Céilí to see to. After a few days of living off the land out in the woods, maybe a civilized meal is in order, even if it is a bit late."

Hakon schooled his thoughts, having already deduced the Gaelic leader had been waiting for this move. Faolán waved to his warriors and moved his chariot aside so his men could escort Hakon and his three fellow outlanders into the dun, sandwiched between the Gaels. Gern, Brynjar, and Haldor followed, seemingly uncomfortable with the escort.

Faolán demanded, "I must know your business on the High King's Road, which we call *Slíghe Mor*. As it leads to Tara, our

Ard-Rí commands that all who arrive without a written travel permit are stopped and questioned. So, while I assume you're eager to be off, my council and I must know what business you're about."

Hakon offered, "Some call me the Dreadlord of Garm, as I'm sure you know. As for my business, I seek my daughter, who has fled into Mide or Laigin."

"Och," Faolán put in. "Daughters can be tricky business. Yet, why such a big party? Four warriors to seek one?"

"For only a girl, you mean?" Hakon answered, playing out the charade. "She has friends with her."

Faolán smiled broadly. "Run off with a boy, aye? Come. Chieftess Falyn will want to meet you. We can talk over ale and roasted boar."

Hakon could only groan; it would be a long night. The Gael leader had deftly maneuvered him into a delay. He would be fortunate if he could negotiate access to the High King's Road by noon tomorrow.

A moment later, a second chariot, surrounded by another *fian,* rode up behind them. Fortunately, it seemed to Hakon that they had not seen his men and hostage on the High King's Road.

◈ Breanna ◈

Corbmac, this time mounted on a horse instead of his chariot, joined Breanna's Band and the Druids within a few moments after setting off from the dun with his two *fians.* Breanna knew that, due to their training, his warriors were fit and could jog for miles on end, so she picked up the pace a bit. As she did, gauging they were out of sight of anyone behind them, she commanded light from her ring and blades so no one strayed from the hard-packed road.

They rode silently for a while before Corbmac mentioned, "Given my Chief intercepted the Dreadlord, I suggest we stop at a settlement that straddles the River Brosna for the night. Then we can ride onto the River Boyne ford first thing in the morning."

Eoin nodded. "Sounds reasonable."

Breanna gave him the same gesture. She found she enjoyed riding her mare versus sitting behind one of her warriors to double up on one of her father's larger warhorses.

Croí Dàn said in her mind, *"Touch your mount between her ears, and I will link her to your thoughts. You can let her know you have chosen her."*

Surprised again at what the gem could do, Breanna obeyed, and the horse snorted, shaking her head to affirm that she had agreed to be chosen by Breanna and her Heart. Breanna addressed Corbmac. "Two things. First, what is my mount's name? And I'd like roughly a quarter-span in the morning for Braoin and me to test our new bows. See how we mesh with them while seizing the *void*."

"Her name is Eimar. And I'll ensure you have a practice area set up, my Hero," Corbmac answered.

"Corbmac, you will call me Breanna or Bre, or you will have to face me in a match, and I will not hold back because you're an old man," she responded tartly, her eyes narrowed.

He appeared to cringe at the thought before agreeing with a nod. "Aye, Breanna."

"That's better."

Inwardly, she commanded her horse, *"Eimar, you are mine! I am Breanna, My Heart's chosen Hero. She has linked us through her magic. Should I need you, you will understand my need and act as I command."*

The mare whinnied again, evidently pleased to be chosen and have a purpose. In mind-speak, Eimar agreed, *"I am yours!"*

"I didn't realize horses could talk."

Croí Dàn chuckled. *"Indeed, they are the cleverest animals in all of Erin."*

"Mares are smarter than stallions," Eimar opined haughtily.

Breanna's Heart added, *"Gaels have forgotten that Tuatha enabled them to speak with animals who inhabit this Emerald Isle as part of their Great Agreement. Yet, while almost all of you do not remember, you can now do this as my Hero."*

The band and their Druid escorts rode with Corbmac's warriors until it was close to midnight. Then Corbmac signaled a few of his *fian* warriors to advance and announce to the settlement's leader that they required shelter for the night.

A quarter-span later, Corbmac pulled into a collection of huts on the west side of the river's ford. Chief Faolán and Chieftess Falyn funded the barracks and those who lived there, ensuring their *fians* had food and shelter when needed as they patrolled the High King's Road. Grooms scurried to life to take their mounts and brush them down.

After pulling their packs from the rumps of their horses, Fergal, Braoin, and Bradaigh were guided to one hut, Eoin and Breanna to another, and the Druids to a larger dwelling that fit their status. The *fian* warriors went to their barracks, which could hold three bands of nine. With one stationed *fian* in residence, the barracks were full for the night. It was only a settlement, but Breanna noted the lodgings were a bit fancier than their own at Dun Arrogh.

As they took their respective packs and bedrolls to each hut, Eoin stepped into their assigned dwelling behind Breanna and commented, "Hmm, only one pallet."

"No problem," she commented to the room. "You were that close to me in the main hall of Dun Uisneach, sleeping on our bedrolls."

"Aye, we were," he answered. "Yet that was before our dance among our blades yesterday and the dance we created beneath the stars earlier tonight."

"True," Breanna answered. "Yet now that you are tied more deeply to my cause through *Mo Chroí*, I trust you more than ever."

And so they turned to strip down, put on their night clothes, and slipped into a pallet meant for two. Eoin could not help himself when he extended one of his well-muscled arms as a pillow for her head, saying, "Sleep well, my love."

Breanna caught her breath before whispering, "You too."

And then *Croí Dàn* murmured in her mind, *"You need to let go of your geas, My Hero, as it no longer fully binds you."*

Breanna only sighed at her Heart as she snuggled up to Eoin, allowing him to pull her closer, front to back, as he wrapped his other arm around her middle. She let his hand slide between her breasts, nudging the Heart of Destiny aside, and wondered if it could be that easy. Before she pondered the notion further, she fell asleep in his arms for the first time.

Lang

Lang crept through the forest, following the sounds of arrows thunking into tree trunks. He'd hoped to glimpse the warriors practicing with their bows south and west of the ford to see if they were something new. Yet the yard from where the sounds came revealed nothing. The Gaels practiced behind a rampart that was more of a dike against floods than something protective, so there was no way to tell who they were. Then he saw several *fian* warriors, each ranging around the settlement, tending to various duties. He counted them, hit ten, and then eleven. So, two *fians* had stopped for the night, adding to the standing Gaels in residence.

A warrior hissed to Lang, "Thorvald and Runa have demanded you provide them with an update."

Lang sighed, controlling his rage as he had pledged, and turned to return to the camp. He found Thorvald and Hakon's völva outside the lean-to she had been sleeping in. "You required my presence?"

"Já, Lang," Thorvald answered. "What word do you bring? What is afoot southwest of the ford?"

Glaring at Runa, Lang said, "I'd have had more to share had I stayed longer, but it seems two *fians* arrived last night, likely along with at least two other warriors with bows. It is not a weapon that *fian* warriors normally carry; they stick with long spears. I was unable to see them and learn their identities."

Runa smiled. "Good work, Lang. There is something in motion that the Gaels are hiding from us. I understand you and the others want to act. Yet if they have three *fians* against our eighteen and some other number of warriors, probably more than two, seizing this moment to attack is not advised. Should we do that and fail, Hakon will spit on our bodies when he comes upon our carcasses."

Lang said tightly, "We should not let them pass!"

Thorval countered, "We will watch closely before deciding. Let's ensure all are ready to ride if it is our quarry we seek. I suspect Hakon will be close on their heels if that is the case. We will be stronger together. And, remember your pledge, the one you made to your Jarl."

He nodded, thinking both were overestimating the threat.

Breanna

Breanna sighed as she awoke with the light of dawn streaming through the hut's leather door, discovering Eoin still had his arms wrapped around her. She found it comforting, yet rolled out of his arms, stretched like a cat on all fours, and then was on her feet, working out the kinks in her muscles from the previous night's ride—she'd have to get used to being mounted for spans.

Eoin groaned. "Ugh, you had to wake me just now?"

"Aye, my Chief. Braoin and I must practice with our bows. What Toal taught me was a start, but I'm rusty. And they are new bows, likely more powerful than the ones I used before with my cousin."

"My Chief?" Eoin demanded with a frown as he rolled over to face her, looking up. "I am stricken, I say stricken. After holding you throughout the night to be called your Chief this morning! I at least merit an endearment, like *A chroí* or *A rún-searc* or *M' fhíorghrá*."

With her hands on her hips and an eyebrow raised, she smirked. "Hmm, *my heart* won't work, given the gem around my neck is my Heart, and I certainly don't think *my secret love* would fit, as it is no secret that you love me. I will think about being your *true love*, though. So stand up, and you'll get a proper hug of thanks for a night of warmth. But, then, I'm off to fetch Braoin, though there'll be no hug for him!"

Eoin smiled as he stood and pulled her into his arms. "Good enough, my true love. That I'll accept."

And then he kissed her forehead.

After Breanna had dressed in her warrior clothes and boots, with vambraces, dirks, a spear, and magical long blades in place, she marched out of the hut with her bow in hand. She found the ground wet, for it had rained while they slept. Not seeing Braoin, she banged on the wooden doorframe where the three warriors had spent the night.

Her half-brother grumbled from inside. "I'm almost ready. A minute or two, please."

Moments later, Braoin emerged with his new bow on his back. "Sorry for the delay. It was a late night, my sister. I had dreams of the lass I danced with yesterday evening."

"It's okay, my brother," Breanna answered with a smile. "Yet you'll find my *geas* and *Ċroí Dàn* are harsh mistresses. I can only go as easy on you as they let me."

"I'll try not to disappoint them."

Corbmac was already up, getting his *fians* moving through their morning stretches. He turned to the pair, saying, "There are two hay bales with targets set against trees across the yard. Have at it, both of you!"

Breanna and her brother turned to the tree. "Aside from our brief time at Dun Uisneach," Breanna said, "I have not seized the *void* while shooting, save for our few shots in the yard of Dun Uisneach. With Toal—who I sure hope is safe with Orla—I didn't use it because I hardly knew how to use either his smaller bow or the *void*. Anyway, I need practice."

Braoin agreed, adding, "Neither have I. Yet we did rather well with Kyle's practice bale of hay. Even if you did show me up."

Breanna grinned as they nocked their arrows, seized the *void*, focused, and let them fly. They landed two center hits on each bale target, thwacking through them and into tree trunks beyond. Both warriors smiled and repeated the action again and again, without a miss.

They strode to the bales once out of arrows to check their scores. They had tied on center hits, but Braoin had scored one better on non-center hits when they aimed for the inner and outer rings. Yet he said nothing as they retrieved their arrows and repositioned themselves.

"I wish we had moving targets to practice on," Breanna said when they finished with tied scores. "Yet, we will have to make do if we engage with our dear old father and his brutes."

"Aye," Braoin agreed. "That we will. Since this is our first evening as a band away from Dun Uisneach, we can hunt down a tasty dinner. Or use our new spears to collect some trout."

The Druids emerged from their larger hut and strode toward them. "Good morning, Breanna," Maoilir said. "I have some reports that the *sight* has opened to me. We have Norvegr outlanders across the river on the north side, lying in wait. They are unsure of our numbers or when their Jarl will arrive. Thus, there is indecision on what to do next."

Breanna held her hand out to stop him and cast her voice toward the huts. "Eoin, Fergal, Bradaigh. I need you out here, now!"

The three warriors emerged from their assigned huts, nearly ready. "What's happened?" Eoin asked.

She answered, "Maoilir says Norvegr outlanders are waiting for us across the river, to the north. No idea on how many yet."

Corbmac approached, adding, "I can confirm that my scouts agree. Therefore, I suggest we prepare to depart. We cannot hide our presence, but our numbers will deter them. The best strategy is to get Breanna and her band on the High King's Road and to the ford at the River Boyne, as the Norvegrs have no travel writ and will have to stick to the woods. Beyond that, the way should be open east and south."

"You think we should challenge them?" Breanna asked.

"Aye, I do," Corbmac answered. "Challenge them to attack. They will not, as they are missing their Jarl. Assuming my Chief uses his diplomatic skills with his usual aplomb, the Dreadlord will not be here for six or maybe eight more spans. Faolán likely played the *I need my council to approve the writ* card when that council is actually just Falyn. If we ride now, we can get you off the High King's Road once we ford the River Boyne. That will be well before they know what you're about or bound."

"And if they respond to my challenge?"

Corbmac smiled, saying darkly, "Then they'll be dead."

A week ago, Breanna might have disagreed. Yet not now, not when surrounded by Corbmac's *fians*, the standing *fian* assigned to settlement, her blooded warriors, and the Druids. She put a firm hand on the old warrior's shoulder. "Let's get this done, grandfather!"

After a quick breakfast, they all prepared for the journey.

Breanna greeted her mount, holding an apple to the mare's mouth. "Eimar, here's a treat. We might ride hard today."

Eimar whickered her approval, using their mind voice, *"I will fly for you, my Hero!"*

As Breanna's Band mounted to head out in front of the marching *fians*, she commanded, "Braoin, nock!"

The two had a quiver on their shoulder and another tied within reach behind them on their saddles. Then they set an arrow to their bows, riding out of the settlement thirty-two strong, the Druids bringing up the end of their train.

She rode from the settlement toward the ford, scanning the forest, her warriors drawing their swords. To their left was a slight ridge that held back Loch Ainninn in the low season, save for where it tumbled over some rocks to make up the beginning of the River Brosna. It created a natural crossing, which they used to ford the waterway. Breanna scanned the lake and river with her mind in the *void*, checking for Tethra's demons. Finding none, she moved her mental probe to the forest on the road's north side, letting it guide her. Eoin rode on her left side, and Braoin on her right.

As her band emerged from the river ford on its east side, Breanna swung her bow toward the woods, using the *void* to explore the darkness. The space between her realm and the Tuatha realm showed her that a Dreadrider, brother to the one she had killed at Dun Garm, hid in the shadows and shade. She was unsure how she could know these things, yet she did.

Croí Dàn informed her, *"Your use of the void is deepening, allowing you to sense auras. You should also be able to read the emotions within any given aura, typically by color."*

Corbmac's *fians* emerged from the shallow ford on the east bank, slipping to either side of Breanna and her blooded warriors, all crouching with their long Gaelic spears at the ready, eighteen inches of sharp, pointed iron on the tips. Then, a third *fian* nestled in behind the first two, also deploying shields and spears.

Breanna saw Lang nudge his mount forward just from the tree line. He stopped, glaring at her. As her Heart had informed her, the *void* showed that his aura was flickering dark red, as if he trembled in rage that she was close enough to kill.

Breanna said defiantly, "Your life is mine if you wish me to claim it. Our arrows will fly true."

An older Norvegr warrior held him back, who nudged his horse next to the young Dreadrider and placed a hand on his shoulder.

Breanna added with disdain, "Same for you, old man. Between my brother and me, you will both be dead if you flinch. We outnumber you—and the rest of your warriors will likely die."

⸺⁂ **Thorvald** ⁂⸺

It was the first time Thorvald had seen his Jarl's bastard. Yet he knew her words were a promise. The dead calm in her voice was something he recognized in his Jarl. His bastard was no different.

He ordered, "Lang, hold."

The younger Dreadrider trembled in an attempt to hold his anger, and feeling it, Thorvald commanded sternly, "Remember, you pledged to honor your oath to your Jarl, Hakon Skadi! It appears that our foe from Dun Uisneach, the wily Corbmac, has his warriors in tow. These Gaels distinctly have the advantage; only thirty yards separate us."

As four Druids guided their horses behind the band, Hakon's Destroyer teased, "I know you, Lang. I beat you once and will beat you again, as I did with your brother at Dun Garm. But I will not take you to Valhalla because I shun your *Asgardian* gods!"

Thorvald was surprised he was unable to hold Lang back as the lad urged his mount forward and raised his blade to point it at his brother's killer with a scream of, "I'll kill you!"

Breanna unleashed her arrow into his sword arm shoulder. Lang spun off his horse and crashed to the ground, cursing. Breanna nocked again, saying, "Do not follow us, Dreadrider, or we will kill you all. You can be certain of that!"

Thorvald watched as Breanna and her band turned their mounts east with the Druids following them. The three *fians* rose from their crouch and thumped their spears on the ground, repeatedly chanting, "Bre! Bre! Bre!"

"Use the High King's Road at your own risk, as we will be watching," Corbmac said as he rode past the Norvegrs. "I know you have no writ to use this pathway. To use it without such a document will mean your death. I have put forth a call to all *fians* to be on watch for you."

His warriors fell behind him as they continued their chant of "Bre! Bre! Bre!" They turned confidently down the High King's Road.

Thorvald spat at Lang, "You deserved that, you idiot! She goaded you and could have *killed* you. Yet she chose not to. Why? Because she is superior to you. You are no match for her. She is waiting to kill you, knowing you will be impulsive again. Is that what you want?"

Runa, who had held herself back in the woods, stepped in. "No matter, Thorvald. I will tend to Lang while we wait for Hakon to arrive. My Runes indicate he'll be here after midday. Then, we can determine our next moves. The Gaels currently protect Hakon's Destroyer, but how far will that effort extend?"

Thorvald answered, "Much further than I ever thought they would. The Destroyer and her band looked well-kitted out. Certainly, they were not the ratty bunch I expected to find, especially not with new bows and spears. With a silver and four gold arm-ringed warriors, backed by three *fians*, they are more than a match for us."

"True." Runa shrugged. "And they now have four Druids guiding them. With my *sight* blocked by the Dark Goddess, this does not bode well for us."

 Hakon

Hakon and his three warriors spent the night in the main hall, sleeping in a small screened-off area with guards on either side. He cursed as he rose in the morning, irritated at the delay. Chief Faolán had informed him that he needed to gather his council to determine the required tribute. It would likely be around midday before he had a resolution.

Near noon, Faolán and Falyn summoned him to their private meeting room.

"Now that we are on a first-name basis," said Faolán, "I must apologize for the delay in getting an agreement on the tribute due for access to the High King's Road. However, our council members from our duns and settlements who attended the Céilí were needed to represent a majority, and they decided on your tribute. It will be a high price."

"Name it!" Hakon seethed.

Falyn smiled. "It is not just gold that we demand, but the *daor aicme* you still hold. You'll need to release one such hostage for each warrior you want to place on the road to find your daughter, with those held longest released first."

"And if we find more Norvegrs have joined you in your pursuit of your daughter," Faolán added, "we will adjust that total. Now that you've left the confines of the territory you originally seized, you will operate under our laws. As to the gold for your passage, we will accept your coins in payment if that is all you have to offer."

"Which will be ten golds per person for those with you now," Falyn informed Hakon. "And twenty more for each warrior you add on your journey."

"We will be watching," Faolán said darkly.

"And if I refuse?" Hakon asked with a hint of menace.

Chief Faolán smiled and then nodded to his Seneschal, who waved a hand as a signal, and nine *fian* warriors swept into the room, each with a long pike in their hands. "I would not suggest that as a course of action, as my cousin, the High King, has given us the authority to end you, should we choose. That would be messy."

Hakon paused before saying tightly, "It would. I will pay the tribute and release four of our hostages."

Faolán smiled as he rose with his mate. "Excellent. It is always best to negotiate. Correct, Falyn?"

Falyn answered sweetly, "Of course, my love. Keegan, our Seneschal, will manage the details of your writ. We do hope you find your wayward daughter."

Faolán and Falyn swept out of the room, and Keegan moved to collect the tribute, along with the written notes confirming the release of four hostages.

After Hakon and his warriors gathered their belongings, they had to wait another span to get their mounts from the stable, as the lads who managed horses were *busy*. Finally, a fuming Hakon and his three warriors were on their way. The Gaels had ignored him as long as he had kept his kind to themselves. Now that he was seeking those of their kind outside his territory, there was no free passage. With the High King approving his vassal to take direct action against him, he knew he had no option except to seek out his brothers in the spring to bring more of their warriors to Erin.

As they rode out of Dun Uisneach and turned east on the High King's Road, Hakon looked for signs of Jotun or Kvasir. He would have to pay more to add those two to his already steep tribute, and explaining their young Gael captive would be another challenge. He needed another plan to get them all to the ford of the River Brosna.

Around a quarter-span after they had taken the road, Dun Uisneach just out of sight, Hakon heard a short whistle, raised a hand to acknowledge it, and said to Gern, "Ride on with Brynjar and Haldor, but slowly. I'll catch up in a few moments."

Hakon shortly found Kvasir and Jotun with their hostage in another thicket. "I have no time to explain," he said, "but you'll need to follow me from the ridge line to the south. Do not take the road as we ride east. We will catch up at the River Bronsa's ford. Hopefully, Thorvald and Lang will have reinforcements. Now, let's be about it."

Hakon rejoined his other warriors on the road and headed after his daughter in light rain. The lands southeast of Dun Uisneach were rolling, with many wooded covers. It boded well for his cause if this continued to be the case. Seeing Kvasir and Jotun had taken to the heights, he expected they would rarely be out of sight. As the afternoon drew on, the oak forest to the south grew denser, and the road descended into a valley. To the northeast, Hakon could now see Loch Ainninn's glistening surface. Then, the settlement built upon both sides of the River Brosna came into view.

As Kvasir and Jotun rode down into the valley with Toal, the ridgeline dropped away, steering them back toward the High King's Road. As they drew closer, Hakon commanded his three warriors to hold their position on the road. He then surged south to meet with Kvasir and Jotun and decide how to keep their hostage a secret. The pair found their Jarl moments later.

"Kvasir, Jotun," Hakon acknowledged. Then, giving Toal a dark look, he added, "While we are at the ford of the River Brosna, I want you to ride south far enough to cross the river unseen, even if it means swimming with the horses. After you cross, head back north toward the road. If Thorvald and Lang are there, I must meet them after we cross the river. We will need them to ride on the north side of the road while you keep to the south side."

"Aye, my Jarl," Kvasir answered.

"I will explain later, but we have a challenge using the High King's Road," Hakon added. "It will slow us down, but we will catch my bastard. Stay in the forest on the south side. We will find you there."

With that, Hakon turned and rode back to the road, joining his other three warriors, and then they rode on.

As they approached the west side of the river crossing, a *fian* spread out to bar the way.

"Hold!" their leader said. "As Norvegr outlanders, we must see your writ of passage, signed by the Chief of Dun Uisneach."

Hakon reached into his tunic and produced the parchment.

The *fian* leader read the writ and then assessed the Norvegrs. He said flatly, "Very well. We know Norvegrs were in the area this morning. Unfortunately, they cannot join you on the road. We will be watching. Unless, of course, you can pay the tribute of gold and hostages for them to join you, as the writ indicates."

Hakon nodded, returned the parchment to his tunic, and rode on. He and his warriors used the ford across the River Bronsa with the setting sun behind them. Moments later, riding slowly, he heard a whistle to the north and signaled to all that they should ride east through the woods. Then another whistle came from the south, and he did the same. Yet the *fian* leader and his nine warriors followed them at a distance like a shadow, ready to enforce his Chief's writ.

Hakon commanded his warriors to ride slowly down the road while he slipped into the northern woods. Moments later, he met up with Thorvald and Runa.

"Good to see you both," he said. "No time for more words for now. I will be brief." He quickly outlined the conditions Chief Faolan had placed upon his traveling party. "Tell me, when did my Destroyer cross the river, and what did they learn of our numbers?"

Thorvald stoically described that morning's encounter with the Destroyer. Hakon narrowed his eyes at hearing how Lang had once again lost control and let her goad him into injury, but he said nothing and soon controlled his own temper. He would deal with his young Dreadrider later.

He turned to his völva and queried, "Runa, anything to add?"

"Nei, my Jarl," was the answer. "Mórrigan's murder of crows still blocks my sight. I have had to resort to using my Runes. The stones were how I knew you would arrive today."

Hakon nodded in appreciation of her efforts as he turned to the road, directing his smaller group to find a camp for the night. He expected the *fian,* who was likely following them from the river crossing, would do the same.

Breanna led her band, the Druids, and Corbmac, with his two *fians* to either side as they followed the High King's Road toward the River Boyne, their mounts allowing them to make good time. The fit warriors trotted behind on a wide track made muddy by the rain showers that had passed over the previous night while they slept. Light rain lingered on and off, dogging them along the way. After a time, Bláth pointed out Croghan Hill, which was in the distance to the south. The steeply sloped mound of earth jutted up as if giant hands had molded half of a clay ball, plopped it on the ground upside down, and then magically caused trees to sprout up its sides.

Near midday, they reached the ford, where they planned to split up. Maoilir and Bodhmall crossed the River Boyne by ferry with help from two of Corbmac's men and rode off toward Dun Tara. Bláth, however, decided to continue her travels with Breanna's Band.

Tadg declared, "I need no guards—my clans are from these parts." Then he headed south to spread the word amongst the settlements there to be on the watch for Erin's Hero should she pass by. That would ensure she and her band had help if needed.

The rest of them dismounted to water their horses, fill their skins, and share a meal of travel rations with Corbmac and his warriors.

As Breanna gave her apple core to Eimar, the craggy old Gael she had called grandfather said, "I expect the Dreadlord will soon be on his way along *Slíghe Mor*, which will put him at the River Brosna ford later this afternoon. We will wait for them here as you ride on to ensure he abides by the writ that I'm sure our Chief and Chieftess bound him to."

"A writ?" Breanna questioned.

"Aye, the High King requires his leaders to collect a toll on all foreign travelers and bind them to terms if they have not tithed to him. Hakon has not done this. I expect those warriors you challenged by the River Brosna will not join him on the road, as he would have to pay a heavy price in gold for twenty more warriors to travel with him on *Slíghe Mor*. That will slow them down a bit."

"Thank you, Corbmac, for helping us." Breanna sighed as her hands rested on his shoulders and her eyes met his. "I don't know much about the ways of the High King, his Chiefs, and his *fian-ceannards*—yet you accepted me. After meeting with the Mórrigan, I do not know where she will send us next."

The grizzly Gael smiled, looked toward Croghan Hill, and said, "Well, I've no instructions from my Chief on what to do next, but given I know where you are heading, which is east and then south, we can follow Tadg south from here and then swing east. Who knows, we might both find ourselves at Dun Eadan, which sits on the northern edge of the *Morachd Moin*."

Breanna asked, "You'd do that for us?"

Corbmac laughed and looked at her band. "Nay, not for them, but for you, my Hero. That said, you cannot challenge me to a match for calling you such, as you previously threatened to do. Grandfathers have no business matching themselves against such magically touched youth, especially one who is his granddaughter."

Breanna stepped forward and wrapped her arms around the old warrior. "I will make no such challenge, my great sire."

Corbmac seemed surprised by the gesture but smiled broadly. Releasing the old bear, Breanna turned to the others and said, "It's time we ride on. The Mórrigan awaits my arrival at her *Well of Segais* tonight."

Eoin, Fergal, and Breanna's half-brothers bid Corbmac a fond farewell. In the past few days that she had known him, she had grown fond of the gruff *fian-ceannard*.

Eoin added, "I am also sorry to leave you and your escort behind, as I have a hunch that Hakon will somehow track us down." He turned to Breanna. "Bre, we should pick up the pace. While the Dreadlord may be a day behind us, we need to be off this road and leave no trail while you seek out the well."

Breanna whispered something to her Tuatha ring, hesitated, and then she said, "*Maorgairme* has confirmed my father and his ilk were well hobbled by Dun Uisneach's Chief and Chieftess, as Corbmac expected they would. We can take to the road at our own pace."

Eoin sat for a moment, scowling, but nodded in agreement.

Leading Eimar toward the river, Breanna acquiesced, saying, "Fine, we can canter once we cross, now that we don't have the *fians* trotting behind us."

Bláth also guided her horse in front of Breanna. "Best to let the women lead the way and leave the men to use their muscles, aye?"

With the ford across the River Boyne being somewhat downstream and no settlement nearby, an uncrewed rope-based ferry was the only way to cross the deep-flowing water. Unfortunately, the raft was on the far side. Accepting the help offered by the *fian* warriors, they brought it back to their side and assisted Breanna and her warriors as they led their mounts onto the sizable raft. Breanna seized the *void*, scanned the river to check for Tethra's demons, and sighed in relief at finding none.

Using the combined muscle of her blooded warriors and their assigned *fian* warrior help, they soon found their way to the east side of the river. Breanna's Band gave Corbmac's men a wave of farewell once they started back to the west side.

As the six left the river behind, Breanna requested that *Maorgairme* alert her when to turn off *Slíghe Mor* so she could find the Dark Goddess at the *Well of Segais*. Then she heeled her mount into a canter, and those with her followed her lead. They worked their way through the hilly terrain, letting the High King's Road guide them. Breanna would occasionally query her ring, but its answers did not alter their course. The air remained cool beneath a forest canopy that opened and closed over them, often showing a moody sky of dark clouds that threatened more rain.

The road sometimes dipped into small valleys, where they found oak planks laid down to form a causeway known as a togher to assist travel over boggy areas. These sections kept carts and horses from sinking in the muck. With six mounts clopping along the wooden track at those times, it silenced any chatter amongst the small band.

As the afternoon passed, *Slíghe Mor* turned northeast through a cut between two tall hills. Breanna caught a signal from the magic in her Tuatha ring as *Croí Dàn* told her, *"Time to throw off any pursuit. Ride single file over other tracks. The turn-off south is up ahead."*

Breanna relayed the command, and they all lined up nose to tail behind her. A short time later, she raised her hand as they needed to head south. A Gael-worn track ran along the edge of a forest-covered slope that rose before them.

Breanna commanded them to dismount to cover their tracks. Braoin nodded in agreement, darted into the woods, and returned with several small tree limbs he had hacked off.

"This will help," he informed the others as he tied a rope around the branches. "I'll ride west for a few moments to cover our hoof marks and return to follow you. Do not ride until you can no longer see the road. That will make it easier to hide our tracks up this path."

Braoin leaped into his saddle and turned his horse west, dragging the limbs behind him while the others led their horses by their reins south along the softer trail that rose in a semi-circle around a hill. When they could no longer see *Slíghe Mor*, they pulled themselves into their saddles and kept a slow pace. Breanna noticed another trail—one less traveled, more likely a deer path—that split off and would lead them higher up the hill, and she commanded them to wait for Braoin.

A quarter-span later, her brother appeared with his horse, the tree limbs still dragging behind him, and confirmed all was well as he cut loose the branches. Then, her band followed the deer path, which eventually circled to the southwest as it rose higher, heading to one of three sources of the River Boyne headwaters.

Eoin asked doubtfully, "Is your ring guiding us?"

"Aye," was her reply.

Croí Dàn chided him, commanding, *"Have faith in your Champion. She is my Hero!"*

Eoin shook his head. "I find your Heart's ability to speak into my mind unsettling. I need to school my thoughts better."

Breanna smirked. "With *Mo Chroí*, good luck with that!"

Croí Dàn chuckled. *"Silly man, you're mine as much as she is."*

Breanna signaled to everyone that it was time to stop and set up camp beneath a copse of oak trees and added, saying privately to Eoin, "It does appear we now make up a strange triad."

After they had rubbed down their mounts and made a picket for them to graze under, Braoin said, "Sister-mine, shall we see if we can hunt up some game for dinner?"

Noting it was about a span before sunset, Breanna pulled her bow over her shoulder and answered, "Aye, brother-mine. It will let me stretch my legs and scout the terrain. I must meet our Dark Goddess here this night. Yet, we can test my new archery skills one more time."

Eoin said, "We will gather wood and get the fire going once the sun sets. Use your Heart to let me know if you find trouble."

Breanna nodded, leading Braoin uphill, as she expected that was the way she needed to go to find the *Well of Segais*. With their bows strung and nocked, they climbed slowly through the woods. Nothing moved under the brush, and they circled upward as they skirted black oak trees. They emerged onto a small, grass-covered plateau with a moderate-sized, yet deep blue pond in the center, from which a stream flowed out on its west side.

It was one of the headwaters of the River Boyne. The Mórrigan's well and her altar would be nearby. Seeing trees around the pond, Breanna wondered aloud, "Could those be the Nine Hazels of Inspiration from the tale of Fionn Mac Cumhaill? Legends say that when the nuts ripen, they drop into the pond and impart wisdom to the salmon who eat them. Fionn supposedly ate one of these Salmon of Knowledge and became a wise military leader."

"That's quite a tale," Braoin said as he slowly walked forward. "Be ready. There might be game birds in the grass."

Breanna nodded, seizing the *void* as she raised her bow, using her new ability to detect hidden life force auras. She was surprised to see small golden patches glowing in the grass. A moment later, a pheasant burst into flight to her left, and she spun, tracked it for less than a second, and loosed her arrow. The bird tumbled to the ground. Still holding the *void*, she felt for life around her and said, "Head left. I can see more over there."

As they moved toward her downed bird, Braoin stirred another pheasant into flight and sank his arrow into a raised wing joint. They retrieved the two birds and their arrows before moving on to the stream side of the lake.

As Breanna flushed out two more with direct hits by both, Braoin asked, "How do you do that? See them before I do?"

"I'm not sure, as it is new to me. It is an aura. *Mo Chroí* showed me the way this morning when we faced the Norvegrs."

Ćroí Dàn chuckled. *"You're a bright one, Braoin."*

"Wait! What?"

"*Mo Chroí* likes you. Just go with it."

"Aye, maybe I should, as she is so full of light!"

After claiming two more birds, they declared victory and slung the bows in their harnesses. Once they removed their birds' heads so they could bleed out, the pair proudly returned to camp, each with two pheasants in one hand and one in the other. They arrived at sunset and found Eoin had already started the evening fire.

Bláth had rummaged through their packs, picking out some bread, onions, carrots, and parsnips. With the fire going, she set a small pot of water on a flat stone Eoin had placed near the flame for her. Bradaigh, Braoin, Fergal, and Eoin each took a pheasant and began ripping off its feathers.

"Sister," said Bradaigh, "were these six all taken in the air?"

"Aye, and no arrows lost," she answered her brother with a cocky smile. That brought a whistle of appreciation. Breanna handed over her hunting knife to her other brother, as they needed to gut the birds. Then she snatched up his small axe, adding, "I'll find us some limbs to make spits with before the twilight is gone. Roasted pheasant sounds mighty fine for our first dinner on the trail."

Later, after the birds had been cleaned and gutted, they all sat around the fire, watching the pheasants cook. Bláth rose to turn the spits and stir her pot of vegetables. Then, after handing each of them a piece of bread, she asked Breanna, "You found pheasants in the woods?"

"Nay," she answered. "Braoin and I climbed to the top of this hill and found a good-sized pond on a grassy plateau ringed by hazel trees. We flushed the birds out there. There's a stream on the west side of the pond. It must be one of the headwaters of the River Boyne."

"Ahhh," Bláth remarked. "You found the *Well of Segais*."

Breanna said in surprise, "Really? It looks like a pond."

The bard just smiled. "We use the word *well* to throw people off who have no business seeking out the Mórrígan."

"And the Dark Goddess's altar?"

"It lies across the stream where the water leaves the lake," Bláth said as she turned the birds on the spit again and stirred the boiling vegetables. "It can only be seen at midnight of a full moon."

Breanna pointed at the rising moon that showed itself through broken clouds, stating, "Then we timed it right. Tonight, I seek the Dark Goddess."

"Alone?" Eoin asked.

As Breanna turned to him, her tone broaching no argument, she answered, "Aye, alone."

Then Fergal asked, "Does *Croí Dàn* have any insight into where the Dreadlord is?"

The Heart of Destiny and her magical ring sent a pulse to her Hero, and Breanna answered, "It appears he has left behind the River Bronsa but has had to stop for the night, as his men in the woods cannot follow him in the dark."

As they waited for the birds to finish cooking for their evening meal, Bláth strummed her travel harp to life with soothing notes. When the roasted fowl were ready, the Bard and Braoin passed bowls of stew and a pheasant to each of Breanna's Band. They all fell silent, diving into their meal with gusto.

After cleaning up from the greasy mess the bird left on her hands, Breanna turned into her bedroll to hopefully sleep before heading back up the hill to meet the Mórrigan. It did not come easily as the clouds began to break, allowing the full moon to shine through the tree canopy.

After tidying up the camp, the others took to their bedrolls, with Eoin beside Breanna. She sighed when he wrapped her in his arms, yet he added nothing and let silence rule.

What seemed to be a short time later, *Croí Dàn* said in her mind, *"Wake, my Hero. It is time we met Badb Catha."*

As she rose and settled her harness with the *Lann Dàn* on her back, Eoin whispered, "Stay safe, *Mo Ghrá*."

Breanna turned, saw the concern on his face, and let slip a small, confident smile. "I will."

This part of her quest was just another step; what the end would bring was yet to be seen, but it would not end tonight, no matter what happened with the Dark Goddess. And she had magic to guide her to the right path. She turned into the black night, almost drifting through the forest as she ascended the hill to the *Well of Segais*.

Maorgairme and *Lann Dàn* glowed fiercely, but the light was still not nearly enough to show the way. She commanded more luminance, and the ring and her blades responded by casting indirect *balefire* and not its blasting form. Each time she turned in the wrong direction, her ring would fade. Its otherworldly *balefire*, captured inside the small gem, kept her moving upward through the woods. Knowing who she would soon face made it hard to stay calm, for all her childhood tales about the Dark Goddess had focused on battles and death. The Mórrigan, mother of crows, was fierce and dark.

Breanna progressed through the forest, circling west and north, rising as she had earlier with her half-brother. She soon came upon the plateau they had visited. When the cloudy sky broke apart, the pond glimmered in the light of a full moon, and Breanna's gaze turned more to the left through the grassy area between the woods and the lake. Then the moonlight illuminated the water flowing from the west. A crow's call made Breanna shiver, and a dark-cloaked figure appeared on what seemed to be a solid stone bridge across the stream, as the Bard had said it would. When the Mórrigan strode to the middle, a stone altar materialized, bracketed by torches.

Breanna could make out very few facial details, aside from the fact that it was a woman with a slightly hooked nose. Next to Badb Catha, sat a sizeable black cauldron that had not been there a moment before, its contents unknown beneath the glassy surface. Both Danu and Lugh had said she should drink from Badb Catha's Cauldron of Knowledge so she would understand the magic of *Lann Dàn*. In what seemed like months, though only four weeks had passed, she somehow stood before the Dark Goddess to learn how to kill her father.

The Mórrigan said tightly, "So, you have come."

Ćroí Dàn indignantly told Badb Catha, *"She is not just anyone. She is Erin's Hero, my Hero. Respect my magic and my choice."*

Badb Catha laughed. *"Ćroí* was the last of the three *Dàns* created. Thus, the youngest, yet the only one made sentient. And very opinionated. Are you not, *Mo Chroí*?"

Ćroí Dàn huffed, *"Auntie."*

The Dark Goddess beckoned for Breanna to join her by her cauldron. "Danu's Sun God thinks a great deal of you and your skills. As do Dagda and Danu."

The notion brought a faint smile to Breanna's lips as she recalled the night of that glorious battle against Tethra's demons. That the Sun God thought highly of her warrior skills was something of which she should be proud. Then she caught herself and frowned. "Aye, Lugh and I fought sea demons together once, though I think you already know that as you watched the battle through your crow."

"I was there, indeed, watching," the Dark Goddess confirmed with a shrug. "Danu had lent you my *Maorgairme*, and of course, *Ćroí Dàn* had already chosen you by that time, which also drew my interest. And now, you have influenced her as Erin's Hero should, as she has with you. I expected as much, given that I advised Danu to make her a sentient being. Something we needed, yet—"

Breanna interrupted her. "While it was a great battle, all that matters is whether you will help me destroy my father and remove his taint from our land. Danu suggested only you had such knowledge. I have brought *Lann Dàn* here as the Mother Goddess and Lugh commanded, and if you grant it, I will drink from your Cauldron of Knowledge to learn what I must do with them."

Badb eyed her critically. "You have strengths and weaknesses you do not yet know of flickering through your aura. You are at times recklessly brave, yet fight with courage. I sense deeper things within you that you'll need to draw on. *Ćroí Dàn* has certainly influenced her chosen one." Then she demanded, "Step forward, Breanna Ban Morna of Clan Dálaigh, and truly become Erin's Hero."

Breanna did as commanded and approached Badb Catha and her Cauldron. "I am not yet worthy of that title. Only when I destroy my father will I consider such a thing."

The Dark Goddess held Breanna's eyes steadily for a moment as if once again assessing her mettle, and she intoned, "Before you can truly know what you seek, you must know what will come to pass if you fail and what could come to pass should you succeed in your quest."

"How can I fail?" Breanna asked, her doubts returning.

"By not loving your land and your people enough when the time is needed," the Mórrigan said coldly. "Now, drink."

Breanna stiffened but did not hesitate as she took a gold cup from Badb's hand and dipped it under the mirror finish of the cauldron's contents. The vessel came up full of a dark liquid, and she peered into the cup, wondering what the concoction might do to her; if it would help end her father's reign, so be it. Breanna sipped the watery substance, finding it slightly bitter, but it was better than most ales, if not as good as the mead customarily offered at their duns. Then, without hesitation, she tipped the entire cup into her mouth and swallowed, all the while holding the gaze of her Dark Goddess. With that, Breanna returned it empty, waiting for whatever vision might come.

Badb Catha muttered, "Bold and reckless."

"Sink or swim," was her counter.

A wry smile came to Badb's lips. "You're a brave lassie, something I've not seen much of in the Gaels for many years. I watched you fight off Tethra's demons with Lugh, and I have not seen such martial skills since the days of Cuchulain. I'm sure you've heard Our Heart once chose the Hound of Ulaida, but he was still a man with faults and flaws like any other. And Macha Mong Ruad was another, challenged by many but mastered by none. Yet here you are, a young warrior who is only getting better and better, especially at seizing the *void*, and could outshine both if you master your *geas* and the *Dàns*."

As Breanna started swaying under the influence of Badb's draught, the Dark Goddess reached out to steady her, their eyes locked. "I think that Danu has chosen wisely. You possess many dimensions of your personality that Cuchulain had never realized, and you would have challenged and likely bested Maeve and Macha. You are more like Lugh, the first one she chose as Erin's Hero. Maybe it was because you both have outlander blood, Fir Bolg and Gael in his time, and Norvegr and Gael in yours."

Finally, Breanna sank to her knees, her eyes fluttering shut as the *sight* took her. Badb Catha began a chant she could not understand. The world grew dim, the firelight fading. Yet a moment later, the sun rose, casting its blood-red rays across a barren Emerald Isle. A giant white-haired man straddled the River Shannon, and at his feet lay the ruins of her Gaelic people. Around him danced thousands of his minions, each taking their part in laying waste to her land from shore to shore.

Breanna saw her face mirrored in the one towering above her. He encouraged her to join him in his quest to rule his island and beyond. At the corners of his mouth, she noted the barest whisper of a smile that said he did not need her. Enraged at his mockery, Breanna suddenly found *Lann Dàn* in her hands and brought them down onto a small round stone. The world exploded, blinding her, and then she floated over Erin again. Her land was green and lush this time, holding no taint of the giant outlander.

Breanna's eyes opened a moment later, and she whispered in awe, "*Lann Dàn* are the keys that unlock the *Cycle of Time* through the Stone of Destiny. And the vision I saw has to be one of the possible *cycles* turning, one with him in it and one without."

"Aye, it is. You are a clever girl," Badb Catha whispered.

"That round, clear stone I saw is something I don't know how to use yet," Breanna stated. "It could only be the Stone of Destiny."

"Now that you have seen what will become of our land if your father lives, I will tell you how you can stop him," the Dark Goddess said softly. "You already have two pieces of what you need—the first is *Lann Dàn*.

"The second you wear around your neck—*Croí Dàn*, created by Danu as a sentient being who can choose her Heroes as needed, enables you to love your land more profoundly and ensure this isle's people love you, giving them courage.

"The last piece, the original magic of the *Triple Dans*, was the first. It is called *Lia Dàn*, also known as the Stone of Destiny. It holds the *Cycle of Time*, Erin's time, and access to other possible timelines. *Lia Dàn* is something beyond the world of man, created by Danu before we came to Erin. It indeed governs the *Cycle of Time* for this land, as it holds Erin's destiny, and for those who know how to use it, it gives access to other times and places.

"Together, the *Triple Dàns* make up a magic more powerful than any other god or goddess has ever created. It is magic so potent that even I have never dared to use all three together.

"Yet Danu deeply believes you must do what I have not. Only with the *Triple Dàns* can Erin's Hero write a new destiny for her land—your land. When combined, whatever image you hold in your mind when you link *Lann* and *Lia Dàn* will be made real and cast by *Croí Dàn* across our land—like an image without Hakon Skadi. As if he had never arrived."

"Something I've never known," Breanna interjected, but the Dark Goddess only shrugged and said no more. Frustrated, Breanna probed, "So what will happen when I hold this vision of Erin with no Dreadlord in my mind and bring *Lann Dàn* and *Lia Dàn* together? And *Croí Dàn* spreads that vision?"

"Hakon Skadi will be no more."

"No more?"

Badb Catha eyed her critically. To Breanna, it was as if the Dark Goddess questioned why a more profound response was required. Then she answered, "Aye, no more. Through the magic of the *Triple Dàns*, you will remove the Dreadlord's destiny from Erin's *Cycle of Time*. It will be as if Hakon never existed here, never traveled here, never defiled our land. Where he will go, I know not. Only that he will; maybe he will be cast back to his Norvegr homeland."

"But he's my father," she whispered. "If he never existed, then I would never have existed."

"Once more, you show you have a quicker mind than I first thought, lassie."

Breanna was stunned into silence; Badb Catha was indeed a darkly callous figure. When words finally came to her mouth, she could only say, "It is a steep price to pay."

In a voice as frosty as the coldest winter night, the Dark Goddess grated, "Sometimes life costs much more than it should, but you cannot change that cost. It costs what it costs. A true warrior who loves her land will make such a choice and pay such a price."

Breanna was silent for a time. "And where will I find the *Lia Dàn*?"

"Seek the Standing Stones to the south."

"The fairie home of the gods?" Breanna squeaked. "Danu's home?"

Badb Catha informed her, "While I understand the fairie tales of *Tír na nÓg* are dark, you bear our Heart; she will keep you safe. The Standing Stones are doorways to the otherworld, the Tuatha realm. The closest one is across the *Móin Mórachd*, in the foothills of the Wicklows. Go southeast from here. There's a settlement on the edge of the great bog—they know the safest path.

"Your ring can guide you once you're in the Wicklows. When you find the Standing Stones, use the Blades of Destiny to rap on one of them. A door will open to our realm and lead you to Falias.

"After Danu gives you *Lia Dàn*, return here," Badb continued. "Do not let the two blades touch the stone until you're ready to change the *Cycle of Time*."

Breanna acknowledged breathlessly, "Okay, no touching of the *Dàns* while traveling. And return here."

"Well, not exactly here," she responded. She pointed west. "It is Croghan Hill that you seek. It is the current *magical center* of our land. At the top, you will find an altar surrounded by large monoliths on which to set the Stone of Destiny. Then, with *Lia Dàn* in place, you must touch the tips of *Lann Dàn* to the Stone while holding your vision of a land without the Dreadlord in your mind."

Breanna nodded dubiously, trying to assimilate all she had learned. She passed a hand over her eyes to rub away the weariness, and when her eyes opened again, she found the Dark Goddess had disappeared.

Somewhere in the dark, a crow cawed, and Breanna could not suppress the shiver that ran down her spine. What had she gotten herself into?

Croí Dàn exclaimed in her mind, *"I will save you, My Hero! I will not lose you!"*

A Steep Price

Eoin

Eoin watched his Champion's lithe form fade into the night. Breanna's bravery these past few weeks had been a fierce thing to witness. Now, she faced gods, slayed demons, and manipulated Druids as if they were different instruments to play while she fulfilled her *geas*. Whatever magic their former Fáidh had worked at Breanna's birth had been potent. Or maybe it was her new role as Erin's Hero.

While he was proud of her, it was a bittersweet moment, as he had to let her be Erin's Hero. Eoin could not support her when he felt she would need him, whatever the Dark Goddess demanded of her. Eoin dourly turned back to watch the fire, feeling impotent and wondering how she could thread such a needle with so little room to maneuver and yet love another. To be consumed by such pure hatred for her father made him glad it had not been he on whom Beatha had cast that *geas*; it was not the first time he doubted he could kill his sire, even if the man were named Hakon Skadi. Yet now, with new magic in play via *Ćroí Dàn*, there might be hope, as his lifelong love had taken up the mantle as Erin's Hero.

The night was cold, and he huddled closer to the fire to get warm while the others slept around him. It was easy for him to lose himself inside the flames and dream it would all be over one day. That one day, Breanna would be able to return his love.

———⁓❧ **Breanna** ❧⁓———

Breanna silently slipped back into her bedroll next to Eoin, her mind swirling with the visions imparted by the Cauldron of Knowledge and the words she had exchanged with the Dark Goddess. And the finality of her fate. To love her land enough to make her father and herself no more.

Ćroí Dàn said fiercely to Breanna, *"I will not lose you. I am one of the Dàns. I don't know how to save you, but I will find a way!"*

Eoin stirred to life as if sensing her presence and rolled over to face her. In the flickering firelight, he whispered, "What haunted you to make you look like you just spoke to the dead? I can see Badb Catha came to you, and whatever the Dark Goddess has said, it was not good."

"Aye, she did, and it wasn't," Breanna confirmed in a hushed voice. "I am tired. We'll talk about it in the morning. There's more travel ahead of us, and we need the rest. Just hold me and keep me warm."

Eoin wrapped an arm around her and pulled her close to him. Breanna didn't drift off to sleep for several spans as Badb Catha's words kept churning through her mind. Her life was a steep price to pay for ridding her land of the Dreadlord and his kind. A true warrior would make the sacrifice. That was easy for a goddess to say. Thinking of her father, destroying him seemed like the right thing to do. He was a monster who would ruin her land and people if someone didn't use the magic of the *Triple Dàns* to stop him.

Knowing her Chief would disapprove, Breanna decided she had to hide the Mórrigan's confirmation that when *Lia Dàn* erased her father's existence from the land of Erin, it would do the same with her own. It would be best to leave it at the fact that Badb Catha showed her how to remove the Norvegrs from their land.

Hakon

After setting up their camp on the north side of the High King's Road, Hakon commanded Jotun and Kvasir to bring Toal across from the south side so they could make plans for the next day. Upon meeting with Thorvald and his völva, he told Runa, "I need you to ride with me in the morning. Hopefully, we can spot this hill you briefly saw in your vision."

Runa nodded.

"If we find it, do we leave the road?" Thorvald asked.

"Yes," Hakon responded instantly. "Maybe we can catch her at the top, pen her in."

"What do we do with Lang?"

Runa interjected, "His shoulder injury will take, at best, a few days to heal before his sword arm can be ready for action."

"That's not the focus of my question," Thorvald said.

Hakon nodded. "He's unstable."

Thorvald concurred, "Já."

"Keep him on a short leash," Hakon commanded.

The following morning, Runa replaced Gern on the road. She continued to scan the terrain. The others trailed in the woods to the north, save for the four. After a half-span, Runa caught sight of a tall forest-covered hill to their south, saying as she pointed at the mound, "There is the place we seek—Croghan Hill."

With that, Hakon signaled for his warriors to head south.

—◈ **Breanna** ◈—

A few spans after a cloudy sunrise, Breanna was up and about, complaining about sore muscles. She nodded her thanks as Eoin handed her some warm tea and a bowl of porridge, and he then went about finishing the camp cleanup with the others.

As Breanna ate and drank, she worked through her thoughts about what to share with her band. Finally, she explained, "I'm sure you're all wondering what happened at *Well of Segais*. Badb Catha did indeed appear. She informed me that the magic of the *Triple Dàns* she created to tie the Blades, Stone, and Heart together would destroy the Dreadlord. I have to bring them to Croghan Hill."

Fergal muttered something about distant gods, but Eoin's stern look quelled him. Yet he had to defend himself, saying, "Apologies, Breanna. Old thoughts sometimes still arise unconsciously and escape me."

With the *sight* tugging at her, Breanna nodded and said, "I understand. You will change as I have. I'm unsure how, but it will happen. The future is unclear, but we all have a role in this adventure.

"Our path leads to the other side of the Great Bog, fording the River Life to seek the Standing Stones in the Wicklows. My blades can open the *door* to Failias."

Bradaigh couldn't suppress a shudder, saying, "The tales have it that Fomorian and Fir Bolg spirits and demons haunt the *Móin Mórachd*. If that weren't bad enough, you seek *Tír na nÓg?*"

Bláth ignored the warrior. "Let me get this straight. First, we all are to cross the Great Bog, ford the River Lífe, and seek the Wicklow Standing Stones. Then you must open a door in those Stones that will lead you to Falias. Do I have that right?"

"Aye, you have the gist of it," Breanna agreed.

"All so that the Mother Goddess can give you *Lia Dàn*?" the Bard added. "After that, you must bring the *Triple Dàns* to the top of Croghan Hill. And do what?"

Breanna gave Bláth an annoyed look as the Bard was getting close to forcing her to say how the *Dàns* worked together. And that would let them all know the price she must pay.

"Badb Catha said the *Triple Dàns* must work together to cast the Dreadlord out of Erin. It was all a bit complicated, but she said Croghan Hill is the *magical center* of our land and the best place for hers and Danu's magic to work."

Cróí Dàn commented dryly, *"That was a nice deflection."*

Bláth

Bláth was markedly unsatisfied, but let the matter drop for now. She knew the legends of each *Dàn*. The Blades protected against dark magic; the Stone allowed those with the *sight* to touch the *Cycle of Time*, and the Heart inspired bravery in their Gaels. What had the Mórrigan done to combine their magical aspects? And how would joining magic that repels dark powers, time, and bravery work together? How could it remove the Dreadlord?

She was concerned that the Dark Goddess had commanded Erin's Hero to seek out the third magic of the *Triple Dàns*. She knew she would need a master Seer's guidance and seized the *void*, calling to Maoilir, *"You need to ride south to Dun Curragh."* Then she summed up the new revelations about the *Triple Dàns*. She added, *"This matter needs your insight!"*

The Master Fáidh responded, *"This is all very strange. Our gods warned us away from doing any such thing."*

Bláth answered with, *"I know. Breanna is hiding something."*

"I will leave Tara at once. Even though the High King is arranging a new raid on Cymru, he knows what is at stake. He also knows that Ćroí Dàn has selected Erin's Hero, and that she has chosen Breanna. Fortunately, stormy seas postponed his planned raid on Cymru. Either way, I can be there in two nights."

Bláth sighed in relief. None of this made sense.

Breanna

Breanna's Band broke camp shortly afterward and headed southeast as instructed. Breanna led the way, retracing the same faint path she had followed to their camp below the *Well of Sigias*, though the pace she set this time was leisurely. She knew they were nearing the Great Bog, where the ground turned soft. Changes in the terrain here could be deadly. Her ring guided her.

Shortly before midday, a driving rain forced them to take cover beneath a cluster of black oaks. It was a cold downpour that lasted most of the afternoon, and the only positive note any of them could find was that it had not started the night before. While not soaked, they were soon wet enough that delineation mattered little. Between the late start and the rain, they had not covered as much ground as Breanna had hoped.

When the deluge finally eased to a drizzle, they mounted up. Breanna said nothing as she rode, following the muddy track southeast toward the *Móin Mórachd*--the Great Bog. Well before sunset, she spotted a combination of dun and settlement.

Bláth informed them that it was called Dun Eadan, a damp area near the bog, with ponds scattered here and there. Tethra's demons were never far from Breanna's mind when she was near water, and she insisted on peering into the murky surfaces for a moment to touch the *void* as if to assure herself no demons were staring back at her.

Nestled in the crook of hills they had just descended through, they found a dun. It had spread beyond the original defensive ring and thrived with activity. It could hardly be called a ringfort any longer.

Her Heart informed Breanna, *"Dun Eadan is located along a trade route between Dun Uisneach, the High King's palace at Tara, and the southern populations in Lagain, which certainly helped Dun Eadan thrive. Being close to the High King's Road, which carried wares east and west, made this dun a gateway to the southeast."*

Breanna concluded, *"Thus, given that Slíghe Mor also made foot and horse traffic commonplace, travelers could easily swing south of the road to stop for the night. Those traveling up from the south or down from the north use it as a waystation to trade across the Great Bog."*

"Correct, my Heart!"

Eoin dismounted before the dun gates and claimed Guestright for them using his Celtic Knot armring to gain respect; the multicolored cloak that signified he was a Prince of the Blood also helped. Then Bláth joined him, letting her Master Bard status lend weight to their appearance.

Breanna was pleased, for it was the place Badb Catha said she should seek before heading south across the Great Bog. "The Dark Goddess commanded that we head for the Wicklows after stopping here. We will leave in the morning to find the Standing Stones."

As they rubbed down their mounts and settled them into the stable, Dun Eadan's heavy-set Chief entered with his Seneschal in tow and bowed to Bláth as a Master Bard.

The portly man said to her, "Welcome to our dun. Your fellow Druid, Master Tadg, said we should expect you. He mentioned that the Heart has chosen Erin's Hero once more to deal with Norvegrs to the northwest."

The Bard said dryly, "Chief Conn."

Breanna stepped beside Bláth, hoping to downplay the whole Hero thing. "Aye, that would be me. Yet more urgently, we, at the command of the Mórrigan, need to reach the Wicklows. We thought to cross the *Móin Mórachd* directly."

"Ahh, if it's urgent," Conn replied, scratching his chin. "Then best to run the bog's edge. First, to the northeast, then south, to Dun Curragh, where my cousin is Chief. Then, across the River Lífe and into the Wicklows. Not only is it safer, but it is also faster. You will walk horses as much as you ride them through the Great Bog."

Breanna narrowed her eyes but let the advice pass, as she didn't know if she should trust his advice; few had good things to say about this Chief.

Conn added, "We can spend more time on this topic around my high table. Please use my baths, and we can review your plans further at dinner. My Seneschal, Tynan, will look after your needs."

With that, they made the bathhouse their next stop and laid out their wet clothes to dry near the hearth. Breanna was pleasantly surprised to find the tubs heated. A few spare moments to soak out the cold in her bones was an unexpected treat. Her male bandmates allowed the two women to bathe in one of the larger tubs set apart from those they had chosen for themselves.

Bláth whispered, "I know you're hiding something."

Breanna arched an eyebrow. "Indeed."

"I know the lore of the *Triple Dàns*," the Bard added. "Combining their magical aspects has always been—well—not anything our gods encouraged."

She shrugged. "I wouldn't know."

"Och, you didn't know it before, but you do know it now since meeting Badb Catha," Bláth surmised in a hushed voice. "She told you how they work together. She told you what their combined magic would bring forth. Something that will destroy the Dreadlord."

Breanna held the Bard's eyes in a cold, dead glare, saying, "You may be right, but you'll not hear it from my mouth."

She turned away to untie the green beaded thong that held back her hair and finished her bath, washing out the detritus collected during her time in the woods and on the trail.

Bláth stared after her, asking in a hushed tone, "What magic is so terrible it would cause you to be so evasive?"

Breanna did not answer, rose from the tub, and left the Bard behind.

Eoin

When the six presented themselves to the Chief of Dun Eadan, they were each given a chair at the high table near the hearth. The portly *Ceann-cinnidh* was of Clan Ceallaigh, another cousin of the High King. Eoin noted his main hall was not as sumptuous as Dun Uisneach's, and its Chief had dressed himself in pale yellow linens rather than fine blue silks. Even his cloak, which lay draped over the back of a chair, featured a simple striped pattern of green and gray, with the same pale yellow used for the fringe.

It spoke of him as a Clan Chief and no more. Still, the cook served fresh-baked trout, brown bread, and good dark ale. Breanna, as always, requested mead, and Bláth followed suit. Dining here was much better than trail rations; they ate their fill and some more.

Knowing they had crossed from Mide into Laigin, Eoin commented, "I could grow accustomed to claiming Guestright."

Warmed by the fire, Breanna's Band finally relaxed despite the stares they received from others in the small hall. As at Dun Uisneach, only the young women of the dun seemed interested in the traveling warriors for purposes other than gossip, and once more, Eoin noted Breanna showed some subtly jealous signs over the flirting glances he received. Braoin, Bradaigh, and Fergal certainly did not mind the attention.

Chief Conn commented, "So, my fellow warriors, I understand some of you are from North Mide. A long way to travel."

Eoin had been expecting this, for warriors seldom strayed far from home when they had a family to protect. Trying to be polite without saying too much, he offered, "Aye, a long way. Breanna Ban Morna, my Champion, and my cousin, Fergal Mac Conall, agreed to help with her quest. Then Braoin joined us, as did Bradaigh, and Dun Uisneach stood behind us, as the Heart of Destiny declared Breanna as Erin's Hero."

Conn looked at Breanna, his eyes lingering a moment. He stated blandly, "You are distinctly Norvegr, at least partly. Yet you wear a gold armring. And you are your Chief's Champion. Braoin and Bradaigh also have Norvegr blood in them. Both blooded warriors are bound to you. While Tadg agreed, what kind of quest would Druids send a Gaelic Chief on?

Breanna asked, "I know I command my *Aos Dána*, and when it's the other way around, it spells nothing but trouble."

Her comment made Eoin want to groan—he had thought himself clever to try to direct any questions away from Breanna.

Bláth saved the moment, asking darkly, "Are you insinuating the Druids of Dun Uisneach do not have the support of Chief Faolán and Chieftess Falyn?"

Conn's mouth moved like a fish seeking water when there was none as Bláth continued. "One who is a cousin of the High King and the other a cousin to our High Queen? If you doubt who sits at your table, I suggest you think again."

It was a direct challenge. Conn looked at Bláth harshly, but one such as he, even as well placed as he was, did not challenge a Master Bard. She could ruin his reputation with a few songs.

Croí Dàn informed Eoin and Breanna, *"I like her!"*

Seeing the change, Eoin knew their story needed refining and answered in as soothing a tone as he could manage, "While I may be a Prince of the Blood, I'm not an appointed Dun Chief yet, just acting, so such latitude is not mine to command.

"This is a quest and a challenge to the Clans Mórdha that we must undertake. The Heart of Destiny commanded us to travel to the southern side of *Móin Mórachd* to seek out a Druid hermit, whom some think has been touched by the Tuatha gods. He supposedly lives in the foothills of the Wicklows and dwells in a cave or some such near some Tuatha Standing Stones."

Conn shuddered. "As I mentioned, my cousin is *Ceann-cin-nidh* of Dun Curragh, just northeast of the River Lífe. He may have heard of this Druid. Have you a name?"

"Nay, but we would appreciate it if you knew a safe path through the bog," Eoin countered, glad of an opportunity to change the subject. "One that could get us across in a day if we rode hard."

Chief Conn puffed out his cheeks. "A day at this time of year? You saw the rain today. Even with riding hard—which there'll not be much of—that would be a challenge. Chariots get stuck frequently, and even horses falter in the bog. Many break their legs. Even the iron bog miners despise this time of year."

"Can we ride on horseback?" Fergal asked.

"So, horse riding has even spread to the outer reaches of Mide," Conn commented, his eyes alighting. "It's become all the rage in Tara, and even many of the king's *fianna* leaders now come by on horseback regularly. My cousins drew me to it and sent me fine horses, though I've only tried riding them a few times. With the bog around us, it proves of little use, except on the *Slighe Mor*. Maybe you can show me how to improve my skills before you leave?"

Eoin shrugged. "While we've ridden hill ponies for years, our new steeds are true warhorses, so we've only just learned ourselves. The High King's *fianna* leaders might be better for such instruction."

Conn sighed. "Ah, well, it was but a thought. Anyway, to have an even chance of making it to the southern side of the Great Bog in a day or so, you must follow the track that leads east of here until you see Adhlaic Hill directly to your north. Then, follow a fork in the path to the southeast and round the shoulder of the bog. After several spans of moving in and out of that dangerous terrain, the ground will rise as the bog pulls away to the southwest.

"You'll then be in the *An Currach*, as it forces the *Móin Mórachd* into itself. There is a path—if one can call it such— between those two points. My cousin's fort, Dun Curragh, lies in the hills beyond the end of the bog. Give Chief Miach this token, and he will help you."

Conn offered it to Eoin, his palm up. Eoin reached for the piece of green Connemara marble, noting how a fire flower had been carved into each side and painted red. He was about to ask something more when a Bard cleared his throat and dragged his bow across his fiddle to get everyone's attention. That ended any conversation as the servants removed the remnants of the evening meal.

Bláth offered to play a duet with the dun's young Bard, which noticeably pleased him, as playing a song with a Master Bard was a rare opportunity. As she took out her small travel harp, the pair began to tune their instruments.

The dun's Bard played the first song with Bláth, an upbeat jig. Once finished, she returned to the high table with a big smile, saying, "Always fun teaching young ones a thing or two."

"You're not that old," Breanna chided.

While Conn's Bard was not as skilled as Bláth, Eoin and his companions stayed and listened respectfully for a time. When Breanna claimed fatigue from their journey, Eoin led their band, sans their Bard, to the dry stable loft where they were to sleep. Indeed, it was not the welcome Eoin had hoped Conn would offer, but it would work. He had chosen it over staying in the main hall, saying they were tired, and the dun's residents still had much of the evening left to entertain themselves. Not to mention that they needed to be on their way at sunrise.

Braoin

Braoin whispered to Fergal and Bradaigh, "I see Breanna has maneuvered us away from the young women of the dun once more."

His half-brother added, "It's not for us that she does this."

"I noticed she keeps Eoin pretty close when such female distractions are at hand," Fergal agreed. "I know he's smitten with her, but I expect there is more to her affections for him than she seems to be willing to admit."

With that, the three followed the pair into the stable.

Once settled in the loft, Braoin heard Eoin whisper, "I still don't understand how the magic of the *Triple Dàns* can remove the Dreadlord from Erin."

Breanna responded with, "It's magic. I'm just a warrior."

Eoin's response was an explosive sigh.

Braoin could only shake his head, convinced Breanna was not being entirely truthful about what the Dark Goddess asked of her. His sister was hiding something, which had to be an ominous outcome. He understood his *geas*, but not hers. What had the Badb Catha asked of her? It had to be significant. Since he felt compelled to protect her, he wondered if it was the Heart of Destiny's influence. With that thought, sleep took him.

Hakon

After finding a path off the High King's Road that led south, Hakon led his men and the völva toward Croghan Hill. As he drew nearer, it seemed as if the gods had thrust up a fist from deep within the earth to form the strange mound, its steep forested slope towering over them. The ascent would be difficult for their horses to master, so Hakon ordered his warriors to dismount and spread into four groups to search the base of the hill before they sought its summit.

Hakon helped Runa climb, albeit slowly, up and up through the hard-to-traverse hillscape. After a span, he heard no signals from the other groups that any had found his daughter. He was beginning to wonder if his völva had been wrong or misled.

When they finally crested the top of Croghan Hill, they found a trio of ten-foot stone monoliths in a small clearing of trees surrounding a shorter bowl-shaped altar filled with water, toward which Runa hobbled.

Hakon demanded, "What is this place?"

Runa reached out to it, laying her palm on the water, before answering, "Tuatha magic. This altar feels like it is the center of their island. Not literally, but magic-wise."

Hakon saw her good eye roll up as the *sight* took her.

A moment later, she sighed. "The Goddess of War can no longer block my inner eye. Her murder of crows did not greet me. I can now try to find your Destroyer or the path she will follow."

"Do it!" he commanded.

Her eye rolled up again. When she lurched back into their world, she had to steady herself on the altar before saying, "I thought Croghan Hill was Breanna Ban Morna's destination, but that was untrue. With the full moon passing last night, the Destroyer received new instructions from the Dark Goddess, telling her to go around the Great Bog to the southeast and into the foothills of the Wicklow Mountains. It was unclear what she should seek there, but it must be more Tuatha magic. I only know it is the Destroyer's destination."

Runa added, "Your daughter is east of here, yet far enough away that we cannot catch her, even if we leave at this moment to pursue her directly. Instead, we need to try to intercept her. If she makes it across the River Life, nothing can stop her before she obtains the Tuatha magic the Dark Goddess commanded her to seek out."

She turned from the short monolith altar and continued, "You should be able to intercept her there if you ride due south and then veer southeast when the Great Bog ends."

"How much time do we have?" Hakon asked.

"To intercept her, two, maybe three nights."

"Will we make it in time?" he probed dourly.

Runa answered, "You will if you allow me to trail after you with one of your lesser warriors to ensure he looks after me."

Looking at the western-leaning sun, Hakon shook his head. "Nei, I would rather have you with us. If our path remains as solid as it has been today, it should only be a day's ride, maybe two, to the river ford. I left you behind before, and that was a mistake."

He commanded, "Gern, sound the horn to regroup at the base of this hill—south side. And see that Runa gets down safely. We leave at first light."

A rain shower passed over, making their descent treacherous. Despite the inconvenience, Hakon finally had a firm direction and a plan to overcome the Tuatha God's magic cast in his path. With that, his resolve solidified.

⬥ Corbmac ⬥

With Breanna's Band well on their way east, Corbmac looked to the broken cloud cover. It was now just after midday, and he and his *fians* were getting restless waiting for the Dreadlord. Hakon should have ridden down the road to the Boyne River ford by now. Something was amiss. Corbmac soon had his men moving west, following his chariot. When they came across a section of churned-up road, he signaled two scouts in each *fian* to search north and south of *Slighe Mor*.

The scouts reported that more than twenty riders and a chariot had crossed the road and headed south toward Croghan Hill. Corbmac had them follow him south along the Dreadlord's path. He looked up at Croghan Hill; it was not hard to guess where they were going. Why they were seeking that place was another matter.

Within a few spans, Corbmac discovered those he sought had stopped and split up to surround and likely ascend Croghan Hill. With none of the Dreadlord's warriors in sight, he ordered his men to position themselves to the southeast of the steep rise.

Corbmac thought that since Breanna was to meet with the Dark Goddess, placing his *fians* between the Dreadlord and the *Well of Segias* would be best. Once she met with Badb Catha, he suspected she'd head to Dun Eadan.

A horn sounded as the sun headed west, which, from Corbmac's experience, was a Norvegr signal to regroup. Then another horn sounded from the hill's south side, a sign that all should gather there.

Corbmac smiled, as it seemed likely they would head south in the morning. If they did indeed so, it was under the guidance of their völva, which meant his Hero would do the same. Yet from where she was now, she would have to go east of the *Móin Mórachd* while the Dreadlord would ride down the west side. And he would be sure to follow.

Breanna

When morning came, Breanna and her band headed toward Adhlaic Hill, following the rolling terrain northwest as Chief Conn had directed. As expected, the track was still a muddy mess from the previous day's rain, but the sky was no longer full of angry gray clouds, which was a pleasant surprise. Even the air seemed to hold a hint of warmth that had been absent since the last time they had trained in their Grove of Instruction near Dun Arrogh.

It seemed a lifetime ago that Breanna had become Eoin's Champion, not little more than two fortnights. Never in all her imaginings would she have believed that Chiefs, Druids, and Tuatha gods would be at her beck and call. Yet there wouldn't be a moment's hesitation if Breanna could have traded her life shadowed by her *geas* and her father for something mundane.

A life in which she could do more than hate. A life in which she could love.

Adhlaic Hill appeared to the east, and their track turned southeast. As all had told them, the bog to the southwest looked dangerous. Even their current path was so wet it had to have a layer of oak-wood planks toghered in places to provide a sound footing for horses, carts, and chariots, such as they had crossed while traveling the High King's Road. When the forest around them was thick and tangled, they could not help but cast wary glances from side to side.

Tales had spread far and wide about how Fomorian and Fir Bolg spirits haunted the area around the Great Bog. Breanna pressed on, unconcerned but alert for other signs of danger near water, as the path veered around numerous small ponds and lakes. Several times, she was certain Tethra or his demons were nearby. Only the presence of the sun in a broken sky of clouds assuaged her fears.

Then the trees ended abruptly, and the land opened into fields of heather capped with blue and purple flowers. The track pushed them eastward to the edge of these fields as the ground beneath them had to be toghered with timbers again. Breanna could not imagine how they had thought to pass directly through the *Móin Mórachd*, as their path was a muddy mess even here, their mounts kicking it up and covering them in filth. After that, they reached a new patch of forest, followed by more boggy terrain. The day wore on in this manner, alternating between forest and heather patches.

At midday, they stopped to eat the fresh bread from Dun Eadan, the remnants of the more portable pheasant pieces, and some grilled pollan—a native freshwater fish in Erin—the Bard had collected from last night's serving dishes.

Breanna queried, "A Master Bard as a scullion?"

"All in their time," was Bláth's response. "Like you."

"Meaning?"

"I know you're hiding something."

Breanna scowled and turned away from the Bard.

Croí Dàn offered to the Bard, *"Tread carefully."*

Breanna added, "My Business, not yours!"

Hearing that, Bláth stated flatly, "That sounded like a warning. Yet, my Hero, I am not your enemy. Your father is."

Finally, as the sun slid into late afternoon, the land rose, leaving the Great Bog to slide away to the northwest. Seeing the foothills called *An Currach* in the south of *Móin Mórachd* bolstered Breanna's confidence, as they had made good time and could see the River Lífe glittering between *An Currach* and the Wicklows. With the sun setting, they pulled their mounts to a stop. They had not reached Dun Curragh, but it seemed they were close.

Eoin dismounted. "Now that we are safely around the Great Bog, we should seek Chief Miach in the morning. Hopefully, the *Ceann-cinnidh* knows where we can find these Standing Stones. Somewhere southeast of River Lífe covers a great deal of territory."

Bláth slipped from her horse with practiced ease, interjecting, "No need to rely on anyone for directions. I had to visit all of the standing stones in Erin as part of my training. With our mounts, it will take us a day to get there. I can also guide you to Dun Curragh. That said, it would be a good idea to request the support of one of his *fians* until we are across the River Lífe safely."

Trying to mend a fence, Breanna gave the Bard a wink and said casually, "I knew having you with us would come in handy."

Bláth just shrugged as they settled beside their fire after setting up camp in a small clearing beneath a cluster of oaks. Once they assembled their dinner with strips of boar jerky, cheese, and bread,

Bláth pulled out her travel harp and played a few relaxing songs. Twilight faded into the night as the band drifted off to sleep.

——⊰ **Hakon** ⊱——

The morning following his climb to Croghan Hill's summit, Hakon found the sky cloudy and chilly, with a threat of rain in the air. Lang was sullen as he prepared his mount, and Hakon knew it. Yet he still had to organize his pursuit to intercept his daughter and had no time for such a grievance.

He told his warriors, "Men, we must stop our Destroyer south of the Great Bog, reaching her before she can obtain the magic that will challenge our right to be here, to even exist in this land. We ride for the River Lífe shortly to protect our lives."

Runa confirmed, "Já, it is as our Jarl says, and at the river's ford, we might have some help from a local Fomorian god and his demons. If you see them, stay back."

As Hakon's warriors set about breaking camp, he quietly asked his völva, "Anything else before we depart?"

"Unfortunately, we do not know what magic she seeks."

"What is it, and how does it work?"

"That I cannot say yet," she replied. "I felt the Tuatha magic at the hill summit and discovered some, but not all, of her story. There is more afoot than we know. I cannot pierce the veil of what Breanna has in play. Maybe I can try again tonight."

Hakon held his völva's good eye and saw she was tired. She had spent much energy obtaining those scraps of knowledge. Yet there was no time for rest. "We must lay a plan to stop her."

"I have no more information, save that the Destroyer is seeking the Wicklow Standing Stones."

Hakon frowned. "You mean those old monoliths we see occasionally?"

"Gates to the Tuatha underworld," Runa explained.

"This is where my daughter will find the other piece of magic she seeks?"

Runa nodded. "Já, and those in the Wicklows are the closest."

"Could she seek this Tuatha realm anyplace else?"

"There are more Stones to the southwest, but they are farther," Runa answered. "And some lie just northeast of Loch Gowna."

"Again, too far from here," Hakon put in, his concerns appeased for the time being. "Then it's to the Wicklows if the Destroyer eludes us at the next ford?"

"As I foresaw, she will ride southeast of the Great Bog," Runa said. "We must ride the west side. I'll be along in a moment."

With that, the völva turned away and stepped into the wood to take care of her morning ablutions. When Runa returned, Hakon mounted his horse, his men joining him, and she climbed onto her chariot, with Jotun handling the reins for her.

The day started well, and to Hakon, it seemed his men were taking the trek in stride. When it began to rain heavily just before midday, Hakon would not let it deter him, but the downpour did slow their pace. Later, when the deluge had slackened to a drizzle, he found the muddy track more hindrance than help. Hakon was pleased with his decision to keep Runa with him, as she had slowed him down no more than the weather had. Yet, more than once, he questioned her vision about his Destroyer's destination.

Nonetheless, Hakon growled to himself and stayed the course, lashing his horse into a trot. Unfortunately, he soon had to pull back due to another cloudburst releasing more sheets of water down on them, falling hard on his collection of warriors. He knew that pushing the mounts farther today would be useless. It was a dark sky, and his men were tired from the slog through the afternoon downpour. And he certainly didn't need one of their mounts pulling up lame. Shaking his head in frustration, he decided to call it an early day. Half his warriors made camp as the other half rubbed down the horses.

Toal

Toal constantly sought a chance to escape and thought the River Boyne crossing might be the best option. Yet they had veered off the High King's Road, and now he was bound, heading south, and certainly couldn't be any wetter or colder. He was still riding with Gern, who had not taken kindly to the last attempt he had made to flee. Also, his eye still hurt, but the more significant problem was that his hands were still tied. The river would have been the perfect spot, as Breanna had taught him how to swim after saving his life a few years back from drowning. He had tried to escape during the River Brosna crossing by throwing himself from the back of Gern's saddle and into the water. Yet he couldn't drag the Norvegr after him. It would now not be easy to outrun any pursuit in his present circumstances on soggy land.

Once stopped for the day, Gern lashed a rope to Toal's bonds, though it barely mattered. He no longer had the energy to escape after a day of soggy travel, and he collapsed with everyone else as Hakon Skadi ordered his men to make camp.

Yet to Toal, they had just lain down their heads when Hakon roused them, looking feral in the morning light. It was as if he sensed his prey was close at hand.

They soon rode again and took a southeasterly course after a few spans. The great bog still lay to their east, but its influence on the land was fading, with the ground growing firmer and the weather improving. With Runa leading the way, they came to the River Life by midafternoon. It was too broad and deep to ford in any shallows, so they followed it northeast, looking for a way across.

When they came to a ferry that could take them over to the south side of the river, the Dreadlord's völva proclaimed they had reached the spot where the next meeting with the Destroyer would occur.

Toal thought that was doubtful.

"You're certain of this?" he heard Hakon demand.

"The *sight* revealed it to me at the top of Croghan Hill," Runa confirmed. "My goddess will not be wrong."

"Then we lay our trap on this side and wait for them. Jotun, seek out the ferryman, tell him we expect visitors from the far side, and ask him to wait there. This way, the Destroyer and her band cannot easily escape us."

Toal could only groan at his inability to help. There had to be something he could do. Maybe find a way to alert Breanna?

Breanna

Breanna was the first to rise. She restarted their fire, using the still-smoldering coals from the night before, enough to spark the dry timber she had found. Her half-brothers and their Bard stirred next, followed by Eoin and Fergal. They again had their breakfast meal of trail rations, which were as tedious as ever. As she chewed on a strip of dried boar, Breanna thought wistfully of the gooey eggs she'd eaten at Dun Uisneach and the trout Dun Eadan had served them. Perhaps they could hunt down some game or stop at a stream to catch fish. Otherwise, their meals would remain monotonous.

They found they had camped in the shadow of a tor about the same height as Croghan Hill, though it covered a larger area. To the southeast lay the rising land of *An Currach*, which kept the great bog in its place. Somewhere beneath the canopy of the trees that covered those foothills was Dun Curragh, and hopefully, there they would find additional protection via the Standing Stones that would lead them to the fairie world of *Tír na nÓg* and *Lia Dàn*.

Once they were all mounted up, Breanna led the way as they followed a forest line trail; it was nothing as refined as the High King's Road. The flat land of the bog returned for a short time, and the air was pleasantly fair. They rode quickly, following paths when they could and forging through a forest when the path led them that way. Their destination, the Wicklow Mountains, loomed higher and higher to the southeast. The band stopped when they came to a stream, as their mounts needed to be cleaned and curried with the chilly water after their ride along the muddy track, not to mention themselves.

Breanna's mount, Eimar, whickered her approval at the attention, saying through the Heart, *"You are selfless, my Hero."*

Breanna just laughed at her mount and handed her the core of an apple she had just munched on, and Eimar whickered her approval again.

Ćroí Dàn chided, *"You spoil her!"*

Breanna smiled. *"Aye, I do."*

A few spans later, their band encountered a *fían,* all fledglings, bold lads on foot, brandishing their spears while trying to look fierce. Breanna noted the mounted young commander had a red beard that was little more than fuzzy red stubble, and his blue eyes were twitching as he looked around for possible threats. Then, it was clear to her that he had realized three of them were white-haired Norvegrs.

When the Commander, wearing his two-colored cloak that proclaimed he was a Chieftain's son, took in the fact that one of the warriors was draped in a five-colored cloak and rode a large warhorse, it took some of the puff out of his chest. Upon seeing that all five wore gold Celtic Knot armrings, another gust of wind went out of his sails. His men wore only plain bronze arm rings, which bore no artwork.

They were all clearly of the warrior class, and the gold indicated considerable skill with a blade. And three of them were outlanders, with the woman covered in weapons, and that was cause enough to be wary. Yet there was also a Master Bard among them, which was confusing. With a hand on the hilt of his sword, he demanded, "What business does a Prince of the Blood have in *An Currach*, and to whom do you swear your loyalty?"

Eoin raised his hands, saying, "Peace be with you. All deserve respect. We seek Chief Miach's dun, and the *Ard-Rì* in Tara is the only man with the right to claim any man's loyalty in Erin. We were recently guests of Chief Conn, and since our quest brought us south, he suggested we contact his cousin for help."

"How do I know it is the truth you speak?"

"Conn himself gave us this token," Eoin said, taking the piece of green Connemara marble with the red-painted fire flower from his cloak.

The Commander held out his hand for it, but Eoin did not move to give it up and just let the other eye it from his mount. "My name is Eoin Mac Cairbre, and this is my cousin, Fergal Mac Conall. Next to him is my Champion, Breanna Ban Morna, and her half-brothers, Bradaigh and Braoin. The last of our band is Master Bard Bláth from Dun Uisneach."

The *fian-ceannard* hesitated, looking from one of them to the other and back again. While the Bard's name was familiar from a distant memory, as he stated, "I am Mahon Mac Miach. The Chief you seek is my father. May I ask where this quest takes you?"

"We search for a Druid Seer rumored to live near some Standing Stones in the foothills of the Wicklows," Breanna put in. "Would you know where we might find these Stones and thus the Druid?"

Mahon turned to the Prince's Champion. "Aye, south and east of the River Lífe's ford. We maintain the ferry for the crossing."

"Can you show us the way to Dun Curragh, Mahon?" Eoin asked, moving his warhorse next to the lad's crossbred hill pony, offering his arm in respect. "I would appreciate your honor. We request aid from your father, as we need a *fian* to escort us across the river."

Mahon took Eoin's arm, proud that a Prince had asked for his honor and didn't demand it. He was more than a bit relieved that these warriors were friends and not foes. Knowing he and his men would be guiding them to the ferry crossing, he said with a smile, "Aye, follow me."

"Let's ride and get acquainted, shall we?" Eoin offered.

Mahon Mac Miach nodded and turned his mount to fall in at Eoin's side while his *fian* spread out to trot beside them.

Bláth said from behind them, "Mahon, I think your father would be aghast that you don't seem to remember me."

Breanna spoke up. "Och, please grant some pity on the lad, Bláth. Let's overlook that foible."

Despite her words, Mahon appeared stricken. Once she spoke, memories of her alto voice singing in their hall many years ago came flooding back. "Apologies, Master Bard!"

Bláth laughed, "I think Breanna's right, Mahon. Forget it."

Full of youth and vigor, the *fian* warriors ran tirelessly beside the riders, bobbing and weaving through the trees while their commander took the path. Eoin told Mahon, "Watching your men keep this pace tells me you keep them well trained, much like Corbmac does with his Dun Uisneach *fians*. While I consider myself in good shape, your men have endurance beyond any I could muster."

Mahon smiled at the compliment. "You know the old commander of Dun Uisneach?"

"Aye, we do, and my Champion has claimed him as her grandfather, as she has had none to call her own."

Mahon made small talk with Eoin, inquiring about their quest, dun, and anything else that came to mind. They reached Dun Curragh around midday, and as they passed through the gates, those in the yard froze, wary of the strangers. Mahon called out, "Father, we have guests sent by Chief Conn!"

Chief Miach strode through the hall door and greeted them with a bellowing, "Welcome, travelers! I hope my cousin treated you well. He's a miserly *mac soith!*"

Bláth

Bláth laughed at the insult flung at Chief Conn by his brother as she dismounted, turning to Dun Curragh's Chief. "Miach, you ancient war wolf—it's been years! The Druids of Dun Uisneach don't get this far south often, but I hope one of ours has reached you."

Miach answered, "Aye, Maoilir arrived late in the evening. He was a little the worse for wear, but the old Fáidh has recovered from his long ride from Tara."

"Good to hear," she answered. "We ride for the River Lífe ferry crossing as soon as possible, as we must make it into the Wicklow foothills before tonight."

"What is this all about?"

Bláth sighed. "Sorry that Maoilir tends not to share enough, especially with our *Ceanns*. The Heart of Destiny has chosen Erin's Hero once more."

The Bard added, "Please meet Breanna Ban Morna."

That announcement caused a stir in the yard, with Miach's people, who had returned to their chores, now taking more interest in the newcomers. Whispers abounded about the fact that she was the one whom the Heart of Destiny had chosen as Erin's Hero.

Breanna dismounted, followed by her band, and stepped between the Bard and Chief. She said as she extended her arm in greeting, "Pleased to meet you, Miach. Your son was most helpful in guiding us here."

As Miach took Breanna's arm, Bláth added, "Aye, Mahon was the perfect guide. As to our new Hero, I know she looks a bit like a hedgehog with her weapons bristling about her. Yet you'll find her approachable. Homegrown in northeastern Mide."

Miach released his grip, saying, "You are welcome to my dun. I am to understand *Croí Dàn* has chosen you?"

"Aye," came Breanna's answer as the ruby gem pulsed her magic in agreement. "This is my Chief, Eoin Mac Cairbre."

Eoin offered his arm in greeting, then handed his counterpart the fire-stone, "Your cousin, Chief Conn, said you would help us."

Miach nodded, waving away the chit. "That I will, regardless of what my miserable cousin offered. Knowing that *Croí Dàn* has chosen a new Hero, Erin's Hero, is enough for me."

Maoilir strode to the Chief's side, saying abruptly, "Bláth, we must talk before we ride to the Wicklows."

"Please excuse us," the Bard offered apologetically and went off with the Fáidh, wondering what had knotted the old Seer up.

Breanna

Breanna also noted the rudeness, though her thoughts about the Druid were more vulgar; her opinion of him had not improved. Yet she turned brightly to her other warriors, saying, "The rest of my band is Fergal, Eoin's cousin, and my two half-brothers from Mide, Braoin and Bradaigh."

Miach clasped arms with each of them. "Let's have a midday meal. We would typically dine inside at this time of year. Yet, given the day is fair and we were cooped up with each other for several days due to the recent heavy rains, let's have a small celebration in the yard."

Breanna, noting the whispers of curiosity persisting from Miach's people, turned to them and said, "I know having Erin's Hero walk the land once more is surprising to you all—I can assure you I was more surprised than you when *Croí Dàn* appeared around my neck and proclaimed me as such. Yet, I am still just Breanna Ban Morna from northeastern Mide. Please, call me Bre!"

With that, *Croí Dàn* sent out a pulse of love and welcome.

Several people came to greet her before they began setting up an outdoor luncheon. Soon, the kitchen workers brought out several long tables and benches. They started serving various dishes—sliced venison, boar, grilled pollan, cheese, mashed tubers, and fresh bread. And, of course, ale.

Breanna declared, "Make me happy with mead instead!"

Miach laughed. "Of course!"

"Bláth will want the same."

As they ate, more people stopped by to introduce themselves and ask about her diamond blades and the heart-shaped ruby. Breanna blushed a bit over the attention.

Mo Chroí chimed in, *"I sent them your love of this land and its people. They are just returning it."*

Breanna enjoyed her moment with these southerners of Laigin, feeling them warm to her, folks who welcomed her like one of their own. It was a new experience compared to Dun Eadan, save for the *fians*.

The two Master Druids soon rejoined them after their private consultations and filled their trenchers. While Breanna eyed the old Seer curiously and wondered what they talked about, the Bard smiled and said, "Thank you for saving me from the ale."

After the meal, they reprovisioned their packs, and it was time to move on. Miach announced, "My son and his *fian* will escort you to the river crossing."

Breanna exclaimed, "Then let us be off. Miach, thank you for your support and the escort!"

"Of course, my Hero!" he answered with a wave of farewell.

Corbmac

Corbmac and his two *fians* quickly followed the Dreadlord and his warriors along their southern track as they pressed along the edge of the Great Bog. Then, the trail turned southeast toward the River Life ferry crossing.

When they caught up with the Norvegr and his twenty-plus warriors, they were lying in wait on the north side of the river crossing, all hidden in the woods. Corbmac silently signaled for one *fian* to spread out and flank their opponents to the far right. The other *fian* would take up their position along the path that led to the river's edge.

It was time to wait and be ready to strike out at the Norvegrs if Breanna's Band attempted to use the crossing as he expected.

Breanna

The sun was in the afternoon sky when Breanna spotted the River Life in the distance below them. The ribbon of water was moving swiftly eastward with the recent rains, and its width would be challenging for their mounts if not for the ferry crossing. She and her band finally dropped out of the *An Currach* foothills and made their way along an easy woodland path. As it widened, she saw the river's edge through the foliage roughly a few hundred yards ahead.

Breanna rode next to Mahon, with Eoin on the other side of her. When she heard a low whistle, she raised her hand to bring them all to a halt. Mahon returned the call, and another *fian* emerged from the woods, led by Corbmac as he maneuvered his horse around some trees in his way.

"Well met, My Hero," he stated with a broad smile, clearly happy to see her. "And hail, Mahon Mac Miach, it's good to see you again—it's been a while."

Mahon looked around warily. "What brings you to lead a *fian* here from a distant Dun Uisneach?"

Before he could answer, Breanna nudged her horse forward, speculating, "It is not good news, I expect. Aye, Grandfather?"

"You are correct. The Dreadlord has somehow sussed out your plan to cross the river and made it here before you. He waits with his men on the west side of this path near the river's edge and has sent the ferryman across the river. I have one of my *fians* flanking him, and you see the other here."

Maoilir and Bláth nudged their mounts next to the old warrior, the former saying, "We must get Erin's Hero safely across the river. Can it be done?"

"Aye," Corbmac confirmed. "I believe so. We now have three *fians* to defend her with."

"You are referring to the Norvegrs who settled northwest of Dun Uisneach?" Mahon questioned.

Eoin said, "Aye, the one and only, and one who is our bane in the north. We need a plan first to surprise them and then make it clear we outnumber them."

Mahon advised, "Might I suggest Corbmac and his *fian* circle in the eastern woods and be ready to emerge behind us as we clear the tree line? Then his other *fian* can appear behind them when these Norvegrs show themselves."

Corbmac nodded. "Agreed. That will allow us to present eighteen long pikes as an iron wall in front of them and another nine behind. Maoilir and Bláth, you two ride with me and keep back. We do not need to be concerned about your safety while we stare down the Dreadlord."

The two Druids agreed to follow Corbmac, and Breanna added, "Then let's be about it. We will lose the light if we don't step up the pace. And I don't want to see what might be in the river after sunset."

"Something I should be concerned about?" Mahon asked.

"Aye," Breanna said, "The Dreadlord has made a pact with the old Fomorian God Tethra to set his water demons after me. Yet they shun daylight, so we must make haste."

After the first group was in place, Mahon signaled for his men to ready their pikes and form a line on the right side of the wide path; the mounted warriors took the left.

Breanna commanded her band, "Braoin, ready your bow with me, and you three, ready your swords. Let's ride."

As Mahon's warriors marched double time down the narrow road, the band nudged their mounts into a trot, keeping pace. When they burst into the cleared flat of land along the river's edge, Corbmac and his *fian* emerged behind the riders and split up to either side of them, his men thumping their pikes on their shields and taking up the chant, "Bre, Bre, Bre! Bre, Bre, Bre!"

When they broke through the tree cover, the raftsmen on the far side noted Mahon and the riders. The pair started to pull their sturdy raft across using a massive rope tied to a similar oak on the other side. The swift current tugged at the collection of lashed logs as if hoping to pull it downstream, but Mahon waved off the older man and his son, as he did not want them entangled in a possible battle just yet.

Breanna's Band stood ready, facing west with a wall of pikes guarding them. A swarm of white-haired warriors emerged from the woodlands west of their position, all mounted on warhorses. The Dreadlord sat between them on his big black steed, with one Dreadrider to each side. On Corbmac's previous order, his other *fian* moved when they saw the Norvegrs emerge from the woods, flowing from the forest nearly simultaneously, forming a shield wall and lowering their pikes toward their enemy's backs.

When Breanna saw Hakon, her first thought was to goad Lang. She said to Braoin, "Nock and seize the *void*. I think we are about to take down a Dreadrider."

Once the bows were ready, she yelled to the warrior she had wounded twice, "Lang, are you ready to die like your brother?"

When the brash Dreadrider heeled his mount forward around the Dreadlord's front line, Breanna whispered to her half-brother, "Loose."

Two arrows flew true, one taking Lang in his good shoulder and the other high in his thigh, knocking him from his horse.

"Stand down!" the Dreadlord commanded in a tone that brooked no room for exceptions. His warriors froze, along with everyone else. Then he said, "Breanna Ban Morna, I see you have me outnumbered, but I have your cousin, Toal Mac Kyras. Put up your weapons, or he dies!"

Breanna turned toward the voice that had echoed in her mind since their first meeting. She saw Toal sitting behind one of her father's mounted warriors. Groaning, she slung her bow on her saddle's horn and slid off Eimar, pulling *Lann Dàn* from her sheaths, their blades glowing brightly with *Maorgairme*, and strode to the iron wall the *fians* presented. Their muscle would not help her without *Lia Dàn*. Yet the Stone of Destiny lay far beyond her reach. Knowing she needed to stall, she spat, "Didn't have the guts to face me yourself, did you, Father? Had to hide behind a boy?"

"I know better than to be goaded by you, child," Hakon said as he dismounted. "Jotun, see to my fool of a Dreadrider."

Breanna looked around to assess possibilities, but there were few, especially with the river to her left. With three *fians* backing them, the odds were clearly on their side if it came to a full-out battle, but Toal's life hung in the balance. As the sun slid toward the horizon, she looked again for options, as she did not like the idea of being near such a large body of water. Time was running against her.

Given this, she tapped the shoulders of two *fian* warriors to open a hole for her in their shield and pike wall. Eoin, Fergal, and her half-brothers dismounted to follow, swords still in their hands.

The Dreadlord walked toward her with another warrior leading his big warhorse, though she could not read his carefully guarded face. When she raised her blades, he stopped ten paces away from her. His sword remained sheathed, and his tone was neutral as he held up a hand. "Hold, I would bargain with you, daughter, not battle."

"You expect me to trust a *dubhchaile*?"

"Nei, just listen to one," the Dreadlord commanded, ignoring her insult. He signaled an older woman with his hand, one Breanna recognized as his völva, to join him. She knelt beside the wounded Dreadrider, tending to his wounds. Once the Norvegr named Jotun had helped Lang limp away, she rose and moved to Hakon's side.

Hakon continued, "I know you have a *geas* that makes you seek my destruction, and such a course can only lead to one of our deaths. It is a fate that is not cast in stone, Breanna. I will let your friends return to Dun Arrogh if you allow me to show you that I am not the monster you think I am. I will even give you Dun Arrogh, with no tribute due as long as you live.

"As for you, Runa has agreed to try to show you the nature of your *geas*. Remember, I said that understanding *what* drives you can help you understand *why* it drives you. Let her help you understand your *geas*, and then together, we can make Dun Garm into a place other Chiefs and even the High King will envy."

Croí Dàn infused Breanna with courage, saying derisively, *"He is an arrogant arse, isn't he? I can see why you hate him."*

Breanna smiled at her Heart's commentary and turned to Eoin, but he could do no more than a shrug. It was something she would have to decide. Looking past her father, she saw that Toal still sat behind Hakon's warrior, trying vainly to avoid her gaze. She demanded, "Let me talk to the boy."

Hakon frowned, and Breanna was sure he had not liked that she had diverted him. Yet she saw her father wave to his man, who rode toward them. Breanna took in her cousin, who had his head hanging in shame.

As the horse stopped before her, he said, "Sorry, Bre."

Breanna looked him over, noting the black eye. "What happened?"

"I made it to the woods that night you rescued Eoin, but I ran into a tree trunk that knocked me senseless," Toal answered. "The Dreadlord's men caught me in the morning."

"I surmised that much," Breanna said tartly. "I was referring to your eye."

"Oh, that," Toal said with a bright smile. "First, my arrows flew true, wounding several, and then I tried to escape. One of them didn't like it."

Breanna turned to her father, her expression narrowing. "This is how you treat my Gaels, the ones you hold hostage. I've seen them at my dun and yours. You are cruel, a man shaped by your hate. You survive in my land, but you don't love it. You love nothing but yourself. A cruel man is not something I can abide by, so having you escort me to Dun Garm is out of the question. And I have numbers on my side."

Breanna noted Hakon's face had darkened, and she knew she was testing his temper as she added, "I see you don't like someone so young, especially a woman, defying you. For some reason, you think I can help you rule this land. You think your Runa can stand up against my gods?"

Hakon rejoined, "I was not with the boy when Gern hit him. It is not something I would condone, but my warriors can be single-minded. Still, as a token to show you I am not a total ogre, the boy can go free. Maybe that will change your mind. Yet know I cannot let you reach the top of Croghan Hill."

She answered, "You can only try, Father."

Then Breanna watched the warrior named Gern turn his horse to circle his mount back to their line of warriors and hand Toal down to the warrior holding the reins of her father's horse. Then he dismounted and untied the lad's hands.

"Toal, come, stand behind Eoin," Breanna said. Her cousin did as she commanded, and Eoin gave him a friendly hug in welcome.

Toal said as he glanced warily over his shoulder at the river, "Thank you, cousin. But standing near rushing water while the sky is darkening, is it a wise action? Given, you know, what happened last time."

Breanna glanced at the water warily, looking for signs of the black otherworld things that had attacked them where the River Shannon entered Loch Aillionn. The water was swirling, making it difficult to distinguish between what was natural churn and what wasn't. "Good point."

Then she turned back to her father. "Thanks to you, Hakon, we must cut this little chat short, as I know you set Tethra's demons after—"

A massive black shape erupted from the river, holding a long black blade, and as Breanna whirled toward it, the demon lunged, its blade aimed directly at Toal's heart. Her cousin tried to twist aside, but the otherworld sword ripped into his chest.

"Toal!" cried Breanna as she dove at the demon. Her long blades glowed white-hot as they sank into the shimmering ebony form. The thing exploded in a shower of muck, but she was too late—the demon's black sword lay buried in Toal's right lung. Breanna turned back to her cousin, and he looked up at her with an expression that held both surprise and shock; he was not ready to die.

The world around Breanna faded for a moment, and she saw herself standing next to a young boy who danced with glee through the green meadows surrounding Dun Arrogh, a young boy who had faith in her ability to stop the Dreadlord only because she said she could make it so. And then the burly smith, who was his father, appeared over her, and she was promising to protect Kyras's son and keep him from harm.

Blood welled around the black sword, and a spasm made Toal cough up more, bringing Breanna's attention back to her cousin. She had failed them both.

Toal sputtered, "I thought I saw something in the water. I should have guessed. Stop him, Bre, stop the Dreadlord!"

With that, his eyes glazed, and his *anam* fled his body.

Breanna turned to her father, screaming, "You planned this all along! You want us all dead, but could not dare to do it yourself! Curse you!"

"No!" Hakon bellowed back.

Yet there was no time for more words as nearly a dozen more demons sprang from the water. Breanna cut down the one closest to her and jumped over its dissolving body to take on the next. One of her blades briefly locked with an otherworld black sword, but she spun clear and drove in with her other. The thing howled as *balefire* ripped into it and exploded into a mist like its brethren. She wanted to yell at Eoin, Fergal, and her half-brothers to run, but ten more demons replaced the two she had just killed. Fortunately, she remembered Lugh's advice and commanded the Blades of Destiny to let their *balefire* flow, to arc across them.

As some of their horses fled up the path, her Chief, his cousin, and half-brothers raised their iron blades to fend off the black swords flicking around them. However, they found that their counterstrikes did not stop or even slow the demons.

Seeing her mount at her side with front hooves raised, Breanna commanded Eimar to withdraw from the battle. *"These are demons that you cannot damage!"*

"No!"

Breanna screamed mentally, *"I command it!"*

Eimar whinnied but withdrew, following the other mounts back to the path away from the river.

Hakon

Hakon, once more mounted, was surrounded by his men, who formed a semi-circle before him to keep the strange demon attackers from flanking them. Their horses were jittery in the presence of such creatures. The Norvegrs found their blades could do no better than the Gaels' as they sank them into the black otherworld flesh without inflicting any damage, so they withdrew closer to the woods.

Hakon watched Breanna take the point with her magical blades, cutting off the legs and arms of Tethra's demons and burying her Blades of Destiny in anything near her. Each time she did so, the Tuatha magic would erupt with white-hot flares of fire that spelled death. When the demons hesitated under her relentless assault, he saw that Breanna had pushed them back nearly to the river's edge.

Hakon realized that she stood over Toal's broken body, the black sword that had taken his life still buried in his chest. She wrenched it free and hurled the otherworld blade into the water. Whirling back, she screamed at him, "You will die for this, my father! I will erase your stain from my land."

Then he saw the River Life was churning with demons again, and at the center was a much larger one than the others of Tethra's spawn. Runa said, "It can be none other than Balor of the Baleful Eye himself."

The great misshapen demon and one-time king of the Fomorians rose from the water and made for the riverbank.

Breanna

Breanna stepped back, nearly tripping over Toal, as she took in the demon that once had been Lugh's grandfather. Having watched Balor and the Sun God battle, she knew she was in trouble. Once more, he held his great black blade, but now there were no gods to stop him.

Her heart grew cold. Her cousin had always loved her unquestioningly, believed in her, and trusted she would keep him safe. While she had failed him in life, she was suddenly determined not to do that same thing in death. Those who opposed her would die for what they had done! Starting with Balor of the Baleful Eye seemed as good a choice as any. Then would come her father.

"Bre, run!" Eoin called, but she ignored him. It was not the time to run—it was time to kill or be killed!

As Fomorian demons regained their courage and renewed their attack, Breanna let her rage pour into the Blades of Destiny, and its *balefire* swept across them. They died by tens, then twenties, and maybe more before Balor strode from the river. Looking for weaknesses, Breanna took a step back. Tethra's head demon was twice as tall as she was and several times wider. That made his reach much more significant, leaving only agility and her opponent's arrogance in her favor. There would be little room for error with what she had in mind; for once, she was within his reach, and one of them would not escape their fate.

Breanna let Balor close to within three steps. With her sense of the *void*, she ducked the black blade that swept toward her head, then surged up to ram her magical blades into his stomach and push them into his dark demon heart, driving them as deep as she could through his cold black hide.

Tuatha *balefire* surged through *Lann Dàn*, augmented by *Croí Dàn* and her rage, and that staggered the demon-king as his great chest exploded in a shower of stinking muck that knocked Breanna backward several yards. She landed on her back with a thump that had left her momentarily breathless. Then she scrambled to her feet, her blades held before her.

A muffled groan rumbled from Balor's mouth, yet he did not fall. Around him, his horde of demons faltered in their attack. The once great Fomorian king growled, "Impudent one, it is time to die."

Despite the gaping hole in his midsection, he somehow managed to hold onto his massive, shimmering black blade. He let it swing straight down this time. Breana had foreseen his move in the *void*, and she noted that he expected to cleave her in two. Dazed by the Tuatha blast of magic she had previously released, Breanna barely managed to spin aside. As Balor's dark sword buried itself in the soft earth, he nearly lost his balance.

Breanna used the opening to drive one of *Lann Dàn's* blades into his empty black eye socket, the same one that Lugh had put out with his sling when the Sun God ended his grandsire's human life a millennium before. The Tuatha *balefire* erupted again, and once more, *Croí Dàn* enhanced the impact of the blade. Her Heart screamed, *"DIE!"* and Balor's head turned to vapor. He toppled to the ground at Breanna's feet. The otherworldly life the Fomorian god, Tethra, had given him ran out of him like water from a broken pot.

A great wail of pain passed through the host of Tethra's demons, and their attack wavered as it had when she killed nearly a hundred of their kind with sweeps of her *balefire*, but they did not give way completely. Eoin, Fergal, and her half-brothers made it to Breanna's side. Their faces were a study in grimness as they fought valiantly but ineffectively. Her Chief cursed as his blade sank uselessly into the black shapes that assailed them. Yet Breanna retaliated, and *balefire* flowed in great arcs to protect her Chief.

A motion along the forest line caught Breanna's eye, and she saw Hakon and his band retreat into the woods west of the path leading away from the ferry crossing, clearly waiting to see what would happen next.

In a voice edged with barely contained panic, Eoin called to Breanna, "What now? Tethra's demons are still before us!"

Breanna did not answer, for she was looking across the river where the air had coalesced into a fireball. As it moved toward them, waves of heat rolled from the growing apparition, and roaring wind assailed them. The flames grew and elongated until a face formed within, possessing a gruesome expression and eyes that promised death to those who dared gaze too long.

Then, a rough human shape with a grotesquely enlarged head emerged from the swirling black doorway and stepped onto the riverbank. Breanna watched in horror as it could be none other than Fomorian god Tethra who stepped onto the wet grassy bank, fire springing beneath the god's feet regardless of the dampness. He stomped toward Breanna, leaving blackened stains on the ground behind him. With each pace, he grew taller and taller, his towering form quickly surpassing that of his now-fallen head demon. Breanna knew Tethra had come for her because of her father!

Breanna watched the inhuman apparition approach, somehow knowing his touch would spell her death. His followers gathered around the old god, pressing forward. Seeing she was doomed, Breanna held her hand aloft and cried to *Maorgairme*, "Danu, Danu, Danu! Save us!"

Tethra spun about as the Mother Goddess's name rang through the air. The crystal ring flared to life, and the River Life seemed to shudder. Then, the pointed prow of a tremendous luminescent green ship emerged from the water. A single mast came next, and once the stern cleared the waterline, the hull crashed onto the river's surface. It was a sleek craft with few adornments, made for speed. River water sparkled along the sheets, pouring from the mainsail and deck. At the helm stood a tall man dressed in a green seagrass cloak.

A headband of gold was set upon his brow, and strapped to his waist were two short swords. In his hand lay an even longer blade. The shimmering green weapon appeared as if formed from a single emerald gem, yet it was a magical illusion, as the Tuatha steel glowed with power. Around the tall man gathered a host of similarly dressed men with elfish features, and they poured over the ship's low-slung gunwales and began to drive their strange green blades into the Fomorian god's demons.

The Sea God bellowed, "It has been a long time since Answerer has had a chance to drink your black blood, Tethra! Shall we let our blades dance together, my *Fragarach* against yours?"

In the Fomorian god's hand appeared a giant red sword, and he left Breanna behind without a thought as the two gods moved toward each other out on the water while their respective hosts did battle. Upon the surface of the River Life, the gods began their duel of magic and might, and each time their swords met, red and green lightning flew.

Fergal exclaimed, "You summoned Manannan Mac Llyr—our Sea God?"

"Aye, it does look like I did just that," Breanna said darkly. "And he needs our help!"

With that, Breanna threw herself into the fray of Tethra's demons and Manannan's seamen. *Lann Dàn* blazed with *balefire* as they sliced into the shimmering black demon flesh. She came upon one of the Sea God's men as he went down, hacking the dark blade from the demon's arm as it came cutting in. The thing howled as she drove her other long blade into its heart, the Tuatha power surging to cause an explosion of its gruesome innards. Eoin and Fergal were at her side, helping the seaman to his feet while Breanna moved on to another of Tethra's followers.

Eoin

"She has great courage. I'll say that for her," the sea-green merman said thankfully. Then he pulled four pieces of seaweed from his cloak and chanted something arcane. As they turned into green swords like his own, he added, "Use these sea blades instead of your iron. They will cut demon flesh—if you can call their black hides that."

With that, he was off, lost once more in battle. Eoin, Fergal, and Breanna's half-brothers sheathed the iron swords and turned in the direction Breanna had headed, cutting their way through the black shapes in their path. The green blades did not possess the white-hot lances of *Lann Dàn's balefire*, but they at least could mete out damage to Tethra's demons.

It was as fierce a battle as they had ever engaged. They all took slices and jabs but gave better than they got. In all the confusion, keeping close and protecting each other's backs was hard, but the practical, green-bladed weapons put them on the offensive as they rotated in the *void* as a four-pointed star and fought like never before. Their Gaelic warrior blood sang as they claimed their first demon heads—their first demon trophies, which turned to vapor.

Breanna

Meanwhile, Manannan Mac Llyr and Tethra battled on the surface of the River Life. The two gods were trading mighty blows, and Breanna, through the *void*, could see that this battle would end similarly to the one she had witnessed between the

Sun God and Balor of the Baleful Eye—a stalemate. Yet she had defeated Balor, and she was not ready to accept losing to the dark god, for while it had been one of Balor's demons who had taken Toal's life, all these dark ones owed their allegiance and existence to the Fomorian god. As with Balor, he was the one who must die.

She felt *Croí Dàn* directing her thoughts to the tales of the Sea God retold by their Bards in the evenings. Her Heart had her spinning toward Manannan Mac Llyr's ship, fighting her way there. What was it called? *Wave Sweeper*? And he always had two magical spears: one named Gáe Ruadh, Red Javelin, and the other Gáe Buide, Yellow Spear. Her Sea God had used each weapon in previous battles against the Fomorians in the distant past. They would surely be near the helm of his ship.

A demon crossed her path, surprising her, and his blade lashed across her hip as she tried to spin out of his attack. The sting it left behind was familiar, like a bad memory, and she couldn't help hissing as she used one blade for balance and let the other blade take the thing in its throat. As *Lann Dàn* connected, Breanna wondered if her blades had overreacted to her injury, for the flash of white-hot *balefire* was enough to turn the entire demon into vapor. Pressing a fist clutching a long blade to her hip, she moved on and tried to ignore the sticky wetness surrounding the wound.

Croí Dàn's power surged through her hand to heal the wound on her hip, saying, *"I am indeed working in tandem with Lann Dàn, enhancing its power through your rage."*

Breanna had no time to consider that as she approached Manannan's ship. She vaulted over the low railing onto the deck, quickly gathered her bearings, and headed aft, sheathing the Blades of Destiny as she went. As Breanna had hoped, two magical spears were in stanchions on either side of the helm, as they were in legends. Yet they would not come free when she tried to take them.

"*Maorgairme*, release the magic which holds these weapons," Breanna commanded. "I would taste the black blood of that god who is the source of my cousin's death!"

The ring flared, and the dual-pronged Red Javelin leaped into her left hand. Yellow Spear flew into her right. Breanna whirled and sprinted for the ship's prow, noting that the Sea God had his back to her as he battled with Tethra. "Manannan Mac Llyr," she cried, "I suggest you duck!"

Breanna Ban Morna seized the *void*, *Croí Dàn's* power surging through her muscles, and the longer Yellow Spear flew first. Then she let go of Red Javelin with a mighty hurl. Manannan Mac Llyr slid away at the right moment so the two spears could miss him and bury themselves in the Fomorian god's eye and heart.

Tethra roared as the Sea God rose, sending the gleaming green blade all knew as Answerer streaking toward his opponent's neck. A great gout of dark purple fire erupted from Tethra's stump, lighting the darkening sky. The Sea God seized *Gáe Buide* and flung the Fomorian god's head, his howling mouth still open, into the River Life. His demons shrieked in anguish, for they felt their god's pain and death.

Tethra's life spent itself in one last flare as Manannan ripped his magical dual-pronged spear *Gae Ruadh* from the dead god's heart. His misshapen body dissolved in the currents of the River Life; the otherworld life granted to his followers went with him. Their black bodies lost all form, and the foul-blooded demons became simple pools of muddy water.

Silence fell over the clearing around the ferry crossing. After a time, Manannan Mac Llyr turned to see Breanna standing at the prow of *Wave Sweeper* and proclaimed with a chuckle, "Lugh said you have grit, girl, and I must agree! You helped us remove two of our key enemies in one battle!"

Breanna only nodded and leaped from the ship's deck onto the riverbank, drawing her *Lann Dàn* as she landed in a crouch. There was one more foul foe to deal with.

 Eoin

Eoin stepped beside his Champion, his love, and said, "You spent all your magic in the battle. We will have to fight iron against iron, and while we might take most of them, good Gael lives will be lost. Believe in the magic of the *Triple Dàns,* and you will prevail better on that path than seeking vengeance now."

He nodded to where the Dreadlord stood at the edge of the woods. His men had arrayed themselves around him. While Hakon had only lost one warrior in the battle, his men remained outnumbered.

The Sea God was suddenly beside Breanna, saying softly, "Your Chief is right. I can work magic against those of the otherworld, but your father is yours to fight if you choose. Or you can take the course the Dark Goddess laid out for you. Only on that path can you give Toal Mac Kyras a chance to live again."

Breanna looked at the green-cloaked Manannan Mac Llyr and then back at her father. Eoin saw her expression, one as deep as the sea, knowing she was a pawn of their gods. Then she asked darkly, "Manannan, would you not fight at my side as I fought at Lugh's? You truly would let him take us—let his stain remain on our land—after what I've done? You would still be battling Tethra had I not cast Red Javelin and Yellow Spear into his heart and brain. And I slew Balor with *Lann Dàn!*"

Manannan nodded before he answered, "Aye, I probably would still be battling the foul one, and the Fomorian god might even have won the contest. But Danu made it clear that I cannot help you fight your father. My men will defend me, but we cannot aid you in battle with the Norvegrs."

Eoin demanded, "What have you done, and what is it with you and your Tuatha secrets?"

Manannan ignored her Chief, "I can help you fulfill your destiny, though. Board my *Wave Sweeper* and let the river take us to the Standing Stones. Go to Falias, seek out *Lia Dàn*, and return to Croghan Hill as Badb Catha commanded. Only by using the combined magic of the *Triple Dàns* and making the sacrifice the Dark Goddess spoke of will you truly end your father's reign of terror on Erin's Emerald Isle."

Breanna spat, her voice seething, "You're all manipulators."

When she suddenly froze, though, Eoin knew the Tuatha *sight* had taken her. Then Manannan raised a shield to encase the three of them, and Breanna felt as if he pulled them into the in-between. Surrounded by the shimmering green light, Eoin saw they were isolated. While he could not follow her into the *sight*, he was sure Breanna saw something else, maybe a land without the Dreadlord, where Toal walked the forests and meadows around Dun Arrogh without concern. For him, watching her cousin die had all but sealed her father's fate, and likely hers. This magic she had to wield was undoubtedly immense.

Eoin pleaded *Ćroí Dàn, "Help me bring her back!"*

The Heart of Destiny answered, *"Rest easy, she is safe."*

A moment later, Breanna lurched into motion, the Sea God dropped the shield, and the three reappeared.

Breanna turned to Toal's broken body and bent to pick him up. Tears streaming, she cradled him in her arms and said to her dead cousin, "I'll not leave you behind to be picked over by wild animals."

Then she turned her head to her father and, in a voice that held a deathly chill, said, "I vow to number your days. You can do nothing to stop me from erasing your stain from my land."

With that, Eoin watched her board *Wave Sweeper*.

After Eoin thanked Corbmac and Mahon for their help, he joined his Champion and the rest of her band, along with the Druids, on the ship. Manannan Mac Llyr summoned their mounts to the river's edge, and with a wave of his hand, he transported them onto the deck with his magic. With that action, he and his men flowed back aboard. When all was ready, his green glowing ship heeled over, turning to follow the River Life northeast. The sleek craft cut through the water without a wind to push it, as if some otherworldly storm drove the ship.

Into Falias

Runa

Runa watched how Breanna Ban Morna engaged the Fomorrian demons in battle, carefully searching for signs of new Tuatha magic at play, hoping to find some clue that would tell her about the Destroyer's plans. The *Lann Dàn* markedly possessed great power, seemingly only against the otherworld creatures and not living flesh. Then Tethra's Chief Demon entered the fray, giving his followers new life and courage.

Hakon and Thorvald were her shields as they all fell back toward the tree line. Runa took cover behind a tree, for the black shapes did not seem to know friend or foe, and she had no weapon. Balor of the Baleful Eye closed on the Dreadlord's bastard, but she slew him in two blows.

As the Fomorian god appeared, it brought a smug smile to Runa's face, and she told Hakon, "Your *dìolain* will not be able to stand against such a god! Now, do you see that she must die? That with the boy's death, she'll never trust you?"

The Dreadlord just nodded, unable to pull his eyes from the towering Tethra.

She added, "Breanna will undoubtedly fall to the likes of such a powerful god, and you can do nothing to stop it."

Without looking away, he said sourly, "I agree, Runa. Yet I know I have a place in this land. The Tuatha gods will fail. That said, I don't have to like losing such a fine warrior."

Runa glanced at him, surprised. Convinced Hakon had no concept of the powers in play around him, she turned to watch the Fomorian god finish her proclaimed Destroyer.

Instead of buckling, Breanna shouted her Mother Goddess's name thrice as she held a ring aloft. It was the same piece of Tuatha magic Runa had seen that night in Dun Garm. She had not understood its nature, yet now did—the Destroyer could summon major Tuatha gods when she was in great need. That must have been how Breanna had evaded Tethra's first attack with his demons.

Then Breanna Ban Morna cast two magical spears at the battling gods, and Manannan managed to turn aside and let the magical weapons bury themselves in Tethra's heart and eye. Then, the Sea God let his blade sweep off his nemesis's head. Could nothing stop her?

Hakon turned to her, asking, "Now what? Do we fight the seamen?"

Runa shook her head, raising her hand to withhold any action. Silence settled over the remaining warriors as if time stood still. If Manannan Mac Llyr had not acted by now, he likely could not have joined in the battle against mere mortals. And that made it the Gaels against the Dreadlord and his fighters.

Yet the Destroyer had somehow managed to have the odds stacked in her favor. It was still thirty-plus against their twenty-something.

She turned to listen to what the Sea God and her Jarl's bastard were discussing with her Chief, but they disappeared. Runa felt it was a magical barrier and reached for the *sight* to help her, using that unique space to hear what others around her could not. It was a talent that set her kind apart from her fellow humans, and Runa knew she would need every bit to save Hakon Skadi.

With hearing augmented by seizing the *sight*, Runa picked out some of Manannan Mac Llyr's words, confirming her suspicions that he could not assist the Destroyer in battle with her father. Then he said something about finding *Lia Dàn* and returning it to Croghan Hill. Only that way could Breanna hope to remove the Dreadlord's presence from Erin.

The *sight* told her that this would do more than impact her Jarl—it would remove them all from the Gaelic Isle of Erin! Then Hakon's daughter said as much in her own words. Nothing could stop her from eliminating the Dreadlord's stain from her land. If *Lann Dàn* meant Blades of Destiny, *Lia Dàn* could only be the Stone of Destiny. Surmising both pieces of magic were required, Runa reached deeper into the *sight*. And she was stunned by the portents it revealed to her.

As Hakon watched his daughter climb aboard the strange ship, Runa let go of the power that bridged the realms. "The Sea God is taking her to the Standing Stones and thus to the fairie underworld. Danu will give her *Lia Dàn*, the Stone of Destiny, and then she will bring it back with the *Lann Dàn* to Croghan Hill. She cannot reach the top of that hill; if she does, your daughter can remove your very being—and ours—from this land. And all you've worked for will disappear with you, including us."

"She can do what?"

"The Destroyer can make it so you never lived here."

"If I never lived here, neither did she—she would be killing herself."

"Aye, but I think it's a sacrifice she is ready to make."

Hakon was staggered. "Then, by Thor's hammer, we must stop her—my daughter must die!"

Runa smiled, and for the first time, she believed her Jarl had grasped the magnitude of the powers at hand. Whether Hakon had the grit—and the luck—to accomplish such a feat was uncertain. Runa advised, "We will not be able to stop her from reaching the fairie underworld, so that leaves us to stop her from taking the Tuatha magic to the top of Croghan Hill."

"Then we ride north at sunrise," Hakon ordered. "Until then, we must slip away from these Gael *fians* before they try to detain us."

# Eoin

Breanna stood near the pointed prow of *Wave Sweeper*. Eoin took in her taut form, outlined in the dark by the green glow of the ship, as a breeze washed over his face. At her feet lay her cousin's lifeless body. Manannan Mac Llyr commanded the helm with his seaweed cloak fluttering in the breeze; Fergal and her half-brothers stood beside him. At least, Eoin now understood Breanna's pursuit of Tuatha legends had been more than fanciful dreams. How the magic would help them, she had yet to say. Even though the magical green sea blades had been effective against the black demons, Eoin knew Breanna would need the magic of the *Triple Dàns* to fulfill her quest and seek her destiny.

Yet he now had other concerns, and they were rooted in the conversation he had overheard between Breanna and Manannan

Mac Llyr on the riverbank. Unsure how to address the Sea God, Eoin asked, "Manannan, what did you mean when you told Breanna she must make the sacrifice the Dark Goddess asked of her?"

The Sea God turned to Eoin and said, "It is for her to tell, not me. If she has not explained Badb Catha's plan to remove the Dreadlord's stain from our land, I will respect her reasons for keeping it to herself."

"It involves the Tuatha magic she has found and that which she is seeking, does it not?" Eoin probed as he searched the Sea God's green eyes.

Manannan Mac Llyr held firm. "That you must ask of Breanna Ban Morna, the chosen one of our Heart of Destiny and Erin's Hero."

The Sea God seemed proud to call her that name, and his eyes beamed as he gazed at her motionless figure at the prow of his ship. He added wistfully, "I wonder how many contenders Danu culled through to find her. One thing is clear. Lugh is right—she is a brilliant warrior. Not since the likes of the Hound of Ulaida, Maeve, and Macha Mong Ruad have we seen such talent in a Gael warrior."

Eoin heard *Croí Dàn* snort in Manannan's mind, *"She is much more, and you know it! My chosen one will achieve things no Hero has ever thought possible!"*

Manannan smiled at *Croí*'s feisty opinion and said to Breanna's Band, "Unlike myself, I see you all took a few cuts from Tethra's demons. Rub this salve in your wounds, or they'll fester."

After handing each of them a jar, the Sea God turned to speak with the two Druids, leaving the warriors to care for their wounds. Eoin carried a second jar to the prow. He took his place next to Breanna as *Wave Sweeper* glided through the night. He had no time to ponder how the Sea God guided his craft without wind or light, his mind filled with concern for the love of his life.

Breanna stood deathly still, lost in her grief. Earlier, when they had talked in the fading light on the riverbank, Eoin had noted her eyes held the same haunted look as the night Breanna first met the Dark Goddess. Now, Manannan claimed she must follow Badb Catha's path, one that Breanna was not forthcoming about. The notion of using magic wrought by Badb Catha made Eoin shudder, for the Dark Goddess always claimed something in return. And he had a sinking feeling that her price would be his love's life.

With hardly a whisper, Eoin said, "Manannan said to rub this into any wounds you might have taken. It will stop the festering, and we certainly don't need a repeat of your first illness from Tethra's ilk, the one that Fergal found you in. Especially not if we have to take this other piece of magic back to Croghan Hill."

Breanna finally looked at him, her grief spell broken. It was hard to see clearly, but Eoin was sure she had tears on her cheeks as he set his jar on the deck. Giving his love a chance to compose herself, he began checking himself, trying to recount the slashes he had taken in battle. There was a shallow one on his right hip, a deeper one beneath it, and a series of minor nicks on his left arm and hand. The salve was cool to the touch and erased the residual sting left by the black blades. Then, magically, the wounds faded as if the demons hadn't touched him.

Breanna bent, took a gob of the green salve, and applied it to a slice on her hip that her Heart had mostly healed.

Eoin said, "Here, let me help you with that."

Finding more gashes, nicks, and slices where Tethra's followers had gotten inside her defenses, he tenderly began working the ointment wherever he discovered them. When he finished salving each wound, he asked, "Bre, I must know what this magic you seek will do to the Dreadlord. And to you."

Breanna's eyes were water-rimmed as she said, "Not now, Eoin. Maybe once we reach Falias, I can speak of it. But not now."

As she looked down at Toal, Eoin said, "He shouldn't have died in that battle. It was a steep price to pay. Telling Kyras and Lissa will not be easy."

"Aye," Breanna choked out as they skimmed the surface of the River Life in silence.

Breanna

While Breanna had ended the lives of those directly responsible for her cousin's death, it was a bitter victory, as her father still lived. She could not bring Toal back to life. Not without forfeiting her own life to Badb Catha's dark magic. Thankful that Eoin did not press her with more questions, she fixed her gaze on the misty night before them.

Later, *Wave Sweeper* stopped along the southern riverbank. It was dark save for the moon's waning light that danced in and out of scattered clouds overhead. Manannan Mac Llyr pointed them south and said they would find the Standing Stone shortly if they marched in that direction. Then he said solemnly to Breanna, "You are fearsome, strong, and courageous, and I know you feel deeply about your clans, people, and land. I believe in you, my Hero. Stay strong!"

"Easy for you to say to one manipulated by her gods."

Manannan was unsure how to respond. "You might be right."

Breanna did not thank the Tuatha Sea God who had come to their rescue and just frowned as she turned away to carry Toal's body across a plank of wood that led to firm ground. A few moments later, *Wave Sweeper* slipped beneath the river's surface to return to *Tir fa Thon*, Manannan's realm beneath the waves.

With the Sea God and his seamen gone, Breanna and her band buried Toal on the rise overlooking the river. It was a good place. Yet she wondered if her gods cared about those who worshipped and died for them.

Croí Dàn said, *"My Hero, as I will save you, we will save Toal."*

"As you say, but I am bereft. I promised to keep Toal safe. I failed him, my aunt, and my uncle. I failed in my promise."

Then she called on *Maorgairme* and *Lann Dàn* for light and strode into the night, feeling Toal's death in her core. She cared not about the price Badh Catha demanded.

Breanna and her band soon climbed into the emerging foothills of the Wicklow Mountains. Her crystal ring guided them, dimming when they strayed off course. And true to Manannan's word, they found the Standing Stones within a span. Breanna, dead tired from the battle, dropped to her knees, using one of the Stones as a prop. She asked, "Should we enter now or in the morning?"

"I say now, for the Dreadlord may have been guided this way by his völva," Eoin advised, though he sank to his knees as well. "He may be here at any moment."

Fergal looked around in concern, so Breanna queried *Maorgairme*. She shook her head to say the ring did not expect her father.

Croí Dàn concurred, *"The ring on your finger is correct. There will be no pursuit until you have Lia Dàn in your hand. That said, there is something you must know. Not all of your band can join you in Falias: only two, only those whose clans have mixed with your clan's blood, as your blood unlocks the path. Only Eoin and Fergal. You must tell the rest to prepare to support you again when you return to the land of Erin. Pick a place to meet. I suggest you choose Dun Eadan, which is close to Croghan Hill."*

Breanna said, "My ring and the Heart say we are secure for tonight."

Bláth sighed. "Thank the gods for that. What a battle to witness. I hardly know how to craft a tale that would do justice to describing what happened. The feats of courage and skill. To see her Tuatha Gods' magic that was truly at work in our world. Something surely not seen in eons."

"Indeed," Maoilir interjected, "but we have made it here safely, ensuring Erin's Hero can continue her quest. It is not yet over."

Breanna agreed sourly, "Nay, it is not. And yet, there is more to tell, as *Croí Dàn* has informed me that only two others can join me in Falias. They will be Eoin and Fergal, as their clan has intermarried with my clan over generations, allowing them passage. The rest of you must be ready to support me when I return. You should go to Dun Eadan and wait for our arrival with the Stone of Destiny."

Braoin asked, "Will you not be in danger while traveling from these Standing Stones to the dun?"

Croí Dàn informed her, *"The stones are the only way in for humans, but not out of Falias."*

"The Tuatha gods will ensure my safe return," Breanna answered. "We should start a fire and share a meal and our friendship. Maybe Maoilir and Bláth can say the words to send Toal's *anam* on its way to the afterlife."

Maoilir said solemnly, "Of course, My Hero."

When Maioilr began the passage right, Bláth stepped in. "Given that I am closer to Breanna, I should invoke Toal's passage, Maoilir. Then the Bard led the ceremony, playing a mournful tune on her travel harp, ending with a chant for all to be whole. She said solemnly, "In the hush between heartbeat and sky, your *anam* slips the bonds of flesh and sails the misted path to the stars, delivered into Danu's moonlit arms. May the winds bear you gently, the sparks light your way, the waters remember your name, as the earth cradles your rest. We unbind you, unlacing the cords of time, and open the veil to the ever-turning *Cycle of Time*. As the *Cycle* spins you out, be whole once more."

The tradition of sending an *anam* included those who knew the passed soul, who cast a memory into the *Cycle of Time* so their loved one could find their way to their next life. Eoin and Fergal shared their memories, and then Breanna added, "I—I loved him like a little brother. He inspired me, full of life and light, when I was full of darkness and hate that my *geas* drove. His death burns in me. I will give my life if he can live again."

With that, the service ended, and Toal's *anam* was on its way.

When morning came, the band readied themselves for their separate journeys, where three would travel to the fairie realm, and the rest would head back north. Breanna's half-brothers approached her, and Braoin said, "Sister-mine, we did not get a chance to talk to you about yesterday's events. That battle was unbelievable, and you fought brilliantly. You showed all that you truly are, Erin's Hero. We want you to know we are sorry for the loss of your cousin."

Bradaigh added, "Know that we will stand with you against our mutual father when the time comes. You will not be alone. Stay safe and strong until we see you at Dun Eadan."

Then her two half-brothers hugged her, this time with genuine compassion, and she sighed. "Thank you, both. Braoin, please look after Eimar for me. Bradaigh, please do the same for Eoin and Fergal's mounts. We will need them when we return. I'll see you soon."

Eimar whickered, saying wistfully, *"I will miss you, my Hero."*

"I will miss you as well, my brave mare."

Then Breanna turned away, pulled *Lann Dàn* free from their sheaths, and rapped the butts of her hafts on an ancient Standing Stone. The diamond blades flared, and the hard surface turned suddenly transparent. Since she was already in motion for another rap, Breanna tumbled through the suddenly open doorway and down several steps.

Eoin hurried after her. "Bre! Bre, are you all right?"

"Aye," she sourly answered as he helped her up. "I just didn't expect the door to disappear like that. Damn slippery, this fairie magic is. Hand down our packs, Fergal."

With that done, Eoin bid farewell to those who were unable to join them. "Stay safe, all of you. We'll see you soon at Dun Eadan!"

Behind the three from Dun Arrogh, the door reappeared as solid stone, shutting out the natural light, and Breanna couldn't help rubbing her shoulder as she cursed the Tuatha for their tricky magic. Still grousing, she led the two warriors and followed a narrow passage into the heart of the Wicklow Mountains. *Maorgairme* was still needed to light the way, but it was not long before they passed through a glimmering veil. The rock cave ceiling vanished, and a lush world appeared—the fairie realm called *Tir na nÓg*. How plants grew in the strange greenish light was something Breanna could not fathom.

When they came upon several dozen elf-like individuals frolicking naked in a nearby pond, Breanna noted that the fairies all stopped to look at the strangers. Then, they gestured for the trio to move along in the same direction they had been heading. While Fergal was busy trying to catch a glimpse of the otherworldly women, Breanna seemed to be the only one to notice the lack of children. She commented, "While they seem happy, seeing no young is sad."

Eoin agreed. "Aye, it is. The Tuatha lost the ability to procreate during their war of magic with the Fomorians."

The three marched on, marveling at the fairie place they had entered. Giant oak tree trunks covered with ivy stretched into a sunless otherworld sky, and enormous ferns spread beneath them. A path led them into the ancient forest of old woods. Breanna couldn't help but sense that the trees were alive and had a power she did not understand. It felt like the *void*, yet it was sustaining, giving energy to the realm. The other odd thing was that she saw no animals or birds, and there was no wind. It created an unearthly silence—something Breanna found more than a little disconcerting.

She led Eoin and Fergal into a strange village that was more than a settlement, a great collection of huts, halls, and shops woven from the forest. Branches twisted and turned to form walls, windows, and doorways. Hundreds of Tuatha males and females were among the buildings, which featured elements similar to those they had seen in the pond. Many sat talking while others bartered or played little games invented to pass their endless time in the otherworld realm.

The Sun God, Lugh, strode toward the travelers from one of the living buildings. Breanna knew him immediately, even from such a distance, and it was not just from his shining golden breastplate and bright yellow cloak. Nor was it the long locks of hair that gleamed like they were rays of sunshine. It was something in his eyes, the way the others deferred to him.

Yet when he approached, Breanna showed no such deference. If he had once earned her respect, she had buried that when they buried Toal. She said flatly, "Lugh."

"I see you've brought friends," he responded carefully.

Breanna responded in the same dead tone, "Eoin, Fergal, meet the Sun God."

Eoin offered his arm in greeting, as did Fergal.

Lugh turned back to Breanna, saying more tenderly than she expected, "I cannot help but note the change in your demeanor. The bright young lass is gone. Yet know your loss is our loss. I saw the battle with Balor and Tethra through *Lia Dàn*, and Toal did not deserve to die that way. If I could have done anything to stop it, I would have. As it was, we were hard-pressed to keep my grandsire and his demons off your trail as long as we did. There were several times I was sure they had you trapped."

Breanna hesitated, taken off guard by the Sun God's tone and sorrow. Then she let her iron will assert itself again. "Nonetheless, Toal is still dead."

"Aye," Lugh acknowledged solemnly. "I see your loss lies heavy upon you, more so than your *geas* ever could. Yet, thanks to you, my grandsire went with him. You also helped defeat Tethra, a boon I had not foreseen. You certainly surprised Manannan when you cast his spears."

"It seemed a logical choice," Breanna offered tightly, still unswayed. She could not hide the bitterness in her voice when she added, "Especially since the Sea God didn't appear to be faring any better against Tethra than you did against Balor of the Baleful Eye in the previous battle we shared."

Lugh took the intended barb graciously. "I may have ended my grandsire's earthly life, but ending his otherworldly life was a challenge I had not solved. Your cunning was an approach I could never have used. Many of us who once ruled Erin are guilty of that same overconfidence.

"You used his ego to your advantage and will be honored among our people as his slayer. Balor of the Baleful Eye took thousands of my fellow Tuatha to their deaths, including many of my cousins. That is something he will never do again. Nor will the Fomorian god, Tethra."

"Honor is not something I seek," Breanna said sharply.

Finally seeming to tire of her ill temper, Lugh responded ominously, "Then seek your cousin's birth again. Only through Badb Catha's advice can you accomplish such a feat, using the magic of the *Triple Dàns*."

Breanna seethed. "You want darkness? Then you should know I can show you something far worse than anything you've seen, even from your ancestor, whom I killed, along with his Formorian god! Is that where you want to go?

"You know the cost your Dark Goddess is asking of me. Yet I see arrogance dancing in your eyes as if you think I will blankly accept it. Think again! Maybe I'll cast a future without you in it!"

Eoin asked, "What is going on? You two once fought together against Tethra's demons. Now, you're fighting like two barn cats, only with words. Yet I followed this exchange closely—you're hiding something about your cousin. Can Toal live once more? But how? His spirit has passed on to the otherworld."

Breanna looked at Eoin as if he had just come into existence.

Lugh stated, "So, Breanna has not told you."

All-Father flashed into their space, demanding, "Lugh, your time here is done. We will have words, but not now. You trifle with things beyond a mere warrior god's reach. While you may be Danu's favorite and fought with Breanna before, this one is mine!"

Breanna gaped at the huge man standing before her. "Dagda? Why are you here? And what do you mean that I'm yours?"

Eoin said, "Wait! What did Lugh mean that my Champion must sacrifice herself to end her father's reign in our Emerald Isle?"

"That is something only Breanna can tell you when she is ready," All-Father said.

"Damn you all!" Eoin spat. "What is this secret you and she share? Mannanan was equally cagey. And now All-Father is here defending you against this prick."

Breanna faced her Chief and explained flatly, "I can only end my father's life by using the *Triple Dàns* to change the destiny of our land and make Hakon Skadi no more."

"Make him what?"

"Make it so that he never existed in our land."

"But he's your father," Eoin protested. "If he never lived in Erin—"

"Then I never lived, never was born as a half-breed," Breanna finished for him, her tone bitter, and then she turned a dark eye to the Sun God. "You can get your arse out of my sight."

Then she turned to All-Father, saying, "Dagda, there is something about this place that has drained me. I'm tired and want to sleep. Show me to a bed. Lugh, you can go, well, lie in your shite."

Lugh nodded stiffly.

Dagda motioned for Breanna to follow him and, flicking his wrist as if banishing his brother god, casting him away in a flash. "I am sorry for Lugh's poor reaction to your killing of Balor's demon spirit. Doing that deed by himself has been his *geas* for a long time. Yet you did what he could not and helped our Sea God remove the Fomorian god Tethra from all realms."

The strain of Breanna's quest and battling warriors, demons, and gods had taken its toll. Losing her cousin had not helped her believe in any possible positive outcome for her people. "Just get me a bed!"

Eoin stammered something, but Breanna pretended she did not hear him as she walked with All-Father toward a dwelling.

Trailing behind her, Eoin growled to Fergal, ensuring Breanna could hear him, "My Champion's little more than an ìobairteach *uan*."

"Aye, who would have guessed they'd ask her to be a sacrificial lamb?" Fergal confirmed.

"The Dark Goddess demands a steep price, a fool's price," Eoin added. Even though he strode directly behind her, Breanna did not respond.

Dagda led them through a doorway of living tree branches covered with flowers, then through a garden with a babbling stream that emptied into a small pool. There were a few rock benches and endless varieties of flowers on either side of the rocky path that wended its way through the god's grove. Off to one side were several rooms constructed of twisted branches, like the wall that held the doorway. Each had a soft bed of lacy moss.

With a wave of his hand, All-Father somehow dimmed the ever-present greenish light that seemed to come from nowhere and everywhere. "Danu will want to see you once you've rested and bathed. I'll have new clothes set outside your doors."

Breanna knew his tone left no room for argument—whether she wanted to or not, she would be meeting with the Mother Goddess—but she had no energy to use her sharp tongue. Saying nothing more, she sought one of the rooms and a bed of moss.

She found the living cradle was softer than anything she had ever slept in, especially after shedding her dirty clothes. The supple grass-like surface caressed her skin, and with the hammock-like bed swaying slightly, she was soon dreaming about not being Hakon Skadi's daughter and having her cousin at her side once more.

Eoin

Eoin found his dreams elusive, though he was sure he had slept. As far as he knew, the strange nature of the fairie world was all an illusion, and he had never been awake. Then, there was the sound of water splashing.

Eoin had not remembered rising, but found himself standing in the doorway of his room. Before him lay the small pool of water, and Breanna was bathing herself.

Her white hair was already wet, plastered to her back like many strands of white silk, and her pale skin glistened in the strange light. Eoin had seen his love bathe more than a few times, but she had never looked more beautiful than at that moment. That he might lose her was not something he wanted to think about. Maybe they could pretend the Dreadlord and her *geas* were just dreams, nightmares. Perhaps even this was a dream.

Drawn to her, Eoin left his room behind. As he shed his clothes and slipped into the warm water, he discovered the pool was only a few feet deep at the edges and had a smooth stone bottom. He spread his legs before reaching out and pulling Breanna toward him. Keeping her back to him, she leaned into his muscular chest and let him wrap his arms around her, his hands holding each of her breasts. He leaned against the pool's edge and kissed one of Breanna's ears, nibbling on the lobe.

Eoin felt the heat of his loins press into the small of her back, bringing a little sigh from her. They lay like that for a long moment before Breanna turned her head and used a hand to pull his lips to hers. Twisting in Eoin's arms, Breanna kissed him a second time, this time more passionately. She rose and settled herself on him, smiling at him as he'd never seen before, and he melted back into the soft, mossy bank of the pool with her on top of him. It was a moment he had waited for his entire life. Then she was in his arms, and they let their passions overtake them—several times. A shudder passed through them of a love shared beyond their earthly time when they peaked together repeatedly.

When Breanna left him in the pool and returned to her room, Eoin Mac Cairbre felt they had forged something new between them. He was less convinced that he could talk her out of the madness of her quest to kill the Dreadlord with the Tuatha magic. But that could wait. For now, he just wanted to savor the sweet memories that washed over him.

Lying in the pool, Eoin drifted dreamily in the warm water. He woke later to find himself in the strange bed of moss again. His old clothes lay outside the door, and a new tunic and kilt were beside them. Rising, he noted he had not completed his bath, for some of the grime of battle with Tethra's demons still seemed to cling to his skin. He should have washed before making love to Breanna.

He stepped from his room to find his Champion in the pool again. Yet, as he watched her rub some strange leaves over her skin, he remembered that she had already bathed.

Confused, he asked, "One time in the pool was insufficient?"

Breanna turned, and there was a troubled frown on her face. Then she crossed her arms over her chest and, with flushed cheeks, said, "Cover yourself."

Eoin smiled. "It would be difficult to bathe in clothes."

Seeing he was about to step in, Breanna squeaked, "Give me a moment, will you? I'm not finished yet with the pool!"

"I'd rather join you."

"Eoin, we've gone over this before," Breanna snapped. "And now that we've discovered the nature of the Dark Goddess's magic, it's all the more reason to put aside our feelings for each other. I won't be alive for you to love—you won't even remember I ever existed."

It was Eoin's turn to frown. "But what about last night?"

A hint of recognition crossed Breanna's face. Then she shook her head. "Last night?"

"Aye, when we made love last night, again and again."

Breanna sank into the water and whispered, "Made what?"

"Are you denying it?"

She stammered something about dreams before saying, "This place is playing tricks on our—on your mind. Now, I must meet with the Mother Goddess. *Lia Dàn* is needed to complete Badb Catha's destiny-shaping magic of the *Triple Dàns*, and Danu must give it to me if I am to fulfill my destiny and remove any trace of my father's existence in our realm."

Eoin stood stiffly when Breanna rose from the pool and strode past him. He watched Breanna flee into her room, taking the love they shared with her. Their conflicted relationship was complicated at best. Yet he knew she was under pressures he could not understand, especially those she hid from him.

❧ Breanna ❧

Breanna picked up her new clothes and reentered her room without looking back, then promptly sagged onto her bed, mortified that Eoin had shared the same dream. It was a dream that they had not just made love, but passionate love. And more than once.

While Eoin did not seem to think it was a dream, it had been so easy for her to slip into a world where Breanna's father did not exist, where her *geas* did not rule her every move. Now, Eoin would pursue her like never before, for she had acknowledged her love for him, if only in a dream they both had shared.

Or had it truly happened? The line between what was real and what was not in the fairie world was undoubtedly blurred. It seemed like time itself was twisting her mind. Yet her body told her otherwise, as her nether region was a bit tender. Breanna heard Eoin enter the pool and wondered what he was thinking. Trying to focus on something else, she took her time donning her clothes and was thankful that Eoin had returned to his room when she finally decided to seek the Mother Goddess.

Croí Dàn said, with emotion and tenderness she had not yet used, *"Before you seek out Danu, know that last night was not a dream. I understand you love Eoin, that he loves you, and that what you share can stretch beyond time if you believe in your mutual love. And both of you love your land and its people. Otherwise, you would not have pursued such a quest against such odds this far. Yet you have because there is love in you, for your man, for your kin, and for your land. And your land and its people already love you. So, ask the gods a different question. Ask how you can be mine forever."*

Breanna pondered, *"Is that possible?"*

"All things are possible, my Hero. Just believe!"

Breanna questioned Badb Catha's claim that she must make a sacrifice as she set off with *Lann Dàn* harnessed to her back. The doorway Dagda had led them through earlier loomed before her.

She stumbled into a slender-built man with piercing green eyes. As the two untangled themselves, Breanna asked, "Can you direct me to the Mother Goddess?"

"Aye," the man said. As Breanna took in his handsome features, he added, "Danu said you would be asking after her. I am Cairpre, Chief Bard of the *Tuatha Dé Danann*."

Surprised by his deep, melodious voice, she answered, "I am Breanna Ban Morna."

Cairpre smiled broadly. "I know—we all know—who you are. And that Erin will become whatever you hold in your vision when you wield the power of the *Triple Dàns*."

"That's great, just great," Breanna muttered sarcastically. "What do I know about our land?"

The Bard shrugged and motioned for her to follow. She wanted to protest, but Cairpre's disarming nature made it hard to be cantankerous. His face seemed a mix of warrior and poet, showing he knew the glory and pain of battle. There was a spring in his step as he led her down the main street of Falias.

More of the odd branch buildings lay to either side, and some of the Tuatha folk who had once claimed Erin as their own lingered about their doorways. Those who had been conversing stopped as Breanna passed. A hushed silence followed her wake, as if she were a boat, and the waves made by her passing washed her words away.

Breanna did not like how they stared after her, how their green and blue eyes followed her. Even those playing games or bartering with their neighbors turned to watch her as she passed. It seemed that they all knew of her quest and her *geas*.

Cairpre, as if sensing her uneasiness, asked hurriedly, "Did Badb Catha tell you about the *Well of Segais*? Before you bring *Lia Dàn* to Croghan Hill, if you go to where you met her and dip it into the *Well*, the stone will give you a vision of Inis Fáil—what you call Erin—as it is today. You must change that vision when you touch the Stone with Lugh's Blades, for that picture will only be cast when you do so. And *Croí Dàn* will ensure that vision reaches across Erin's entire length and breadth."

"Aye, she told me that, but I don't know what the land was like before Hakon Skadi."

"Then you must call on Dagda or Danu to show you the land as it was," Cairpre advised. "Only All-Father or the Mother Goddess can give you a vision of your land before the Dreadlord came there. If he is on Inis Fáil soil when you do this, Hakon and his ilk will be no more. It will be as if they had never come across the sea, as if Hakon had never existed in Erin."

"You know he is my father," Breanna countered, catching his eyes. "And that means if I do what Badb Catha commands and make it so he never came to Erin, I will never have been born. She demanded that I make a sacrifice. Knowing that my father will not suffer for what he has done to my land is a bitter pill while my fate hangs in the balance."

"I cannot say for certain what your fate will be," Cairpre honestly said as he held her gaze. "Only Badb, Dagda, or Danu can fathom what will happen, and I think even they may not be sure, as no one has ever wielded the magic of the *Triple Dàns.*"

The Bard stopped at another doorway formed from branches and motioned for her to enter. Breanna found a garden similar to the one they had spent the night in, with the main difference being a small, round crystal sitting on a white stone pillar at the garden's center. Though she could not read the white Ogham letters inscribed on the stand, she knew it had to be *Lia Dàn*.

The Mother Goddess stood behind the Stone of Destiny, but was not dressed as the Silver Huntress this time; instead, a simple white gown was draped about her. As she approached the goddess, Breanna noted that Danu had split her attention between her guest and the stone that held Erin's many possible futures.

"As Badb Catha commanded, I am here for *Lia Dàn*."

Danu responded with an arched eyebrow. "Then take it."

"Just like that? No words of wisdom, no advice?"

"Just like that," the Mother Goddess answered. "You know what you must do. If you fail, your land will fail, as will we. If you succeed, you will remove Hakon Skadi's presence in Erin and restore all who suffered at his hand."

"Including Toal?"

"Aye," Danu confirmed.

"And what of me?"

"As the Badb Catha said, sometimes one must make sacrifices."

Breanna was not surprised by the answer—disappointed, but not surprised. Snatching up the Stone of Destiny, she said bitterly, "Your Bard insisted I ask you to show me a vision of what Erin was like before the Dreadlord came to our shores. Or would you prefer that I create a vision of my own, perhaps one in which we worship a different pantheon of gods? Maybe those of Asgard?”

Danu eyed her critically. “You learn quickly. And as usual, Cairpre is right. Look deeply into *Lia Dàn* to find what you seek.”

Croí Dàn said inside both of their minds, *“I will help My Hero, and so will you, Mother. I will not accept any other response. I heard Badb Catha’s words while my Hero was at the Well of Segias, and I say she is wrong!”*

Danu shook her head. *“Then you and your Hero must seek All-Father. Dagda can help her understand the love needed to rewrite our timeline and yours. Maybe even one with you both in it.”*

Breanna let her gaze drift down to the Stone of Destiny in her hand. Within its depths, clouds swirled, slowly parting to reveal Erin’s length and breadth. Then Breanna let the *sight* pull her into the otherworld existence of *Lia Dàn*, and it focused on the heart of her land, the hills, valleys, and lakes where Breanna lived. It showed various duns alive with activity and children.

Nowhere did she see the Dreadlord or his kind. Nowhere did she see the broken-down lives and duns surrounding Dun Garm. Nowhere did she see *daor aicme* serving her father. Could it be that simple? When the world lurched into motion again, Danu was gone, and Breanna was alone.

Croí Dàn informed her chosen one, *“I will call Dagda as Danu suggested.”*

⟞⟊ Corbmac ⟊⟝

Late in the day, Corbmac watched Maoilir and Bláth ride into the courtyard of Dun Uisneach with Braoin and Bradaigh. He hailed them. “I take it Breanna made it to the Standing Stones?”

“Aye,” the Bard answered as she smoothly slipped off her mount and handed her reins to a stable boy; the two white-haired lads joined her, handing off their mounts and those now in Falias. "It's been three days since she, Eoin, and Fergal entered the fairie realm. We four were not permitted to join her in *Tir na nÓg*, but we know what comes next for Erin's Hero. She will return to Dun Eadan using Tuatha magic, but we do not know when. It appears the gods can return them anywhere they want."

As Maoilir dismounted more gingerly and with Braoin's help, the Druid inquired, "And what of the Dreadlord?"

Corbmac replied, "He and his Norvegrs stopped at Croghan Hill as expected. I have the River Brosna settlement *fian* watching them, as my men needed reprovisioning."

"This is not good," Bláth stated. "Hakon must know through his völva that is the destination of Erin's Hero."

"Indeed," Maoilir agreed. "We must ride to Dun Eadan at first light. I assume your *fians* will be ready?"

Corbmac motioned toward the main hall. "Let's talk further while we have dinner. I assume you're tired of travel rations."

"Indeed!" confirmed Bradaigh. "Though we did manage a few good dinners along the way."

After they commandeered a table, Corbmac waved over a few servers for ale, mead, and trenchers for their meal. He said, "As to your question, Maoilir, I had hoped to give my men another day of rest. Yet I sense that is unlikely. We need to discuss this with our Chief and Chieftess. Once we finish here, you both had better clean up and get some rest. I'll send word once Keegan tells me when Fáolan and Falyn are ready for us."

Later in the evening, the meeting with Dun Uisneach's leaders was short and to the point. Corbmac was to lead his two *fians* east in the morning, then collect the *fian* from the River Brosna settlement that had been keeping an eye on Croghan Hill, and do the same with one from Dun Eadan. Four *fians*, plus Breanna's blooded warriors, should hopefully be enough to win the day. Four blooded warriors at the dun would join them, one for each *fian*, to repel any Norverg who broke through the *fian* shield wall with his sword.

For Corbmac, rousting himself out of his bed the following day was more straightforward than rousting his *fians*. Still, he was their leader, and they had little choice when he commanded their band to move. Only the oldest of his long-time group, a man named Ruaidri Mac Ciarán, a few years his senior, took the inconvenience in stride. He asserted to his commander as he checked his weapons and rations, "Listening to *Aos Dána's* advice has gotten me to a ripe age, something few warriors can claim. If they say we should jump, then we should."

"Aye," Corbmac agreed, though he was not entirely convinced. The younger ones around him grumbled about having to rise at such a span as they tended to their travel packs. Ruaidri, who had already finished with that chore, turned to get the stablehands, helping them ready mounts for their *Aos Dána*, Breanna's two half-brothers, and those required to pull his commander's chariot.

"Does anyone know where we are taking the Druids?"

Corbmac turned to the young warrior who had asked, a fair-headed fellow named Mogue, whose mother was from Albion's coast. "East, to Dun Eadan, and then likely to Croghan Hill once Breanna returns."

Ruaidri replied, "Ah, then we will need to bring her mount, as well as Eoin's and Fergal's."

"And my mount as well, as the chariot will slow us down."

The Fáidh and Filidh arrived shortly after that with Braoin and Bradaigh. Corbmac commanded the guard to open the gates a moment later, and they rode out with the additional four warriors with gold arm rings. Once on the far side of the River Brosna, the Druids wanted to press on, but Corbmac insisted on a break. Though they said nothing, the Druids were not pleased.

Corbmac strolled to where Maoilir and Bláth stood. "Best eat now," he said, knowing his men were doing just that, "just in case there's trouble ahead."

"Why should there be trouble ahead?" Bláth asked, her expression concerned.

"Maybe it's because Hakon and his warriors have surrounded Croghan Hill?" Maoilir questioned.

Corbmac answered, "Indeed."

Maoilir went still as the *sight* took him. He shook his head a moment later and added, "Well, that was interesting. Never had direct communication with All-Father."

"Dagda?" Bláth queried.

"Aye," the Fáidh answered. "We are to make sure our *fians* are at the disposal of Erin's Hero and be ready to meet her at Dun Eadan as soon as possible."

"Good thing we have Corbmac and his *fians* en route already, then," Bláth said dryly.

Corbmac just rolled his eyes.

Eoin

With his mouth hanging open, Eoin could do no more than watch his love walk through the branch-formed doorway of her room. She had essentially denied making love to him! Had it been a dream? The passion of her kisses the night before made it hard to believe. Yet Breanna had evaded the matter. He wondered if her *geas* had driven all ability to love from her. Needing to compose himself and get his mind on something else, he slipped quickly into the pool and began scrubbing himself with the strange leaves that seemed to mimic soap in their land.

After bathing, he returned to his room, though he could not get Breanna out of his mind. And it was not just their recent passionate encounter—it was the fact that she was about to claim the Stone of Destiny from the Mother Goddess, and by possessing *Lia Dàn*, his Champion had the power to fulfill her *geas* and end her own life along with her father's. And he was helping her accomplish that goal!

Sometime later, he heard water splashing in the pool again, but a glance out an open window revealed it was only Fergal. That meant Breanna had already left to seek Danu. Needing to talk with someone—even if it was his testy cousin—Eoin dressed and left his room behind. Fergal lay in the pool with his eyes closed, occasionally splashing the warm water over himself.

Eoin strolled to the edge. "Strange place."

"Aye," Fergal agreed without looking up. "Never thought any stories about the Tuatha and their magic and underworld realm were real. Even after seeing Breanna help kill that Fomorian god and riding on *Wave Sweeper* with Manannan Mac Llyr, I often wonder if this is a dream."

"Dreams," Eoin muttered bitterly. "I don't think so. Breanna's gone to claim the *Lia Dàn* from the Mother Goddess. That means she will be able to sacrifice herself for this cause."

"And your problem is that you can't stop her," Fergal intuited.

"Exactly."

"Eoin, seldom have we seen eye to eye where your Champion is concerned, but I was wrong," Fergal offered as he rose from the pool. Putting a hand on Eoin's shoulder, he added, "Now that I've witnessed her battling demons and gods for our cause, I know she must fulfill her *geas*. And though you may love her, in your heart, you know you cannot try to stop her. Not if our land is to be free again."

Eoin nodded as tears ran down his cheeks. "I know."

Fergal left him to grab some fresh clothes so he could cover himself. Returning, he asked as he slipped on a tunic, "What is next?"

"I truly do not know."

—✶⟐ Fergal ⟐✶—

Moments later, Fergal saw someone standing in the doorway to their garden. A second look revealed a woman of stunning beauty. Fergal hardly noted that she was holding a tray full of food—he only saw that she had locked her green eyes on his. Her glimmering dress did little to hide the curves of her lithe body, and her hair glistened like it was composed of a thousand tiny rubies.

Eoin cleared his throat. "Cousin, finish dressing."

Fergal looked down and quickly positioned the white kilt at his feet over his growing manhood.

Eoin chucked at his cousin's discomfiture. "Thank you, my lady. Or my Goddess, as we are unfamiliar with your ways."

She turned away from Fergal and said to Eoin, "I am Sinéidin. Formalities are not needed. Please eat."

Fergal caught himself staring at her, at the arch of high eyebrows that matched her hair. Her thin nose turned up slightly at the end, and her lips parted when she smiled. And then there was the way her ears crested in a soft point, how she tucked her glimmering red hair behind them. Realizing he had not introduced himself, he said abruptly, "I am Fergal Mac Conall. And thank you for the food. Would there be ale in this place?"

Sinéidin chuckled as he reached for a piece of dark bread and cheese. She answered shyly, "Nay, but can I offer ye mead? Honey is easier to gather here than barley, you know."

Fergal frowned. "That may be, but Gael men drink ale."

The Tuatha woman shrugged, and Fergal saw a challenging grin dance in her gaze.

"Then set your tray down and show me to the mead," he demanded.

With a sparkling smile, Sinéidin handed the platter of food to Eoin, took Fergal by the hand, and pulled him away. As they left, his cousin snatched a piece of fruit with a mischievous wink.

Eoin

Eoin couldn't help being a little jealous of his cousin, even if he knew there was no more than a physical attraction between the pair. He would have accepted it from Breanna, but she denied him even that, saying any such notions were just a dream.

Then, Breanna was standing in the doorway to their secluded grove. A small round stone lay in her hand, and she told him in a hushed voice, "The gods cast my destiny before I was born, and soon we leave to fulfill it."

"And there's no way to dissuade you?" Eoin asked as he took a step toward her. "No way for my love to keep you from destroying yourself? Destroying us?"

"Whatever we feel doesn't matter—only destroying the Dreadlord does."

Eoin could not believe the coldness in her voice as he sank to his knees. And he had no one to blame but himself for loving such a fierce woman.

Croí Dàn interjected, *"Yet Mother insinuated that Dadga can help. Do not despair, Eoin. We will find a way."*

"All-Father will be here shortly," Croí Dàn announced. *"He must teach you something about using the magic of the Triple Dàns. Heed what he shares."*

Breanna sighed, wondering when this would all end.

"Erin's Hero!" All-Father called out as he arrived at their guest abode, made from the trees.

Breanna stepped from her room, eyes narrowed, saying, "Aye, I am here, though I'm not sure where else I'd be."

"Greetings, Daughter!" Dagda said as he marched forward, swept her into his big arms, and spun her around. "You've met our Mother Goddess, the Mórrigan, and my Lugh. Yet, I have not had the pleasure of properly greeting you. Our moment with Lugh was, to say the least, distasteful. You are a wonderful being! Such energy!"

"Put me down! And I am not your daughter!"

"Nay, lass, I will not!" Dagda exclaimed as he held her three feet off the ground. "Not yet. And, yes, you are my daughter. Are you not Breanna Ban Morna?"

"Of course, I am!"

"Then you're my daughter!" Dagda said, smiling. "And Eoin is my son. All Gaels are my children, sons and daughters, all! But you more so than any others."

"Why are you here?" Breanna demanded.

The mammoth god set her down gently and extended a hand to Eoin, pulling him to his feet. "We need to discuss how you can best combine the power of the *Triple Dàns*, as I expect our Heart has told you. With the Blades, you have experienced how to invoke their magic and use it against those who oppose the one who wields it, which has lately been you. When you defeated Balor, your rage enhanced *Lann Dàn's* abilities. With

Tethra, *Croí Dàn's* power surged through your body to empower skills you used to accurately cast the Yellow Spear and Red Javelin, something no human could hope to match. That was well done, indeed!

"Yet with *Lia Dàn,* you'll need love and not rage, love of your people and your land, to cast the vision necessary to remove the Dreadlord's stain. Danu and Lugh told you as much, but that's easier said than done, mainly because of the intent of your *geas* cast by one of my Druids."

Breanna questioned, "Beatha is one of your Druids?"

Dagda chuckled. "All Druids in Erin are mine, as I was the first one. Their magic flows from me. In any case, at your mother's direction, Beatha cast your *geas* as the source of the Dreadlord's ultimate destruction. While you are aware of this, I believe it will hinder your ability to wield the *Triple Dàns* successfully. Since we don't want you to fail, I propose you let me fix it."

"Fix my *geas*?" Breanna questioned. "Why did Danu, Lugh, or Badb not mention this before?"

"Because they are not Druids, just gods," Dagda answered smugly. "I am the source of all Druidic magic manifesting in Erin."

Croí Dàn said, *"My Hero, All-Father is wise. Trust him."*

Dagda smiled at their Heart's interjected advice.

Concerned, Eoin asked, "Will this *fix* hurt Breanna?"

"Och, gods no, lad!" Dagda protested. "Beatha's approach was single-minded, so all I need to do is make some tweaks to make room for what my daughter needs to wield the *Triple Dàns*."

"Then make it so," Breanna said firmly, squaring her body before the big god. Dagda, his eyes drifting closed, lifted a hand and touched her forehead with a finger.

Croí Dàn added, *"All-Father, if I may suggest, have Breanna seize the void. That will open her mind for you."*

Dagda nodded, saying in Breanna's mind, *"Do it."*

Breanna quickly found herself floating in the *void* as she complied with the request. Then she felt Eoin join her in their shared place, where he always found her, and she felt his support and love.

As Dagda worked through the threads of her *geas*, Breanna felt his happy grin in the *void* as he noted Eoin's presence.

Dagda informed her in *mind-speak*, *"I have what I need to weave a new pattern, a larger one, to something greater than what Beatha had cast upon you, Erin's Hero."*

And with that, All-Father was gone, and darkness pulled her into a deep slumber.

Sometime later, Breanna groggily awoke to find herself lying on her bed in their guest quarters. Eoin slept with his arms wrapped around her, holding her tightly as if he let her go, she would vanish.

When Eoin's eyes fluttered open as Breanna stirred, she whispered, "What happened?"

Croí Dàn said to them, *"All-Father was successful."*

"Hmmm," Eoin murmured. "How do you feel?"

"I'm not sure," was her answer. "Something more, like I have room in my mind for more than one thought now, more than one thing. Love is not as abstract as it was."

Eoin rolled Breanna toward him and looked into her eyes. "And that means?"

She sighed. "I can now accept that I love you. I always have, and that thought no longer overwhelms me. I need your touch."

He leaned forward to kiss her lips gently. Then, as Breanna responded more passionately, he pressed their foreheads together, his eyes locked on hers. He whispered, "You are my everything."

Breanna's lips twitched. "I know that, and now you know it's the same for me. This place is magical. Let's enjoy it."

With Breanna lying up on top of the one she now could feel as her lifelong love, straddling his hips, he asked, "Like this?"

"Absolutely like this, my love. Follow me."

With that, Breanna seized the *void*, dragging him with her as she joined her well-muscled man, letting their love fill each other.

When they sated their passion, *Croí Dàn* said, *"Trust in your love. It can save you both as well as your beloved land of Erin!"*

Breanna

Breanna asked *Croí Dàn* where to find All-Father and followed her directions along the main thoroughfare to his abode. She saw him sitting on a stool before the massive tree that made up his home in Falias. He held what she knew to be his giant magical harp, Uaithne.

Dagda was playing a haunting and hopeful tune when he looked up to see Breanna smiling happily. The song sounded familiar, and then she flushed when she realized why the song Bláth had written about her, titled "Erin's Hero Rising." As he finished with a flourish, Dagda said, "Daughter, you grace my humble place with your presence."

"That—that was the tune Dun Uisneach's Bard Bláth played during the Céilí," sputtered Breanna. "It was about the rise of Erin's Hero, my rise."

Dagda laughed. "Aye, my Hero. I wrote it for our people so they know you walk their land as *Croí Dàn's* chosen one. I write many songs that my Bards *compose*, sending them through their dreams. Sometimes it's just a snippet to get them started, and at other times I provide more detailed information. With Bláth, it was only a light nudge, as she's one of my more talented ones. So, what brings you here?"

Breanna said quietly, "I wanted to thank you for giving me more, I guess I would call it space in my head and heart. There's still the destruction driving me, but I now have space to love others, my people, my man, and my land alongside it."

Dagda said solemnly, "I am pleased to serve, my Hero."

"I am not long for this world, but at least I have this."

All-Father shook his head. "You are young. Yet know that *Croí Dàn* will use her considerable influence to ensure you walk our land with her again. While she wasn't *born* as we were, she is one of us and carries as much weight as any Tuatha god. As much as I do."

Croí Dàn said, "Thank you, All-Father. Danu often questions herself for making me sentient and a female being."

"Och, not that again! Mo Chroí, I'll have a word with her. You are a bit young for her to consider you an equal. Regardless, I have big plans for you and your Hero, so stay true."

Croí Dàn just huffed as if annoyed. Dagda smiled at her internal expression, saying, *"Yet she is your Mother, so don't sass her—it is time to grow up and fast. Now, you both have much to learn. Speaking of which, Breanna, you need to practice using Lia Dàn, for you will not have many opportunities after you return to Erin."*

"How?"

Switching to his natural voice, he answered, "Take out the Stone and hold it in your hands. Then seize the *sight* and direct it to show you the wonders of Erin, most of which you have not seen. Think with your inner voice, as you do with *Croí Dàn*, and it will respond. The Stone is like the Blades and will not engage you in conversation as your Heart does. It just reacts to your will."

She pulled the *Lia Dàn* from her inside tunic, where she had tucked it between her breasts. "Okay, then, here goes."

When she requested *Lia Dàn* to see the wonders of Erin, it swept her away, soaring over her island. Forests, rivers, lakes, bogs, ponds, rolling hills, flower-covered meadows, snow-capped mountains, cliffs above sandy beaches, coastal waters, and islands flowed before her eyes like she was a hawk floating on updrafts. It was breathtaking.

Then she rocketed into the sky to see the coast of the Dàl Riata, which had shared lineage with the original Gaels, the sons of Mil, who had sailed north from the mainland many centuries before. Beyond those lands were the Picts, originally Celts from the mainland. Not so far away as she had thought, and if they were so close, Romans or others could invade and be a source of future troubles for her land. Cymru, to the southeast of Dàl Riata, had already faced the Romans and had lost part of its homeland to the One God and its small trinity pantheon. Then, there was Albion beyond the Celts of Cymru, which others would fight over.

There were flashes of the past where key battles were lost, leading to Roman ascendancy. Following that were future wars with Norvegrs, Anglos, Saxons, and others who would fight over that land, each bringing their gods to those battles. In the end, there would be some spill-over invasions into Erin.

Stunned, Breanna withdrew from the Stone of Destiny, shuddering at the immense effort the Tuatha gods faced to keep the Gaels, with whom they had entered into a pact of mutual support, protecting them from the outside world.

She took a deep breath. "That last part was so vast. Especially the idea of going to distant lands to prevent invasions in Erin."

"Add to that," Daga said, "we must keep the faith strong here at home for the Tuatha gods to survive the future. That you could work with the Sea God to end Tethra's rule of the Fomorians in our land is a testament to what you can do with other challenges our Gaels and other Celts will encounter in the coming centuries."

"You ask a lot, my Father."

"Aye, my daughter, otherwise you'd not be Erin's Hero."

"Yet I will not be your daughter when I erase Hakon. Badb Catha and Danu said I must make a sacrifice."

Then All-Father was in her mind, adding, *"Breanna Ban Morna, that word has many meanings. Believe in your land and us. Do this, and I will teach you how to walk along Erin's Cycle of Time to help us protect your land's future, our land's future. Make me proud, my daughter."*

Croí Dàn said resoundingly, *"Mine!"*

Thinking about the warmth and love All-Father and her Heart gave her, she stepped next to the god, still taller than her in his current sitting position, and hugged his massive shoulder. *"Thank you, Father."*

As Breanna turned to leave, a lithe, elvish-looking young woman hurrying to see All-Father collided with her in the open doorway, and they both barely kept their feet under them. Breanna exclaimed, "Och, I need a moment to ensure I'm in one piece!"

"I'm sorry. I didn't know my great-grandpa had a visitor."

Dagda, who had picked up his harp and started playing the same tune about Erin's Hero, turned to the young lady and admonished, "Sinéidin. Show some grace to our guest, please."

"Apologies, my Lady." The goddess blushed as she tried to untangle herself from Breanna. "Wait, you're Erin's Hero! Everyone has been gossiping about how you killed the demon Balor and helped Mannanan end the Fomorian god, Tethra! Fergal told me the tale. It was glorious. Listening to him made it seem personal—like I was there. He's a very virile warrior."

Breanna raised an eyebrow, wondering what Eoin's cousin had been doing with Dagda's great-granddaughter, but said only, "I hadn't noticed. I'll leave you be."

As she turned to leave, she heard Sinéidin say to Dagda, "These Gaels are a wonder! Will they be here long?"

As Breanna walked down the main street of Falias, Cairpre, the Chief Bard of the Tuatha, stepped to her side, matching her determined stride. "So, you have the Heart, Stone, and Blades. I would give anything to see you battle with such magic at your side. Are you ready to use them?"

"You mean, am I ready to sacrifice my own life?" Breanna countered with a raised eyebrow. "None of these magics help in a physical battle while I am in Erin. That's all on my band, save we can seize the *void* where most others cannot."

The Bard said longingly, "Och, apologies, that was insensitive. We don't often get to interact with those in your realm. While life below the land of the living offers certain benefits, there are moments when we long to feel the sun warm our skin, feel the wind on our faces, and watch children playing without a care in the lush meadows we once called home. To have a conversation with someone new."

Breanna looked at him with some compassion. She knew they were all childless, but his voice carried a hint of loneliness. So, she offered, "No apologies needed."

Cairpre sheepishly shook his head. "Sorry, my Bardic desire to spin a tale about your quest blinded me. I've had little cause to use my craft since I came here, and the Tuatha have heard all my stories. Not much new happens here, you know."

"Another Bard said something similar to me when she discovered I was Erin's Hero," Breanna replied. "She was similarly blinded and saw me as a hero—not a person, not a woman—just a hero with a powerful *geas*, a hero with a destiny already cast."

"Aye, it sounds like more than one Bard fell into that trap."

"When I use the *Dàns*, you won't remember that I did so, for none of this will have occurred. There would be no tale to spin."

Cairpre's voice lowered. "Maybe in your world, but time is like a loom here. Once woven into the pattern, events remain on the tapestry of time, like part of an incomplete picture. I will remember you, always, and I will sing a tale of praise in your honor, whether you like it or not. It will be a story the Tuatha have not heard!"

Breanna offered wryly, "Only if I use the magic as planned."

With that, she turned into the doorway to their garden area, with Cairpre behind her, asking. "Is there something you're not saying?"

"I've said enough," Breanna rejoined as she picked at the fruit tray on the grass next to Eoin.

Her Chief said, "Cairpre, *Croí Dàn* informed us you could return us to Erin, where we need to be. Our friends await us at Dun Eadan."

"That would put us one day away from where we need to be," Breanna estimated as she bit into a strange yellow plum. Then, it struck her that she still had to evade her father. Swallowing hard, she asked, "And what of the Dreadlord? Will he know where our quest leads?"

"His völva is adept enough to have foreseen it," Cairpre answered. "I understand Badb Catha had blocked her out with her murder of crows. When this woman named Runa reached the summit of Croghan Hill, the Norvegr Seeress cleared what the Dark Goddess used to stop her for a time."

"Then there's no way to get to Croghan Hill before him," Breanna said grimly. "We will have to battle for the summit."

"Time in the underworld is different," Cairpre advised. "We can make it so that you depart at the same time you arrived, only you'll be in a different place. Since you came during your morning, the Dreadlord must have waited until that morning before setting out. He will have to swing around the *Móin Mórachd* before heading north, which will take two days to reach Croghan Hill. If you travel back to the day you left Erin, you might be able to get there a few spans ahead of him."

Breanna was doubtful. "But then my brothers, the Druids, and likely my grandfather and his *fians* will be where we left them and will not be at Dun Eadan to support me. I have sent them there to await me. Your suggestion will not work. I will meet them as I planned."

The Bard rubbed his jaw. "Then it'll be a race."

Breanna shrugged, letting an uneasy silence settle over them as she finished picking at the fruit platter. She decided it would be best to come from the northeast and possibly surprise her father.

Changing the subject, she asked, "Cairpre, I need something to carry *Lia Dàn* in. Badb Catha said I could not let the Stone touch the Blades until I am ready to use the magic of the *Triple Dàns*. Can you find or have something fashioned for me?"

"Aye, my Hero," the Bard answered and turned to leave. "I'll find a pouch fitting for the Stone of Destiny."

As Cairpre left, Fergal approached Breanna and Eoin with the Tuatha woman. "I'd like you to meet Sinéidin."

"We've already met," Breanna said. "I was visiting with her great-grandfather, Dagda. That's where we ran into one another. Funny thing, that, right?"

Fergal looked between the two women, asking worriedly, "So, Sinéidin, you didn't tell me about your lofty lineage."

The lithe young woman just shrugged. "Not much to tell. Dagda's daughter, Brigid, had three sons. They, in turn, without a female Tuatha, mind you, somehow had Ecne, my father. His three fathers ended up in a feud with Lugh's father, which ended badly for him. Then Lugh took his revenge, killing the three of them, and things settled down. It's a messy family, for sure.

"Anyway, technically, Dagda is my great-great-grandfather, but that is too much to say, so I use Great-Grandpa. It's easier."

Fergal looked a bit stricken and changed the subject. "Bre, since you have the magic you need, when do we leave?"

"Are you ready to do battle?" Breanna countered.

Fergal said with a small smile, "Yes, Sinéidin—ah—healed my wounds. I'm ready when you are. How about my cousin?"

Eoin said bitterly, "I'll never be ready to help my Champion die. Yet, since I can't turn her from this course of madness, who am I to delay us?"

With that, he turned away to his strange tree branch room.

Sinéidin hooked her arm through Fergal's, pouting, "You're leaving me—us, so soon?"

"The fate of Erin lies in our hands."

"Hmmm, I can't say I like it," Sinéidin arched an eyebrow, "but one can't test the Fates. We should recheck your wounds before you go to ensure they won't hinder you in battle. One more Elemental *healing* is likely needed."

As the young Tuatha goddess led Fergal away, Breanna sighed as she felt the weight of her quest on her shoulders. While All-Father had expanded her *geas* to include destruction and love, her need to remove her father had not changed. She must erase Hakon's thread in her land. Extract it from the tapestry of time, or her land could eventually be lost. Her once iron will now felt like it was balancing on a blade's edge, especially knowing failure meant she could not save Toal.

As to Eoin's reluctance, that was something she needed to clear up, and she strode toward Eoin's branch-formed room. Breanna knew he agreed that the Dreadlord must die. While convincing him that the magic of the *Triple Dàns* was the only way to accomplish that goal would be futile, she had to try.

Breanna demanded, "Eoin, face me, as I have words to share with you from All-Father. As you're now aware, I just left him."

Eoin stated, "I am surprised you sought Dagda out, especially given your exchanges with Lugh and what you said about your exchange with Danu. Neither seemed very positive. What was the reason for the visit?"

"To thank him," she answered. "For expanding my *geas* to include not just destruction but love. For my land, for you, and even myself. While I still need to fulfill my *geas* using the magic of the *Triple Dàns*, my Heart and All-Father are working on a plan to save us."

"How?"

Croí Dàn told them, *"You'll have to trust us."*

"All-Father also said something about teaching me how to walk Erin's *Cycle of Time*, whatever he means by such a thing. Sounds like more magic."

"Gods and goddesses and magic," Eoin stated. "It's a bit much, I'll say that."

Breanna let a small smile touch her trembling lips, asking, "I need to know one thing—we still have each other, right?"

"Aye, my love, always."

Lighting up, Breanna demanded again, "Now, stop talking. Let's make time for a little *luigh le chéile* before we leave this place. I need to feel your body on mine!"

"Your wish is my command, my Champion!" Eoin answered, sweeping her into his muscled arms with a big grin. She giggled as he spun her around and flung them into the strange bed of moss.

Breanna's Sacrifice

Corbmac

Corbmac led his two *fians* along the High King's Road with their four blooded warriors, then turned off onto the path leading to Dun Eadan. Not long after that, they met up with part of his third *fian* from the River Brosna settlement, which Corbmac had assigned to keep a watch on the Dreadlord and his men. The *fian's* leader, Tian, informed his commander that the other part of their band was keeping watch farther down the trail.

Just as Corbmac had everyone moving again along the path, the Fáidh of Dun Uisneach commanded them to stop, pulling his mount to a halt moments before the *sight* took hold of him. When Corbmac started to ask a question, Bláth held up a hand to stop him. The three *fians* slowly collected around them. They had been pushing hard throughout the day to reach Dun Eadan, and even the seasoned Ruaidri Mac Ciarán was breathing heavily.

Maoilir jerked into motion again and heaved a breath as Bláth asked with concern, "What is it?"

"It's All-Father again. Very demanding, that one. Our Hero has claimed the magic she needs to end Hakon Skadi's life from Danu's hand herself," Maoilir pronounced as he reached down with both hands to hold his saddle's horn and steady himself. "Now that she carries the magic of the *Triple Dàns*, Breanna will seek the altar between the monoliths at Croghan Hill. Since the Dreadlord's völva can use the *sight* again, we must assume she knows our Hero is coming soon. The Norvegrs cannot be allowed to stop her."

Corbmac's eyes narrowed, and he glanced to either side of their path to Dun Eadan. Looking up at Croghan Hill, he commanded, "Ruaidri, take Mogue and Tian to check if any outlanders are nearby while you fetch the four still on watch. I want to know if the Norvegrs are aware we are here. As for maintaining a watch, it's not likely the Dreadlord is going anywhere. Better to have all of us together to form a plan."

Ruaidri grimaced, saying, "Aye, but I get a break from camp chores this evening for the effort."

Corbmac chuckled. "Done."

Before they acted on their commander's order, each handed their shields to fellow warriors so they could move fast. The trio slipped into the woods to the south.

Bláth asked, "Should we make camp so we can be ready to counter any magic the Dreadlord's sorceress manages to conjure?"

"Nay," Maoilir answered, "we must press on to Dun Eadan. We need one of the *fians* under Chief Conn to join us."

Corbmac said, "But we will take time to make a quick meal as we wait for my scouts. Then we march on."

The *fian-ceannard* went through the supplies to see what they might have for dinner, finding a mix of dried venison and boar meat, which was hardly appealing, along with some leeks, carrots, parsnips, onion, garlic, and peas. Three loaves of not-too-stale bread someone had thought to bring were also in the sack. Corbmac grimaced, but there had been no time to hunt. He could see the sun nearly on the horizon through a patchwork of clouds. That ruled out any notion of catching some game for their meal.

He unhooked a large pot from his saddle before he emptied his waterskin into the kettle and threw the dried meat and vegetables into it. It was a meal his warriors would grouse about, so he commanded his men to build a fire. When the stew had been at a rolling boil for a half-span, his scouts returned from their search, along with the remainder of the Brosna River *fian*.

Ruaidri, Mogue, and Tian were winded and paused to catch their breath before they could confirm that the *Aos Dána* had indeed been correct in surmising the Dreadlord was still nearby. The other *fian* warriors who were keeping watch told them the Norvegrs had settled on the southeast side of the hill, just below the forest line.

Maoilir and Bláth looked at each other for a long moment, with the Bard noting, "The Dreadlord's völva is adept. She will lead him to the summit, where the monolith altar rests. Does the Destroyer come tonight?"

"Nay, it will be tomorrow," Maoilir informed her. "I cannot say from which direction, though. It's like she is part of the land. Still, if I cannot say, neither can Hakon's völva. The Tuatha gods in Falias will likely deliver Breanna, Eoin, and Fergal near Dun Eadan tomorrow evening."

Bláth seemed doubtful. "Aye, that may be true, but I still want to know what magic this Runa can command as she appears to weave powerful spells. She may have hidden Breanna's arrival from your eye."

Maoilir chuckled. "Even she isn't that good. Now, let's eat and march on to Dun Eadan. We will need that extra *fian*."

The Filidh frowned, but Corbmac put in his agreement. One thing he didn't need was to travel all night. A quarter-span later, he was doling out the stew he had thrown together.

After the men had finished their meal, they all marched or rode again toward Dun Eadan. The grizzly warrior decided it was time to retire from his trade. He was getting far too old for such adventures. Especially if the *Aos Dána* lured him into a battle.

Then Breanna came to mind. Had he retired, he would never have met the spunky young woman who called him grandfather and whom he claimed as his granddaughter.

It was late when Corbmac and the large band arrived at Dun Eadan's gates. It took a bit of organizing on Chief Conn's part to get thirty-some warriors both a late meal and all bedded down. Then they would train with the *fian* in residence tomorrow to ensure they could work interchangeably.

⸺✦◈ **Hakon** ◈✦⸻

Hakon finally eased his mount to a stop three evenings after his daughter's battle and two full days of hard riding. Croghan Hill rose before him, framed by fading sunlight. Fortunately, the *Móin Mórachd* was behind them. Riding the edge of the Great Bog had claimed one careless warrior and his horse when he'd given chase while hunting a boar. They had fallen into a bog pit and were sucked beneath the mud before anyone could reach them.

Hakon had been furious over such stupidity, for he could not afford to lose any men if he hoped to prevent his daughter from ascending Croghan Hill and fulfilling her promise. If not for the quick-thinking Kvasir, who would soon be a Dreadrider, they could have lost another young warrior to the great bog. Hakon took to riding point after the mishap and ordered Thorvald to ride next to Runa in the chariot. Having their Jarl near at hand quelled any unbridled exhilaration in the ranks.

As they all dismounted, tired and sore from the long ride, Hakon turned to talk with Runa. Thorvald was pleased to leave his charge behind and mocked Runa's usually dour expression as they passed. That brought a wry smile to Hakon's face. Then he thought of Breanna and her plans to destroy him, and the smile faded.

He urgently told Runa, "Now that we have arrived at Croghan Hill, I need to know where my daughter is. Has the *sight* revealed anything to you? Have our gods told you anything? Is she near?"

Runa looked to the east and let the *sight* take her. A moment later, she said assuredly, "The Destroyer will return tomorrow night from the underworld, from the realm of the Tuatha gods, bearing the magic to end your fate in this land. Yet I cannot say from which direction she will come."

"So, what do you advise?" Hakon asked with the same urgency.

"Since she must seek Badb Catha's place of magic at the summit, where we were before, I'd start for there in the morning."

They all went about making their camp ready for the night.

In the morning, Hakon ordered his men to ready the horses. He held his hand out for his völva to mount up behind him as her chariot horses could not pull her cart up the steep slope. Runa directed them up the eastern side of Croghan Hill, and by the time they worked their way through the woods that ringed the Dark Goddess's rounded mound, it was fully light, yet the dense trees filtered much of it.

The horses were strangely quiet. It was as if the place had sucked the breath from everything living. Runa inhaled. "I feel deeply rooted magic in the altar now, something that was not there before. Like it's waiting for your daughter."

Haken asked, "So the Destroyer must come here to work the destiny-shaping magic of this Stone of Destiny?"

"Já, my Jarl."

"Then she cannot be allowed near it."

Hakon ordered some of his men to prepare fires to ring the area in case his daughter arrived in the darkness, hoping to surprise him. To the others, he said, "We need a gauntlet in place to slow any of her warriors down if they charge us. Cut down small trees to make pickets. And we do not need our mounts – lead them down to the north side if we need to make a hasty retreat."

Breanna

Breanna looked at the shimmering doorway Cairpre had led them to and saw her reflection. She had seen it mirrored in ponds or lakes many times before—a turned-up nose and high cheekbones below blue eyes flecked with red, white hair falling about her shoulders, white brows arching high into her temples, and a firmly muscled figure. But never had it been so evident to her. Never had she realized how much she looked like Hakon—her birth father.

Yet if she carried out Danu's plan, that would change for both.

There was also a strong Gael side to her being, evident in her fine otterskin cloak with the boiled leather pauldrons and her body bristling with weapons.

Appearing suddenly at her side, Dagda said, "Do well to remember that, my daughter. You are now more mine than his."

"Were you reading my mind?" Breanna questioned with an arched eyebrow as she looked up at the big man. Well, *gigantic god* was likely the better term. "A lady must be able to keep some notions to herself."

"Ach, no, girl," Dagda denied. "You were broadcasting it."

"I see, so I must school my thoughts around you," she stated.

All-Father shrugged, saying warmly, "Just wanted to see that you are seen off to Erin properly and with all you need."

"Cairpre has taken good care of us," Eoin interjected, glancing at the suddenly beaming Master Bard, who handed a glittering pouch to Breanna in which to hold the Stone of Destiny safely in her tunic.

Breanna gave Dagda a wry smile after putting the Stone inside it and tucking it between her breasts just below her Heart. "Unless you have a magic apple or something for me?"

"Now there's an idea!" he answered, reaching up as if he were plucking fruit from a tree. A golden apple appeared in his hand, and he tossed it to her.

Laughing, Breanna deftly caught it. "What happens when I eat it?"

Dagda winked. "A little of this and a little of that. Eat it before you ascend to the summit of Croghan Hill, and you'll see."

Motioning for Eoin to add the golden apple to the pack on her lower back, she commented, "Very well, Father. I trust it will be delicious and help my cause and yours. Thank you for what you've done for me, for us, for fixing my *geas*."

"No thanks needed, Daughter, as it was my Druid who botched the casting of it in the first place. She should have been more subtle." He added, "I've expanded the space for you to fill in with what you need and want. I am pleased you chose love."

Breanna blushed. "Then I guess we should be going."

"Indeed, as all is in place, so fair thee well, Breanna Ban Morna," All-Father agreed, stooping to give his daughter a light hug and a kiss on her forehead. With that, he was gone.

Cairpre waved and said farewell as he walked away from the shimmering door. Breanna believed that he, among the Tuatha, might understand her plight best. She looked at her reflected self in the light of *Maorgairme* and the two *Lann Dàn* blades and shivered. Then she stepped into her image and through the strange, otherworldly *doorway*.

Breanna emerged into Erin's twilight, standing in the woods just outside the open torchlit gates of Dun Eadan. Behind her came Eoin and Fergal, and the two warriors were as dazzled as she was by the stars dotting a moonlit sky overhead.

"Take hold of the Stone of Destiny," Croí Dàn instructed, *"and touch the earth with your other hand. Claim your land!"*

In one motion, Breanna knelt, reached inside her tunic, found the Stone in its pouch, and grasped *Lia Dàn*. She held it aloft as her other palm slammed to the ground. A jolt of energy surged out of her, proclaiming to all Druids and any warrior who could seize the *sight* or *void* that Erin's Hero walked their land once more, a Hero supported by Tuatha gods and their magic. It was a call to aid her or be shunned by their gods. It held an intensity backed by All-Father, the Mother Goddess, the Dark Goddess, and the Sun God as if they were one, an announcement echoing across all of Erin: *"Breanna Ban Morna is ours! And yours!"*

Croí Dàn commanded, *"So mote it be!"*

When Breanna's Heart cast those four words, her magic exploded across Erin. She felt her land's acceptance from shore to shore, be it trees, plants, rivers, streams, or animals.

Croí Dàn projected her chosen one's words, *"Beanna Ban Morna calls her people to be one with her land once more, to support our gods as they support us. Invaders are among us. We will end them, yet I need your help to change our ways. As Erin's Hero, I am yours!"*

As her Heart magnified those words, Breanna settled into her role as one who would fight for her people. Filled with confidence, her possible sacrifice the next day no longer weighed as much. Though she was just a back hills warrior, she slammed her hand down again and cast her love for her land. This time, the impact was personal. She felt wonder from some of her people, while others were silent, as they were no longer true believers in the Tuatha gods—that would be a challenge.

When Breanna stepped out of the woods, the three from Dun Arrogh discovered they stood before Maoilir, Bláth, Breanna's half-brothers, Corbmac, and three *fians* flanking them. Through their auras, she could sense their support and belief in her and their Tuatha Dé Danann gods.

Croí Dàn stated, *"With your claim, you can now see who believes in us and who does not through their auras."*

The rough warriors from Dun Uisneach picked up their pikes and repeatedly rapped them on their shields, chanting, "Bre! Bre! Bre!" Then the *fian* from Dun Eadan joined them, all waiting for Breanna to lead the way through the gates.

Bláth stepped forward first, with Maoilir a half stride behind her, and she exclaimed, "That was not the entrance back into our world I was expecting, but well done, Erin's Hero! I see you now possess the magic of the *Triple Dàns* and have undoubtedly won the backing of our gods."

"Aye," Breanna answered, "that I have. And I'm sure you will be happy to know that All-Father played your song, 'Erin's Hero Rising,' for me on his great harp, Uaithne. He was rather impressed by it."

The Master Bard blurted out, "He did what?"

"More on that later," Breanna added as Braoin, Bradaigh, and Corbmac stepped around the Druids to greet their leader with happy smiles.

"Welcome home, Bre!" Corbmac said.

Breanna hugged each of them before saying, "Thank you."

Maoilir added, "You know your pronouncement that Erin's Hero has truly claimed her land and people was strong enough to be felt across the entire width and breadth of our Emerald Isle?"

"Aye, that was the idea."

Fergal added, "Quite the welcome. Can I assume Chief Conn has his high table ready for us? With no meat in Falias, I'm starving for a haunch."

Corbmac laughed, assured them the dinner was ready, and led Breanna's Band and the chanting *fians* into the dun. Then he escorted Breanna and her fellow warriors to the stables to greet their mounts. Bláth slipped an apple into her hand as Eimar whickered her approval at seeing her chosen one. When Breanna raised her hand and gave her beloved mare the fruit, Eimar said, *"Welcome home, my Hero. I am relieved to see you are safe."*

Breanna answered, *"And I for you, Eimar, but much danger lies ahead."*

Her horse responded, *"Yet with us together, we will prevail."*

Breanna had to smile at Eimar's confidence.

They left their packs with the grooms and headed to the main hall. There, Chief Conn awaited them, sitting at his high table. He disdainfully added, "I see you've returned."

"Indeed," Breanna acknowledged with a broad smile, but his aura said he was a non-believer; she needed to change that soon. "I left this land with a bastard Norvegr father and returned with a new one named Dagda. Interesting how life takes such turns."

Chief Conn rose as if to challenge her, yet a narrowed-eyed look from Bláth stayed his retort. Instead, he opened his arms, saying, "I welcome you to Dun Eadan, Breanna Ban Morna."

She smirked. "Of course you do. Otherwise, you'd be upsetting the apple cart, as one might say. And All-Father wouldn't be happy, not that you embrace our gods anyway. I imagine there will be others like you, some who believe our gods have left us. But I can assure you that they have not. Either way, your belief is not required; only your support is—and I will have it.

"Now, I understand Corbmac, through the authority of Chief Faolán and Chieftess Falyn, who supersedes your rank because of their relations with the High King, will be taking control of your best warriors to make up a new *fian* to join my other *fians* from Dun Uisneach. It will take four bands of nine to help rid our land of the Norvegrs. Is that agreed?"

Conn stared down at Breanna. And she stared right back at him. A wry smile crept over her face.

Then *Ćroí Dàn* blasted into Conn's mind, *"Unbeliever! No one in Erin challenges my chosen one, Erin's Hero! No one!"*

Breanna chuckled at the recalcitrant Chief, seeing he was stunned by his first direct experience with Tuatha magic. She chided, *"Mo Chroí, temper yourself. We should not be bullies about this."*

Ćroí Dàn huffed.

Maoilir stepped beside him, whispering, "Conn, Erin's Hero, stands before you. Whether you believe it or not, she is the adopted niece of Faolán and Falyn. They recognize her as Erin's Hero, as does the High King. They have granted her the authority to command your support. Don't be a fool!"

Conn hesitated, then finally nodded. "So shall it be. Welcome to my High Table."

As Breanna's Band dined with the Chief of Dun Eadan, they noticed a positive shift in the mood as the word spread about Erin's Hero claiming her land and people; not all were like the dour Conn. Then Bláth took up the song she thought she had written by her hand, and the crowd stirred to life as she played "Erin's Hero Rising." When the evening meal was almost over,

Eoin rose, removing his sword belt and cloak, and extended his hand to Breanna, saying, "Let's show them some magic!"

Breanna removed her weapons and otter skin cloak, and Eoin led her to the open floor between the Chief's High Table and the lower tables. They both seized the *void* and danced to the Bard's next song to celebrate their newfound love. They spun and twirled, with Eoin again acting as the physical base for the pair and Breanna, the lithe flying falcon, ready to meet her mate in the sky.

Though they reenacted some of the same patterns they had danced at Dun Uisneach, they moved now with even more power, grace, and unity. As the song ended, Eoin caught Breanna in his arms from where she descended after a high-whirling flip and knelt, lowering her to the floor, forehead to forehead, and then a slow kiss.

Croí Dàn cried, *"My Heroes!"*

The *fians* listening from the lower tables thumped their dirks on the oak tops and started chanting again, "Bre! Bre! Bre!"

Breanna and Eoin rose and bowed. "You honor us!" Breanna said. "Yet it is time to plan for tomorrow's battle with the Dreadlord and his Norvegrs, as we will march at sunrise to Croghan Hill. We must take the summit. Corbmac, please gather your *fian* leaders. Bláth, Maoilir, if you will, join us as well."

Breanna turned to the *fian* warriors and added, "You all face grave danger for me tomorrow. I will not forget this."

Corbmac stepped forward. "Nor will we all! For you, Breanna Ban Morna. For Erin's Hero! Our Heart calls to each of us, and we know you honor us by fighting for Erin."

The *fian* warriors thumped their dirks on the oak tables again and once more chanted, "Bre! Bre! Bre!"

Breanna gave them a humble bow, gathered her weapons and cloak, and took Eoin's hand to leave the hall behind. Such faith they had in her, especially now that she had made her claim. It finally felt right.

Corbmac led them all to the Chief's private meeting room, with Conn grumbling, "Someone could have asked before assuming my room was available."

"If it wasn't, it is now," Corbmac countered with a smirk.

The older Chief had nothing to say about that remark as the band entered and sat around his meeting table. Corbmac called in Ruaidri, his second-in-command of the two Dun Uisneach *fians*, summoned by the River Bronsa settlement leader, Tian. Then Conn called for the leader of his *fian* warriors, Taig, to join them.

Breanna went into pre-battle mode once they were in the room. "*Ćroí Dàn*, please ensure Hakon's völva cannot hear us."

All looked around as if the *Asgardian* magic worker presented an imminent danger. Then *Ćroí Dàn* said a moment later, *"Done!"*

Breanna nodded, adding, "We can continue safely. Tell me what resources the Dreadlord has and what we have to counter him."

Corbmac responded, "Ruaidri, as you heard it firsthand, tell our Hero what the Brosna settlement's *fian* warriors informed you about their surveillance of the Norvegrs."

"Ahhh," the old warrior stuttered a bit in the spotlight. "Corbmac ordered his men to watch over the Norvegrs. They appear to have lost another warrior to the Great Bog. That puts them at twenty or twenty-one warriors, as we think he also lost one in the River Lífe sea demon battle. Anyway, they appeared to be concentrated at the summit of Croghan Hill as if to prevent your approach."

Breanna nodded. "Aye, that makes sense. I need to reach a short pillar, the altar representing the center of our land, at the summit. That center point, surrounded by three monoliths, is called Erin's Altar. Only there can I unleash the magic of the *Triple Dàns*. Yet I'll need your protection while I make that happen. And, likely, a diversion."

Sitting next to Breanna, Eoin proclaimed, "We have four *fians*, plus four blooded warriors, assuming that Breanna will have to focus on working the magic of the *Dàns*."

Corbmac added, "My Chief and Chieftess provided four blooded warriors to protect each *fian* against shield breakthroughs."

"Excellent news," Eoin put in. "For the diversion, I suggest one *fian* ascend the eastern slope and another the northern slope. The remaining two *fians*, along with us four, will act as a spear from the western slope to get Breanna to the center of the summit so that she can reach Erin's Altar."

"Good plan," Corbmac agreed. "That will make eighteen warriors distracting and twenty-two advancing, not counting their blooded protectors. That should split them up. The only downside is they have long swords, and our men, at least the *fians*, only have pikes."

Eoin shrugged. "Have them keep a tight formation. I have heard the Romans used this tactic to their advantage in Albion before they withdrew. That formation is advancing with pikes out and shields in, establishing a close, united barrier. Each *fian* needs to appear as if they are seeking the pillar and leading Breanna to it. While it will quickly become apparent that we are the leading spear, it should be too late."

Breanna said, "Don't forget, Braoin and I have bows. And we five have short casting spears to fill in behind the two *fians*. Corbmac's men will not take on the fight alone. It is all of ours to win."

Corbmac said with a wink, "I know you'll fight for my men as you would fight for your band—we are all family now—but no taking unneeded chances."

Eoin flicked his attention to the old warrior. "While I can't argue that Bre should be taking any chances, she makes a good point. Ensure your warriors provide a little space between their shields until they engage the Norvegrs so these two can use their bows. Then it will be a tight formation. We will need shield walls to give Breanna time to wield the magic of the *Triple Dàns*—your blooded additions need to address any breakthroughs, as you suggested."

Breanna asked, "Well, is there any other input?"

Chief Conn demanded, "Who will replace any warriors I lose in this battle?"

Corbmac put in darkly, "You overstep yourself, Conn. All *fians* belong to the High King, not the Dun Chief assigned to them. The highest-ranking regional Chief can command them to perform particular duties like this, but they are not obligated to provide compensation to you. That's why we rotate them around the duns. Chief Faolán and Chieftess Falyn will have an initial say in how any assigned *fian* warriors lost will be replaced. That can only happen by those stationed higher than you.

"And right now, the High King has granted the leaders of Dun Uisneach full authority to deal with the Norvegrs. Do I make myself clear? Or do I need to send word back to my Chief and Chieftess about your lack of support for Erin's Hero?"

"Ahh, no, no, no need for that."

Breanna smiled. "Well then, Conn, since that's settled, I need a bed for my Chief and me for the night. Something private. Please have your Seneschal, Tynan, see to it."

Turning away from the truculent Dun Eadan Chief, she continued brightly, "Thank you all for your support. I couldn't have done this without you. We do not know what tomorrow will bring, but let us hope it will be a new day for all those held *daor aicme* by the Dreadlord."

Bláth inserted herself into Breanna's space as they rose to depart for the evening. "A word, if I may. You mentioned All-Father playing my song in the otherworld. In Falias. How is that possible?"

Breanna chuckled. "As the first Druid, Dagda is always helping his own. Well, maybe only those with a close connection to our gods. Who can say which way All-Father flows into your soul and from you into his? Likely both.

"Anyway, who wrote the song is moot. Maybe you both did, just from different planes. Maybe together. He praised your efforts."

Bláth sighed. "You are a wonder, Breanna. How you accept the magic of the Tuatha and our land with no reservations gives me courage about what's to come."

Breanna smiled again. "It's your song about me, as Erin's Hero, Master Bard. I think you need to take ownership of it. I know Father would never try to claim it. After all, he did say he only sent a snippet."

Bláth threw her arms around Breanna and said, "Thank you."

Surprised, Breanna hugged the Bard and commanded, "It's time to sleep. We shall gather at sunrise."

With nods of agreement, they all sought their beds, Conn's Seneschal leading Breanna and her Chief to a private hut fit for nobles.

Later, Breanna, wrapped in Eoin's arms, sighed. "Hmmm, I'm so glad Father made room for you in my head. This love thing is a wonder. And no matter what comes tomorrow, that we could share it has made my heart bigger. And more confident than ever that we are on the right path."

Eoin smiled. "I like how you said *we* in your declaration."

Croí Dàn interjected, *"You are both my Heroes."*

Breanna responded, *"Mo Chroí, sometimes lovers need some space. Go to sleep."*

Eoin chuckled at such a firm admonishment as Breanna whispered, *"Déan grá aris.* I need to feel us together again to face tomorrow. To face the unknown as one."

"Your wish, my love, I will happily grant that."

Hakon

It was near dark, with all hunkered down in their bedrolls around various fires, when Hakon said to Runa, "What can you report?"

"Your Destroyer not only returned this night," she answered, "but also declared herself as Erin's Hero to her land and people. I'm not sure what that means. The myth and magic of these people are a complex mix. Maybe another piece of Tuatha magic is in play beyond the Blades and the Stone. Regardless, every Druid in this land knows the Tuatha gods have chosen her as Erin's Hero, and probably any warriors who can seize the *void*, too."

"Can you not break through to discover what it is?"

"No, this is a direct mind block," Runa replied. "Unlike the Mórrigan's interference, it is like she has a shield across her mind and those around her, likely more Tuatha magic. It is not good. Yet I do know they will rise at dawn to march on the summit of Croghan Hill. We must be ready."

He had already positioned his men to protect the summit. Given they could face more warriors than he could field, he had them continue to build pickets to prevent full *fian* charges with their long pikes. Hakon could only nod and turn toward his bedroll, hoping for some sign as his men continued to cut down small trees and build their defenses. Yet nothing came as he drifted off to sleep.

When Breanna awoke, she found her good feelings from the night before replaced with dread. Given that only she could work the magic of the *Triple Dàns*, Eoin had built their plans around ensuring she did just that. However, that plan mostly took their best warrior—her—out of the battle. She could kill three, maybe four warriors that a *fian* warrior could take out, and likely two more than her blooded warriors could best. It might be too late if they waited too long to let her engage Norvegrs.

Eoin roused as if feeling her tense muscles. "What troubles you, my love?"

"I am unsure of our plan. I can't see how it could unfold positively. We are missing something."

Eoin said, "The plan is sound—get you to the altar as quickly as possible to work the magic of the *Triple Dàns*."

"Yet we take our best warrior out of the fight. I know that sounds arrogant, but you know it's true. While *fian* warriors are good, even with a blooded warrior assigned to each, they won't be that good against Hakon's long swords. Our advantage is not in talent. Our five blades to match their twenty-plus. No, correct that, because I have magic to work—so that's four. We will be in trouble if anything disrupts your shield wall approach that the *fians* will deploy."

Eoin countered, "The faster you wield the magic, the faster you remove Hakon and his ilk. What would you have us do?"

"Unleash me!"

"Let's talk with Corbmac. Time to address our warriors."

Breanna commanded, "Not a word to the Druids."

"Of course," Eoin said as he softly kissed her forehead.

Even though Croghan Hill was about a two-span march from Dun Eadan, Breanna ensured her band had a hearty breakfast before setting out. They took a westerly course shortly after sunrise with their four *fian* escorts and extra blooded. The collected warriors started marching with smiles, again chanting as they trotted behind the horses, "Bre! Bre! Bre!" Corbmac admonished them, calling for silence.

As Eoin dropped back next to Corbmac to explain Breanna's concerns, Breanna nudged Eimar to move between Braoin and Bradaigh. "A word, my brothers. You know we march to end the Dreadlord's reign using the magic of the *Triple Dàns*. What I haven't told you in plain terms is how it works. Using the combined Tuatha magics, I must remove our father from the timeline he created since he arrived here. It will be as if he never discovered our land."

Braoin said, "Wait, but doesn't that mean if he did not arrive, the three of us would never have been born to this land. Right?"

"Good, you grasp the most salient point I've had running around in my head since meeting Badb Catha," Breanna said wryly. "While that cost galled at first, All-Father said we had to believe in him, and he and *Mo Chroí* were working on a solution to that problem. That said, I need you both to be aware of what could happen. I will understand if you do not want to help me with this."

Bradaigh grunted. "Leave it to the gods. I care about only one thing, Breanna, and that is helping you end our father's life in any way possible. If there's a cost as steep as you say, I will gladly pay it."

"Aye, sister-mine," added Braoin. "We are in this with you to the end. We all have a *geas* that would not let it be any other way. Nonetheless, thank you for telling us plainly how the magic works."

Breanna beamed at her half-brothers. "Thanks for that."

Then she moved between Eoin and Corbmac. "Have you discussed my concerns?"

Corbmac sighed. "Yes, and they have merits. And downsides. Our plan with the three-sided attack is sound. While your concern about the potential for the Norvegrs to interfere with our *fians* and their shield walls is valid, we now have a blooded warrior to support each band of nine. And I could cover a *fian*, giving you another blooded."

"Whoever you choose would not have trained with us."

Eoin took up the challenge, saying, "I agree. Without a way to get you close to the altar undetected, you need to be in the battle plan. Given this, Breanna's Band should form a continuously rotating five-sided star pattern. We all strike and rotate and strike again. In the *void*, we will be near unstoppable. If one of us falls, we collapse at that point into one less."

Corbmac protested, "But you can't fall."

Breanna declared, "Never! And I'll rotate out when I can."

As they reached the base of Croghan Hill and dismounted, Bláth suggested, "I believe the magic you possess can raise a fog. While I'm sure they know we are here, that will keep us hidden from them longer."

Croí Dàn chimed in with, *"The Druid is correct. Hold Lia Dàn; I will use it to command the mists and hide us."*

Breanna reached inside her tunic, finding the pouch nestled between her breasts to take hold of the Stone of Destiny, and after a short while, a white fog began to creep around the base of Croghan Hill. The *fian* warriors murmured in amazement and approval. Each stepped before Erin's Hero one by one, taking a knee before her as if to ask for a boon of courage.

As Breanna put a hand on each warrior's shoulder, *Croí Dàn* whispered in their minds, *"I grant you the courage of Erin's Hero."* The fog thickened and rose when the last *fian* warrior stepped away with a proud set to his jaw and a fierce look in his eyes. Then, the Heart of Destiny reached out to Breanna's Band and conveyed that same boon of courage.

As Breanna and Braoin readied their bows, Eoin said to Corbmac, "It is time. As discussed last night, we advance when the two *fians* are positioned on the north and east slopes and ready to ascend with us on the west."

The Master Bard demanded, "What about Maoilir and me?"

"Safer for you two to stay here," Breanna replied.

Bláth sputtered, "I'll—I'll not be a coward. He can stay behind, but I will not! I have my knife and my Element!"

Maoilir added, "I'm not young and not trained for battle. I'll look after the mounts."

The old *fian* leader shrugged and turned to pass the orders. A short time later, bird-like whistles reached them, and Corbmac ordered, "Press forward, men. And Bard. We fight for Erin's Hero!"

As the two *fians* ascended the western flank, they split and aligned in diagonal lines, forming an arrowhead with a leader at the front and a blooded warrior right behind him. The Bard was at the back, and the others followed behind each line with swords drawn, save for Braoin, who had an arrow nocked like Breanna. Their pace was steady, but the dense tree cover necessitated a slow movement. They climbed higher, and in doing so, the fog rose with them.

Breanna said hushedly, "Eoin, I need a favor. Look in my pack. At the top, you'll find the golden apple Dagda gave me. I think now's a good time to eat it."

Eoin pulled her pack open and handed her the apple. "Do I need to hold your bow?"

"Nay, love, I only need one hand to take bites," Breanna replied. With that, she took her first mouthful and moaned, "Mmm, that is wonderful. You must try it."

She handed Eoin the piece of fruit, and he took a bite, marveling at the sweet taste, before handing it back to Breanna to finish. He commented, "Sort of refreshing, in a strange way."

"Aye," Breanna concurred as she munched around the golden orb.

The next moment, Dagda said in her mind, *"My daughter, you ate my apple! That's good, as it has solidified our bond. As Cróí Dàn is bonded to Danu and has a piece of the Mother Goddess within her, so I have bonded you to me. So you're more than just my daughter, like all Gaels. You actually are my daughter now."*

Breanna stumbled at the sudden intrusion, and Eoin had to catch her before she fell. She said to the All-Father, *"I'm what? And what does that mean?"*

Dagda gave her a mental shrug. *"I'll explain more soon, but let's say you have new capabilities due to our bond. When you crest the summit of Croghan Hill, imagine a cloak of invisibility surrounding you. Then, let your warriors take the battle to the Norvegrs, and you focus on getting to Erin's Altar. The altar is a ring of water that holds the magical center of your land. Submerge Lia Dàn in the water and then set it in the limestone cup at the center, and you'll see what you need to cast your vision."*

Breanna answered dubiously, *"Okay."*

"Trust me, Daughter."

Breanna said to Eoin, "Thank you for catching me. That was Dagda, and he proposed a new plan. I can now become invisible to Hakon and his spawn, so we're back to the original plan. Here, you finish the apple, then take my bow and quiver. You'll need them more than I. Seize the *void*, and I'll give you my archery skills."

With that quickly done, Eoin shook his head in amazement at the skills she injected into his mind.

She added, "You now lead our four-pointed star. Stay safe."

"You, too," Eoin replied. Then added, "Corbmac, we must buy Breanna time to sneak inside their defenses before we all charge in."

The old warrior signaled hold, which rippled through the woods.

Hakon

Hakon whispered, "Is she near?"

"Já," confirmed Runa. "She has more magic, something deeper than before. It's as if she is now part of their pantheon, which is the last thing we needed."

"What can you do?"

Runa shrugged. "Not much. We are over-matched. You and your warriors must fight for their right to be in this land."

As the fog crested the summit, Hakon signaled to his men, saying, "Stand ready. They are nearly here. All is not what it seems."

Breanna

Breann saw a *fian* rise from the east side of Croghan Hill, another from the north, and finally two more *fians* rose from the west. All four units charged forward, with thirty plus against just over twenty, but the pickets on the east and north sides slowed those two Gael units. Yet the two *fians* from the west had the greatest strength, and that was where the pickets were thinnest. They dodged around them, pushing deep into Hakon's defense of the monoliths surrounding the altar. A hole opened briefly as the two western *fian* units spun toward the men Hakon had posted on the southern flank.

Then, four warriors, two with swords and two with bows, quickly filled the gap between the *fians* and his men. Arrows flew, taking the Norvegrs from behind as they turned to face the *fian* warriors. Their blooded warriors followed that up by casting their short spears and several dirks, with more of Hakon's men going down.

Cloaked as the All-Father had directed, Breanna crept as close as she dared to Erin's Altar before stopping. The Dreadlord's warriors had engaged with the *fian* warriors, with swords against their pikes. As Eoin had predicted, the shield-wall formation left little room for the Norvegrs to use their blades, but the pickets set to the north and east had split those *fians* in two, making them less effective.

The fog was thinning, but it still lingered. The Dreadlord's men were yelling war cries in their language and grunting as they engaged the *fian* warriors, with now only some in shield-wall formation. Others were in one-on-one combat, which put those warriors at a disadvantage with a spear against a longsword. The blooded warriors from Dun Uisneach each helped them as best they could.

She briefly caught sight of Eoin, Fergal, Braoin, and Bra-daigh fighting back to back as they spun through the Norvegr warriors, pushing closer to her, four warriors battling as one by using the same *void* space, each making sure she was able to wield her magic as they rotated like clock hands. Hakon's men briefly rallied when a large Dreadrider stepped in to slow their progress. Yet he could not stop them.

Breanna noted that Hakon Skadi was scanning the area as if looking for her. With his back to her, she could fling one of her dirks at him and not even use the magic at her command. She saw the Dreadlord turn and look directly at her, his expression appearing to be concerned, but he did not see through her cloak of Dagda's magic.

Turning her attention to casting a vision of her land, she moved with stealth and cunning toward Erin's Altar. She carefully avoided her father and his men, using the giant monoliths for cover, inching through the fog like a phantom. Beneath her deerskin boots, the dead leaves of the fall season threatened to crunch and give her away. Yet they did not, and soon, two of Hakon's warriors stood not twenty yards to either side of her, each battling with Corbmac's men.

When she finally reached Erin's Altar, Breanna found two more of her father's men guarding the short pillar, each standing five yards away to either side. She quietly sheathed *Lann Dàn* and pulled *Lia Dàn* from a pouch between her breasts. The small, round crystal held a faint glow, like her ring, and felt cold in her hand. She let her hand sink the Stone of Destiny beneath the water's surface.

The water was icy, numbing her skin as she waited for her vision to consume her. She would have sworn she was not holding the Stone if she had not been looking at her hand. Then, a numbness spread up her arm. Breanna tried to pull away, wondering if Runa had poisoned the water and if *Lia Dàn* was drawing that poison into her. Yet her muscles would not respond as if paralyzed by the cold. Her eyelids refused to close, and panic swept over her that one of her father's men would discover her.

Left with little more to do than stare at *Lia Dàn* beneath the surface, Breanna calmed. All-Father and the Mother Goddess would not have let her come this far only to be stopped by a possible poison. The Tuatha magic that was supposed to end the Dreadlord's reign would not allow it.

A mist swirled inside the Stone of Destiny to pull Breanna's attention back to it. As *Lia Dàn* captured her mind and drew her into its depths, she felt herself falling. A light enveloped her, and then all of Erin lay before her and in her. Breanna Ban Morna was one with her land. From the rugged coast in the northwest to the lush plains and misty mountains of the Wicklows in the southeast, from the untamed northeast to the rock-strewn southwest, she was Inis Fáil—she was Erin. Where legends had passed down through the ages, and Heroes were born, when might and magic ruled and the very land held unbounded power, a present where few had the will to be a Hero and the earth, once full of its life-giving energies, was sapped.

She felt all of Erin rise in her heart this morning, her people's hopes and dreams coursing through her veins, and what it meant to them to be called Gaels. The wit of the fox was in her mind, the cunning of the wolf in her eyes, and the power of the stag in her muscles. Her land flowed through her, fish and otters swimming through lochs and rivers as if they were in her veins, and hawks rode the wind currents over her mountains and valleys, all alert for signs of danger as if her arms were wings.

And then she felt the true poison—her father. He was seeping up one arm, poised to take over her entire body, ready to rape her like he had her mother.

That vision ripped Breanna Ban Morna from her trance, with *Croí Dàn* exclaiming, *"My Hero, enough! You have what you need inside you now. Set Lia Dàn in the cup at the altar's center. It will lock on and be safe until you touch it with Lann Dàn."*

Rising as her Heart commanded, she found her body was hers once more, and the numbness the Stone of Destiny had cast in her vision state was gone as quickly as it had come. Breanna let her hand drop to the center of Erin's Altar. There was an audible click when *Lia Dàn* locked in place.

Croí Dàn said to Eoin, *"Now!"*

Runa stood nearby, hands raised as if she were in a trance. Then she pointed at Breanna and waved in her direction, casting her invisibility cloak to the wind. Breanna immediately seized the *void* as the startled guard raised his sword to her right, hoping to cleave her in two. Breanna's counter was quicker—reaching for her waistbelt, she flicked one of her dirks into his throat. He fell backward and clutched his neck, gurgling as he went down.

The other guard to her left had his sword in motion, slashing toward her neck. Ducking low, Breanna reached for her waistbelt again and jammed her other dirk into his groin. As he doubled over toward her, she used another dirk from a forearm sheath to stab him in the eye, and he toppled over.

Breanna was still assimilating what she had seen—no, felt— while held in a trance by Erin's Altar. She had been Erin, her land from shore to shore. The Stone had filled her heart with all her people's hopes to become more. Yet she had no time to think more about it and spun back to the altar, needing to complete her quest to destroy the Dreadlord. With the Stone of Destiny locked onto the monolith, she stepped back and drew the Blades of Destiny.

Before she could drop the tips of *Lann Dàn* onto *Lia Dàn*, a warrior unleashed a bloodthirsty scream of vengeance. It was the Dreadrider named Lang, whose brother she had killed. Behind him came the Dreadlord, moving with rational purpose.

When Fergal separated from their four-point star formation, he caught the Dreadrider's sword on his own, stopping him from reaching Breanna, and their moves spun them away as they battled. She saw Lang counter by throwing a fist into Fergal's stomach, then whirled to strike at her. Yet Breanna had moved, using the flickering sunlight through the trees to mask her movement, and then drove a blade into his left shoulder. He staggered back, struggling to keep his balance.

Breanna said flatly, "Looking for me?"

Fergal had recovered and struck out with his blade, putting himself between the two once more. He demanded, "Go, Bre, you've got magic to work. Go before any of us fall!"

Breanna nodded and, turning back to the altar, saw Eoin briefly face an older Dreadrider. As Braoin and Bradaigh rotated, they took on the burly warrior, and Eoin moved before Breanna so the Dreadlord could not fight his daughter.

She saw Hakon try to sidestep Eoin with a low sweep to make him jump back, but the Chief ensured their swords met. As if sensing her near, Breanna heard him say, "Bre, go!"

Then, Breanna reached the Altar once again.

The Dreadlord pushed Eoin away and turned after her. Eoin managed a weak swing at the outlander's feet, and the flat of his blade caught a boot to trip the Dreadlord. Then Lang charged toward Breanna with a growl while Hakon climbed back to his feet and turned to face Eoin again.

Fergal

"No!" cried Lang, and he tried vainly to push Fergal out of his path, but the Gael would not let him get away without a fight. The two struggled for a moment, their blades meeting a second time. Enraged, Lang spun away for some space and began pounding at Fergal with powerful overhand blows that forced him back. With Fergal's mind in the *void*, he met each stroke delivered by the feral Dreadrider, countering them repeatedly. He could not fail, as Breanna needed time to win everything for them by using the magic of the *Triple Dàns,* and they could finally be free of hated Norvegrs.

Lang threw an overhead strike that Fergal deflected into the ground. His counter slash opened a shallow slice on Lang's off arm, and he noted his opponent stagger backward. Yet the

Dreadrider recovered and swept up his blade to meet Fergal's again. They circled and clashed once more, but neither found an opening.

Growling with the thought he had to win this fight for Breanna and Eoin, he spun away to set up another strike. Another of Hakon's warriors behind him, fighting with Braoin, got skewered and was knocked back into Fergal. That weight pitched him forward, and he lost his balance, allowing one of Lang's strokes to come in wide of Fergal's guard and open a deep gash on his forearm.

The next blow came in just above his collarbone as his sword fell from his hand, and blood sprayed from his neck. Pain exploded from the area, and Fergal groaned. As he watched Lang's blade slice toward him again, he wondered what dying was like.

The Dreadrider cried, "For my brother!"

With that, Fergal's head was cleaved from his neck.

Breanna

Breanna didn't see Fergal die but knew he must have been vanquished by the Dreadrider when she felt Lang's rage-filled mind closing in on her through the *void*. She rolled to the ground with perfect timing as his blade slashed the air just above her head. Her fury over losing Fergal to the Dreadrider powered her muscles as *Lann Dàn* swept up before her. Her blades caught his hard overhead strike on their axis, and she twisted to force Lang's sword into the ground. Spinning away, one of her blades slashed up across the side of his face, opening a gash from his jawline to his temple.

Lang cursed as she anticipated his next move in the *void* and went low, leaving his sword to find only air. She raked his back with a blade as the motion of his heavy sword carried him around.

That drew an angry hiss from his lips. He aimed his next strike at her neck, which she rolled under as she slashed the back of his lower thigh deeply, cutting muscle and tendons.

Breanna spun and rose to one knee, her blades pointed up. Lang's leg folded as he turned toward her and lost his balance. The Dreadrider fell forward, impaling himself on the two sharp glowing blades. His sword fell to the ground, and he grabbed the shafts buried in his stomach and chest. For a long moment, they just stared at each other. Breanna saw hatred, rage, and begrudging respect in his eyes, and then blood began to pour through his fingers. As he toppled over, she came to her feet and stood over the Dreadrider. Lang groaned as she twisted her blades free and said, "Time to meet your gods without me."

With that, Breanna drove her blades into his gut and heart, and his eyes glazed with death. Satisfied she had avenged Fergal, she headed again for the monoliths surrounding the altar. Fighting between the two sides raged on, with Braoin, Bradaigh, and now Corbmac forming a three-pointed star while Hakon was still engaged in battle with Eoin. Only Runa stood between Breanna and her destiny.

The völva held her small jeweled sword and spat, "I'll not let you destroy us!"

Unable to hold in her disdain, Breanna feinted with her left and let her other long blade flash across the old crone's neck. Runa stumbled away with her hands clutching her throat, blood flowing, leaving Breanna alone at the altar.

Hakon and Eoin were still exchanging blows in her peripheral vision. She felt each of them in the *void* as they struggled for supremacy. She had not known the Dreadlord could use such magic. Her lover did all he could to stop the Dreadlord from reaching her, but her father was undoubtedly winning the battle.

Then Hakon Skadi whirled and removed her Chief's legs from beneath him, fortunately with the flat of his blade. Eoin stumbled and crashed to the ground, trying to keep himself between Breanna and the Dreadlord. She saw Hakon kick him in the groin and turn back to finish him, but Eoin toppled into him first, knocking the Dreadlord to his knees before falling beside him onto his own back. With that, her father reared back with his blade.

With *Lann Dàn* held high, Breanna knew Eoin would die in a second if she did not act, so she demanded, "Stop, Father!"

She was surprised when Hakon's arm froze, and he looked up, his eyes catching her with a feral gleam in the backdrop of the sun glistening through the woods. She was poised to use the magic of the *Dàns*.

His voice held no emotion when he asked, "Would you spare me?"

Then she heard Bláth, standing a short way from the Altar, whisper, "You are one with the land. Do what you must, Erin's Hero, do what you must to save it!"

Breanna was unsurprised to find the Bard hovering over her father's downed völva, with Bláth's bloody hunting knife in her hand, having ensured Runa didn't rise again. Yet she knew that using the magic at hand was not something she was doing to save her land.

To protect her Chief, her lover, Breanna began conjuring an image of Erin, without the Dreadlord, without her father—a land whole and pure, one uncorrupted by his dark hand. It was a time when her mother and the man who should have been her father were still alive, when she and Eoin Mac Cairbre could have walked hand in hand, and there was no *geas* on her soul.

She spat at her father, "Spare you? How can I spare you after what you've done to me, my mother, and my land?"

"Then I'm dead either way."

With that, she watched in horror as her father's blade plunged into Eoin's chest, his blood pumping onto the ground around him, and screamed, "No!"

Then Hakon was flinging his sword at her, at her own heart. It was an improbable cast, one that should not have been close. Yet she could see the blade finding its mark, see his iron blade driving deep into her chest if she did not act. What did it matter if she was lost as well? Nothing would be the same without Eoin at her side, and Toal and Fergal had paid the same price. She would sacrifice anything to fulfill her quest and rid her land of her father. And restore Eoin, Toal, and Fergal, as she no longer mattered. Only removing her father from Erin would be acceptable. If her gods saved her, who would she be—without being who she was? If only she could walk away with Eoin's hand in hers.

Heartbroken, Breanna Ban Morna accepted her fate and let the tips of her glowing long blades drop onto the Stone of Destiny with her new vision of Erin in her mind. When *Lann Dàn* touched *Lia Dàn*, pain seared into her heart and mind, and the world around her swirled as if the combined magics of the *Triple Dàns* had flung her backward and into the air.

Croí Dàn demanded, "*Remember your last grant of help from my Mother's ring!*"

Devastated and desperate, she thrust *Maorgairme* into the air and cried in her mind a final thought, "*Danu! Danu! Danu, save us!*"

With that, Dagda said, "*We've got you, daughter-mine.*"

EPILOGUE

Danu

The Mother Goddess of Erin sat beside the white pillar that had always held the Stone of Destiny, but *Lia Dàn* was still absent. Danu had often discussed her plans for Breanna Ban Morna to use the magic of the Triple Dàns with Dagda, Lugh, and Badb Catha. They had assured her it was the only way to hide *Inis Fáil*, what the Gaels called the Isle of Erin, from the white-haired Norvegrs and others who would come from beyond the Ninth Wave.

Removing their existence would ensure their gaze did not once again fall toward the Emerald Isle until a stronger *Ard-Rí* was again seated in Tara. That would also keep the Gaels worshipping the Tuatha gods, as they had promised many years before.

Lugh approached her with a look of concern etched on his face. "What troubles you?"

"I just hope giving the Stone of Destiny to Breanna Ban Morna was the right choice."

He rejoined, "If Badb Catha's magic works as expected, *Lia Dàn* will return to Falias, along with the two other *Dàns*, the Blades and the Heart."

"You know the Dark Goddess often creates fickle magic at best. Who can say how the *Triple Dàns* will react to their combined magics and send themselves afterward?"

He said, "You have been sitting here since Breanna left. Watching an empty pedestal won't bring *Lia Dàn* back any sooner."

"True," Danu answered with a sigh, glancing at him briefly. "But, it seems time is something we have much of while we wait."

Lugh watched her gaze wander back to the empty pillar. A moment after she spoke, *Lia Dàn* was suddenly there, as if the Stone of Destiny had never moved, had never been lent to Erin's Hero, had never been brought to the center of Erin for Breanna Ban Morna to wield.

The two gods reached for the crystal orb simultaneously, but Lugh deferred to his mistress and let her see what their chosen one had wrought. Then *Maorgairme's* magic was pulling hard at Danu. Breanna had used the magic of the *Triple Dàns* and Badb Catha's crystal ring simultaneously. And then their sentient *Croí Dàn* was demanding that Danu save her Hero!

Danu slipped from her seat and onto her knees with a deep groan. The combined magic of the *Triple Dàns* ripped through her as Breanna's vision reshaped the center of their land, where her Gael worshippers had lived under the Dreadlord's rule for seventeen years. The Stone of Destiny was still alive with images of the final battle between Erin's Hero and the Dreadlord.

Drawn by Breanna Ban Morna's third and final invocation of Badb's ring, the Mother Goddess reached into *Lia Dàn*, attempting to smooth out the raging currents of the new timeline Erin's

Hero had brought to life. While the magic within the strange ring compelled her to save her Heart's chosen one, Danu would have done it anyway after seeing the sacrifice she made for her land.

Then the All-Father joined her in spirit, saying, *"I can help, as she is now part of me."*

With *Ćroí Dàn* screaming in their minds—*"Mine! Save Mine!"*—the Mother Goddess and the All-Father felt the changes wrought in the *Cycle of Time* by the magic of the *Triple Dàns* rippling through the land. They struggled to find the right threads and weave them into a solid pattern. It was *Ćroí Dàn's* task to spread Breanna's reshaped vision, and the Heart of Destiny included her Heroes in her casting as the two had privately discussed. The magic reinserted most of those who had died because of Hakon's presence back into place as best it could.

Then, finally, Danu, Dagda, and *Ćroí Dàn* pulled Breanna's soul into the new timeline created by the Dreadlord's removal.

It was a difficult struggle, and many loose threads were left in the new life the Mother Goddess and All-Father had woven. Finished, Danu sat back with a sigh and released her mind's hold on *Lia Dàn*, and they let Breanna Ban Morna settle into the new pattern they had woven for the warrior, for Erin's Hero, slipping her back into Erin's new *Cycle of Time.*

A moment later, Badb Catha's strange ring, *Maorgairme,* appeared on Danu's finger, and *Lia Dàn* came alive with a view of the Mother Goddess's work. At her knees lay the twin blades of *Lann Dàn,* though there was no sign of *Ćroí Dàn.*

Lugh knelt to help Danu to her feet, having to hold her a moment to steady her so she could center her balance after the tremendous magic she and Dagda had wielded. He stooped to scoop up the Blades of Destiny, saying with a smile, "It seems I need to retrieve Breanna's set of iron long blades from that cave she left them in so she could win these."

"Aye," Danu agreed, a smile touching her lips for the first time in a long while. "Blades she won and wielded with skill and sacrifice while giving her own to the Heart of Destiny. Likely, it is why *Croí Dàn* did not return to me. She believes Erin's Hero still has work to do."

Badb Catha appeared suddenly, commenting, "Sister, I see from your worn look that the magic of the *Triple Dàns* took a toll on you. I'm just glad it wasn't me you had to pull through such a timeline change. And you, Lugh, hand those blades over to me."

As the Sun God started to protest, the Dark Goddess raised a hand, commanding, "*Lann Dàn* needs some refinements to support our Hero in the world of man. Goibhniu and I created them at a time when magic was the dominant force in the land. They need a *magical sharpening* to be useful to her now in the mortal world."

All-Father appeared next, adding, "Aye, they do, my love, as there is, indeed, still work for Erin's Hero, especially now that she has a part of me in her."

"She has what?" the Dark Goddess erupted. "What did you do now?"

Dagda shrugged, "Like Danu bonded with Our *Croí*, I bonded with Breanna. Since we consider our Heart one of us, I'd say Erin's Hero is now at least a Demi-Goddess and likely more, and I will be the one to train her."

"You are going to meddle with *things* again. I know it!"

"It's what I do best, woman!"

"Gah! You bugger things up more often than not!"

"Woman, you wound me!"

Danu and Lugh looked at each other and could only roll their eyes at the bickering All-Father and the Dark Goddess. Danu was pleased that All-Father had made Breanna Ban Morna one of them.

One of their own. Yet could Erin's Hero reshape history to save her people and fellow gods from what was to come, not just her people, but the remaining Gaels and Celts scattered across the mainland and Pretannia?

Yet that future can only become real if Brenna masters walking Erin's *Cycle of Time*!

Here ends *Lia Dàn* – Stone of Destiny
Dàn Cycle Two

This epic tale of the Gaels continues in:
Ćroí Dàn – Heart of Destiny
Dàn Cycle Three

**For those interested in a sneak peek of
Heart of Destiny, turn the page!**

Acknowledgments

want to thank Marty, Chris, Cindy, and Kimberly for their contributions to developing the original storyline many years ago, as well as all of my early readers who provided valuable input on what was a rough draft at the time. Marty, Chris, and Cindy are still with me, giving feedback on the various editions of Dàn Cycle One and Two, as well as Dàn Cycle Three and Four (and possibly Dàn Cycle Five).

While the First Edition *of Dàn Cycle One and Two improved over the original work, I required additional* editorial input for this Revised Edition. I am delighted to thank Holly Atkinson, who runs Evil Eye Editing (www.evileyeediting.com). For authors who do not believe they need a content editor, think again! Holly and her team have been fantastic!

A big thank you goes to Nadiia Kolpak, a talented illustrative artist from Ukraine, for producing my book covers and the website artwork; she also created the print and eBook layouts. I found Nadiia on Upwork.

As the Tuatha Gods spread my musical talents to other, more worthy humans, I want to recognize Claire Odlum and Muse

Cill for evolving our jointly created lyrics and compositions of the songs in the Dàn Cycle Novels and on the website (www.destinycycle.com, via YouTube links). I found Claire and Cilla on the Airgigs website. I even gave them the honorary title of *Dàn Cycle* Bards!

Guide to the Gaelic Language

While this novel is set in fifth-century Ireland, I primarily use modern Gaelic for specific words rather than early or old Irish versions. Yet, even with this, there are Irish and Scottish Gaelic variations to consider. Because certain vowels and consonants in Gaelic have no equivalent in English, it can be a complex language to read. A Gaelic-English dictionary (or an online source) helps to translate between the two languages.

Below is a summary of some differences that can assist with the pronunciation of these words. I have included phonations in parentheses to aid in sounding out names on the Central Characters & Places and Glossary pages. For those less inclined to make such an effort, sound out the word as you like. How it sounds to you will not insult the Tuatha Gods! I can't say the same for native Gaelic speakers, though.

Vowels & Vowel Combinations: Individual Gaelic vowel sounds are as follows: *a* is typically pronounced *ah*, as in father; *á* or *à* takes on a longer sound, as in Dàn taking on the sound dawn (note: the author chose Scottish Gaelic spelling of Destiny over the Irish Gaelic spelling, as cinniúint is too lengthy); *ae* takes on the sound *i*, as in high; when words end in *e*, it is always sounded out, as in fairie; *i* rarely takes on the sound *eye* and instead is usually an *ee* or *ih* sound, as in feel.

Some vowel combinations take on different sounds from English to Gaelic; *aoi* takes on a long *e*, as in peel; *ao* takes on *ay*, as in pay; *au* takes on the sound *ow*, as in pow. Accents such as `and ´ lengthen the sound of a letter.

Consonants: As with vowels, a few Gaelic consonants also take on different sounds from English; *c* always takes on a *k* sound, as in Celtic being pronounced Keltic; *ch* and *kh* are guttural, as in ache; *g* sounds are hard; *h* is not strictly a letter, but rather it's a function to aspirate or lengthen a consonant, and thus *lh* would take on the sound full.

I hope you have some fun with Gaelic!

Central Characters
& Places & Terms

Aife (Ee-fa) – Mate of the former Dun Arrogh Chief Cairbre, a Princess of the Blood from Dál nAraidi, and Eoin's mother.

Aos Dána (Ays Daw-ah) – Led by All-Father, wise ones of the Celts known as Druids; comprised of four sects, each wielding Tuatha powers such as the *sight* and *void*, with others controlling the five Elements.

Ard-Rì (Ard-ree) – The High King of Ireland, the Chieftain to whom all Clan Chiefs swear allegiance.

Bards – History keepers, storytellers, and master musicians of the *Aos Dána*.

Bean-Sidhe (Banshee) – *Sidhe* women who are young and beautiful and wail or keen over the dead or those soon to be so; often referred to as harbingers of death; another name for similar fairies is *Sìthiche* (Shee-uh-khe), who can be both benevolent and malevolent; note the Irish and Scottish Gaels spell the word for fairies differently, with it being *Sidhe* and *Sìth*, respectively.

Badb Catha (Biv Kah-ha) – Goddess of Death and Knowledge, commonly called Goddess of War, and The Mórrigan, often taking the form of a battle crow on the earthly plane.

Beatha (Bay-uh) – A Fire Elemental Druid Seeress, called a Fáidh, near Dun Arrogh, one of the *Aos Dána*.

Bláth (Blaw) – An Air Elemental Druid and Master Bard of Dun Uisneach; Bards were a sect of Druids known as Filídh in Gaelic.

Bradaigh (Brad-ee) – Bastard son of Hakon Skadi and a Gaelic warrior who joins Breanna's Band.

Braoin (Breen) – Bastard son of Hakon Skadi and a Gaelic warrior who joins Breanna's Band.

Breanna Ban Morna (Bree-an-na Bawn Mor-na) – Initially a Red Branch warrior from Dun Arrogh who is of Clan Dálaigh (Daw-lee) and the daughter of Morna and Nevan, with her actual father being Hakon Skadi. The Heart of Destiny chooses her to be Erin's Hero.

Brede – Dreadrider of Garm and the oldest of Hakon Skadi's warriors; he is also one of the Norvegr leaders known as Dreadriders.

Breitheamh (Breh-huv) – Judicial sect of the *Aos Dána* that acts as judges, lawmakers, interpreters, and negotiators.

Cairbre (Car-bree) – Former Chief of Dun Arrogh, mated with Aife and Eoin's father; killed by Hakon Skadi soon after the Norvegrs arrived.

Celts (Kelts) – People who once occupied a significant part of Europe and the Northern Isles; those from southwest France and northeast Spain, specifically those from Galicia, were considered the ancestors of the Gaelic.

Cilla Ban Calla – Daughter of Calla, Dun Arrogh's cook.

Claimh Solais (Kly-vuh Soh-lish) – One of the Four Treasures or *Jewels* brought to Erin by Dagda and Danu and wielded initially by the Sun God, Lugh; he gifted it to Nuada of the Silver Hand, one-time King of the Tuatha; once unsheathed, no enemy could resist the Sword of Light or escape from its path.

Corbmac (Korb-mak) – Commander of the *fians* in the south part of Mide; *fían-ceannard* (fee-un kyan-ard) in Gaelic.

Ćroí Dàn (Kree Dawn) – Created by the Mother Goddess, Danu, and known as the Heart of Destiny, *Ćroí Dàn* is a heart-shaped ruby pendant that endows heroes of the land to rise above their mortal beings, become true defenders of Erin, and rally clan warriors to their cause.

Cycle of Time – The Stone of Destiny's magical bridge through time, allowing those with the *sight* to see the many possible timelines of Erin and the world. Also, the Druidic yearly cycle of Winter Solstice, Imbolc, Spring Equinox, Beltane, Summer Solstice, Lammas, Autumn Equinox, and Samhain.

Cuilcagh Mountains (Kwil-cah) – Northwest of Dun Arrogh.

Dagda (Dahg-duh) – All-Father of the Tuatha pantheon, Dagda is the God of Life, Death, and Fertility over the land and its people; he is also the first Druid and a master of all things magical, often considered wise, witty, and wily. Dagda typically resides on the Tuatha island of Murias.

Dál Riata (Dawl Ree-uh-tuh) – An area claimed by Gaelic Clans that became known as Scotti territory in ancient times of the many Celtic tribes of Albion; it once comprised the northeastern part of Ulaida in Erin and the Northwestern part of what is now Scotland, then known as Argyll.

Danu (Dah-noo) – Mother, Earth, and Moon Goddess of Erin, also known as the Triple Goddess and the Silver Huntress, when she takes her wolf form; she is co-creator with the Dagda of the entirety of the *Tuatha Dé Danann* pantheon.

Druid (Drew-id) – *Aos Dána* are Dagda's masters of law, music, foreseeing, healing, and Tuatha magic, such as the *sight, void,* and *Cycle of Time*. Some, known as Elementals, can also manipulate the elements of Air, Earth, Water, and Fire.

Dun (Doon) – Earth mounds and pickets that usually surround a settlement of several clans for defensive purposes; duns or ringforts typically consisted of the main hall and several small conical-shaped huts serving as living quarters.

Dun Arrogh (Doon A-ruhg) – A moderate-sized ringfort where Clans Mórdha and Dálaigh splinters settled.

Dun Uisneach (Doon Ish-nach) – A substantial Gaelic ringfort located in southwest Mide along the High King's Road, also known as *Slíghe Mor* (Slee-geh More). Chief Faolán and Chieftess Falyn oversee the formidable fortress.

Dun Tara – The seat of the High Kings of ancient Ireland, located in eastern Mide.

Eoin Mac Cairbre (Owen Mak Car-bree) – Dun Arrogh and Red Branch Chief of Clan Mórdha, cousin of Fergal, and a Prince of the Blood from Ulaida

Erin (Eh-rin) - Four primary provinces or kingdoms comprised what the Gaelic called old Ireland. Connachta (Kon-akh-ta) is in the northwest; Mummu (Moo-moo), later called Munster, is in the southwest; Ulaida (Ul-ay-duh) is in the northeast; and Laigin (Lay-gin) is in the southeast. Royal Mide (Roy-uhl My-de) was carved out of the original provinces by the first-century High King Túathal Techtmar, and led the land from Tara. Unfortunately, this last kingdom did not survive as a province on its own after the heroic period of the fifth century passed; High Kings would not reemerge for four to five centuries.

Falias (Fah-lee-us) - One of four fairie islands where the Tuatha resided with Danu and Lugh; often called *Tír na nÓg* (Teer-na-a nug) by the Gaels.

Falyn (Fa-lyn) – Chieftess of Dun Uisneach and mate to Faolán; her children are Dáithí (Daw-hee), Oisín (Uh-sheen), and Teagan (Tea-gan).

Faolán (Fae-o-lawn) – Chief of Dun Uisneach and mate to Falyn.

Fáidh (Faw-ee) – The prophetic sect of the *Aos Dána,* typically called Seers or ovates.

Fergal Mac Conall (Fur-gul Mak Koh-nawl) – Dun Arrogh Red Branch warrior of Clan Conall, a subordinate clan to Clan Mórdha (Mur-dha) and cousin of Eoin Mac Cairbre. Eventually, a Warrior of Destiny and Sinéidin's mate.

fíanna (fee-un-nuh) – Initially, freeborn Fir Bolg warriors – and after a time, interbred Gaels – formed into the first army by Fionn MacCumhaill and served the High Kings in Tara; Fionn formed the *fíanna* into *fíans* (fi-anns), or bands of nine, who eventually served local Chieftains and kings when the first reign of the High Kings ended.

Fir Bolg (Feer Bulg) – The original people of Erin who were subjugated first by Fomorians and then by the Tuatha.

Fomorians (Foh-mawr-ee-uhn) – A race that settled in Erin after the fall of Atlantis; subsequently defeated by the Tuatha.

Fragarach (Frea-gar-thach) – A sword, also called Answerer, brought from the otherworld by Lugh, the Celtic God of the Sun; known to be able to pierce any armor, and later gifted to the Celtic God of the Sea, Manannán Mac Lir.

Gaelic (Gay luhk)– A people who came to Erin after the Tuatha, arriving from a part of the Celtic empire known as Galicia, also called Gaels.

Hakon Skadi (Hah-kon Skah-de) – Dreadlord of Garm, son of a Norvegr Jarl, and killer of his father; Norvegrs later became known as Norsemen or Vikings.

Erin | Éire (ay-rah) – The Emerald Island, also known as Ireland.

Kyras (K-eye-rass) – Dun Arrogh Smith of Clan Dálaigh, brother
of Nevan, mate to Lissa, Toal's father, and Breanna's uncle.

Lang – Dreadrider of Garm, brother of Lunt; killed by Breanna.

Lann Dàn (Lanna Dawn) – Blades of Destiny, created by Badb
Catha, the Goddess of War; they were a pair of long dia-
mond-bladed weapons with oak hafts imbued with the power
to battle invaders wielding magic.

Laoch (Lay-ukh) – The nearly forgotten name for the Warrior
Druid Sect, once referred to as Laoch Draíochta (Dree-ukh-
tah), or Warriors of Magic.

Lia Dàn (Lee-ah Dawn) – Stone of Destiny, a round crystal brought
to Erin by the Mother Goddess Danu. It enables those holding
it to see both the past and possible future timelines via the
Cycle of Time.

Lissa – Mated with Kyras, Toal's mother, of Clan Dálaigh.

Lugh (Loo) – Sun God and wielder of Tuatha's magical *Jewels*
and other items of the *Tuatha Dé Danann*, sometimes seen
as a great white stag in his animal or familiar form known
as Cernunnos.

Lunt – Dreadrider of Garm, brother of Lang; killed by Breanna.

Maorgairme (May-or-gair-mee) – An amulet ring created by the
Dark Goddess to aid the bearer with fickle magic and summon
the Tuatha Gods in great need.

Mórrigan (Mohr-ree-gan) – The name of the Goddess of War, Fate,
and Knowledge, also known as Badb Catha or the Dark Goddess, when she takes her crow form.

Morna Ban Cahir (Mor-na Bawyn Kah-hee) – Mated with Nevan,
mother of Orla, Ronat, and Breanna of Clan Dálaigh.

Nevan – Warrior mate to Morna, brother of Kyras, and of Clan
Dálaigh; by Hakon Skadi soon after the Norvegrs arrived.

Niall Noígíallach (Nye-al Nee-Gal-ach) – The High King in
fifth-century Ireland, also known as the *Ard-Rì*; the ancestor

of the Uí Néill dynasties, which governed significant parts of the Emerald Isle for many centuries; his son, Lóegaire Mac Néill, followed him as the next High King.

Ogham (Oh-am) – Typically only used by the *Aos Dána*, it is the written language of the Celts.

Ollamh (O-lam) – Healer sect of the *Aos Dána*.

Red Branch – A band of warriors in old Ulaida led by Rory the Red; in Gaelic, they were called *Craeb Ruad* (krayb roo-ad); it was a name resurrected by Eoin Mac Cairbre of Clan Mórdha when he organized the young warriors in Dun Arrogh to fight the Dreadlord.

River Shannon – Divides the Kingdoms of Connachta, Mummu, Laigin, and Mide.

Rune Stones – Black stones used by *Asgardian* magic wielders like Runa, etched with symbols to help divine the future.

Sidhe (shee) – What the Gaelic people call fairie or Tuatha mounds and living places; also spelled as *Sith* (shee) in the northeast part of Ireland and the western coast of Scotland, in the region once known as Dál Riata.

Sight – A common name for the vision state of the *Aos Dána* used to touch the *Cycle of Time* to see a past or possible future.

Tir na nÓg (Teer-Na-Nug) – Alternate name for the Tuatha realm of Falias.

Toal Mac Kyras (Toe-al Mak Ky-rass) – Dun Arrogh Red Branch warrior of Clan Dálaigh, cousin of Breanna.

Tuatha Dé Danann (Too-ah-ha Day Dah-nahn) – Magical beings who came to Erin after the fall of Atlantis, some known as *Sidhe or Sith*, often mistaken as faerie or fae, which originated in the 1500s. In Destiny Cycle, the author used the spelling fairies to depict these Tuatha beings.

Tuatha Dé Danann Islands – Falais (Fall-eece); Findias (Fin-dee-us); Gorias (Gore-us); and Murias (Mord-us)

Urghabháil an neamhní (ur-guh-vawl un nyow-nee) – Means to
"seize the *void*." This state allows some of the warrior class who
have reached mastery level to access the magic of the Faerie
realm, similar to the *sight* typically used by other Tuatha *Aos
Dána* sects to access Erin's *Cycle of Time* through *Lia Dàn*, the
Stone of Destiny.

Ulicia (You-lee-see-ah) – An Earth Elemental Druid and Healer,
known as an Ollamh in Gaelic, and one of the *Aos Dána*
assigned to Dun Arrogh.

Mythology & Legends

The *Dàn Cycle* series, you now know, revolves around Gaelic and Celtic mythology, especially that of the Irish. Their myths, legends, and lore have been interpreted in many ways over the centuries. For authors in such a genre, we pick which thread lines to present among those posited by many historians. For those who follow Fae fantasy themes (which I also love), those myths emerged over a thousand years after the Tuatha legends envisioned here. Thus, I used a setting as close to semi-historical as possible to build this world.

As for the characters, I based some on historical figures and others on fictitious characters. The same goes for titles like Erin's Hero. The names of gods used in this series come from well-known myths and legends, and some have multiple formal names that require capitalization.

Speaking of capitalizing words referencing gods, I use the following conventions: Tuatha gods, gods of Asgard, Asgardian gods, or any general god. The names with proper titles are: Tuatha God All-Father, just All-Father, Sun God (with or without a name like Lugh), Mother Goddess, Dark Goddess, Goddess of War, One God, Goddess of Language, God of History, etc.

Additionally, Gaelic words for Druids and their English counterparts are capitalized, thus Bard (*Filidh*), Healer (*Ollamh*), Seer/Seeress (*Fáidh*), and Lawgiver (*Breitheamh*). Similarly, the Druidic Elements powers are Air (*Aer*), Water (*Uisce*), Earth (*Talamh*), Fire (*Tine*), and Aether (*Eitear*).

About Gael Druids & Sigils

I n the *Dàn Cycle* series, the first Druid was the Tuatha God All-Father. In the days when the Gaels first came to Erin from the coastal region of the Spanish region once known as Galicia, Dagda created five sects. He passed his magic to them once the *Tuatha Dé Danann* and the Gaels forged the Great Agreement, where they both would halt their battles in exchange for the Gaels paying homage to the Tuatha Gods. In turn, the Tuatha ceded the land of Erin to the Gaels, with some Tuatha remaining in the underhalls of Erin that Danu, All-Father, Badb, and Lugh had created. Others chose to retreat to their magical island realms. Dagda's Druids were the skilled guides who ensured the Gaels remembered the myths and legends of the Tuatha and continued their worship of the adopted gods.

Dagda's five Druidic Sects are Lawgivers, Healers, Seers, Bards, and Warriors, where he passed specific knowledge to each sect, along with how to seize the *void* and the *sight* when they needed to connect the realm of Erin with the Tuatha realms. Using the high council of each Druidic sect, All-Father also passed on the secrets of manipulating the five Elements: Air, Water, Earth,

Fire, and Aether (the energy of life). Details on each of these sects can be found below.

Fáidh: Seers used their *sight* to touch the *Cycle of Time*, seeking to understand possible future timelines and listen to the voices of their *Tuatha Dé Danann* gods. Seers and Seeresses often would have an affinity for the Water and Aether Elements and wore green and red robes.

Filídh: As history keepers, storytellers, and master musicians, a Bard used the *void* to retrieve the mass of words that comprised the entirety of the Gaelic people's experience; none could recall that much knowledge without it. They wore yellow and green robes and tended to be Air Elementals, which helped them cast their voice.

Ollamh: Healers could seize the *void* to draw on the deep understanding of healing and pull power from the Tuatha realm to mend the sick and wounded. They wore green and red robes, typically commanding Aether and Earth or Water Elements to heal.

Laoch: Warriors focused on ensuring their Gaels had the expertise to protect their people. The most proficient of these warriors bore the title *Laoch Draíochta*, a Warrior of Magic. They could seize the *void* in battle and typically wield one of two Elements, such as Earth and Water or Air and Fire. Their strategy and blade-work skills made them Battle Masters, with the most senior among them commanding all the physical Elements. Their sect has all but disappeared from the Emerald Isle.

Sigils of Power: Using the Druidic (rune-based) language of Ogham, Druids create sigils as amplifiers of intent and typically incorporate one or more of the five Elements. They would etch them in wood, metal, or stone. Applying woad on one's skin (called woading) could also have been used by a Druid to leverage such sigils. The sigil below represents the five Elements.

About James

I grew up on a small lake in the upper Midwest of the USA, exploring the natural surroundings that embraced me, with miles of trails and waterways branching out from my family's home on the lake. I could travel across my lake, slip into a tributary creek or river, and go up or down it for hours with my small boat and its little outboard motor. My trusted dog sometimes joined me, standing at the prow like a warrior sentinel. At other times, he would rather sleep in the comfort of his lakeside home.

He was often fickle like that, sometimes deciding he needed a "Canadian Walkabout" in the neighborhoods around the lake and getting into trouble. Our family has a long line of Quebecers, and women in our line used a euphemism to describe their men who would go roaming the land in search of *adventure*. Anyway, I remember the little rascal fondly.

Like many during my youth, I experimented with some forbidden things, which quickly grew old. Esoteric matters caught my attention for a time, and I found a young lady with similar thoughts on reincarnation and karma. As I pursued college and tried my hand at fine arts, I discovered my left hand was not so good at the *fine* part. I got married and entered the technology sector to make a living. Then, I switched my major from fine arts to English with a focus on Creative Writing.

After a failed first attempt at writing a set of great fantasy novels, work, raising a family, and life took over my time. Writing faded as a priority. Yet it resurfaced years later with this Gaelic adventure set in Celtic Ireland, which started as a dream - literally. We traveled across the pond to see that land and its people, and they captured my heart and imagination.

Being a quarter Scottish of Clan Ferguson, the Gaels became my people; their history, legends, and mythologies became mine. The Celts of Europe, especially Galicia, where the Gaels originated, became mine. The Druids and their gods became mine, as did the injustices inflicted on my people, which became a vision.

What if the Gaels of Ireland could change the history of the world by changing the Isle of Erin's timeline? And Britain's, starting with Rome's first-century invasion?

It would take a Hero and the *Tuatha Dé Danann*, who backed her, to make that happen.

Welcome to *Dàn Cycle,* or in English, Destiny Cycle.
I hope you enjoyed reading this adven-
ture as much as I did while writing it.

It is where Gaels Rule!
www.destinycycle.com

Interested in a sneak peek of Heart of Destiny?
Turn the page!

Croí Dàn - Heart of Destiny: Preview

Loose Threads

Breanna

Breanna Ban Morna let her long blades flash in toward Eoin, who deflected the first one and swirled just out of range of the other before attempting a riposte. His sword swung wide of her as she spun outside of his reach, her flaming red hair flowing behind her. They clashed several more times, with no successful touches. When Eoin tried another backslash, she cast the word *shield* into the *void* so he could not see her counter in the space they shared and deftly rolled beneath his sword.

The grassy meadow cradled her shoulders briefly as she regained her footing, letting a haft flick out to catch the back of Eoin's knee. When he tumbled to the ground, Breanna was quickly on top of him, straddling his hips, her ancient long blades crossed over his exposed neck.

Eoin puffed out a breath, protesting, "No fair! You cut me out of our combined space in the *void*!"

"Then get better at using it! You rely on sharing too much."

"Aye, I should," he rejoined with a grin. "Though if I have to lose this bout to you, I prefer it end with you on top of me over any other."

Breanna blushed, realizing their respective positions. "Och, you oaf, I should draw a little blood for that comment—to show the others I beat you again! I'm sure you'd rail at me if I ended up on top of a Connachta raider like this to slit his throat."

"Aye, I might do just that," Eoin replied. "Seeing my wom— Champion bestriding anyone would be troubling."

Breanna caught his slip of the tongue. Now and then, she would think she and Eoin might be able to build a life together, but then he would start on one of his diatribes about what a woman should and shouldn't be. She hissed, "You only get that way when I show you up after we have fought off a Connachta raiding party, especially when I take out more warriors than you. I hear the rumors, you know, that many other clans fear me in battle. I was born to be a warrior. We both know it!"

Bristling with sheathed dirks, she rose above Eoin, nicked his neck with a long blade, and angrily spun away from him, only to come face to face with Ulicia. She gruffly demanded, "What do you want?"

The Healer Druid ignored her tone, save for a raised eyebrow. "Bre, it's your mother. She's taken a turn for the worse."

"No," she murmured and turned to speed toward Dun Arrogh.

Later, after the sun had set, Breanna sank to the rushes on the packed earthen ground, her heart heavy as she held her mother's frail hand in hers, a hand that had carried her throughout her childhood. Their wattle-and-daub hut felt empty. Tomorrow, she realized it would be even more so. Her sisters, Olra and Ronat, had spent time with their mother earlier, so they were alone. Everyone in Dun Arrogh knew Morna wouldn't last the night, that on the eve of Samhain, they would be burying another Clan Dálaigh matriarch.

She gazed at the fire as her mother stroked her lustrous, red hair. When Breanna looked up, she saw her mother smiling faintly, her eyes glistening with tears. Morna whispered, "You remind me so much of my younger self, though that white streak in your hair is a mystery."

Breanna brushed her fingers over the white shock, her frown deepening. "I always wondered about it, but it's not important now."

Morna added more intently, "Bre, I sense a fresh scent about you that speaks of blooming youth, one destined to burn brightly."

Breanna's skepticism flickered to life as she looked up to catch her mother's gaze. "I don't know how that could be. Sometimes, I feel lost, like a leaf tumbling in a fall breeze. And now, Ulicia says you'll be gone by morning, and I don't know what course my life will take, save I want to be a warrior."

Morna sighed. "Just yesterday, you were a tiny bundle in my arms, your father beaming with pride beside me. So many years lost—but our Druid Healer has it right. I'm fading. I don't have the will to send you away, but it's probably best you let me go peacefully into the night so I can find Nevan once more."

Breanna whispered, her voice quivering, "I wish your *anam* peace during your journey to find him, Mum."

She had lost her father to a sparring match gone wrong just after she was born. No memory of him survived her childhood, save for tales that others told her of his bravery with his long blades. They had been her grandmother's before that—the same blades passed down to her.

"Thank you, my lovely daughter. While I realize Kyras is busy with his forge, he and Lissa will look after you. If only you and Eoin could find a workable arrangement, I would go more peacefully."

At their previous Beltane Festival, Breanna had turned down Eoin's suggestion that they join as mates, and Morna knew why. Breanna looked away. "Mother, find solace in Ronat and Orla making good matches with their mates. I must find my destiny somehow and somewhere in our land."

Morna wheezed, drawing Breanna's eyes back to her mother. "I never puzzled out where you got your green eyes from. I remember them as blue when you were little, and no one on either my father's or your father's side has those glowing red flecks. It's like they were a gift from the Mother Goddess herself."

Breanna shrugged, unsure of what to say. "Much of my life feels like a mystery, save for being a warrior. Our Druids can only shake their heads over my strange ways of sensing things I shouldn't be able to, especially in duels or battles. Perhaps our ancient gods hold the key to my fate. I'd certainly like to know what Dagda and Danu had in mind for me when they cast my lot."

"Few of us know such things, Bre, but you must find a way to move forward," Morna advised. "You'll soon have to accept the man who loves you. It is time to start a new life."

"A man who loves me," Breanna echoed, dropping her gaze to the rush-covered floor as if it held the answers she sought. Then she looked up and added bitterly, "A man like Eoin Mac Cairbre, who wants me as his mate, expecting me to abandon my dreams so I can stand beside him! I bested him again in our match today, and he made light of my victory."

"Bre, I tolerated your passion for battle—even when you insisted on winning a gold Celtic Knot this past summer. Much like your father did, and before him, your grandmother, all wielding those ancient long blades with pride."

Morna grumbled, "Maybe I shouldn't have. Yet you must understand that men can feel threatened by a woman who battles as fiercely as you. That said, Eoin, our next Dun Chief, is certainly invested in you."

"A woman has every right to fight as fiercely as any man—"

"We've had this discussion before." Morna raised a hand, her voice faltering as a cough seized her. "Now, it's time to let me die in peace. Leave me with a kiss, my sweetest child."

Breanna leaned down, pressing her lips to her mother's forehead, a mix of sorrow and love swelling within her. After a lingering hug, she rose and picked up her long blades. Next to them lay a new spear, a bow, and a quiver full of arrows. She grumbled to herself, as she couldn't recall how she'd acquired those weapons. Then Breanna slid her blades into their harness and shrugged the supple leather construct onto her shoulders.

Looking at her mother one last time, she found her asleep and stepped out of their small hut, her refuge throughout the years. A thick fog clung to her memories, obscuring the vibrant moments of her past and leaving only vague impressions. It was a life woven with the struggles of her kin, the whispers of ancient spirits, and the enchantments that shaped their fate. She asked the night sky, "Why do I feel so unmoored? By the stars, what's happened to me?"

Breanna stood amongst the huts, looking across Dun Arrogh's yard to the central hall. Smoke rose from two round vents at each end, one for the ovens and one for the fireplace. She wondered why her life seemed jumbled as she took in the gloomy firelight from various torches.

Breanna caught sight of her sisters, who stood in the hall's doorway. They had been chatting with their Druid Healer when they looked her way, their expressions dour as always. Prepared to abandon the dun for a time, she turned away and abruptly ran into her cousin Toal.

He hesitated, momentarily holding her arms, then said, "Sorry to hear how badly your mother is ailing, Bre. Our family will miss her. If I can do anything for you, you will let me know, right?"

When Toal's earnest gaze told her he needed acknowledgment, Breanna pulled him into a hug, something she rarely did. He stiffened for a moment and then hugged her back.

"I will. You've always been my favorite of our clan. Thanks for those words." Untangling herself from him, she added, "I need some fresh air. I'll see you in the morning."

Breanna Ban Morna, the fierce and feared warrior of the Clan Dálaigh, headed away from the huts and walked to the gates alone. The familiar weight of her well-worn oak hafts pressed against each shoulder as if they were an extension of her body, a legacy passed down through generations, each warrior forging a bond with the long blades, always kept as sharp as she could make them.

When she reached the gates, she stopped. Thick clouds blanketed the chilly black night, an apt sign of the weight she felt upon her. The layer hid what would have been a nearly full moon, the body in the sky that Mother Goddess claimed dominion over.

She lifted a hand to her neck, took a deep breath, and pulled her heart-shaped ruby pendant from her tunic. It felt familiar, as if holding secrets of another time. She could not remember who had given it to her, but every time she closed her hand around it, the gem seemed like something she had always worn, almost as if it had known her and could talk to her. Yet, that could not be—jewels couldn't speak. Could they?

Their Druids claimed the barrier between the living and the dead was at its thinnest during the Harvest Festival, and few would spend the night beneath the sky with the many spirits of the Tuatha Dé Dannan walking the land. Breanna held her head high, for while there were truths in those tales, she was unafraid. Though the source of her certainty eluded her, an unshakeable instinct told her such spectral creatures could not and would not touch her.

Strangely, that was another of her many memories that seemed blurred. Breanna shook her head, hoping to clear the cobwebs, unable to fathom why nothing made sense. Why did it feel like she had lived a different life?

As the evening deepened, a couple walked through the gates, arriving late for the ancient festival called Samhain. All living nearby, in both settlements, or those living alone, were welcome to the communal gathering at Dun Arrogh. This pair was likely the last to arrive for this evening. She recognized them as being part of Calla's clan, who frequently visited their cook's family. Yet, the promise of more revelers would come with the dawn. The two mates nodded respectfully at her, which she returned in kind before her gaze drifted back to the enveloping shadows, a hint of unease flickering within her.

A voice Breanna recognized broke the silence, pulling her from her tangled thoughts. Eoin, her staunch friend—and would-be lover if she ever accepted him—offered quietly, "Ulicia says your mother's *anam* will seek her next destiny by morning. I'm truly sorry, Bre. Her absence will echo in our hearts. And I am sorry for my ill-timed words after our match this afternoon."

"It's okay," she replied, her voice barely above a whisper, unwilling to meet his eyes. She wished to be alone, yet she lacked the strength to send him away. The thought of solitude sent a chill through her bones, a reminder of the soon-awaited emptiness.

Turning that concern aside, Breanna wondered why she could battle as she did, understanding that not only could she seize the *void*—what their Druids called the *urghabháil an neamhní*—but her abilities were unmatched. Only Eoin came close to being her equal in blade skills from time to time. Their Fáidh, Beatha, insisted their gods had touched her at birth.

Yet Breanna's memories seemed full of holes. She looked down at her fine boots, sleek dirks strapped to each of them, not remembering when she'd bought them or where the money to do so would have come from. There were dirks sheathed to her vambraces and two more on her waistbelt positioned to each side. She also wore simple yet flexible boiled-leather pauldrons to protect her shoulders. Then, there were the expertly crafted spear and bow with a full quiver and gloves back in her hut.

With a shake of her head, she asked, "Eoin, I know this will sound strange, but I feel like a hedgehog. Where did all of this fine weaponry come from?"

Eoin looked at her quizzically. "You don't remember? It was a great moment in your life and a prodigious honor for Dun Arrogh."

She looked up at him with pleading eyes. "No."

"At the Dun Uisneach summer games, you were declared the Annual *Comórtas* Champion," he stated.

"That doesn't seem right."

"Then Faolán and Falyn, the dun's joint *Ceann-cinnidh* and *Ceann-feadhna*, showered you with praise and gifts of new weapons, armor, boots, tunics, leggings, and that fine otter skin cloak. It has been six generations since a wielder of long blades bested one with a sword, and longer still since it was a woman named *Comórtas* Champion. You did both, and everyone started comparing you to former legends like Macha and Maeve. You quickly bested Bradaigh and claimed your grandmother's golden arm ring."

"Hmm," Breanna said. "That's not how I remember the moment. It was a tie."

"No, Bre, it was not a tie," Eoin countered. "It was not even close. Rather, it was an exhibition of a warrior with complete command of the *void*. Somehow, later that day, you showed us your path to reach the place between the realms and wield the *void* as you do. Certainly not as well as you, but much better than before."

"Us?"

"Me, Fergal, Toal, and someone else, a warrior about your age named Braoin, who hails from the south end of Loch Síleann," Eoin informed her, his gaze concerned.

Breanna commented, "I remember Braoin and his twin swords. He moves swiftly and is certainly much easier to get along with than that brawny Bradaigh."

"When we returned to Dun Arrogh, we started teaching our younger warriors about your way. Yet now I am concerned that something is very awry with you. We need to seek out Beatha."

"Aye," she agreed. Then Breanna stiffened. "Yet the Seeress has always meddled in my life. I'm not sure I truly trust her. My mother once mentioned that Beatha cast a *geas* over me before I was born, but I can't remember why. Then she left us to her bumbling apprentice, Aodhfin."

"What are you talking about?" Eoin asked. "Beatha and Ulicia have shared the same hut for years. While Aodhfin is still, indeed, a bumbling fool, I'm very concerned about you, Bre."

When she added nothing else, Eoin sighed. "What will you do now?"

Breanna knew what that question meant. Could she accept his proposal to join hands and dance around the Beltane Tree with him in the coming spring? Yet, how could his mother, Aife, a Princess of the Blood, accept a half-breed like her into their clan? *What? Half-breed? Who was a half-breed?* Unsure where that thought came from, she shook her head.

Breanna finally answered, "I don't know. Rumors have it that the *Ard-Rì* is seeking fían leaders to assist him in monitoring the followers of the One God. I was thinking about going to Tara and seeing if I could fight my way to the leadership of a band of nine. Then I can roam the countryside, enforcing his laws. Or maybe the High King will take me abroad, and I can help him trade with and raid other lands. He is said to like such adventures."

Eoin shrugged. "While others might question those dreams, I can understand them. You always wanted to be a warrior first, not a Chief's mate. I suppose there's nothing I can do to change that. Today's match proved that yet again."

Breanna nodded, surprised he had acknowledged her desire. She knew how others saw her, for they had often mentioned the way her graceful steps around her opponents seemed choreographed to some strange music that only she heard. Her flaming red hair, with a white slash at her left temple, flowed behind her with each swift step. The calm and icy demeanor with which she fought made it seem like their gods had cast her destiny.

Yet her Chief—no, her Prince—wistfully added, "A lonely life, but being a *fian-ceannard?* That's beneath you, my love. We could be like Faolán and Falyn, joint *Ceann-cinnidh* and *Ceann-feadhna*, joint leaders, here at Dun Arrogh. You saw what they had together at the games. She is his *Taoiseach.* I want something like that with you."

"You could join me," Breanna suggested, turning her eyes on him. "We can renew our ties to Dun Uisneach on the way, yet still strive for more."

Eoin sighed. "Everyone's expecting me to be *Ceann-cinnidh* once my father dies."

"That won't be for years, and he's not so old and still fearsome. Maybe just for a season?" Breanna suggested hopefully. Doing such a tour would be a dream come true. "While you're better than Fergal, you could use more—well, seasoning. Since I am your Champion, your father will know that no single combat challenge would put you at risk from becoming the next Chief of Dun Arrogh."

"Fergal would not be happy."

"Och, well, he is often unhappy with his life." Breanna shrugged. "Anyway, it was but a thought. It might have been fun battling together while the seasons cycle from autumn to winter to spring, showing the world we are the best warriors in our land."

"Aye," Eoin answered with a smile, his eyes shining. "That would be glorious, wouldn't it? Yet, what about Breanna's Band? They would want to join us. It would be a great experience for them, but my father wouldn't let all of them go with us."

"Breanna's Band? You mean your Red Branch?"

"What are you talking about, Bre?"

"We created our own Red Branch—because the younger ones needed training in our warrior ways. To fight off, um, invaders. Only yesterday, I bested Fergal to earn the right to be your Champion."

Eoin frowned and shook his head. "Nay, once you won the *Comórtas* this past summer, Fergal resigned. He declared that your way with the *void* made you his superior, and that's when we all started calling Dun Arrogh's warriors Breanna's Band."

"What?" she demanded. "How can that be?"

"It just is," came his answer. "Fergal and Toal can confirm it. We must talk with Beatha in the morning."

Breanna was silent for a time, wondering what was making her feel like she genuinely had no right to be his Champion due to her tainted blood—but tainted by what?

Eoin broke into her thoughts, saying, "For tonight, sleep in my clan's roundhouse so you can let your mother pass on in peace."

Breanna could only nod as Eoin wrapped her in his strong arms. "Please take the lead with Beatha," she requested. "I don't fully trust her, and I don't know why. In the meantime, seize the *sight* with me."

As they did so, she felt the land around them, and all was at peace like she had not felt in a long time, as if she and the land could be one. Yet, to the east, something was off. Something was not right—something near Tara.

What could be wrong in her land? Wait! What? When did Erin become her land? That notion made her shudder.

Danu

The Mother Goddess stood in the same grove where she had first met Breanna Ban Morna via the Druid Beatha. It was where *Croí Dàn* proclaimed her Erin's Hero, on a night that surrounded her with nary a light to see by. With a blanket of clouds overhead, despite a full moon, she had bounded into the clearing where Beatha had started a fire and met a warrior who made Erin whole. Now, using the *sight*, Danu watched the meeting between Dagda's brilliant young warrior and Eoin Mac Cairbre play out for another moment before she pulled her attention from *Lia Dàn* and placed it in a pouch on her belt.

Even though she knew Breanna had fragments of memories from her life as the Norvegr Destroyer, Danu was pleased with what she had wrought. When the *Cycle of Time* was about to sweep away Breanna's *anam*, at that precise moment between life and death, Danu accomplished what was needed, what her conscience demanded. Thanks to All-Father's help. Without him, she might have failed to save Erin's Hero, especially now that she knew about his bond with her. Together, she and Dagda could do more. Yet it was early in Breanna's return to her land. The effort needed to make Breanna whole by working through the young warrior's dreams would not be easy.

Standing supportively beside her, Lugh commented, "As I watched you work within the newly woven pattern that now makes up Erin's Hero, pulling a thread of time here and there as if weaving a tapestry, I have to say it was magnificent. It was as if the *Cycle of Time* sang to you."

"Thank you, but it was not all me. Without Dagda and *Croí Dàn*, Breanna would likely not be here. We all spun her *anam* away from the *Cycle of Time*. If it had seized her, we would not have won."

"Are you sure you should have left the Heart of Destiny with her?" Lugh queried. "She was mine at one time."

"Jealous, some?" Danu chided. In the Stone of Destiny, she knew Lugh had seen that their land was no longer threatened by Norvegrs, at least not as long as the magic of Erin's Veil stood in place.

The Sun God protested, "Our Heart is—inexperienced."

Danu sighed. "As I said, *Croí Dàn* was not ready to come home to me. As Dagda often reminds me, I agreed for her to have a piece of me so she could be sentient. I can no longer dictate her path and must let her decide on how to chart her way with her Hero. She's grown significantly since choosing Breanna and casting the vision her Hero held while wielding the *Triple Dàns*. Not to mention helping create Erin's Veil. It's all tied together and will collapse if my Heart's chosen one passes back into the *Cycle of Time*. It is why they need to be together."

Lugh cocked his head. "Still, what Breanna has done is locked inside her—a part of her *anam*. Her *geas* may no longer be an influence, but the warrior part of her that dealt with the Dreadlord very much is. She is going to need, well, a tutor to learn about the magic she bears. Maybe it would have been better to let her go."

"Dagda would not have allowed it," Danu answered. "As for a tutor, All-Father will take on that role. You already know we did not take lightly the fact that we pulled her through that life to this one. *Maorgairme* compelled me when Breanna used it with her last breath. Because of her sacrifice for her land, I might have done it regardless. We certainly need her to rise once again to defend our Gaels. Few in Erin have such courage or such heart."

"Then she deserves to know what she has done and why she is so driven," Lugh said firmly. "You and Dagda pulled all impacted by the Dreadlord's presence into a new timeline envisioned by Breanna, one without the Norvegrs, but the *Triple Dàns* didn't completely rewrite time. That will be a challenge for anyone with memories that don't quite fit, as they haven't truly lived those lives."

"Aye, it will likely be an issue. Yet it's not like we knew exactly what Breanna's wielding of the *Triple Dàns* would bring about. Even Badb Catha didn't know and declined to wield it. Breanna's troubles now, though, might be due to her being the one who cast the vision."

Lugh was critical. "Likely best not to have used that magic."

"Water under the bridge, Lugh, but when Breanna pieces enough together and calls on me, I will answer," Danu insisted. "Yet it must be of her accord. That said, given his bond with her, Dagda will be a better choice to help her with any concerns she may have. I don't think he'd have it any other way, especially since he gave her a piece of himself as I did with my Heart."

"What of Eoin and the others in her band? Those warriors will likely need a sign from us to ensure they know that the Breanna they once supported needs their help again."

"Not Eoin, for he is also Dagda's, but do what you will for the others," she commanded. "All-Father will see to Breanna's mate."

Ćroí Dàn interjected cautiously, *"Mother? I can feel it when you're nearby, in this realm. I have to thank both you and Dagda for saving my Hero. Yet I'm unsure why you are here?"*

"Daughter," Danu offered warmly. *"There has been no opportunity to say this, but well done. You've grown, and I'm proud of you. Breanna will need your help to settle into her new timeline, which I'm sure you'll manage perfectly. As to why I'm here, that also involves you. Your Hero must claim her land as she did in her previous life if she is to have any chance of changing the Gaels' ruling class. While not her primary goal, I expect she will want this outcome. When she asserts herself as your Hero, I will lead my wolf pack to support her, as Badb will lead her crows and raptors, Manannán his creatures of the sea and waterways, Étaín her wild horses, and Lugh, his deer herd. We did not do that in the before-time as we should have."*

"Thank you, Mother. *Breanna needs to be Erin's Hero once more!"*

**Ćroí Dàn – Heart of Destiny is available now!
Get your copy today!**

Available at Amazon, Apple, Barnes & Noble,
Google, IngramSpark, & Others

Formats: eBook, Paperback, Hardback
(Amazon only), and Audiobook

And do not miss **"Bards of Destiny"** on Spotify, Apple,
YouTube Music, and other streamers for paired music!

Sign up for my <u>Fan Club</u> at
<u>www.destinycycle.com/about-james</u> to get updates!